BENEATH
THE
STAIRS

BENEATH THE STAIRS

A NOVEL

JENNIFER FAWCETT

ATRIA BOOKS

New York   London   Toronto   Sydney   New Delhi

An Imprint of Simon & Schuster, Inc.
1230 Avenue of the Americas
New York, NY 10020

First Atria Books hardcover edition February 2022

ATRIA BOOKS and colophon are trademarks of Simon & Schuster, Inc.

For information about special discounts for bulk purchases, please contact Simon & Schuster Special Sales at 1-866-506-1949 or business@simonandschuster.com.

The Simon & Schuster Speakers Bureau can bring authors to your live event. For more information or to book an event, contact the Simon & Schuster Speakers Bureau at 1-866-248-3049 or visit our website at www.simonspeakers.com.

Interior design by Kyoko Watanabe

Manufactured in the United States of America

1 3 5 7 9 10 8 6 4 2

Library of Congress Cataloging-in-Publication Data

Names: Fawcett, Jennifer, author.
Title: Beneath the stairs : a novel / Jennifer Fawcett.
Description: First Atria Books hardcover edition. | New York : Atria Books, 2022.
Identifiers: LCCN 2021053617 (print) | LCCN 2021053618 (ebook) | ISBN 9781982177157 (hardcover) | ISBN 9781982177171 (ebook)
Subjects: LCGFT: Horror fiction. | Novels.
Classification: LCC PS3606.A925 B46 2022 (print) | LCC PS3606.A925 (ebook) | DDC 813/.6--dc23/eng/20211105
LC record available at https://lccn.loc.gov/2021053617
LC ebook record available at https://lccn.loc.gov/2021053618

ISBN 978-1-9821-7715-7
ISBN 978-1-9821-7717-1 (ebook)

For the real Abby, wherever you may be

One not need be a Chamber—to be Haunted—

—EMILY DICKINSON

prologue

SPRING

One of the girls found out about the house first. It was always this way; one heard the story and told the others, and so the secret was passed down, girl to girl, generation to generation. She heard her mother talking about it, about something that had happened there before the girl was born, something bad. This secret place still existed, hidden in the woods, waiting to be found again.

And so, one spring afternoon, the girl led her friends around the curve in the road where the field stopped and the woods began. Partway along, she slowed down, searching for the spot where the fence was only hooked over the nails. Easy to pull back; easy to hide. They hid their bikes just inside the woods and followed the old road. Insistent undergrowth pulled at their legs like barbed seaweed, but they kept moving deeper. "Why would you build a house in here?" "Are you sure this is where she said it'd be?" "Maybe it's gone now." None of them were willing to say that they wanted to turn around, that as soon as they'd crossed into these trees, they knew this wasn't a place for them. And then they tumbled into the clearing. And there, alone and asleep, was the Octagon House.

They went inside. Of course they went inside.

Their feet crunched over decades' worth of broken beer bottles, leaves, animal droppings, and scattered remains of garbage, all of it turned a uniform shade of dust. The girls shivered and wanted to hug themselves but didn't. They walked carefully around the two large rooms on the first floor. They glanced up the decayed stairs to the second floor. They looked at the strange door, too large for a regular door and made of metal instead of wood. "It must lead to the basement," they said. They wiggled the latch, but it was broken, the door firmly shut. The girls were quietly grateful for that. They wandered back into the old kitchen where they had started, kicking at the garbage, wondering what to do next.

But the one who had brought them returned to that metal door. It was once dark green, but rust had spread over most of its surface, slowly gnawing its way through. Nothing stays hidden forever, she thought. And then she remembered how her mother had sounded when she'd talked about this house, that old fear coming awake again. She heard the others and turned to follow them. Just as she did, there was a click, and the door began to slide open. The air that escaped was cold and wet and smelled of earth and rot. Go, she thought, they're leaving. But her legs wouldn't move. The door opened farther, and now she could see the top of old wooden stairs.

She wanted to look.

She didn't want to look.

She dared herself to look.

Only darkness, but there, on the lowest stair: something. She leaned into the doorway and looked down. She took out her phone and shone the light into the darkness, but that only made shadows, so she turned it off again. And in that millisecond, the instant between the light and the dark—

Help me.

The voice was inside her head, but it wasn't hers.

Her friends called out to her: "Are you coming?" They were already at the door, stepping out of the grip of the house like it was nothing. She was alone.

Help me leave this place.

She pulled herself away and ran to them.

———

The girls bolted across the clearing, giddy with adrenaline and release. And as they disappeared into the woods, the door shut. But it would open again. The house was awake now.

She would come back. They always came back.

1

FALL

I'm back.

I'm sitting in my car in the almost empty parking lot of the Sisters of Mercy Hospital. The sun has long since dipped behind the low peaks of the Adirondacks, and the last traces of light are leaving the sky in the west behind me. The car engine cools down, ticking, metal settling into its resting state.

I've been inside this hospital twice before: the first time when I was eight, to say goodbye to my mother; and the last time when I was fourteen and my best friend, Abby, was rushed here, catatonic with fright. And now she's here again, and so I am too.

I don't want to get out of the car yet. Getting out means I'm here. I need to stay in the bubble that carried me here for a little while longer, the same bubble I stepped into twelve hours ago when I put the padlock on the storage locker holding the contents of my life—what Josh left me— and drove east. Just before I slammed the locker door shut, I looked at the pile of boxes and mismatched furniture. I didn't recognize any of it. Is this all there is of me? Barely enough to fit in a ten-by-sixteen box on the outer edges of Chicagoland. When I stopped for gas in Indiana, I crumpled the scrap of paper with my lock combination and threw it away.

Clare, I'm writing from Abby's account. I hope you still check this address . . .

Three nights ago, Mrs. Lindsay's email woke me up.

Abby went back to that abandoned house in Sumner's Mills.

In the early days of my relationship with Josh, I used to turn my phone off at night, not just silent but completely off. But now those late-night messages, even though they're almost always spam, they let me know I'm still here.

Overdose . . . Attempted suicide . . . Brain injury . . . Coma.

Once I open the car door, the night will rush in and push out the last of my old life, my Chicago life, my life as someone who left Upstate New York far behind. I don't want to be there anymore, I'm sure of that, but I don't want to be here either. I'm not staying. There's no reason for me to stay. I'm just here to help an old friend, and then I'll go somewhere, anywhere, else. This is what I've been telling myself ever since I decided to return to Sumner's Mills—the backdrop to my girlhood, the town that holds the Octagon House.

In the summer of 1998, right before we were starting high school, I went into an abandoned house with my three best friends, Monica, Lori, and Abby. The house was in the shape of an octagon and had been abandoned in the sixties after a man killed his family there. It was a few miles outside of Sumner's Mills, the village where we grew up, and it was hidden from the road by trees, so unless you knew how to find it, you wouldn't. Despite that, there have always been a few kids in each successive generation who've learned about it and dared each other to go in. Absence and neglect have a gravitational force of their own. If we had gone just once, everything would have been fine, but later that night Abby and I went back, and she went into the basement alone. Again. She never entirely came out.

Now she's done it again.

The doctors put her in a medically induced coma to bring down swelling caused by a lesion in her brain. She was barely conscious when they got her out but she said your name.

I didn't reply to Abby's mother. I didn't make any promises about showing up, but I came, I came right away, because I know why Abby said my name.

I inhale the stale air of my car one last time, put my hand on the door, and swing it open. The cool evening air snaps me out of my stupor. All I have to do is walk across the street, go into her room, then leave again. I can do this.

The glass of the hospital doors glows orange with the reflection of the fading daylight behind me. Parts of the sky have turned that deep blue of early fall nights, when darkness returns minute by minute each day. I'm twenty feet away when the orange glass slides apart and a little girl runs out. She's probably six, blond hair tangled around her face. A green scarf trails out of one arm of the coat that is open and flapping behind her—a bird wild with the joy of sudden release. She's coming straight for me, and then her mother comes out, three steps behind her. The girl stops at the edge of the sidewalk. Her mother stands beside her, glances both ways, then, without even needing to look, takes her daughter's hand.

It's nothing. It's everything.

I stop.

Muscles, breath, and heart all hold.

Hold, hold.

And then the pain rises from my gut into my lungs and my throat like water. But this is ghost pain, only a memory of pain, I tell myself. It's been five months. How long is this going to hurt?

When I can move again, the child and mother are long gone. I turn around and walk to my car. I can't go in there to see Abby now.

Abby needs you, Clare. Come back and wake her up.

What happened to her is my fault. What happened to me is her fault. Logically, that may not be true, but logic has nothing to do with any of this. Abigail Lindsay and I are tied together, and I don't know if my coming here ties that knot tighter or is a way to finally disentangle ourselves for good.

2

I turn the car on and get on Route 5. I could take the interstate and be in the village of Sumner's Mills in two exits, but I'm in no hurry. Route 5 takes me along the river. The winding road, the close trees, the rocks towering overhead—as much as I don't want to be here, my body settles into the familiar geography of my childhood. I never was able to get comfortable under the open skies of the Midwest.

Coming into my hometown this way, I pass the shuttered remains of Sumner's Metals and Lubricants. It was founded during a boom in the early 1900s and held on, through all the lawsuits and accusations, until the mid-eighties. When it was finally shut down, it almost took the whole town with it. The appliance store and the ladies' clothing store on State Street were the first to go, then the bakery and the hardware store a few years after that. When I was a child, I thought boarded-up storefronts were the norm. The old brick factory buildings are slowly caving in, and when they go, they'll fall into the river they tower above. When *The New York Times* writes about the bucolic charm of the small upstate towns with their craft breweries and farmers' markets, Sumner's Mills is not the place they're talking about. Its one claim to fame was being the setting of a low-budget horror film shot in the early 2000s, now a cult classic, a fact Josh delighted in, being a lover of all things B-movie. But when he asked my father about what it had been like to have Hollywood come to Sumner's Mills, he was disappointed to learn that the entire cast and crew had spent as little time as possible in the actual village, preferring the less authentic but more comfortable tourist towns farther south. Despite all this, sometimes a developer comes up from the city, and there's talk of turning the factory buildings into condos, artist studios, or a luxury resort, but they never get far. All it takes is a little investigation into the area's history, the cancer rates, the birth defects, the lawsuits from environmental groups, and they leave. Sumner's Mills doesn't like outsiders and never has. If you dare to come here and stay, it will cost you.

I drive through the village and out the other side, winding along the road for another mile, until I come to my childhood home. Dad moved away last spring. He'd talked about it for so long, but it still came as a shock last Christmas when he told me he was moving to South Carolina. That was the last time I saw him, standing in the driveway while Josh attempted to repack the car for the third time, being one of those firm believers in the ability of hatchbacks to carry anything if you just got the engineering right. Every time we visited, Dad insisted I take some memento of my childhood or box of dishes or kitchen gadgets; when he told me he was moving, I finally knew why. He was slowly disconnecting me from this place. It shouldn't have been a surprise, but my first response was anger. Of course, I knew I was being childish. I don't want to live here, and it wasn't fair to expect he would, but I couldn't say that.

"She's not here, Button," was all he said. I hadn't mentioned my mother. I hadn't said anything at all, but he knew. "You and Josh have your own home now," he said, nodding to Josh and our overflowing car. "But I won't put it on the market until you're ready." And true to his word, here it is, empty and waiting.

I lean over to dig through the glove box. The key is where I left it all those months ago when Josh and I drove back to Chicago, having no idea what was about to happen. Dad had stayed in the driveway watching us go until we rounded the turn, and then I imagined him in the empty house, putting the kettle on. My father is in a perpetual state of making tea, shuffling around in a slumpy cardigan. Quiet and constant. I can't picture him any other way. I can hear Josh telling me, "Childhood trauma can lead to an unrealistic desire to hold on. You can't blame your-self." I shrug off his voice. Josh is gone. That too is my fault. Maybe I'm not so good at holding on after all. Maybe I'm better at letting people slip away.

I move through the rooms by rote, turning on every light until I'm out the back door and looking at the yard, the house a beacon behind me. My parents bought this place when they were first married and "house poor," as Dad used to say. It had been a wreck inside, so they got it cheap, and slowly, room by room, they ripped out the wood paneling and pulled up the matted rugs and made it into a home. Mom planted flower gardens all around, but the real masterpiece was in the backyard, where she grew her lavender. She had plans to launch a line of organic cleaning products long before they were trendy, and for a few years she sold lumpy homemade soaps at local farmers' markets. Dad's vegetable gardens were beyond the lavender, his neat functional rows of quiet order and utility in contrast to my mother's wild bushes of perfumed wonder. My earliest memories are in those gardens: the local public radio station chattering quietly in the background, the sky purple above me in the summer twilight, my mother on her hands and knees digging in the earth, and me, happy and filthy, beside her. Maybe it was all that time with her hands buried in the poisoned soil that made her so sick. I never said that to my dad, even in my angriest moments, because I knew how much it would hurt him. He was the one who fell in love with the rocks and the trees and the ruggedness of Upstate New York. He con-vinced my mother to move up here with the dream of living a simple life, of home-grown vegetables, flowers, and honey. She embraced that dream completely. He was the one who brought her here, but she was the one who got sick. I don't think he's ever forgiven himself for it either.

After my mother died, Dad let the lavender go, but it just kept blooming and spreading every year. If the breeze blew in the right di-rection, I'd smell lavender in my bedroom. I know I should hate that scent, but I don't—I can't. That smell is her. Every spring, Dad would talk about tearing the plants out and reseeding the lawn, but he never did. Just like I know he won't sell. Not until I'm ready.

I'm not ready.

But I don't want to be here either. This is just a stop on the way to . . . something else. I haven't thought of my plans beyond now. Mrs. Lindsay's email gave me direction: come here, do this. So, here I am. Tomorrow I can figure out the rest.

I'm stiff and tired from the drive, and the panic from the hospital has left behind a residue. There's no internet or television to distract me, so I throw my bag on the sofa, dig through it for my gear, and head out for a run. It's the best way—the only way—I know to clear my head. It's dark now, but I don't mind. In the past few months, I've taken to doing late-night runs, turning down streets I know I shouldn't be on, music pounding loud enough to make me deaf to what's around me. I run until I hurt, and only when my thighs are burning with lactic acid do I turn around and head for home.

Habit sends me back toward Sumner's Mills. In the center of the village, at the T-junction where State Street meets Main, I turn right and then I'm heading north out of town. I pass our old school and the road forks and I veer right. Soon the rhythm of my feet on the dirt shoulder and the even in and out of my breath work their magic, because I'm not thinking about anything, I'm just breathing and moving forward, noting only enough of my surroundings to move into the ditch when a car speeds past. Then I stop short and realize two things: I'm no longer sure where I am, and up until the last wrong turn, I have been running toward the Octagon House—at least where I think it is.

Abby went back to that abandoned house in Sumner's Mills. The last she'd been seen was at the store in the village, three days earlier. The police think she was in that house the whole time.

Three days in the Octagon House. What the hell were you doing, Abby? My heart beats in my throat. The air is cold and my breath steams around me as I stand on the side of the empty road. It's paved, but I swear it used to just be gravel, and I've passed houses that I'm sure weren't there when I was growing up. I don't know where I am, but I know I'm close, within a couple miles of that house. I suddenly feel exposed. Seen.

I turn around and run toward the village. It's dark except for a few scattered streetlights and the glow of the gas station, which also serves as a general store and ice cream counter in the summer. This is where Abby stopped.

There's one woman behind the counter. A television plays silently above her, and she only gives me a glance when I step inside. I must look strange, my face splotched pink from my run, my hair a frizzy mess falling out of its ponytail. I duck into the bathroom and splash some water on my face.

What are you doing? My heavy breaths fog up the spotted mirror, erasing my face into a blur.

I spend a long time examining the store items while I get up my nerve to ask the woman about the house. About Abby and what happened recently. I lived here four more years after we went inside the Octagon House, and knowing it existed didn't bother me then. *Because you actively worked to forget it,* the voice in my head says. And I did a good job. If it weren't for Mrs. Lindsay's email, I would think that we had dreamed the whole place up as kids.

I've been staring at the meager selection of cereal for a long time, and the woman is watching me now.

"You looking for something particular?" she asks. Her voice is scratchy and low, the sound of a lifelong smoker.

I grab a box and a few cans of soup and put them in my basket before walking toward her. There's no one else in here, but I don't want to ask this question across the small store.

"I was wondering if you know about an old house around here. It's the shape of an octagon."

She looks at me for a moment and I can't read her face, then she starts taking the food out of my basket and ringing it in. "You new around here?"

"I grew up here. I don't live here anymore."

She nods slightly. "That's lots of people." The cash register beeps methodically. I'm about to repeat my question when she asks, "What do you want to know about that place for?"

"So, you do know about it?"

She shrugs. Indifference or reticence, I can't tell which.

"Have you ever seen the house?"

She snorts. "No point in going near that old place." She finishes shoving my food into a bag and drops into her chair—a faded lawn chair that doesn't look like it will hold her for much longer—and picks up her book, pointedly ignoring me. Lined up on the shelf behind her is a row of troll dolls. Some are facing straight out, staring forward with their wide-open painted eyes, while others are randomly angled toward each other, as if in conversation. One in the middle has two heads.

She glances up and sees me looking at them. "They're not for sale."

I nod. Underneath them is a handwritten sign saying as much. "It's just, my friend went to that house and—" And what? And something went wrong? What went wrong, went wrong years ago; at least that's what I thought. The truth is, I don't know. "And I heard she stopped in here first. She was asking directions. It would have been about a week or maybe ten days ago. I'm just trying to figure out what happened."

I hear myself say it. Am I trying to figure out what happened? *Don't get involved.* But instead of taking my groceries and leaving, I'm unable to move. It suddenly seems important—essential, even—to trace Abby's last few steps. I know where they end, but I don't know the path that got her there.

The woman looks up at me, and I can see her considering whether or not to indulge me. Then she says, "It wasn't a big conversation."

I've been holding my breath and exhale slowly. "But you do remember her? You were the one who talked to her?"

"I told her it fell down years ago."

"You did? But—"

"Didn't seem like the type who should be going into places like that. She got real upset when I told her that. Told me that *I* was wrong. I said, 'If you're so sure it's still standing, what do you need directions for?'"

"What'd she say?"

She narrows her eyes but stands up again and leans over the counter toward me. "So, you're what, friend of the family?"

"She was my best friend."

Her expression makes it clear she's not impressed.

"I mean, when we were kids. We grew up here, but it's changed. Some of the roads are different from what I remember."

"I told her roughly where it was at," she says. "Just to get her to calm down."

"Did she ask anything else? Or say anything?"

She looks down at her book and closes it with a sigh. "She bought gas, got a Coke, and asked for directions to that house. Like I said, it wasn't a big conversation."

I feel like I should be asking more, but I have no idea what. It's a four-hour drive from Buffalo to Sumner's Mills. Abby gets here and realizes, as I did, that she doesn't know how to find the house anymore. She stops in and makes conversation with this woman; buys a Coke so she'll talk. I keep seeing her mother's message: *Three days. The police think she was in that house the whole time.*

"How about you tell me something, since she's your friend?" the woman says. I can't tell if she's being friendly or challenging, but she looks like she's enjoying herself now. "Why'd she put a full tank of gas in her car if she was only going to drive a couple miles and leave it on the side of the road?" My breath catches in my throat. "She didn't strike me as the type to spend money if she didn't have to."

"What do you mean?"

"Because she didn't have any. Paid in cash but didn't have enough, so she had to put the food back. I told her to take the Coke. She looked like she needed it."

I don't know how much she knows about what happened. She must know something, though, since she was questioned by the police. "Did you tell the police about the gas?"

"They said it don't mean anything. It was pretty clear what she'd gone there to do. I got a cousin who's a state trooper. He's one of the ones who found her. Told me she had an empty pill bottle in her hand." The woman's eyes narrow as she adds this detail, daring me to contradict her or letting me know her thoughts on people who choose to overdose, I'm not sure which.

"Did your cousin tell you where they found her? In the house, I mean?"

She looks like she's deciding whether she'll tell me, whether I've earned this bit of information. But the Octagon House and what happened there is mine—mine and Abby's—and she doesn't get to be a part of this. "Look," I say, lowering my voice, "was she in the basement? Did he tell you that?"

Her nostrils flare. "How do you know that?"

An old man comes into the store and glances at me, registering the newcomer, then he nods in her direction. We both wait until he's moved toward the far end of the store.

"It was just a guess," I say, because I'm not going to tell her the real reason. I've known it ever since I learned Abby went back there. I can see her, the way she'd been when we found her the first time, curled up in a ball on the floor. There's so much I can't remember, but that picture is etched in my memory.

The woman sits down again and picks up her book, the conversation clearly over. I'm half out the door when she says, "It's private property. In case you were thinking of going too."

For a moment, it looks like she's going to say something else, but then she shrugs and says, "Next time you go for a run, bring a light. Don't want someone to take you for an animal."

I glance down at my battered blue running jacket. I could point out the a reflective strip across the back, but I don't think she's telling me this out of any actual concern for my safety. She just wants to remind me that what I'm doing doesn't fit here. *I* don't fit here. "Thanks for the advice," I say. The bell on the door jangles as I shut it behind me.

The walk back to my father's house is pitch black, and the plastic bag of food bangs against my leg. I can't stop thinking about the full tank of gas. A full tank of gas and an attempt to buy food. That doesn't seem like what you'd do if you're going to kill yourself. But if Abby didn't go into that basement to swallow a bottle of pills, what was she planning to do?

3

I'm lying on the couch, trying to muster the energy to make some of the soup I bought, when my phone buzzes with a Facebook message from Lori.

Heard you might be around. Let's talk. And then her cell number.

My first response is to ignore the message. Lori and I connected a few years ago on Facebook but never communicated beyond the occasional birthday greeting. In my rare visits home to see my dad over the years, I never stayed long enough to get in touch. This is what I always told myself. Habit would have me put the phone on the coffee table and continue staring at the ceiling. It is almost ten, after all. Instead, I reply:

Just got to town. Long drive.

She sends me a picture of a baby crying, which I'm assuming is meant to be me, and tells me to come over for a drink, then texts me directions. Much to my surprise, I find myself looking forward to seeing her. My brain's just running in circles, and although I'm tired, I'm not going to sleep anytime soon.

When we were in grade school, Lori, Monica, Abby, and I were a foursome, though in reality, it was two and two: Abby and I following Lori and Monica, the strings that held us together as fragile as spider thread. It hadn't started that way. There's a picture of Lori and me, knock-kneed and squinting up at the camera with big grins. Kindergarten graduation. We're each holding a dripping ice cream cone in one hand and a homemade diploma, complete with a shiny gold star, in the other. We were the first person the other found when we left the comfort of our little world and ventured, alone, onto the yellow school bus. Lori was always taller and stronger, her hair in perpetual pigtails, her stubborn face focused toward whatever was in front of her. In my eyes, she was fearless.

A few grades later, Monica came to our school, and our easy twosome became a more delicate triad. Even at the age of eight, Monica understood the importance of her audience and always dressed, spoke, and acted with an awareness of how to maximize the effect. That was the year my mother died, and Lori and Monica swooped in to stand guard over me after I returned to school, sharing the best parts of their lunches and rebuffing the blunt curiosity of our classmates. Lori's clumsy compassion was genuine, but Monica's turned to resentment after the value of playing best friend to the saddest girl in the school wore off. And then the next September, Abby arrived and the dynamic changed again. She was younger and smaller than the rest of us because she'd skipped a grade. She and I snapped together like magnets.

Friendship for Abby and me was easy until it wasn't. I can't blame what happened at the Octagon House for causing the crack between us because it was already there when we went in. Whatever happened to Abby to set her on the course that has now landed her comatose in a hospital, it happened because all those years ago she went into that house without the shield of her best friend to protect her.

Despite seeing recent pictures of her online, when I think of Lori, I see the girl she was at fourteen, but as soon as she answers the door, that picture scrambles. She is a little wider and rounder, her hair in one of those functional short haircuts, and there are a few more lines on her face, but when she smiles, I can still see the girl I remember. She is probably doing the same with me. I try to see myself at fourteen: curves due more to residual pudginess than puberty, hair in a permanent ponytail, skin in some combination of sunburn and explosions of freckles. For our reunion, I'd pulled on an old pair of jeans and an oversize sweatshirt, and I suddenly wish I'd gone to a little more trouble to look like a grown-up.

"Come on in. Excuse the mess," Lori says, kicking a squawking toy robot out from under her foot and walking toward the brightly lit kitchen in the back. "Don't worry about your shoes," she calls over her shoulder. "Between three kids and two dogs, you're safer with them on."

In the kitchen, she motions to an empty chair at the table and pushes aside a mess of math worksheets and a half-finished LEGO project. "You want a beer?"

"I'd better not," I say. "Maybe tea?"

She wrinkles her nose. "Don't have any tea. I can do instant coffee."

"I'll go with beer."

"Wise choice." She grins and pulls two bottles out of the fridge, depositing the one she was holding in the sink. "My husband, Matt, is a long-haul trucker. He drinks that instant shit by the gallon. He says the caffeine hits him faster than regular coffee. I can't stand either of them."

"He must be away a lot," I say.

"The schedule he's on now, he's only here about five days a month." She shrugs. "I kind of get used to it being just the kids and me. We have our routines. When he comes home, we're always bumping into each other, you know? Takes a few days to get used to, then he's gone again. He wants to start his own trucking company, sell the farm."

"You'd sell this place?"

"You can't make any money farming. We'll need it if this business of his is going to happen. We'll see. It'd be better for the kids to have him around."

"But hasn't your family lived here forever?"

"About a hundred years. It's not forever." She shrugs again. "I'd be happy not to have to deal with the fucking Octagon House, I can tell you that."

I haven't been sure how to bring it all up, so I'm relieved she said it first. "It's over there, right?" I point in the direction that I believe is across the road, toward the majority of the farm property. Lori was the one who originally brought us to the Octagon House and told us about the murders that happened there years before. It was hidden in a patch of dense woods that ran along the back fields of her family farm.

"If you cut through the fields, it's about a mile, but if you drive around on the roads, it's closer to two," she says. "Honestly, I forget about it most of the time."

"The roads have changed," I say. "I was trying to figure out how to get there from town."

"Why?" Her eyes narrow. "You're not planning to go there too, are you?"

I laugh, but she doesn't join me.

"Did you come home because of Abby?"

I nod. On my way over, I didn't know if I wanted to talk about Abby or distract myself with gossip about classmates whose names I wouldn't remember and details I wouldn't care about but could pretend I did. Even when I was a kid, I knew I wanted to leave Sumner's Mills as soon as possible, but now, being in Lori's kitchen—cluttered with the debris of children and dinner, the gallery of family photos covering all the walls—and sensing her security in knowing *this is me,* I wonder what it would have been like if I hadn't run as fast as I could. And now I've done it again, leaving behind my life in Chicago, because even with ten years of memories woven into it, there wasn't enough to hold me there.

Lori's looking at me. "Strange to be back?"

"Different. My dad's not here anymore, but our house is. I feel like a ghost haunting a place that isn't mine anymore."

"I've been in pretty regular contact with the Lindsays since it happened. That's how I heard you might be coming. You got here quick." Lori was never one for small talk.

I shrug. "It seemed important."

"How did you find out?" she asks.

"Her mother. She asked me to come."

"So, you just dropped everything . . . ?"

"There wasn't much to drop."

"Oh." She takes a swig of her beer.

I realize in the silence that I haven't talked to anyone about what's happened in the past few months. Josh and I had friends, but they were couple friends, and when we broke up, they went with him. No, that's not quite true. I encouraged them to go to him. It's a lot easier to punish yourself if you're not talking to anyone, if you can just live in your own head for months. The thought of even starting to talk about it all now is too overwhelming. And pathetic. Instead I ask, "How's Monica? Are you guys in touch?"

"We're Facebook friends," she says. "She lives in Brooklyn, or maybe it's Queens. I can't remember. Matt's family is down there, so we're in the city a couple times a year. Each time I think, Hey, I should look up Monica, but then, you know . . ."

"Yeah," I say. Maybe this is being directed at me.

"It's hard when you're doing the family-visit thing," she offers.

"Does she have kids?"

Lori thinks for a moment, then says, "Yeah, two. Girls, I think." She shivers. "Imagine, two more Monicas out there."

I can't tell if she's joking.

"You and Abby stayed close, right?"

"Not really," I say. "I mean, there were a few messages over the years but nothing much. What about you?"

"First time I heard anything about her was when the police showed up at my door. She goes there to kill herself? I mean, what the fuck? There's nowhere in Buffalo to OD? Sorry, I know that's probably not the 'correct' thing to say but . . . seriously?"

"Maybe she didn't want anyone to find her," I say, but as soon as I do, I think of the emails.

Five one-line emails that always arrived in the middle of the night. Five emails from Abby that marked the beginning of me losing everything. But maybe that wasn't the beginning; maybe the beginning was here, all those years ago when we were kids. My stomach squeezes into a cramp and I don't know if it's hunger or the other. Lori sees my hand go to my abdomen and looks like she wants to ask but doesn't.

"Well, it feels personal," Lori says. "She knew that house was basically on our property."

"What did the police say?"

"They wanted to know if I knew her, if I'd had any contact with her. Which I hadn't."

"That was it?"

"They asked if anyone had been with her, or if I knew of anyone else who'd been out there."

"Why would they ask that?"

"They didn't want to say at first, but I'm in a hockey league with two of the officers' wives, so I kind of, you know, leaned on them a little, in a friendly way. I mean, I'm living here essentially by myself with three kids, I have a right to know."

"So, what'd they tell you?"

"You know she was found in the basement, right?"

I nod.

"Do you remember the basement door?" I close my eyes and try to picture it, but all I can see is darkness. I shake my head. She looks at me strangely. "How can you not remember that? After what happened . . . ?"

"Sorry, it was a long time ago." I remember flashes of our visit to the house, the first one with the four of us and then the second, at night, but only flashes. They don't feel any more real than a memory of photographs, or maybe that's wishful thinking. So much of my life here has been filed away, but the memories are waking up now. I feel them stirring.

"It's metal, like the kind of heavy industrial door you'd see in a restaurant or something," Lori says. "Like the kind that leads to a walk-in fridge. It's a weird fucking door to put in your house, is my point. Anyway, on the basement side of the door, there's no latch or anything."

"Okay . . ."

"Well, think about it."

"Oh. Shit. If you're in the basement . . ."

"How are you going to close the door on yourself?" she finishes.

"And the door was closed when they found her?" But it wasn't a question. The door had been closed. Abby in that darkness, again.

"It took three officers to get it open."

A memory jumps to life in my head: Lori, Monica, and me, all desperately trying to get the basement door open, and I shiver involuntarily. "Yeah. It's really heavy. I remember that now."

"There's some kind of suction effect, at least that's what the police officer I spoke to thought."

"At the gas station," I say, "the woman who works there—"

"Looks like a pug dog crossed with a weasel?"

I laugh. "Yes, now that you mention it. The one with the trolls."

"That's Rhonda. Been there forever. Every year, I swear, she looks a little more like them." Lori squishes up her face and pulls her ears out wide. "I don't have the hair to pull off the look."

A laugh that's more of a bark comes out of me, and I clamp my hand over my mouth, thinking of the sleeping children overhead. "Anyway," I say, wiping the beer that's spilled out of my nose. "She said that Abby went in there asking for directions and that she filled up her car with gas."

"Okay . . ." And then Lori realizes. "Oh. But why would she . . . ?"

"Exactly. But when she told the police, they said it didn't mean anything, it was obviously a suicide attempt."

"It was," she says quickly, like she's trying to convince herself. The room's gone still again.

"But the gas? And now the door?"

"You know, she tried to kill herself a bunch of times. I've talked to her parents a lot in the past week. She was really sick. I guess she had been for a long time. And she ate a bottle of pills. And . . ."

"And?"

"Well, nothing else makes sense, right? There's no other logical reason. There probably is a way to pull that door closed from the inside, but then once you do—" Suddenly she holds up her hand to stop me from saying more. "Taylor?" she calls out, then says, "Kid radar," quietly to me.

A girl comes into the kitchen doorway, one of those gangly tweens who's all limbs and hair.

"Why are you out of bed?"

"Can't sleep," the girl says, looking at me.

"This is Clare," Lori says to her, then turns to me. "This is Taylor, my eldest."

"Hi, Taylor," I say, hearing the immediate perkiness in my voice. That's teacher Clare. It just kicks in automatically, even after all these months.

"You know the woman who tried to kill herself?" she asks me in response.

"We were friends when we were your age. Your mom too."

"She's not my real mom," Taylor says, still talking pointedly to me.

"Yeah, well, I'm the one with your phone charger," Lori says, getting up and ushering her out of the kitchen.

"Why'd she go in there?" Taylor asks me, ignoring Lori. "Is she all right?"

"She's in the hospital, but I think she'll be okay," I say, hoping that's enough to get her to leave.

"Taylor, bed. Now."

Taylor glares at Lori, then turns and stalks away. Lori watches the empty doorway for a moment before turning to me.

"I'm the evil stepmother in this scenario, as you may have noticed."

"Ah, I see," I say.

"Never mind that her actual mother is a drunk who abandoned her when she was less than a year old. She lives somewhere downstate, and she 'found' Taylor online last winter. Ever since then Taylor's been such a little shit to me. I mean, not all the time, but as soon as I do something she doesn't like, it's all 'You're not my real mom.'" She sighs. "And Matt's like, 'It's hormones, it's typical mother-daughter stuff.'"

"Do you think she heard what we said?"

"Probably enough of it. She used to be this sweet kid." She shakes her head. "And this sneaking around, trying to listen in on conversations— she never used to do that. This past spring, she and some of her friends went into the Octagon House."

The sharp intake of breath is automatic. Taylor is just a child—way too young to go into a place like that, and yet we were only a few years older. We thought it was just a game, a dare. We had no idea what we were walking into.

"Did anything happen?" I ask.

"Like did one of them fall through the rotten floor or something?"

"No, you know, like did they see anything strange?"

Lori gives me a look as if to say that this is a preposterous idea. "Like what?"

"No, not—I don't know—just, you know, strange."

"No," she says firmly.

Maybe it's my imagination, but I sense the possibility of doubt underneath her certainty.

"I only know they went in because she started asking me all these questions about it and I was able to pry that much out of her." She rubs her forehead. "Not that she's going to tell me anything while she's in this phase. God, I hope it's a phase. What is it with that house and teenage girls? How old were we when we went in, thirteen? Fourteen?"

"That sounds about right. Summer between eighth and ninth grades."

"Taylor thinks she's twelve going on twenty."

"Does she know what happened there?"

"She knows enough. She was here when the police came."

"No, the other stuff, from before," I say quietly, in case Taylor is still eavesdropping.

"I haven't told her anything. I made her promise never to set foot in it again because that place is a death trap. I don't know if that really got through to her, though. We spent a fucking fortune to send her away to camp for part of the summer. Just trying to . . . you know." She looks off and chews her bottom lip.

"Has she tried to go in again?" I ask.

Lori looks at me sharply, then she returns to her beer. Picks up the bottle, examining it. "It's like—" She stops herself again and sighs. "Something changed with her last spring. She spends hours up in her room, which is new. Couple of nights ago, I went to check on her and she was just sitting on her bed, staring off at I don't know what. She's started sleepwalking too. That started at camp. I got an angry call from the camp director telling me that she'd been found at the edge of the woods. Said they couldn't keep her there because of the liability. I had to beg." She looks up at me and gives me a weak smile. "Sorry, you don't need to hear all this."

"Maybe it's because of her mom," I say, but is that what I really mean? In all the years the Octagon House has been sitting there, the kids who've known about it have gone into it. The garbage and broken windows that I remember attest to this. I'm sure most of them thought it was cool or scary, but that was that. But for some, it has a stronger effect. Taylor is Lori's daughter, even if not by birth, and as far as I know, Lori was fine after we went in. But there was something about the girl, the way she seemed so hungry for answers, that I recognize.

"The sniping at me started after her mom, but this is different," Lori says. "Now it's like she's not even present half the time. I'd take the bitchy-teenager act over this any day."

"What's your husband think?"

"He's going to have a conniption when he hears about Abby almost dying in there. He says we should get a bulldozer and knock the house down ourselves. The old lady who owns it is about a hundred, so it's not like she's going to be out there checking up on it, but someone could. Besides, I don't think it's quite legal to bulldoze other people's houses, even if they are a pile of shit."

"But it's on your land."

"The fields all around, yes, but the woods aren't ours. That's why we can't touch them. Trust me, we've been trying to for decades. My grandpa begged the old lady to knock the house down after those murders. He was worried about people getting curious and then starting a fire or something. There's enough dead trees in those woods that if it's dry enough, a fire could spread quick. Take our crops with it. Only thing she agreed to was letting him board it up and put the fence along the road."

"I don't think I ever put together that your family was here when those murders happened."

"My dad says he remembers it. He was a kid. When was it . . . mid-sixties, right? So, yeah, he was about the same age Taylor is now." She drops her voice low again. "Did I ever tell you, the night it happened, the husband showed up at our house? They didn't have a phone, so he came here and used ours to call the police."

"Holy shit." I can't help but look around at the crowded kitchen, the same as it has been for generations. The old green phone is still on the wall, probably where it was then.

"My grandpa and a bunch of other men from town went into the woods and our fields searching for the killer—"

"Wait, I thought the guy killed his own family."

"He did, but he *said* that it was someone else. Just trying to put them off his trail."

"And he was here?" I shiver. "Maybe the woman who owns it is related to the family that died. She's being sentimental or whatever."

"No. They were from somewhere else. The woman who owns it is a Sumner."

I look at her blankly.

"Sumner's Mills? They used to own everything: the factory, half the village, all the land around here."

"Yeah, but that was, like, years ago," I say.

"Trust me, this lady was ancient even when we were kids. And she's not called Sumner. Her last name is Janssen."

I shake my head. The name doesn't mean anything to me, but that's not a surprise.

"I only started dealing with her when I took over the farm. I told her leaving that house there was a lawsuit waiting to happen, but she didn't seem to care. You want another beer?"

I'm only halfway through the one she's given me, but she gets up anyway and takes two more out of the fridge, opening one for herself.

"Way back when, my great-grandpa bought all this land from the Sumners, but they would not sell the woods. If they would have, we could have got the fields all the way to the road. Would have made it a hell of a lot easier to get into the north end of our property."

"Did they say why?"

"Spite? I don't know. Apparently, the Sumners were a weird family." She shrugs. "This was long before my time. Once, though, my great-grandpa was working in the back fields close to the woods and he thought he heard, I don't know, cries or something."

"Did he go and look?"

"No way. Great-granddad was hella superstitious. Those old-world Scots don't mess with no wood fairies."

"So . . ." I can't tell where she's going with this.

"Aren't you glad you came home?" She grins and clinks her beer bottle to mine.

"If they had a house in there, makes sense that they wouldn't want to sell the land around it," I say.

"The Octagon House wasn't built then. It was built . . . end of the thirties, I think? This would have been before then."

"Those cries were probably just an animal."

"Probably."

But then why would it have become family lore? Lori's family, from what I knew of them, were not ones to go in for fantasy. "Is any of this for real?" I ask.

"Of course." I can't tell if she's trying to get me worked up or if she's telling the truth. "I will tell you one strange thing that happened there. This was years later, like after the murders, when my dad was a teen. He used to go into those woods with his BB gun, hunting squirrels. He wasn't supposed to but, you know. So, this one time, he was in there and he saw this man. He'd been focused on a squirrel or whatever, and he turned around and this man was like right there. Just looking at him. Close enough he could touch him."

"What'd he do?"

"He just about shat himself and then ran, are you kidding? Guy didn't follow him or anything. Dad said he was just there, and then when he looked again, he wasn't. Like a fucking ghost."

Lori's father, from what I remember of him, is a big man, over six feet tall with a gut that sticks out over his pants and a thick beard. Baseball cap pulled low, muddy boots that he'd leave outside because they were always covered in something organic. It's hard to imagine a man like him being scared of anything, even as a teen. "Why are you telling me all of this?"

"What, you don't like spooky stories?"

"Did you know all this when we were kids?"

"No. I just knew we weren't supposed to go into those woods 'cause it wasn't our property. Then I overheard my dad talking to someone about an old house in there and told you guys."

"Do people know about the house? Like, in general, in the town?"

She shakes her head. "I don't know. I feel like the old-timers do. They were all here in the sixties, but since then? Some kids always seem to find out about it. We did."

"If I'd known all this, I definitely wouldn't have gone in there."

"You guys would have been fine if you'd just gone in there the one time with us. It's because you and Abby went back. I never understood that."

She gets up, scraping her chair on the floor, and opens the cupboard doors but just stands looking at the contents. Her back is to me when she says, "But why would she go there to kill herself?"

"Maybe she didn't," I say, and immediately regret it. The beer is hitting me harder than it should.

She turns and squints down at me. "What do you mean?"

"I don't know." This idea that has been gnawing at me has become a real question. "It's just like I said, there's some things that don't add up. The gas in her car and then the door being closed—"

"Don't complicate it. There's no other logical explanation."

We're both still for a moment in the quiet kitchen. The tap is dripping into the overflowing dishpan, and somewhere deeper in the house, an old clock is ticking. Lori rummages around in a cupboard and throws a half-full bag of nacho chips on the table between us. "Here. I've got salsa somewhere, maybe. You look like you haven't eaten in a while."

"Thanks," I say, taking a chip out, but I can't eat it. I just methodically break it into bits on her kitchen table.

"Tell me again, why did Abby's mom ask you to come all the way back here? That's like halfway across the country."

"She thought I might be able to help her."

"Nothing personal, but didn't Abby have any other friends? I mean, if you guys haven't been in touch in twenty years, it's a little strange, don't you think?"

"She said my name."

Lori gives me a disbelieving look. "When? People in comas don't talk."

"No, before they put her in the coma. I guess she was conscious when they got her out, but just barely."

"Well, the last time she was in that house was with you, so maybe she was reminded or whatever. That doesn't mean they needed to drag you all the way out here."

"I don't know, okay? I didn't ask. I guess I should have."

I didn't ask because I wanted it to be true. I needed to think I could actually do something to help, even if it was only coming home.

"How was she?" Lori asks gently. When I don't answer, she says, "You have been in to see her, right?"

I shake my head. "I'll go tomorrow. I just got in. I wanted to but . . ."

"I get it. And it's great you came, like really. I wasn't trying to imply it wasn't. But there was probably serious damage done with all the drugs she took. I mean, if it was bad enough they had to induce a coma . . ."

"I know."

"If she does wake up—"

"What do you mean, 'if'?"

"Fine," Lori says. "*When* she wakes up, she's not going to be who she was—"

"I'm aware of that."

Why is it that some people—mainly women, my own age—feel the need to patronize me? It usually happens with the ones who are mothers. It's like my not having kids, not being married, and now not having a job keep me in some kind of childish state in their minds.

Lori puts her beer down and smiles at me. "Go and visit her, be a good friend, and then get the hell out of here. Go back to Chicago."

"No. Not there."

"I envy you. You could go anywhere. You have nothing holding you down. You have no idea how lucky you are."

The tears are welling in my eyes before I have a chance to stop them. I want to put my head on Lori's sticky kitchen table and sob until I fall asleep. I bend over to take my phone out of my bag and wipe at my eyes while I'm hidden.

"I should go," I say, keeping my voice light. "You must be up early with the kids."

"You okay to drive? You can stay here, if you want."

"I'm fine. I've barely touched that second beer." But I don't think it's the beer she's talking about.

We're standing at the front door while I fish for my keys when she asks, "Are you going to go back to that house?"

"Why would I do that?"

"You tell me."

"I haven't decided yet," I lie, because ever since I started running there, something in me has known that I'm going to have to go into the house again.

"Clare," she says. "Don't."

"I'm not fourteen. I'm not going to do anything dumb." I'm trying to keep the annoyance out of my voice. "I feel like I should, for Abby."

"Abby's a fucking vegetable. Just leave it alone." Maybe we're both more on edge than we realize. "Promise me," she says, grabbing my arm, hard.

"I'm not going to—"

"Promise me."

"Okay," I say. "I promise."

She lets go and nods curtly. Then she throws her arms around me. "It's nice to have you here," she says quietly.

In all our years growing up together, I don't think Lori and I ever hugged like this. It just wasn't something we did. Monica wouldn't think twice to reach out and touch your shirt or fix your hair, and Abby and I would sit close to each other when we watched movies and take turns giving each other braids, or we'd hold hands when we were walking. It wasn't something I even thought about, it was just how we were. But never Lori. I hug her back and we stand like that, locked together for a short moment, then we separate and I'm grateful that the hallway is dark.

"See you, Clare," she says, opening the door. "Give me a call if you want to get together again."

===

While I'm getting in my car, a movement in one of the upstairs windows catches my eye. Taylor's pale face is pressed against the glass. I raise my hand to wave, but she doesn't move. I turn around to see what she's seeing. There are no clouds and the moon is bright. Across the road are the fields, harvested now and ready for winter. They disappear into the dark, but beyond those fields are the woods, and inside those woods is the Octagon House.

As I drive away, I catch a glimpse of Taylor in my rearview mirror, still by the window, watching the darkness.

4

BEN

He lies in his blank, silent room, hovering between sleeping and waking. Sleep brings dreams, and in those dreams, he is back at the house on that night in August 1965. His family is inside and it's all about to happen and he cannot warn them. He cannot stop it. Sometimes in the dreams, he's the one holding the rifle, just like the police told him he was. First the police said he killed his family, then the newspapers, then the lawyers. It would have been easier to give in and believe them, just for the simplicity of it.

"If you didn't do it, then tell us what happened, Mr. Fischer? How did those bodies end up in the basement? Doors were locked, you said. No sign of forced entry. Only your prints and your wife's on the rifle."

He's never been able to give them an answer. For all these years.

For all these years he has been trying to put the pieces together in a way that would make sense, and he's never been able to do it. In prison, time slipped past the walls of his cell while his body grew old and weak. Now they've moved him here, to a nursing home, or so they tell him. To him, it is just another room. At some point, a long time ago now, he stopped trying to remember. He tried to make his mind blank, to forget the sounds of that gunshot echoing in the night, the sight of his wife at the bottom of the stairs, his daughters hidden deeper in that dark basement.

And then that woman came to talk to him. What was her name? Amy or April or . . . Abigail, yes, that was it. Abby. She had been in the house too, and something had happened to her; she had seen something. She was looking for him because she thought he could give her answers. Now, after years of trying to forget, he is desperately trying to remember, to stitch that horrible night back together again, and this time, this time, he will see what he missed. The death he's been longing for is finally coming, but he can't go without knowing what happened. Can this young woman give him the answers the police couldn't?

She asked him to remember everything, so he has to clear his head, which means hiding the little blue pills they give him every twelve hours. It's easy enough to keep them under his tongue until the nurse leaves, then spit them into his hand. They know where he was before he came to their facility; he doubts any of them care about the quality of his sleep. And so here he lies, night and day blurring. The pain helps him remember.

Abby said she'd come back, and the next time she comes, he'll be able to tell her the story of that last night with his family in their strange house shaped like an octagon.

He turns to a new page in his sketchbook and writes, "August 22, 1965. Morning." The words look like the writing of an old man, shaky and unsure. But words aren't what his hand is aching to make. Balancing the pencil between his fingers, he wills his hand to become that of a younger man, and as he begins to draw, his hand loses the shakiness. The picture pulls itself out of his pencil and onto the page—demanding to be remembered, to be seen.

═══

They had moved into the house in May 1965. By June, he'd found a job at the local plant—Sumner's Metals and Lubricants. It was a horrible job, mind-numbing in its monotony, and the men he worked with made it clear that he would never belong. It didn't matter. There was no other option. Moving upstate was supposed to have been an escape from the city's noise and congestion that were making his wife sick, but as soon as they moved in, she started complaining of the isolation. At first the idea of a house shaped like an octagon was charming, but then Natalie's list of repairs kept growing. There was no money left after buying the house, not enough money to hire an electrician to fix the Depression-era wiring or pay for the phone lines to be brought in from the main road. As that summer went on, the pressure grew in his head like a black fog, reaching its fingers into his brain to squeeze and squeeze.

That August morning, he and Natalie had been arguing about the rifle again. He hated the thought of a gun in the house with two young children, but she had started talking about wolves and bears and "God knows what else in those woods and there's no one around." He'd told her the worst was probably some coyotes, but that hadn't stopped her from worrying. "I'm the one who's here alone every day and late into the night, Ben. No car. There isn't even a damned phone. What am I supposed to do if some animal comes around and I'm here alone with the girls?"

He knew it wasn't just animals she was afraid of. She'd started complaining about strange feelings in the house too, but she was just overtired. All Joanie's talk of sounds in the night was rubbing off on her.

Joanie, their eight-year-old, was up every night whining about a mysterious sound. If it had been Molly who was too frightened to sleep, it would have made sense. His wife had endless patience for the needs of their three-year-old daughter, but there wasn't much left over for their older girl complaining about imaginary noises at night. So, he gave in and bought a rifle off a man at work, hoping it would make Natalie happy, but that just led to another argument about where to keep it so the girls couldn't get it.

That final morning, he'd been rushing out the door with a piece of toast in his hand when he felt a tug at his shirt. He turned around and saw Joanie. Even now, all these years later, he can remember his eldest daughter so clearly: the spray of new freckles that had appeared over her nose from her first country summer, her coppery brown hair the same color as his. She had chopped it off one night in a fit of rebellion against her mother, and though he could never tell Natalie, he loved the way it made her look even more like a pixie. His daughter had endless curiosity, wanting to turn over every rock and climb every tree; the sunken dark circles under her eyes were the only sign of her nighttime troubles.

"Dad," she whispered to him. "I found something."

"Oh? Something good?"

"It's a secret," she answered, checking to make sure her mother wasn't listening.

"Did you record it in your book?" he asked, and she nodded solemnly. For her eighth birthday, he had given her a leather-bound notebook. "A place to record all of the things you're finding here," he had told her. Ever since her younger sister was born, he and Joanie had started going to the park to look at birds. He would draw them and teach her how to recognize them, and now she was learning to draw them too.

"But it's not a bird," she told him. "Or an animal." She smiled mischievously.

"Mmm," he said. "Where did you find this mysterious thing?"

She glanced back at her mother again, but Natalie was on the other side of the large kitchen helping Molly spoon jam on her toast. Just to be safe, Joanie leaned toward him and whispered, "In the basement."

Hearing her say that word had made the hairs on the back of his neck stand up. But he had ignored that warning. "Your mother doesn't want you going down there," was all he'd said. Why was that all he had said?

"Can I show it to you tonight?" she asked.

"No. I won't be home until you're in bed."

"Then I'll wait up."

"I said no." He reached out to touch her, but she pulled away. "On Sunday," he offered. "We can go down there together when Mom's doing Molly's nap."

"I can't wait that long."

How he longs to be able to reach out and tousle her hair. To hug her to him and tell her, "You must never, ever go down there again." But he didn't say that. He was already turning to rush out the door.

Just before he got in the car, he had turned around and looked at his family through the window. Joanie was at the table, Molly was beside her now, and Natalie was moving around them setting out breakfast dishes. That was the last time he saw the three of them like that, and now his sketch shows them there, frozen in time in the kitchen. He lays his old man's hand over the picture, trying to protect them from what was about to happen that night.

5

CLARE

July 25, 1998
2 P.M.

The proposal to visit the Octagon House happened at Abby's. Her house was hardly ever empty, and it wasn't a preferred hangout for the four girls, but Clare liked it that way and felt uncomfortable having Monica and Lori there now. It wasn't her house, sure, but she spent enough time there that it kind of felt like it was, and she liked knowing there was a place just for her and Abby. Abby's mother worked from home and one of her older brothers was often around, usually with loud friends in tow, but on this particular afternoon, the house was empty and therefore was ripe for an investigation.

"Where is everybody?" Monica asked, already starting to walk upstairs.

"My mom's shopping, I guess," Abby said, watching her from the bottom step. "My dad had to go to a meeting. I don't know where Paul is. Do you guys want a snack?"

"I'm not hungry," Monica said, continuing up the stairs with Lori behind her. Clare and Abby were at the bottom of the stairs, watching the other two move ahead without them. Clare knew where Monica would go first; she always started with the parents' room. They needed to get up there to . . . to what? As far as she knew, the Lindsays didn't have any secrets. But Abby was just standing frozen, which wasn't going to do any good should interference be needed.

"Come on," Clare said quietly. It was always easier to just go along.

Abby gave her a desperate look, but they both knew there was nothing to be done to stop this. Best to let it happen and then they could move on to whatever was next.

"Where's Mitchell?" Monica asked. She was almost at the top.

"He's working evening shifts this week, so he might be sleeping," Abby said.

Mitchell's door was the second on the left, marked with a painted cursive M, the handiwork of Mrs. Lindsay, who was a devoted reader of *Better Homes & Gardens*. Monica stopped outside his closed door and looked at it. "Really? He's asleep?"

"Does he sleep naked?" Lori asked. Monica giggled and put her ear against the door.

Clare had to stop herself from yelling, "Don't." That would have been disastrous. Abby was with them now, out of breath from having bolted up the stairs. "We're not supposed to wake him up."

"I'm not going to." Very slowly Monica put her hand on the doorknob and began to turn.

"I'm thirsty," Clare said in a voice that she hoped sounded neutral. "Let's go downstairs."

"Not yet," Monica said. She gave Clare a look that could have meant "I know your secret" or might have been just a more general "chill the f out." But she took her hand off the doorknob and continued walking down the hall.

The others followed in single file.

Sometimes that summer the four of them were joined by another girl or two from their class. Then, when they got tired of biking around, Monica would casually ask if anyone was home at the new girl's house and if they could go there to hang out. The girl, flattered, would always agree, not knowing what would happen next. When Clare didn't know the girl well, it was easy to join in and let Monica open the dresser drawers and try on the mother's jewelry, but here at Abby's house, she didn't know how to fit herself into this investigation.

Monica always started in the parents' bedroom, since, she claimed, that was where the best stuff was hidden. Porn and lacy underwear were the best finds but disappointingly rare. More often they might find a well-thumbed romance novel. Once they found an opened box of condoms, to the host girl's horror. "Size large, 'for a generous fit,'" Lori read off the box. Later, Monica revealed that she had taken one and slipped it into her jean shorts. Of course, they had all sat through the awkward but memorable health class demonstration, but knowing there was one in her pocket, "just in case," was far more titillating to think about.

Monica would lie on the parents' bed and ask whose side was whose, then open the bedside table drawers. And the host girl would answer all of her questions, usually offering more information, hoping it would satiate her curiosity. The girl's parents had left their room that morning, like any other morning, not knowing they would be invaded and examined, and so no matter how many times the host may have gone into this room herself, she had to be vigilant. No matter how mundane, there was a thrill to opening something that was meant to stay closed. Even if it was just the mother's carefully folded sweaters or the father's junk drawer: coins, doorless keys, almost-dead batteries, and plastic parts long since separated from their functioning whole.

All of it suddenly revealing. Suddenly delicate.

Abby's parents' room was at the end of the hall next to the bathroom. The bed was piled with pillows: circular ones, tubes with lace on either end, square quilted ones, and more behind those. The wallpaper's swirling pattern of blues and greens and a rug on either side of the bed matched the pattern. There was a television facing the bed, and sometimes, when the TV in the basement was being monopolized by one of Abby's older brothers, her parents would let her and Clare watch in their room. The girls would make themselves a fort out of all the pillows and settle in for hours.

"Holy overkill," Lori said. "Paisley, anyone?"

Abby's father's dresser was in the far corner: squat, brown wood, piled high with stacks of old mail, single socks, and other odds and ends.

"Doesn't your dad ever throw anything out?" Monica asked.

"I know. My mom's always complaining about it."

Mrs. Lindsay's dresser was on the opposite side of the room, cream-colored and crowded with framed family photos, jewelry boxes, and piles of neatly folded clothing in one stage or the other of sorting. Monica opened the top drawer. Lori went over and peeked in. Clare stayed by the door so she could keep a lookout while Abby sat on the bed, looking miserable.

"Ooh." Monica had found an old wallet and pulled out a picture. "Is this your dad? Totally creepy mustache."

"That's what Paul would look like if he grew a mustache," Lori said.

Monica glared at her and threw the wallet back in the drawer. "Parents always think that if they hide shit behind their sweaters, no one will find it."

"If I was going to hide something, I'd put it with the underwear," Lori said.

"The *dirty* underwear. Then no one would want to touch it."

You keep dirty underwear in your dresser? Clare thought but didn't say.

A car turned in to the driveway. Abby jumped off the bed and went to the door. "Let's go to the basement. We can watch TV."

"There's nothing on TV now, just soaps," Lori said, then turned to Monica. "Oh, I forgot, you like those."

"Shut up—you were totally into it when we watched it."

"I was just trying to make you feel better for liking something so lame." Lori grabbed Clare and pulled her close. " 'Jackson is cheating on me—I know it. I'm going to *kill* him if it's the last thing I do!' "

Clare snorted and the two of them doubled over giggling. Even Abby smiled.

"You're a horrible actress," Monica said. "I hope you know that."

"Whatever," Lori said, rolling her eyes at Clare.

"You should have seen her," Monica said, turning to Clare and Abby.

"The whole time we were watching, she was like, 'Who's that?' 'Why's she saying that?' 'Is she cheating on her husband?' It was so annoying." But Monica was smiling too. She opened another drawer and slid her hand in, feeling under the clothes.

"Come *on*," Abby said as the back door banged shut.

"Relax, Abigail. We're three steps away from your room. Oh, what's this?"

From downstairs, Abby's mother called up, "Abby? Girls, are you up there?"

"So much for being quiet," Lori said.

"Hi, Mom," Abby called out, trying to keep the high-pitched worry out of her voice.

"I saw your bikes. Are you hungry?"

Monica carefully extracted a flat box from the drawer, making sure not to rumple any of the folded clothes. Written on the front in swirling blue letters it said "Our Family."

"We'll be right down, Mom."

"There's food in the fridge," Mrs. Lindsay called up, but she already sounded farther away. The back door banged again as she went out to get more groceries.

"I should probably go down and help her," Abby said.

"Go ahead."

But Abby stayed.

Monica opened the box and removed a book held together with a pale blue ribbon. "Ooh, baby pictures," she said, opening it up.

"Why's your mom keep those hidden?" Lori asked.

"How would I know?"

Monica opened the book and read: " 'Mitchell Theodore Lindsay, eight pounds, seven ounces, born at two thirty-four a.m., January twelfth, 1982.' Ah, look at him. And look at that tiny footprint."

Lori and Clare crowded around her and she kept turning pages.

"Oh my God, he's so cute. Look at this one. 'Mitchell's first tooth,' 'Mitchell's first swim'—"

"He's totally naked!"

"You're such a perv." Monica kept flipping. "Halloween, Christmas . . ." She turned a few more pages, each heavy with baby pictures. Taped to one there was an envelope that said, "First haircut."

"Is that hair?" Lori asked. Monica was opening the envelope and looking in.

"Be careful," Abby said.

"My mom did that," Clare said. "She put some of my baby hair in a locket that she used to wear."

Clare's mother was forbidden territory, so Monica put the envelope back and kept turning the pages.

"Oh, here's Paul," Monica continued. "My mom told me that's called Irish twins."

"We're not Irish," Abby said.

"It's when two babies are born super close together 'cause the Irish aren't allowed to use birth control." Monica gestured to the photo. "He's kind of an ugly baby."

"That's not nice," Lori said, and glanced at Abby.

"I'm just being honest," Monica said. "My cousin was a weird-looking baby, but he's fine now. Oh, look at this one—I love their little matching cowboy outfits. Can you imagine your brothers dressing in matching outfits now?"

"Not really," Abby said. She chewed her lip and looked in the hall.

Monica kept flipping through the book. "The eighties were such a gross time. Like, seriously, the styles were the worst. Ooh, here's little baby Abby." She turned the page and it was blank. "What the hell? That's it?"

"There's more in the photo albums downstairs if you want to see them."

"Uh, no, that's fine. I'm just observing there's a bazillion pictures of your brothers and then, like, two of you."

"There's not as many of Paul as there are of Mitchell," Clare said.

"But there's still a lot," Monica said.

"My mom says she was lucky if she got to shower once the twins were born," Lori added. Her twin brothers were eight-year-old terrors. "There's no way she'd have time to put together a family album."

"So you don't think it's weird?" Monica said to Lori, like she really was concerned about this. Her tone was almost hurt. "I mean, obviously Abby was the accident but, like, she still counts."

"I wasn't an accident," Abby said.

"Oh," Monica said, turning to her like she just realized a damaged child was in the room. "I didn't mean it like a bad thing. It's pretty typical with a third child. Plus, there's a gap between you and your brothers. So probably your parents weren't going to have more, and then surprise!"

"No, they wanted a girl," Abby said. "My dad told me—"

A door opened down the hall.

"Oh no," Abby whispered, running to the door again and looking into the hallway.

"Close the door," Monica said quietly. Footsteps went past the bedroom and into the bathroom. Monica slid the photo album back into the drawer and walked toward the bedroom door, peeking into the hallway. "Guess who's awake and left his room open," she said, smiling.

"No." Clare and Abby said it almost at the same time.

In the bathroom, the shower started. "I just want to take a little peek," Monica said, and started walking toward Mitchell's room. Lori pulled herself off the bed and started to follow.

"I can show you something else," Abby said suddenly. "It's good, honest." They all stopped and turned to her. "But can we please go into my room? That's where it is."

They crowded into Abby's room, picking their way over the clothes and books all over the floor. Clare took her usual place on the faded beanbag chair by the window. Lori and Monica sat on the bed. Abby looked nervous.

"Okay, well . . ." she started, then looked at Clare.

"What are you looking at me for?" Clare asked. She had no idea what secret thing Abby could possibly have that would be interesting; Clare assumed nothing, that this was just a tactic to get them away from Mitchell's room, but then Abby took an envelope out of her desk drawer and handed a picture to Monica and Lori.

"Whoa," Lori said.

"What is it?" Clare asked, getting up and coming over.

"I'm sorry—I was going to tell you," Abby said, looking at her.

Monica looked up from the picture. "Is this Clare's mom?"

Clare grabbed the picture, but she didn't have to look closely to know. It was a black-and-white picture of her mother taken when she had been eight months pregnant. In it, she was naked and sitting by a window. Her hair was long and covering her breasts, and her hands were folded over her belly like she was holding the baby through her skin. She looked soft and young, and bursting with amazement at what was happening to her. Eight years later that same body would be suddenly and savagely destroyed by disease. Was it in her with me? Clare wondered. She put her finger on her mother's bare shoulder, trying to feel the warmth of that skin. She shivered. The others were looking at her, waiting to see how she'd respond.

"Why do you have this?" she asked Abby.

"I just wanted to look at it for a bit. She's so beautiful—"

"You took it from my room."

"You said I could look at it."

"I didn't say you could take it."

"I was going to give it back. And I took really good care of it."

"What if my dad noticed it was gone? I'm not even supposed to have it."

Abby's lower lip was quivering. "I'm sorry, Clare. I was really careful with it."

Monica and Lori were watching the exchange between the two of them. Clare suddenly felt shaky—too shaky to say anything else. She would not cry. It had been a long, long time since anyone had seen that, and she wasn't going to start now.

Monica reached out and touched her arm. "Here, sit down."

Clare sat between them on the bed while Abby stood in front of them. "I'm really sorry," she started to say again, but Monica held up her hand and stopped her, then turned to Clare.

"Are you okay?"

Clare nodded. It felt good to sit here between the two of them. It felt like it first had, so many years ago now, when her mom had died and Monica and Lori had stood by her through all the questions and strange looks from her classmates. They had claimed ownership over her grief in a way that felt good at first, like these two eight-year-old girls could protect her from any more hurt. But then they had grown tired of her mourning and wanted her to be past it, like they were, and that was when she'd learned the price for showing her grief. So she learned to hide it and promised herself she'd never cry in front of them again. And then Abby's family moved into Sumner's Mills, and Clare found a new ally. The attention was lifted off her and it was a relief to be with someone who didn't see her as weak. All of this went through her head in that moment as Monica and Lori watched her and Abby looked at the carpet.

"It's okay," Clare said. "I was going to show you anyway."

"She's so young," Lori said, gently touching the picture.

"She was eighteen," Clare said. "She finished college at night school when I was little."

The girls looked at the woman in the photograph again. She was only a few years older than they were, yet the distance between her rounded body and theirs seemed impossible. Clare turned the photo over. It said, "Julie, May 1984."

"Scandal," Monica said in a singsong voice, but it was gentle, like she was impressed. "I remember your mom. She was so pretty. Like, even when she was sick."

"She really was," Lori said. "She was super nice too. Remember when I slept over at your house—we must have been, what, seven? It was my first time being away from home and I got super scared, but your mom was so sweet and she sang that song . . . What was it?"

" 'You Are My Sunshine,' " Clare said quietly. She hadn't thought about that song in so long. For a moment she felt a lump burn in her throat again, but then Lori smiled at her, one of her old unselfconscious kid smiles, and the lump went away.

Abby said nothing. She hadn't been around for Clare's mother's illness, or her death, and this was the point. She was biting her lip and keeping her focus on the carpet. How had they gone from a forgettable summer afternoon hanging out to this? Clare sighed and said to her, "It's okay. Just ask next time." Abby looked up at her then, and she could see the tears threatening to spill. She didn't want Monica and Lori to see Abby cry any more than she wanted them to see her cry. They weren't little kids anymore. At some point—she didn't know when—crying had become a private thing.

"Yeah, who knew you were such a little klepto," Lori said, but she was joking. "I'm going to have to keep my dad's porn collection away from you."

"Gross," Monica said. "Like anyone would want to touch that."

"That's not what you said when I showed you that *Playboy.* You couldn't stop talking about her boobs."

"Because they were totally fake, hello."

Clare breathed out and slid off the bed. She put the photo in the envelope and put it in her pocket, hoping it wouldn't get bent. They heard Mitchell walk down the hallway and close his bedroom door again.

"Damn," Monica said softly. "There goes my chance."

"His room probably smells bad, anyway. All teen guys' rooms smell like feet," Lori said.

"How would *you* know?" Monica said. "Oh, right, 'cause that's how your room smells."

Clare was suddenly grateful for their ability to let the attention come back to themselves.

"I'm thirsty," Lori said. "Do your folks have decent iced tea?"

Abby led the way downstairs with Lori following, but Monica turned around and stopped Clare in the hallway. "That was not cool," she said quietly.

"It's okay," Clare said. She didn't know if it was okay or not, but she did not want to discuss it with Monica. She felt angry with Abby and protective of her at the same time.

"I'm just saying," Monica said. "If she does something like that again . . ."

"She won't."

Monica looked at Clare for a moment, then turned and followed the other two down the stairs.

Mrs. Lindsay directed them to a new box of Popsicles, and after they'd picked out their favorite flavors, they went into the basement. It was dark and slightly damp and felt like a relief after the bright sun of the bedrooms. At the base of the stairs there was an old couch with some overstuffed chairs, a shag rug from the seventies, and a big box of a TV. There was a Ping-Pong table, loaded with laundry from the washer and dryer under the stairs, and beyond that were stacks of boxes, skis, old lawn furniture, camping equipment, piles of board games, and all the other remnants of a family of five.

Lori ate her Popsicle in bites, seemingly immune to the cold, and was done within a minute. Monica licked hers delicately, biting off tiny pieces from the tip. And Clare and Abby alternated between the Popsicles and licking their wrists as the sugary juice dripped down their arms. At some point, after the Popsicles had been finished, they started talking about haunted houses and whether or not they were real. Abby believed in them absolutely. Monica did not. "I'd go into any place people said was haunted," she said. "I guarantee you won't find anything in there but a bunch of garbage and dust."

"So then it's not haunted after all," Lori said.

"Yeah, but if everyone says it's haunted—" Monica said.

"But it's not brave to go into a place that isn't actually haunted. You just said that you'd go into a place that is haunted, and then you said that it wouldn't be."

"What?" Monica's tone had the edge that made Clare's stomach jump, but it didn't seem to faze Lori.

"Whatever," Lori said, crumpling up her Popsicle wrapper and throwing it on the table. She picked up a *National Geographic* and began flipping through it as if to say she was also bored of the conversation. She was looking at a picture of sea turtles when she suddenly looked up and said, "I know a place."

At fourteen and three months, Lori was the oldest, and she was fearless. Even her questions were a defiance of sorts. Now, with the clarity of hindsight, Clare would say that Lori probably was afraid, and her way of handling that fear was to run up and knock it in the face before it could get to her.

"Where?" Monica asked.

"It's on our farm, but it's way out past the back fields."

"We would have seen it."

"When have you guys ever been in our fields? You can't see it from my house. It's off Route 31."

"Our school bus used to go down that road," Clare said.

"You have to know it's there. It's surrounded by woods. You've passed it a hundred times and just not known."

Clare shivered, but Monica leaned forward. "Okay, show us," she said.

"Now?"

"No!" Abby's voice was high-pitched.

"Sure," Lori said, returning to the photos of sea turtles. "Unless you're too scared." This was said to Abby.

"Can we go in?" Clare asked, immediately regretting the question.

"Why not? No one's lived in it for ages."

"Why haven't they torn it down, then?" Monica's skepticism seemed brave. The same question out of Abby would have only shown more fear.

Lori shrugged. "It's a weird shape. It's an octagon. My dad calls it the Octagon House."

"Original," Monica said. "Have you seen it?"

"What, don't you believe me?"

"I was just wondering."

"It's cursed. That's what my dad says."

"Cursed?"

"We shouldn't go in, then," Abby said. Sometimes she didn't know when to shut up.

Monica turned and looked directly at Abby. "Why not?"

"Why's it cursed?" Clare asked.

"A woman was murdered in the house. And her kids." Lori's voice dropped lower, and instinctively they all leaned in. "The husband did it."

"Was his wife having an affair?" Monica asked. "Maybe he caught them doing it."

"Then why'd he kill the kids too?"

"No witnesses," Abby said, her eyes wide. "Right?"

"It was during Vietnam, so my mom said the husband might have been crazy. That's not something they ever talk about on Veterans Day, but it happened a lot."

"My stepdad knows a lot of guys who came home and were totally messed up because of what they'd seen," Monica said.

"Did the man confess why he'd done it?" Clare asked.

"He said he was innocent. But no one believed him."

"How'd he kill them?" Abby asked.

"Shot them."

"There'll be bloodstains. I bet we could still see them," Monica said.

"It was ages ago. Those'd be gone," Clare said.

"There'd have been too much blood. You can't get bloodstains like that out."

"Yeah," Abby said. "I had a nosebleed a few years ago that dripped on the carpet and the stain is still there."

"That was two years ago. This was like decades."

"It's a real-life murder scene."

"Your dad should have just torn it down," Clare said.

"He can't, 'cause it's cursed," Lori said. "Like I said before."

"You actually believe that?" Monica said.

"If a place is cursed, you shouldn't touch it. You could disturb it," Abby said.

"Disturb what? Everyone's dead."

"Let's go there and find out," Lori said. "This is boring just talking about it."

No one moved.

"My grandparents are coming for supper," Abby said.

"So, what, you want to invite them too?" Lori said.

Monica snorted and Clare almost started laughing too. The tension was making her giddy.

"It's broad daylight," Lori said. "What, are you scared?"

"Don't be. Curses don't exist," Monica said, stretching her legs and standing up. With that, the matter was settled and, as with any dare, the challenge had to be answered.

But none of them were convinced.

6

CLARE

July 25, 1998
4 P.M.

Because this was Lori's suggestion, she took the lead. They followed the usual road to get to her house, but instead of turning in to her driveway, they went past it and connected onto Route 31, which ran along the north end of her family's fields. Monica biked next to her in her usual spot while Clare and Abby trailed behind.

"What if the husband comes back?" Abby said.

"He'd be dead by now."

"He'd just be old. It was only thirty years ago."

"Well, then he's probably still in jail."

"So, what if he gets out and he comes back? Maybe he hangs around the house looking for his family or something."

"Why would he be looking for them if he's the one who killed them?" Clare said.

"Do you believe in ghosts?" Abby asked.

"No."

"They could exist. There's lots of stuff we didn't know and we thought couldn't be real but then it was."

"Like what?"

"Like, I don't know, other planets and stuff."

"That's different," Clare said. "Ghosts don't exist. You're just going to freak yourself out."

"Is it because of your mom?"

"My mom's not a ghost." Clare kept focused ahead so she didn't have to look at Abby.

"But what you told me before, about her leaving you signs."

"Stop talking about my mom, okay?"

Clare clenched the bike handles and pedaled harder to catch up to Monica and Lori, letting Abby trail behind. First the picture and now this. How could Abby let her mother's picture become the same as Lori's dad's porn? Something to be ogled and judged. Abby was always asking questions about her mom, and usually Clare liked it, but she never should have told her about the signs. It was the one thing she had left of her mother, and Abby talking about it made it sound childish. Childish and impossible.

One afternoon during that terrible spring six years ago, her mother had called her over to the couch, where she was cocooned in her nest of blankets, pill bottles, and hospital paraphernalia. "I dreamed that I was a bird flying over you, Clarabelle." That was her mother's special name for her. "You know I will always be watching over you."

At the time, she hadn't understood what her mom was telling her. It was only later, when it was too late to ask questions, that she understood.

A few months after her mother died, Clare was getting dressed for school, and she saw a bird sitting on the ledge of her bedroom window. She stopped, expecting the bird to fly away, but it didn't move, so she crept closer to the window. The bird looked at her, and that was when Clare remembered her mother's dream. "Hello," she said, putting her hand on the glass. The bird bobbed its head twice and flew away.

After that, she started to see little signs from her mother: a cluster of wildflowers growing where she'd never seen them before, a dollar bill folded into her jacket pocket that she had no memory of putting there, a copy of her favorite book from when she was little—the book her mother had read to her so many times—lying open on a library table. Each sign came with that feeling, the sureness that it was her mother saying, *I see you.* But when was the last time she had gotten a sign from her mother? She couldn't even remember. What if her mother thought Clare had forgotten her?

And now she had betrayed her by showing that picture to Abby. Abby, who couldn't keep a secret and just blabbed whatever came into her head. Clare had felt annoyed with Abby lots of times before, but this was different. Earlier, she had been too discombobulated to feel anything other than a stuttering embarrassment, but now the anger simmered low and hot in her stomach.

After a mile or so, the road curved slightly, and on one side the fields were broken by a large patch of dense forest. Clare had seen it many times before, never paying attention to it. Lori slowed down, scanning the woods, then quietly said, "There." She rolled her bike into the ditch, then walked up to the wire fence that ran for acres, bordering her family's land. She went to a fence post with a faded strip of white paint—almost invisible from the road—and unhooked the wire from the post.

"It's marked?" Monica said.

"My grandfather marked it a long time ago so he could find the old road," Lori said. She squinted into the forest. "Well, there used to be a road. Let's leave our bikes inside the trees just in case anyone drives by." She peeled back the rusty wire to let them pass through.

The sky was blasted pale blue in the heat of the July afternoon, but as soon as they stepped into the forest, the warmth and color were choked out. Lori led them along the old road, little more than an overgrown path now that would be reclaimed soon by the forest. They walked carefully, in single file, eyes jumping from trees to ground to trees, looking for movement. There was none. The smells of wet leaves, mold, and moss rose as their feet disturbed the layers of dead vegetation beneath them. The humming and ticking of insects that formed the white noise of midsummer were gone, and in the sudden silence, Clare heard her own breathing. The forest closed behind them and the road disappeared from view. They kept walking. Then the path turned and Lori said, "It's through here." Clare saw light and space beyond the trees. They stopped at the edge of the clearing and stayed hidden.

The house crouched on a small rise in the middle of the clearing. It was covered in clapboards that had once been white, but years of weather had turned them a brownish gray with streaks of black running down to the ground. As Lori had told them, the house was a strange shape. From where they stood, they could see three sides. Each side had two windows, one on each floor. The windows on the bottom floor had boards nailed haphazardly across them as if someone had been in a hurry to cover them up. The windows on the second floor were bare, and their broken panes hung jagged and sharp. The roof was covered in brownish-red tiles with patches of gray wood exposed. Above it all, and miraculously intact, sat a small lookout that reflected the bright sky in its windows.

All around, the forest waited. And then Clare took a step and a stick broke beneath her foot. The sound was sharp, and three birds shot up from the trees across the clearing, hovered anxious in the air, and flew away. Their presence was now known, and the house, which looked like it had long ago exhaled its life, was, sleepily, awake.

"I want to go home," Abby said.

No one said anything. No one turned back.

Keeping to the edge of the clearing, they crept around the perimeter. On the far side, there was a large door that must have been the front entrance. Like the windows, it had thick boards nailed across it. A sagging porch wrapped around this end of the house. The pillars that had held it up were snapped like twigs, and parts of its roof were bowed to the ground.

"Screw this," Lori said when they'd reached their starting place again. Without looking to see if the others were following, she crossed into the clearing, walking directly toward the dark opening that faced them.

Monica started to follow, then stopped and looked back at Clare and

Abby. "Come on, you guys." It was almost gentle, like she was saying, "We all have to do this." Clare started walking. She didn't have to turn around to know Abby was behind her.

The doorway closest to them had no door. What had been the door was lying shattered and half rotted into the ground. Someone had taken a crowbar or hammer to it, and the splintered pieces of wood hanging off the frame reached out like fingers to brush whoever entered.

"Someone wanted to get inside, bad," Lori said.

"Maybe it was the murderer," Abby added.

"Oooh, come back to look at the scene of his crime," Monica said. "I saw this show on TV that talked about that. It's how they catch them sometimes."

"But they already caught him," Abby said.

"Maybe they did, maybe they didn't." Monica shrugged. "I mean, the husband *said* he was innocent."

"Stop trying to freak everyone out," Lori said. "Let's just go in." She turned around, ducked under a cobweb, and stepped into the darkness. Monica followed her.

"Wait." Abby reached out and grabbed Clare's arm as she went to step in. Her fingers dug in to her skin and left little white marks when Clare pulled her arm away. *I'm not waiting for you.* She shook off Abby's small hand and stepped inside.

The room had been the kitchen. It was spacious but dark, with only a little light coming in through gaps in the wood that covered the windows. Everything was gray and filmed in a thick layer of dust. The cupboards had been ripped from the walls, but the lines of rusty nails and ruined plaster showed where they once hung. In the years since the home had been lived in, many people had been in this place, slowly stripping it of any sign of the previous occupants.

Now Clare felt a hush in the room, like a memory that hung in the air.

She closed her eyes and tried to imagine what the kitchen had looked like the night of the murders.

In this room, hours before she was killed, the wife had probably made supper. There might have been a large table in the middle of the room. Were there children? Yes, Lori had said there were two. Maybe they were given simple jobs like mixing flour and setting the table. What had their last supper been? What night of the week was it? All of it would have seemed so normal.

Clare stopped. Blinked. She could see this mother, later in the evening now, leaning over the sink and doing dishes as it grew dark outside, checking out the window—for what? Her husband to come home? Maybe he was later than usual this evening. Clare imagined one of the children coming into the kitchen and rubbing her eyes. Wanting a glass of water. No, she was afraid of the dark; the glass of water was the excuse. No, that was me. Clare shook her head. The images disappeared and were replaced with the broken gray room of the present. She'd seen it all so clearly, but it was her own kitchen she was seeing, right? That young woman was her mother. Clare was the one who was afraid of the dark.

Who had lived here? What had actually happened? The ruined kitchen didn't give any clues.

"I thought there'd be blood on the walls or something," Monica said, wandering along the perimeter. She moved quickly and confidently, and the glass crunched under her tennis shoes.

"Maybe this isn't where he killed them," Lori said. "Besides, it would have been all cleaned up, don't you think?"

"But still, I bet there's a clue somewhere. I wonder where he did it."

"How do you know it's a he?" Abby asked. "I mean, if it wasn't the husband."

"You think it was a girl? A jealous lover? The husband was cheating and he wouldn't leave his wife," Monica said. It was hard to tell if she was serious.

"You have *got* to lay off the soaps," Lori said.

The stairs to the second floor were in the middle of the house, dissecting the kitchen and the living room. At the bottom of the stairs, Monica and Lori were debating the likelihood of the second-story floor being rotten. Clare went toward the opposite doorway to go into the other room, but then she saw an unusual metal door. She stopped. This one was larger than it should be and out of place with the rest of the house. She put her hand on the latch and pulled. At first it didn't move, but then the door began to swing open, seemingly on its own. The air that came out of the darkness was wet and cold and felt like something long forgotten was exhaling on her. She had found the basement. Get away, get away, get away, her mind screamed, but she couldn't move.

Something down here for you.

Those words flashed across her head. It was a feeling, a knowing, like she was reading the words, not hearing them spoken. The feeling was strong and sudden, and that made it feel like it must be right.

That meant it was a sign.

No. There couldn't be a sign here. There hadn't been a sign in so long. She stared down the stairs to where they disappeared into blackness.

She had been thinking about her mother because of that picture, that's all it was. Wasn't it? She felt for the photo, still in her pocket. I can be brave because she's with me.

She stepped down to the top step. As if she were walking into cold water, she felt the darkness moving up her legs. The thick stench of the air clung to her. The basement was smelling her, touching her, absorbing into her—or was she being absorbed into it? Everything else about this place was empty: the house, the dry, cracked ground of the clearing, even the woods, but this hole, this hole at the center of it all, was filled with something. It wasn't alive, but it was present. Standing on those stairs, she knew this as surely as she knew anything. Then the light shifted, and she saw something at the bottom of the stairs, something small and—

Eyes.

"What are you doing?" The voice was behind her. Abby.

Clare jumped back. She looked down, but it was just darkness again.

"I thought I saw something," she said, and stepped away from the doorway.

"How can you see anything?" Abby said, squinting into the dark, then pulling back. "Ugh. It stinks."

Why would her mother leave her a sign here? Was she trying to ask for help or warn her? Something was wrong. Something was very, very wrong. She'd felt it as soon as the basement air touched her skin.

Seconds passed, and the feeling that had been so clear was getting cloudy. If her mother was trying to tell her something, Abby was in the way, just standing there. The anger rooted in Clare's stomach rose up, sudden and sharp.

"You should go down there," she said.

"Are you crazy?" Abby laughed a little, but she kept looking into the darkness.

She should pay for touching that picture. That's what Monica had been telling her. Abby had gone too far and should be punished.

"There's something down there," Clare said.

"Yeah, right."

"There is."

"How would you know? You can't see anything."

"I just saw it for a second, but you blocked the light."

"I don't see anything."

"I dare you to go down there."

Abby jerked away from the doorway and turned to face Clare. "Why me?" She sounded scared now.

Good. Let her be scared. "Because."

"Clare—"

"You kind of owe me."

Abby just stared at her.

Clare sighed. "Fine, we'll both go. We don't have to go all the way. I just want to see what it is. It's on the stairs."

"How about we go halfway," Abby said. "I mean, the stairs might be rotten. There's no banister, I don't want to fall."

"Sure," Clare said. "You go first."

Abby took a tentative step down, then another. "The smell is getting worse, isn't it," she called back.

In one motion, Clare stepped up out of the stairway and pushed the door shut. For a second there was nothing, just relief that the basement was closed off. Clare's hands were shaking. Her anger had disappeared as soon as the door closed, and she felt giddy. She'd done it. It had been a split-second decision, and she'd acted so fast, she'd surprised herself as well.

Then Abby started screaming. "Clare? Clare?"

Abby sounded far away, her voice muffled by the thick door. Her screams grew more desperate.

Panic exploded in Clare's gut. She needed to pull Abby out. She pushed the handle down and pulled. The door didn't move. She pulled harder.

"Clare. It's so dark. Please—"

"I'm trying," she shouted. "The door's stuck." She pulled harder. Abby's screams were high-pitched and staccato. Terror made into sound. "Push on the door," Clare yelled.

Monica and Lori came crashing into the room. "What's going on? Why are you yelling?"

"It's Abby—she's in the basement."

"Holy fuck—"

"I can't get the door to open. It's jammed or something."

"She actually went down there?"

"We were both going to go, but the door just closed."

"Abby!" Lori called. She banged on the door. "We're getting you out, don't worry."

"Did you close the door on her?" Monica asked.

Clare couldn't tell if it was an accusation. "No. I must have hit it with my shoulder."

Lori had one foot up on the wall to brace herself and was using all her body weight to pull. "You guys, help me."

"You're going to pull the handle off," Monica said.

"How else am I supposed to get it open?"

Abby had stopped screaming. Her sudden silence was worse.

"I don't understand," Clare said. "I just opened it a minute ago." She was going to throw up; the panic was in her throat now.

"Help me pull—"

"Oh my God oh my God—"

And then with a whoosh of air, the door swung open. Lori fell backward into Monica and Clare, and they all stumbled away from the opening. Abby was standing five steps below, her arms wrapped tight around her, her eyes huge.

"Are you all right?" Lori got up and stood tentatively on the top stair, reaching out.

Abby shakily gripped Lori's hand and climbed up. For a split second they were silent, and then they all started talking at once.

"I'm so sorry—" Clare blubbered.

"Oh. My. God. That was—"

"It *stinks*. How did you not throw up?"

"Holy fuck, I bet there's like dead animals down there—"

"That was in*sane*."

"Why are you crying?" Abby asked Clare.

"Yeah, if anyone should be freaking out, it should be Abby," Monica said.

"I don't know what happened," Clare said. All of those thoughts that had come into her head—come in from where?—they couldn't have been real; they couldn't have been her. It had happened so quickly, and then the thoughts had been gone just as suddenly. So maybe they hadn't been there at all. Maybe she *had* really bumped against the door and it had gotten jammed.

"What was it like?" Lori asked. She was rubbing her sore hand.

"Really effing dark," Abby said.

Lori laughed. "No kidding." She peered again at the basement. "You couldn't *pay* me to go down there."

Monica threw her arms around Abby. "I'm so glad you're okay. Rambo over here"—she indicated Lori—"almost ripped the handle off."

Abby grinned. "Really?"

"Yeah, because unlike some, I'm not worried about breaking my freaking nails."

"You got all butch. I'm just saying."

"I totally didn't mean for the door to close," Clare blurted out. She was standing on the edge of the group, letting them push her away. "I must have hit it with my shoulder and it just swung shut and then we couldn't get it open and—"

"Yeah, right," Monica said.

"No, I swear—" Clare said.

Abby stared at her, blank.

"Honestly, it just happened."

"You were getting back at her for before," Monica said matter-of-factly.

"No—"

"Don't worry," Lori said, holding her hands up in defense. "Message received. Don't mess with Clare." Maybe she was joking, but Clare couldn't tell.

"I have to go now," Abby said. "My grandparents are coming to my house."

They stepped apart, giving her space to move past them. Clare desperately wanted to leave too, but Abby had earned her exit. Clare hadn't.

"Okay . . . well . . ." Abby reached up to tuck the loose hairs behind her ear, something Clare had seen her do a thousand times, but now her hand was shaking. She must have realized in the same moment because she dropped her hand, hair untouched, and stuffed it in her pocket. Clare suddenly longed to take that hand, to hold it and press it and take the shaking away.

Without looking at any of them, Abby turned and walked out of the house.

The three girls stood still for a moment after she left, listening to the silence, waiting for what would happen next. Clare couldn't be the one to speak first; she had to wait and see how Monica and Lori decided to handle her now that Abby was gone. What had she done? It wasn't real, she couldn't have possibly done it.

But it wasn't my fault.

Yes, it was.

Finally, Monica spoke and broke the spell. "This whole place stinks now." She moved over to the fireplace at the far end, each step softly crunching the leaves and garbage scattered across the floor.

"It's sulfur," Lori said. "It's in the water. The basement in the old part of our house is the same."

"Now that you mention it, it does smell a bit like your house," Monica said.

The three of them wandered around the kitchen, kicking at the garbage on the floor, avoiding the gaping hole of the open basement door. Clare was sure they were just waiting for a chance to talk about her, to speculate on whether it had been on purpose or not. She wanted to be alone to sort out her thoughts.

She walked over to the bottom of the stairs that led to the second floor. "Did you guys see anything good up there?" Even from the base of the stairs, she saw more light coming into the hallway.

"The room on the roof is cool," Monica said. "You should go up there."

"Be careful, though," Lori said. "The floor's kind of weak in places."

The upstairs had four bedrooms leading off the hallway and a small bathroom in the middle. Most of the windows were broken, and a light breeze blew through, lifting motes of dust into the sun. The bedrooms seemed enormous in their emptiness, but the one on the end was the largest and must have been for the parents. The wallpaper was faded but wasn't damaged like on the first floor. It had thin blue stripes with tiny, almost invisible green vines between them. She walked over to a door, thinking it was the closet, but when she opened it, there was a flight of stairs flooded with light. She smiled. She had found the room on the roof.

The stairs were plain wood, not painted like the rest of the floor, and they still seemed clean after all this time. They were steep and narrow, and she had to crawl up as if climbing a ladder. The room took the shape of a mini octagon with a window in each small wall, so its upper half was almost all glass. It was as warm and bright as a greenhouse, and Clare felt the panic and nausea loosening their grip on her. She sat down and closed her eyes. Whatever had happened downstairs had been an effect of the day and the creepiness of the house. She hadn't seen anything in the basement. The door jammed because it was an old house, no other reason. And the feeling that there was something down there . . . that was just her imagination. It was peaceful up here. She could fall asleep. The heat was making her drowsy . . .

Wake up.

She made herself get up. A movement outside caught her eye, and she saw Abby standing at the edge of the clearing. Abby was looking at the house; then she'd turn to look at the trees and then back to the house again. Why hadn't she left yet if she was in such a big hurry? She was back to looking at the house, but then she must have seen something because she immediately slipped into the woods. In another moment, Monica and Lori walked into the clearing. They were leaving without Clare. That's why they had told her to go upstairs, so they could leave her behind. The thought of being alone in this house hit her as if all the air had been siphoned from the room.

She half ran, half slid down the steep steps into the bedroom, then into the hallway and down the stairs into the kitchen. *Don't leave me behind. Don't leave me behind.* Her eyes hadn't adjusted to the dimness downstairs, and the room was filled with shadows. She was almost at the door when she heard a scraping sound, the sound of something heavy being dragged over grit. She stopped—*GO GO GO,* that voice was screaming in her head—but she turned and moved toward the sound. Only a few steps. Only enough to see the basement door slide shut with a soft *thunk.*

All on its own.

She ran for the bright light of the doorway and the world outside.

———

Clare sprinted up behind the girls.

"Whoa—you see a ghost or something?" Lori's mouth half raised into a smirk, but she'd looked startled when she noticed Clare. They were almost back in the woods.

"No. I thought you—" She was having trouble getting enough air to speak, and there was a sharp stitch in her side.

They looked at her.

"You guys are leaving?"

"We called up to you."

"I didn't hear you."

"Oh." Monica shrugged. "Well, we did." And they turned and kept walking.

As soon as they crossed into the woods, they moved into a single line. Walking behind Lori and Monica, Clare stopped and watched them picking their way down the old trail, either unaware that she was no longer with them or not caring. It felt strange seeing them continue without her—strange yet reassuring, as something that she had always suspected was now confirmed. For Monica and Lori, Clare's presence was inconsequential. But not for Abby; she would have noticed right away. She would have stopped and turned around, cocking her head to one side in that way she did when she was confused.

Tears started to well in Clare's eyes. She felt sick again. What was wrong with her? She looked at the other girls, far off now, barely visible among the trees. If she waited a moment longer, they would disappear, and she really would be alone. She wiped her eyes and ran after them.

7

From my childhood bed, I follow the geography of cracks in the ceiling, imagining, like I did when I was a girl, that they are rivers I'm flying high above somewhere near the Arctic Circle. The plane will lower, and soon I will hear the crashing of water over rock.

In the past few months, I have learned about stillness. If I am still long enough, I can sift through memories as if reaching my hand into one of those imagined rivers and tracing my finger along the bottom. At first the usual sediment will rise. These are familiar memories, the first ones. But if I wait, if I'm still and let those first ones move away in the river water of my mind, there are more underneath.

My life since Josh and I broke up has been silent. I have no job and I haven't been able to face trying to find a new one. I have some savings and there's unemployment. When I moved into my new apartment, I didn't bother to unpack most of the boxes, only what I needed: sheets and basic kitchen supplies, my oldest clothes. No one to impress. I ran each night through dark streets, tempting something to happen, but nothing did. I started to wonder if I was becoming invisible, my only interactions with people kept to the bare minimum. I didn't mean for the memory sifting to happen. It just did.

Last night when I came home from Lori's, I couldn't sleep. I tossed and turned and dropped my phone under the bed, and when I went to retrieve it, I found the wrapper of an ovulation test strip from last

Christmas. Josh and I were trying to get pregnant, but despite ovulation tests and taking my temperature each morning, which felt very grown up and decidedly unsexy, trying to have sex quietly in my childhood bedroom with my father down the hall had made me feel like a giddy teenager. Now my fingers fold and unfold the wrapper. Had my father seen it under the bed? He'd been in my room packing boxes. Maybe he'd known. Maybe that was why he felt like he could finally move; what he'd meant when he'd said that we were making our own home.

Josh and I met at the Chicago Field Museum of Natural History. He was working on an exhibit about South American moths; I was there on a class trip. It was a rainy Monday in March. I was standing in the cavernous lobby with seventeen ninth-grade girls around me, our bus having just driven away through torrential rain. Water dripped off our hair and our coats, forming deadly invisible puddles on the marble floor. I was nervous; it was my first year teaching and my first field trip. The older woman behind the information desk informed me that our guide was sick, and there was absolutely no way could we do a self-guided tour of the exhibit we were there to see. I glared at her, but the effect was ruined by a large drop of rain rolling off my hair and into my eye. Josh said the black line of wet mascara, slowly inching down my face, gave me an undeniable warrior look.

"You were so brave to offer to be our guide," I'd told him later.

"Well, Helen is one of our most dedicated volunteers."

"Helen's a stickler for the rules and has clearly never organized a field trip with teenagers."

"And I was worried you were going to punch her."

So, Josh, who happened to be passing by and heard our predicament, stepped forward and offered to give us the tour. It took only about half an hour, and we had another two hours before the bus was due to pick us up. I was trying to figure out how to rescue the rest of the trip when he asked if we wanted to see something "really fun." He led us down to the basement level, to a part of the museum no one but staff sees, and he showed us specimens. He had been sweet and funny while giving us the tour of marsupials, making no effort to hide the fact that he was reading the information cards at the same time we were, but when he brought us into the specimen room, something in him lit up. The students all picked up on it, and even the ones who'd been looking for a getaway crowded around him as he pulled out drawer after drawer of moths, butterflies, and bugs the likes of which we'd never seen. He answered their questions and let them open any drawer they wanted, and before I knew it, it was time to get on the bus and we had totally gone over our lunch break. Josh walked us back to the main lobby, and while the girls ran ahead, he stayed beside me and invited me to his exhibition opening that Friday night.

He wasn't my type, that's what I kept telling myself. He was crazy about bugs and moths and was like a kid with a science project who just wanted to show whoever was interested. But the museum at night was totally different from that rainy field trip. I spent most of the evening standing with him under the papery wings of flying moths, protected by an invisible dome. People approached him to congratulate him on the exhibit, or to take him to meet donors, but he always came back to me, each time bearing a bite-size dessert he'd snagged from a passing caterer, or another glass of wine.

That was six years ago.

Everything with Josh just clicked into place. There weren't any games; there wasn't any guessing. He was smart and funny and kind. He loved the outdoors and introduced me to camping. He even tried, disastrously, to teach me how to fish. After two years, we moved in together. We got a cat, Thompson, who had different-colored eyes and six toes on one of his feet. We bought furniture and it wasn't a big deal, it was just something we did. We talked about getting married, but there was always something else to save our money for, something else to plan for, like a trip to Costa Rica or canoeing in the Grand Canyon. Everything was just easy.

Is easy boring? Easy is grown up, I told myself. Easy is what you want.

"Let's have a baby," he had said. Half-completed vegetarian sushi was spread out on the counter in front of us, our contribution to a Thanksgiving dinner party we would never attend. Outside, the first major snowfall of the year was blanketing Chicago. Other friends were already texting, letting us know they were bailing on the party too. Cars were buried, snowplows were hours away from the smaller streets, and who knew how long this was going to last.

We had talked about having children, but whenever it came up, something balled up inside me, bracing for impact. I knew as soon as the word "baby" was spoken that it also meant the possibility of loss. Because if something happened, that new grief would wake up the sleeping grief of my childhood, and together they would make something so monstrous, so huge, that it would swallow me whole. So, whenever children came up, I deflected.

But that night, and for the next two days while the snow kept falling and the city shut down, I pushed the knot down. We ate the sushi in bed, hours later. Then we put on our snowshoes and went outside into a city transformed. The sky was orange and purple. All the hard lines and angles had been smoothed out and softened. I felt soft too. And in that softness, in the magic of days that were dark with snow clouds and nights bright with reflected city lights, time lost its meaning, and I pushed the knot so far down that I convinced myself it was gone.

And then having a baby was all I could think about. But getting pregnant wasn't as instantaneous as my high school health teacher had made it sound. I stopped drinking and cut my caffeine, and I religiously tracked my temperature and tried to get the ovulation timing right. We tried for over a year, and last February, it finally worked.

Now I wait for the familiar pain to start, but instead there's something else: a memory I didn't know I had. I must have been only five or six years old. Memories from then are mixed with photos in the albums my dad has packed away somewhere. But there's no photo of this picture that has suddenly surfaced in my mind.

Stiffly, I get out of bed. I didn't turn the heat on last night, so I pull a blanket off my bed and wrap it around me, then pad down the hallway to the closed door at the end. It's to a little room filled with boxes, suitcases, and all the things you would stick in an attic if you had one. The suitcases are gone now, and there are fewer boxes, but it's mostly undisturbed. I squeeze through to the back wall and push aside a pile of old blankets, and there it is: a mural my mother was painting of rabbits and mice and other small creatures frolicking along a river. Once, long ago, I was going to have a little brother or sister.

She had copied the pictures from the Beatrix Potter books she'd read to me: *Peter Rabbit, Tom Kitten, Jemima Puddle-Duck.* I trace my finger along the old paint, trying to feel her in this. Lower down on the wall are some flowers she had sketched for me to paint. The red I'd chosen is faded now, and the color crosses over my mother's careful pencil lines. She never finished it because there was no need. I know now what I didn't know then because I was too young. Had I been home when she'd lost the baby? Was she out in the garden or reading me a story, or had it been late at night, as I lay sleeping in the room down the hall? My parents must have kept it hidden from me, and I was too young to fully understand and believed whatever they told me when they shut this room for good. I haven't thought of this phantom sibling in all these years. Did they try again? Or maybe the cancer was already in her, and that's why her body couldn't hold on to the baby, because it was already filling up with disease.

I lean my head against the wall. My mother would have known what I was going through last spring. She would have driven to Chicago and held me through it, and maybe things would be different now.

My hollow place. That's what I called it when I was a child. It is a hole inside me so huge it could swallow me. If I let myself go inside, black water will seep out of the sides and rise over my head and I will never get out. This is the danger of swimming in deep memories alone. I scramble up from the floor and walk out of the little room, closing the door without looking back.

The other lesson that these past few months have taught me: the antidote to stillness—and the memories it holds—is to keep moving.

Visiting hours at the hospital start at ten. My stomach rumbles, and I need coffee, but Sumner's Mills is far too small to have a decent coffee shop or even a chain. For that, I have to head toward the interstate. I'm taking the scenic route back through the village and to the hospital—no chickening out this time—when I see a girl walking on the side of the road up ahead. Her back is to me, long hair twisting around her in the wind, small body huddled tight. Her backpack looks like it was made for someone much larger. I glance at her in my rearview mirror, trying to see her face. Taylor.

I don't want to frighten her, so I pull over a little way ahead of her and get out of the car so she knows I'm not some creep.

"Taylor," I call out and wave. "It's Clare. From last night."

She'd stopped walking when she saw me pull over, but now she starts moving slowly toward me, probably worried that I'm going to get her in trouble for not being in school.

"Can I give you a ride?" I ask when she gets close enough. Despite the sun, there's a bite in the wind, and she looks cold in her thin jacket. The girls at my old school were the same; the wind would come off the lake and rip across campus, and they'd still be walking around with bare legs and bomber jackets.

"I'm okay," she says, but she shivers while she says it.

"Can I drive you home?"

"Not going home," she says.

"Look, at least get in the car for a moment and warm up. I'm freezing even if you aren't."

I get back in the car without looking to see if she'll follow. After a moment's consideration, she comes around the passenger side and slides in, jamming her backpack down by her feet. "Thanks," she says. She looks out the window and chews her lip while I blast the heat and finish the last of my coffee.

"Are you coming from school?" I ask.

She nods.

"Long walk." She wasn't heading toward the village, which would be the fastest way to get to her house, but I refrain from mentioning this.

"Do you have kids?" she asks.

"No," I say. I try to keep my voice light. "I was a teacher, though. I taught girls your age and a bit older."

"That explains it."

"Explains what?"

She shrugs. "I don't know. You sound like a teacher. Or a mom."

I take another sip of my coffee, even though there's nothing left.

"So, why aren't *you* in school?"

"I lost my job."

"Why?"

"Some, uh, stuff happened to me—some of it had to do with that house your mom and I were talking about."

"What happened?"

This makes me smile, but I stop it before she sees. I lean back, keeping my face looking out, not at her. This is what I miss most about teaching. She's pushing me, I know she is, but she's looking for an opening. She wants to say something, but she can't just come out and say it. She needs me to lay the groundwork.

"Abby, the woman who's in the hospital—well, you know who she is—she sent me a bunch of strange emails last spring. I started having really scary nightmares about that house. So I stopped sleeping. And when you don't sleep, you go kind of crazy. And it makes your body really sick. And I was pregnant and I lost the baby."

I can say this to her, to this young girl I don't even know who's sitting in my car looking at me with such openness in her face. She's not going to give me the horrible clichés about God wanting another angel or my baby being too good for the world. She's not going to look at me with pity either, because no matter what, I'm still the adult, I'm the one who is supposed to know more and be able to do more than she can. It feels good to be able to say it and let it hang between us.

"That sucks," she says after a moment. "I didn't know grown-ups got nightmares. I thought that was a kid thing."

"Nope."

"I've had nightmares about that house."

"Oh?" I'm trying to sound neutral, but she turns and looks right at me.

"They were . . . real. Like normally, when I have bad dreams, they're scary but I kind of know they're a dream. These were different."

"Mine too." My throat is dry.

"My friends think I'm crazy, but I'm not."

"I'm sure you're not."

She takes her water bottle out of her bag and flicks the tab open, then closed. Open. Closed.

"Where were you going?" she asks.

"Hospital. I was going to go see Abby. I should've gone yesterday but I chickened out."

"Why?"

"Just don't like hospitals."

She considers this. "I've never been to one."

What I want to say is "You're lucky," but I know from experience the fastest way to lose a kid is to tell them how what they don't have is good for them. "Look, I need to take you back to school."

She slumps down in her seat.

"Or I could take you home."

"Can I go to the hospital with you?"

It's tempting. Bring someone as an ally. I don't know why I'm thinking of it that way. Abby isn't the enemy.

"Maybe next time. Or if your mom goes, you could go with her. But right now, it's got to be school or home."

She groans. "Home, I guess. I wish I could just find a way to get directly to my bedroom without having to listen to *her*."

"Well, the school's probably called already. That's how it would have worked at my school, anyway."

"No, she would have called me in, like, half a second. I was there for homeroom, and that's when they take attendance. My fourth-period class is math, and Mr. Poleski is *way* too lazy to notice. Then it's lunch, so I'm good until twelve forty-five."

"You've planned this out."

"Sort of. Not really, I guess. It was farther than I realized."

She's waiting for me to ask her where "it" is, but I'm pretty good at this game, or I used to be. I turn the car around and start driving back toward the village. "Do you want music?"

"There's no good stations here."

We drive in silence for a bit. It's only going to take five minutes to get to her house, so I slow down.

"I'm sorry about your baby," she says suddenly. It catches me off guard and I can't hide the sharp intake of breath. She's looking straight at me. "I saw a show about it. It was really sad."

"It was," I say, finding my voice again. "It still is."

We're driving through the village now, past the boarded-up storefronts, the post office, one of the three churches. A woman who looks way too young to be pushing a stroller is moving slowly along the side of the road.

"I can't wait to get out of here," Taylor says quietly, more to herself than to me. I turn onto the road that will take us to her house.

"So." I'm trying to keep my tone light, conversational. "I'm guessing you weren't just going for a midday walk."

"Not really," she mumbles. She's playing with her water bottle again.

"I know you don't know me, but I've got a bit of a history with that house. Things have happened to me there. More than your mom." It's a cheap shot, I know, but it's also true.

"I don't know why I was going there, okay?" She turns and looks at me, challenging me to disagree with her.

"I get it." I signal and pull over to the side of the road. When she looks confused, I say, "You said you had some time until the school called your house." And then, because I know what she's thinking, "I won't tell your mom."

"Stepmom."

"Right."

She chews her lip again and shifts uncomfortably in her seat, the decision of whether to give in and finally be able to tell someone playing out on her face. "It's just—ever since we went in, I've known I had to go back. It's like this . . . *feeling*."

"Go back to do what?" I ask, but I think I know the answer. She saw something and she needs to know if it was real.

"And then that lady—what happened to your friend—that freaked me out, and I thought that would be the end of it, but it's just made it stronger. You can't tell my stepmom. She'll, like, lock me in my room or something."

"I won't tell her."

"Last spring my friends and I went to that house. I heard Mom talking about it and I told them. I didn't think they'd want to actually *go*, but they did. It wasn't that big a deal. Kailey was freaking out that it was going to collapse on us, but she's a total drama queen, like, it's stayed up this long, you know? So we went in. It's mainly just a bunch of garbage and dead leaves. You can't go upstairs. We were only in there for a few minutes. The others were leaving, but I went back to that weird door."

The basement door.

"Was it open?"

"It was closed. We tried the latch. I was standing right by it and—" She swallows.

I start to reach out to touch her arm, but she looks so terrified that I pull my hand back. My awakening memories roared to life in my dreams last night. That door. In my dream, I kept finding myself standing in front of it. A metal door that's too large, too heavy; that doesn't belong.

"I've seen it move," I say. "On its own."

"You have?" Her eyes are huge.

"When I was a kid. I never told anybody."

"I thought maybe I just imagined it but . . ."

"So did I."

"Okay." She turns and looks at me, suddenly hopeful. "That's good. I mean, not good but . . ."

She holds my gaze for a second, but her lip starts quivering, and she turns away quickly and stares into the fields beside us. She squints into the flat light as if she's trying to see the woods and the house that are out there. I instinctively look too. There's nothing to be seen but the skeletal remains of cornstalks and the few birds looking for scraps left behind.

"I don't know why I went back to it. Like, it's just a stupid door. I thought maybe I'd try it again. And then it opened. I was barely touch-ing it and it just opened. The smell—"

"I remember."

"The door just slid open and I—I don't know why I did it—I do stu-pid things sometimes, like I dare myself and then I have to do it, but this wasn't even like that. I just went and stood at the top of the stairs and I looked down and . . . and . . ." She's staring at the fields, but I know what she's seeing is that darkness, feeling it pulling her down. This time I do reach out and put my hand on her thin arm to bring her back into the car. She's shaking. "I took out my phone and turned on the flashlight. There was something on the stairs."

"What was it?"

"I couldn't get my light to hit it, it was just making shadows, so I turned it off. It was less than a second, like that split second when the light's still in your eyes but it's not there, like your eyes adjusting. I saw a—I saw a—" She starts taking big gulps of breath like she's hyperventilating.

"It's okay," I say. "It's okay." I roll the windows down and cold air rushes in, breaking the moment.

"My friends say I'm mental. They won't talk to me, and they're saying all these things, and everyone's acting like I've got some kind of disease."

"You told them?"

"I wanted them to see, but when we went back, the door was closed and wouldn't open." She's clenching and unclenching her fists, her nails leaving red crescents in her palm. "There's this Twitter survey someone made about me, and then I heard you guys talking last night—"

"I'm sorry you had to hear that."

"No, it's the first time . . . like I was starting to think that they're right, I am crazy, but when I heard you talking to my mom . . ." She's crying now, big unselfconscious tears with snot running down her face. I dig around and find some napkins and pass them to her. "I just want my dad, but he's gone all the time."

"I don't think you're crazy. If that's any consolation."

She shrugs. "I just want to get away from here. From that house and that school. I don't know how much longer I can take it."

"Your parents have been trying to get the woman who owns the house to tear it down."

"Doesn't change what everyone thinks about me. I just wish I could *do* something. That's what sucks about being a kid. I can't do anything."

I wait for the worst of the crying to pass, then pull onto the road and travel the last quarter mile to her house. Lori comes to the door as we're getting out of the car. Taylor angrily wipes at her eyes with the remains of a paper napkin. She pushes past Lori and disappears inside.

"Okay?" Lori says, shaking her head as the door slams upstairs. "You want to come in?"

"I don't want to intrude," I say.

She sighs. "She's going to be in her room for a while. I just need to call the school and let them know where she's at. Come on in." She doesn't wait for me to follow.

When I get into the kitchen, she's hanging up with the school secretary. "Sorry, this room is doubling as my office." She takes a pile of papers off a chair and adds them to another pile on the table. "So, I'm guessing Taylor didn't call you to take her out of school."

I glance behind me, but there's no sign of her lurking in the hallway the way she did last night. "I was on my way to the hospital and saw her walking. She was about a mile away from the school."

"Did she tell you where she was going?"

"Not exactly. I think she was going to the Octagon House."

Lori makes a sound but clamps her mouth shut. She goes to the fridge, opens it, and stares inside, then slams the door shut; school notices and kids' artwork fall. Then she turns and looks at me. "You're so fucking lucky you don't have kids. No. Not lucky. Smart. Very smart."

I'm trying to keep my face from showing anything, but I feel my jaw tightening. I know she doesn't know. I know she's not even talking about me. But I am so over the casual pronouncements, the judgment of people who think they know. The anxious humming of Josh's mother that I could always hear through the phone when he was talking to her.

I always knew when the subject came up because he'd leave the room. I couldn't hear what he was saying to her, but I could hear the tone. Soothing. Reassuring. "Soon, Ma, soon." The mothers of the kids I taught who judged me. *Sure, she's a great teacher. Sure, our kid is thriving in her class. But she's not a mother, so she can't really know.*

I look around at Lori's chaotic kitchen, unfinished bowls of cereal on the counter, the peanut butter jar with a knife sticking out of it, a half-full bag of baby carrots, bread crumbs everywhere. My stomach squeezes and twists. Maybe this is why I've been living the way I have for the past few months, keeping my space to the bare essentials. It hurts too much to be in this beating heart of family life.

I stand, pressing my fingertips into the table to keep myself steady. "Can I use your bathroom?"

When I come back, Lori is loading the dishwasher. She seems calmer. "You okay?" she asks. Her back is to me as she bends over to fit the bowls in the bottom rack.

"I'm fine."

"You looked a little green."

"I should go."

She straightens up and gives me a look. "Have you eaten?"

"You don't always need to feed me."

"I know. But I got these cinnamon buns. They sell them at the store in town. I stopped for gas after I dropped the kids off, and I couldn't resist. Come on. Split one with me so I don't feel so guilty." She doesn't wait for me to answer but instead puts two plates on the noticeably clearer table. "I even found some real coffee." She indicates a coffeemaker bubbling away.

"Lori."

"Just sit, please."

I'm still standing where I was when I came in, jacket in hand. Part of me wants to get out of here—the old instinct. I'll go home and go for a run before I head into the hospital. Try to run these memories and feelings out of me. But the other part wants to stay and forget myself in the minutiae of another family's life.

"It's just been tough lately," she says, putting a jug of milk and a sugar bowl on the table. "Taylor's going through something, obviously, and I can't get through to her, and the younger two are always at each other, and Matt's doing all these extra runs to make money. Sorry if I—"

"It's okay," I say, and sit down. "Food would be good."

"So," she says, putting an enormous sticky bun on a plate and attempting to saw it in half, "tell me about the last twenty years of your life."

=====

It's easier to talk to Lori than I thought it would be. She tells me about taking over the farm, and about the company she and Matt want to build. She asks about my father and tells me about her parents, retired and living nearby, "and trying to keep their noses out of what we're doing."

"They know you're going to sell?"

"Yeah. They get it. They don't like it, but they get it. And it's not like my brothers want the place."

I tell her about moving to Chicago and meeting Josh. As I'm talking, my life in Chicago stops being a series of punishments I've been enacting on myself. She asks about teaching, and I find myself missing it in a way I haven't for months as I tell her about the books I chose and my belief that young teen girls are capable of so much.

More coffee is made. At some point, she heats up soup and makes cheese sandwiches. Taylor stays in her room. Lori goes to check on her but comes back down saying that she's fallen asleep. Before I know it, it's almost three, and Lori is scrambling to go pick up her two younger kids, Jake and Chloe.

I'm putting on my coat when she says, "I hate to ask, but would you mind staying here while I'm gone? I don't want Taylor to be alone in the house when she wakes up."

What she isn't saying is that she's afraid of what Taylor will do if left alone.

"I'll be back in about twenty minutes. Visiting hours go till eight, right?"

I assure her there's lots of time. She gives me the Wi-Fi code and instructions for how to work the remote, but I don't want to watch television, and there's no need to check messages on my phone—there won't be any. The past few days have been a whirlwind. I just want to sit in the kitchen listening to the clock.

8

Five minutes after her mother leaves, Taylor stands in the kitchen doorway rubbing her eyes. Her hair is pushed into a rat's nest on one side, and her face has pink lines from lying on a crumpled pillowcase.

"Where's Mom?" The makeup she'd been wearing—makeup I'm pretty sure is forbidden—has been rubbed off through tears and sleep, and she looks much more like the child she still is than the aloof teen she's trying to be.

"She's gone to get your brother and sister. Are you hungry?" I look around at what's available. Everything in this kitchen is bursting, and every available space is covered with food or cooking implements or kid stuff. Multiple generations of hungry people being fed and protected; thousands of hours of meals and conversations and homework and *life* are soaked into every cell of this overstuffed room. It hurt to see before, but now that I've been sitting in it for these past few hours, I feel it pulling me into its chaotic comfort. "I can make you a sandwich."

She shakes her head and chews on her lip.

"What about toast? That was always my go-to." Cinnamon toast with a cup of hot cocoa was my dad's cure-all for every hurt and scrape when I was growing up. Mostly, it worked.

She nods and pulls out a chair, then collapses into it. "I missed a history test."

"Oh well," I say as I start opening cupboards looking for the ingredients I need. The spices are a mismatched assortment of industrial-size plastic containers and tiny plastic bags wrapped with twist ties, only half of which are labeled. I find cinnamon and get the bread in the toaster and then begin the search for brown sugar.

"That's a strange thing for a teacher to say."

"Yes. But you'll come to learn that tests and grades and pop quizzes—all of that stuff is just a means to a bigger goal."

"What I learn?" She says it sarcastically, but it sounds more like a kid trying out a way she thinks she's supposed to speak than something that she actually means.

"Exactly. Where's the brown sugar?" I've given up my search and the toast has popped.

"Most of the baking stuff is down there." She points to a corner cupboard with a big lazy Susan. I've already looked there, but I give it another attempt and find what I need.

Taylor eats the first piece of toast in silence, licking the butter and sugar off her fingers, and I make her another and wait for the kettle to boil. I pass her the cocoa and slide into my seat. Her eyes have lost the lidded, hurt look. It feels so normal to be doing this, feeding a child and giving her some space to say what she needs to say. I remember those spontaneous one-on-ones with the kids when they were finally able to put something into words. Those were the best parts of teaching. But it's not just that. A ripple of longing for my dad, his unshakable belief in the healing power of toast, goes through me. For my own kitchen, wherever I'll end up.

"Taylor." I reach across the table, not to touch her arm—touching her would make her jump—but to close the distance between us. "Can you tell me why you were going to that house today?"

She shakes her head violently.

"You're not in trouble."

Her lip starts to tremble and she's going to start crying again. All of the work of sleep and comfort food undone. "That's it," she says in a whisper. "I don't know."

"What did you see?" But before Taylor can answer, Lori's car pulls in, and the dogs, who have been sleeping somewhere in the house, wake up and start barking excitedly.

Taylor looks at me with wide eyes. "Please—" she starts.

"It's okay," I say. "I'm not going to say anything."

"I don't want to go back there, but I'm scared I won't be able to stop it. That pulling feeling is getting stronger."

I can hear the kids arguing about something loudly in the driveway. Car doors slam and the voices get closer to the house. I grab a piece of paper and a crayon from a pile on the table. "You have a phone, right?"

"It's one of those lame ones that doesn't do anything," she says. "Kailey has a new iPhone and—"

I scribble my cell number on the paper and push it across the table to her. The kids burst through the front door, complaining to their mother about needing snacks and wanting to watch television. "If you find yourself going to that house again, call me. Anytime. Okay?" She nods. "No questions asked, I promise." She nods again. "I'm serious. You can't go back there, especially by yourself."

She takes the piece of paper and shoves it in her pocket as her brother and sister crash into the kitchen with the dogs and Lori behind them. The noise level spikes immediately.

"How come you weren't in school?"

"Are you sick?"

"What'd you eat? Mom, can I have what Taylor had?"

Lori looks at me and raises her eyebrows.

"All good," I say, getting up and grabbing my jacket and bag off the chair.

"Thanks for staying. I hope—" Lori nods toward Taylor, who's helping her sister get a bag of Goldfish out of the cupboard. Her face has returned to the look I saw last night: closed off, guarded.

"I made her some toast."

Lori walks me to the door, leaving the chaos of the kitchen to sort itself out. She seems edgy, distracted; the ease of the past few hours has evaporated. "Did she tell you anything?" She leans against the doorframe, looking like it's holding her upright. She closes her eyes and pinches the spot between them.

"We just talked about school."

"You're sure?"

I feel a jolt of anger at the sudden suspicion. "Where is this coming from?" I ask.

"Come on, Clare. I know you're weird about that house."

"No, I'm not."

"I appreciate you bringing her home—"

A clamor rises out of the kitchen and then dies down again.

"But I can't help her if I don't know what's going on," she continues.

"I know, but she didn't tell me. Yes, she was going to the house, but she said she didn't know why."

She sighs. "Do you know why I don't sleep? Because if I fall asleep, Taylor might walk out of the house. So I sleep on the couch. That way, if she walks past me, I'll know. I've thought about putting a lock on the outside of her door, but I can't because she'd have a fucking fit, and I don't want to be a prison warden in my own house. And now she's leaving school in the middle of the day to go there? What do I have to do, park outside her school all day? What is it about that place that makes people so obsessed?"

"I believe her. I don't think she knows."

"Bullshit. She knows."

This isn't about me, even if it feels like it is. This is a mother who is frightened for her kid, more frightened than she's letting on. I take a breath and try to keep my tone even. "Why do you assume she's lying?"

"Because she's my daughter and I know. Just . . . be on my side here. Okay?"

She looks straight at me and her anger is gone as quickly as it came. I see the bags under her eyes, the desperate way she's looking at me, as if I can help her. Just like Mrs. Lindsay thinks I can help Abby.

I think about that slip of paper. If Lori finds it, she'll see it as such a betrayal. But her daughter opened up to me—I can't break that trust.

If the trust will stop her from going into the house again, isn't that worth it?

And how long do you plan on sticking around to make sure she doesn't do that? a voice in my head asks. *You can't even take care of yourself.*

Suddenly, the dogs explode into another chorus of barking and tear past us to the door. A car is pulling into the driveway behind mine, and sitting in the driver's seat is Mitchell.

Abby's brother.

Lori's face immediately brightens, and she pushes the door open, releasing the dogs into the yard. Mitchell is smiling as he gets out of his car, holding out his hands for them to sniff and lick. From the way they greet him, I can tell he's been here before. I stay behind the door so he can't see me.

"Sorry to just drop in on you," he calls out. "I didn't know you had company."

"Good timing," Lori says, walking toward him. "I just got home—"

They're too far away for me to hear the rest. Lori looks back at the house, and from the shocked look on Mitchell's face, I can tell she's just told him that I'm here. I step outside. Heat rushes up my neck and I walk toward them slowly, hoping the chill in the wind will keep the deep pink at bay. All I want to do is get in my car and drive away, but Mitchell's car is blocking me in.

"Hey, Clare," he says. "What a surprise."

"Ditto," I say. It comes out more stiffly than I mean it.

"You two remember each other?" Lori says. If she's caught anything, she's pretending otherwise.

"Sure, yeah," he says. "Mom told me she'd reached out to you about Abby. They'll be glad to see you."

"I was just about to head over to the hospital."

"You wanna come in?" Lori asks him. "The kids'll be in front of the TV."

"Nah, it's okay. I don't want to intrude." He smiles at me, but it's hesitant.

"I was just leaving," I say. Why is Mitchell here? Why do he and

Lori seem like they know each other so well? From Lori's mood swings to this, everything is moving too fast, and my head feels foggy trying to put the pieces together.

"I just came by to say hey. I was at the hospital and couldn't face going to the hotel yet. Thought I'd go for a drive." He turns to me, probably guessing my questions. "Lori's been kind enough to keep me sane through this."

She snorts. "If by sane, you mean drinking beer in a dirty kitchen, sure. How's Abby?"

"The same."

"Any news on when they'll transfer her?"

He shakes his head. "They want her to stabilize more. Said it could be a few more weeks until it's safe to move her." Turning to me, he says, "My parents want to get her to a hospital at home."

"In Buffalo?"

"Yeah, there's a big one there that specializes in brain injuries."

"The offer still stands," Lori says. "The spare room's just sitting there. Matt's home in a couple days. He'd be thrilled to have a Bills fan around. There's a game this weekend."

Mitchell laughs, then glances at me. "Thanks. My parents want to stay close to the hospital, just in case anything changes. I should stay with them."

"Mom!" Lori's son is standing at the door holding a cereal box. "Taylor said I'm not allowed to have Frosted Flakes, and Chloe's hogging the remote, but it's supposed to be my day."

"Excuse me," Lori says to us and heads into the house. As soon as it's just the two of us, I find it hard to look at Mitchell.

"Hey," he says softly. "How are you?" He reaches out to touch my arm and I automatically pull away. As soon as I do, he pulls back too.

I need to get out of here, now.

"It's nice to see you," he says, but he sounds stiff. The relaxed hanging-out-drinking-a-beer vibe is gone. He doesn't want me here. He's probably trying to figure out if he should encourage me to stay, hoping I won't.

"I'm sorry about Abby," I say. And before I know I'm going to say it, "I'm sorry about everything." Something's rising in my throat and I'm either going to throw up or cry. I move past him, fumbling with my car keys to get the door open.

"Clare. Hey, wait—"

In the car, the heater blasts so I can't hear him. I know I'm being an ass. Part of me hovers above all of this, watching like it's a movie, and I have to keep reminding myself that it's real. I'm in Sumner's Mills, at Lori's house, with Mitchell standing there, staring at me, but I can't stop now. I can't turn the car off and laugh about it and say, "Hey, I'm great, how are you?"

Backing out isn't an option, so I do an awkward eight-point turn and manage to get myself turned around without driving on Lori's lawn. Halfway through, Mitchell clues in and holds up his hands to say "stop," motioning to his car, probably telling me he'll move it. But I keep going and he's forced to just stand to the side, watching my undignified exit. Lori comes out of the house, confused, and yells something in my direction. When I'm finally straightened out, I floor it out of the driveway and don't look back.

Wow. Congratulations. You've just made everything worse.

=====

Needless to say, I don't go to the hospital. Again. I drive home and go for a long run. I'm in the last mile when my phone buzzes with a text from a number I don't recognize.

Hey, it's Mitchell. Sorry about before. Can we talk?

I stop on the side of the road, staring at the phone, my chest heaving. There's a stitch starting in my side, and I press my free hand into it instinctively. If he texts again, I'll respond. I know I'm playing games, and it's not what I want to do, but I can't take anything more right now.

Sunset isn't for another hour, but the temperature is already dropping quickly. The chill starts to creep into my back. There are no houses around me, only dusky woods that make it seem darker than it is. Not the woods that hide the Octagon House; I've been careful this time which roads I turn on. But still. Anything could be in there, watching. Deer, coyotes. Or— I shake my head. Stop it.

It's clear Mitchell isn't going to text again, so I shove the phone in my pocket and sprint the rest of the way home, pushing my legs until they burn.

———

I need a distraction, something to break the mental loop of Mitchell's and Lori's faces while I made an idiot of myself. My cell is dead and there's no TV, so while the last of my gas station groceries warm up on the stove, I rifle through the pile of junk mail that I pushed aside last night when I arrived. Amid the catalogs and credit card applications is a pink envelope with my name on it. There's no return address and no stamp, just my name in big block letters on the front. As soon as I see it, I know who it's from: Abby. She must have stopped here on her way to the Octagon House, assuming my father was still living here and would send it to me. I want to rip it open. And I want to throw it away without looking at it. This is going to change things. I don't know how, I just know it will.

On the back in the same block letters, it reads, "PLEASE SEND TO CLARE." I tear it open. Inside is a sheet of paper, torn out of a notebook and folded into a square like we used to do when we passed notes in class. I tug the corner and it unfolds like an accordion. It's covered in looping handwriting that I recognize from years ago, one word blurring into the next and going right to the edge of the page as if falling off:

Clare,

You told me it was in my head. You told me I was just confused.

I tried to believe you. I wanted you to be right.

But you were wrong.

The dreams came back this spring. Someone woke her up and now she's in my head again. Did you hear her too when you were down there? You will lie and say you didn't. You shouldn't lie about things like this.

If she can't escape, neither can I. If I can't escape, neither will you.

Go back to the beginning to find the end.

~ Abby

9

The next morning, my eyes open the moment sunlight hits the bed. No sifting of old memories this time. I don't feel like I've slept. My brain has been busy all night, turning over what I've learned: Abby put gas in the car, the basement door closed on her, the note. *Go back to the beginning to find the end.*

"What do you mean? Why do you have to talk in circles?" I say to the room, but the dust motes have no answer; they only bob in place as my voice disturbs the air. And Taylor. Taylor who is so terrified but keeps being pulled to the house in her sleep and now in the day. And then I land on it: what woke me up. Taylor saw something else down there.

I sit up in bed. What exactly did she say? Something about the moment when she turned her flashlight off, the memory of light in her eyes. That had to be it—just a trick of bright light and darkness on her retinas. I can sit here all morning and try to convince myself it was that, but it's not going to work. I need to know more about the house.

I could search the Internet, but I don't even know what I'm looking for. It's not like "the Octagon House" is the actual name of the place, it's just what we called it. I could try to find out what actually happened to the family who died there in the sixties, but I don't know their names either.

Lori said the woman who owns it lives in town. She's probably not the original owner, but she might at least know something. After yesterday, I'm not quite sure how to approach Lori. I decide to be direct. It's what she would do.

Hey. Sorry about yesterday.

I don't know how long it'll take for her to reply, but Lori didn't hold grudges when we were kids, and it doesn't seem like she's changed. Within seconds, my phone dings with a message.

Next time they're holding auditions for Fast & Furious in my driveway, let me know. Lol

I give her a thumbs-up, then text back. **Old woman who owns the house?**

Her answer is immediate. **Marion Janssen.** Followed by witch hat and black cat emojis. When I ask for a phone number, she only sends directions. **Big house top of Mill. Good luck!**

Should I ask if she wants to sell?

She texts a selection of emojis that make no logical sense and I laugh out loud. Despite her outbursts, which, given the circumstances, are understandable, it feels so easy to slip back into this childhood friendship.

Don't get comfortable, the voice in my head says. *You're not staying here.*

———

True to Lori's directions, Marion Janssen's house is a brick block that sits at the dead end of Mill Road. In front of it are the late-fall remains of a half-empty garden filled with clumps of dried mums in a perfunctory row. Behind them are taller, wilder rosebushes—brown now but probably impressive when they're in bloom. "Every garden tells a story," my mother used to say. My mother was always telling me stories about animals and magical creatures that lived hidden all around us. This garden says that it is currently being taken care of by someone who does the bare minimum, but it was once tended with love and skill.

I ring the doorbell and hear it chime damply somewhere deep in the house. The curtains are all drawn and there's no car in the driveway. I half hope no one's home. I ring the doorbell one more time and make myself stand there for a slow count of ten, then turn and start down the steps. I'm halfway down the walk when I hear the heavy front door slide open. I turn around and there, standing in the doorway, is a tiny, shriveled woman squinting into the sunlight.

"Hello," she calls out. Her voice is high and watery, frail, like her.

I walk back to her but don't go up on the steps. If I did, I would tower over her even though I'm not tall.

"Mrs. Janssen?"

She looks at me, blinking.

"I'm Clare."

She's wearing a dusty-rose cardigan, buttoned all the way up to the top, with the lace edges of a blouse sticking out around the collar and the sleeves. Her pants are gray with a sharp crease and look like wool or something else that's well made and timeless. She has on pearl earrings and a gold locket. No wedding ring. Instinctively I start smoothing down my clothes as her eyes scan over me.

"Clare. Clare who?"

"Madden, Clare Madden. I'm sorry to just land on your doorstep like this, but I was looking for some information on local history, and I was told you'd be the person to ask."

"Who told you that?"

My mind goes blank. I haven't even made it inside and I've screwed up. If I tell her Lori, she might make the connection to the house. "I've been asking around, and your name has come up a few times. I don't know the names of the people I was talking to."

"It has been a long time since anyone was interested in the history of this town," she says. "I have tried to keep track over the years, but when I'm gone . . . I wonder what will happen to it?" I'm not sure how to answer, but it doesn't seem like she expects me to. She nods. "Come in. We will have tea."

She disappears into the darkness beyond the doorway, and I come up the steps and follow her inside. A small foyer opens into what I think is a living room, though it is hard to tell. The curtains across the windows let in no light. The house is thick with stale air. Large pieces of furniture clutter the room, but they all have sheets draped over them. I blink in the darkness for a moment, allowing my eyes to adjust, before I close the door behind me.

Mrs. Janssen is making her slow, careful way into a hallway that leads to the rest of the house. On the wall to my left, there's a black-and-white picture, blurred around the edges: A girl with long braids sits in a large chair. Her hands are folded in her lap and her ankles are crossed, but her legs aren't long enough to reach the floor. Her dress comes down to the middle of her high-laced boots. Standing stiffly to the side, his large hand on her shoulder, is a man in a suit, with jet-black hair. It's parted in the middle and slicked down. They both wear serious expressions—the way people did in old photos. But the girl looks like she's going to burst into a smile at any moment. The man, though, stares into the camera, and my immediate response is to step back. I feel like he can see me.

From down the hallway, I hear Mrs. Janssen banging something that's probably a kettle, which pulls me out of the picture.

The hall beyond the living room is narrow and pitch black, but then a door at the far end opens and I can see Mrs. Janssen silhouetted in bright sunlight, the kitchen behind her. When I step in, I see that everything in the kitchen is yellow: the walls, the cupboards, most of the old appliances. It's like a different house.

"We don't use the front part of the house much anymore," she says. "Such a big house for only two."

Laid out on the table in front of her is a squat yellow teapot, two pale yellow cups on matching saucers, and a plate of biscuits.

"Oh," I say. "You didn't have to—"

"I was about to have my tea. It is not difficult to put out another cup and saucer." She goes to lift the teapot and I immediately step forward, worried she's going to break her arm. "No. You are the guest."

It seems ridiculous, this frail woman insisting on hoisting up a teapot that must weigh almost as much as she does, but she obviously won't do anything until I sit down and let her serve the tea.

The teapot shakes as she pours, but she manages to do it without spilling too much.

"Milk or honey? I have no lemon."

"Black is fine, thanks," I say, and she nods approvingly. Her tea is also black.

Mrs. Janssen sits down and picks up her teacup, closes her eyes, and sips. I almost start speaking but then stop myself. Something tells me there is a ritual to this that should not be interrupted.

"Are you from the area?" she asks when she opens her eyes again.

"I grew up here," I say. "Out on Conway Road, about a mile west of town, but my family isn't from this area."

"I used to have students who lived on Conway Road. A big family, the Albertsons."

"You were a teacher?"

"For forty-six years. I taught whole families—parents as children, then their children, and even sometimes grandchildren."

"That's amazing," I say. "You must have known them so well."

"People didn't move around as much before. Now, when they grow up, they can't wait to leave. No one has any sense of place." She lifts her cup again, closes her eyes, and takes another sip of the scalding tea.

"I'm a teacher as well," I say. Without the pedigree of multiple generations of family living in Sumner's Mills, I need to find an opening. "You said 'we' before. Is your husband . . . ?"

"No, dear. My husband passed away thirty years ago. It's just me and my daughter, but she's working right now. Do you have children?"

"No." Another disappointing answer. Somewhere behind me, a clock ticks. I take a breath and say, "That photograph by the front door . . ."

"That's me and George. My brother. That was a long time ago." She gives a little smile, then nibbles a biscuit. "You said you were curious about local history. Are you writing a book?"

Her question catches me off guard. I don't want to get too far into a lie I can't carry on. "No. Well, I mean maybe, someday. But this is just a personal interest."

"I've always thought someone should write a book about this place.

It didn't used to be like this, you know. You're too young, but there was a time when Sumner's Mills was a real community. But then we lost the train station and the factory and . . ." She doesn't continue; instead she takes another bite of her biscuit. "I have a box. It's my own kind of archive of the goings-on in Sumner's Mills. I'll ask my daughter to find it when she gets home, and you can come and take a look."

"That sounds wonderful, thank you."

"My family were the founders of Sumner's Mills several generations ago. Janssen is my married name. I'm a Sumner. So, some of what I have is personal family history, and some is the history of the town. My father and my husband were both managers at the metals plant."

I take a notebook and pencil out of my bag—I figure I might as well make this look realistic—and scribble a few notes as she talks about the wonders of the metal plant, ignoring that fact that it poisoned everything around it. Mrs. Janssen's version of Sumner's Mills is of a little piece of utopia nestled among the rocks and river that no one else seems to recognize. It gets to a point where I'm only half listening.

"I don't want to take much more of your time," I say after a while. "There's actually a specific house I was wondering about."

"Oh?"

"It's shaped like an octagon. It's not in the village. In the sixties a family was—"

"I am aware of the house you are referring to." Her tone is immediately cold and clipped. She narrows her eyes. "Why do you want to know about that house?"

"Last week, my friend . . . She went into that house and she, well, she almost died."

"I have already spoken to the police. I have no comment."

"Oh no, I'm not a journalist, that's not why I'm asking." We look at each other across the table. I take a breath and smile. "When we were kids, we discovered that house and were immediately fascinated by it. We had never seen anything like it, and you know how kids are. I know we shouldn't have, but we went inside."

Her eyes narrow again. "No. You shouldn't have."

"I know, and I'm sorry, but like I said, we were kids. We didn't know and were just so curious. About ten days ago, my friend came back here, and she went into that house, and, well, if you've talked to the police, you know the rest. She's in the hospital now, in a coma. We don't know if she's going to pull through. Her parents are looking for answers—they're desperate, Mrs. Janssen, and I promised that I'd help try to understand why Abby went in there again."

She looks at me for another long moment. *Tick, tick, tick,* behind me. I can't tell if my story has softened her at all, then she says, "I am sorry that your friend is not well, but that house has nothing to do with what happened to her. The police told me what she did to herself."

"No, no, of course. Abby wasn't well—isn't. But I'm trying to make sense of why she went there, specifically."

"When people go where they shouldn't, what happens is their responsibility."

I force some lightness in my voice. "I absolutely agree. I am just here . . . as a friend of the family. I want to help. Her parents have so many questions—I'm sure you can understand. I just thought, if I could learn something about the history . . . Am I correct that you own the house?"

Despite the sunlight coming in from the tall windows, a suffocating heaviness weighs down on the kitchen. Fine cracks spiderweb their way up the walls, over the cupboards, and across the ceiling. Mrs. Janssen's thin bones seem to sag, pushed down by an invisible force. She gazes at something beyond me, her face unreadable. Sadness? Regret? Or a long-suffering acceptance of events that happened in the distant past?

When she speaks, her words are slow and measured. "My brother, George, built that house in 1936, and I have kept it for him as best I could. The rest . . ." She picks up her teacup and saucer, but her hands shake, so she sets them back down. "It was a beautiful house that never got to be a home. That is all."

I wait for her to elaborate, but she just looks at her teacup, keeping her hands in her lap.

"When you say it never got to be a home . . . ?"

"George wanted a big family, lots of children running around. That is why he built it, but that was never allowed to be."

"So he never lived there?"

"He never had the chance. He was building it for his bride, but then she disappeared. It broke his heart, and he couldn't bear to even go in it after that. When the war started in Europe, he volunteered, and he never came back."

"I'm so sorry, Mrs. Janssen."

"He never should have trusted her," she says curtly. "Women like her can't be trusted. But George was such a sensitive man . . ." She looks away. "I do not advertise my connection to the house, nor do I deny it when asked. My brother left it to me, and I have held it for him." She sighs. "George is gone now. And that house is the one part of him I have left."

"And then there was the family who lived there in the sixties?"

"Yes, it was a mistake to sell it, but it had been sitting empty for so long, and it isn't good for a house to be empty. My husband insisted we sell. And she needed a family."

"She?"

"It's something my brother would always say." She smiles for a moment, but then it's gone.

"So, you sold it to this family, but now you own it again?"

She purses her lips, obviously annoyed by my questions. I can see why Lori got nowhere with her. Mrs. Janssen may be outwardly frail, but there's a stubbornness in her that shoots through like a rod of steel. "The family had only lived there for a few months. As soon as I sold it, I regretted it. And then . . . Well, after that terrible business, the bank didn't want it on their hands, so it was easy enough to reverse it all. I never should have let it get away from me in the first place."

"You couldn't have known what was going to happen."

"Of course, I didn't know that."

"But are you saying that those deaths had something to do with the family being in that house?"

"No, of course not. I just meant that the house didn't need any more tragedy. If George had come home, how would I have explained that to him?"

"Did you know them? Do you have any idea why that man killed his family?"

"How would I know that?" Mrs. Janssen leans in. "What exactly is it you want to know about: the house or that family?"

"Well, both, I guess. Whatever you can tell me would be helpful. I don't even know their names." I'm speaking too quickly, but it's hard to slow down. I know nothing about the Octagon House. I didn't realize how much I didn't know until now. For me and my friends, it had burst into existence on that long-ago summer afternoon, but of course it had a history. Someone had built it. People had lived there and died there. If I could look past its crumbling state, what had it been like to live in those rooms? What had it been like when this family arrived? Did the kids run into every room, each claiming a bedroom? Did they hang pictures on the walls and leave their toys scattered on those dusty floors now covered with broken beer bottles and dried leaves?

Something went horribly wrong, but was it a wrongness they brought with them? Or was it the house itself, something they blindly walked into? And if it was the house, when did they start to notice that it felt off? I realize my leg is bouncing and put my hand on it to control it.

Mrs. Janssen sighs. "Their name was Fischer. Benjamin Fischer, his wife, Natalie, and their daughters, Joan and Molly."

There it is, after all these years. The names hang in the air between us like ghosts suddenly called into existence. Knowing their names changes the story. Their names make them real people and, so it follows, with real deaths. The events that caused their deaths were real too.

That is what still hums in the air of that house; that is what we felt that summer long ago.

"They weren't from here," she continues. "They came up from the city. They were . . . different. Well, he was. Claimed he was an artist. No one really knew Mrs. Fischer or the children. They weren't here long enough. The children hadn't even started school yet."

"You said they'd only been there a few months when it happened."

"It was all so fast. They bought the house in early summer, and by late August it was all over." For a moment she is somewhere else, remembering something. "I met the wife once, and one of the girls, Joan." She shivers and shakes her head. "After I got the house back again, I told my husband to lock the door and let that be the end of it."

But it wasn't the end, at least not for Abby or for me. And how many other kids have stumbled into that house since then? I think of Taylor, the way she was standing in her window last night, watching the darkness.

"Mr. Fischer worked in the metal plant. He didn't fit in," Mrs. Janssen continues.

"How so?"

"There is a way with men who have grown up together, just as there is a way with women who share a similar outlook . . ."

"He didn't fit in because he wasn't from around here?"

"He hadn't served. That was the real difference."

I do a quick bit of mental math. "In Vietnam?"

"Almost all of the boys from this area went over and a good number of the men too. There was one unit that got hit hard. We lost eleven boys from this village. Some of them had only been there for three weeks. Their first letters home arrived after the funerals. It changes a place when so many of its young are killed. Most of the men at the factory had sons over there, sons who were just a little younger than Mr. Fischer. They understood the cost of it. It was hard for them to understand why Mr. Fischer hadn't made the same sacrifice."

"So, he was a draft dodger?"

"No, he would have had to go across the border. He got out of it some other way." She looks at me, expecting me to make the connection. When I don't, she continues: "There were several reasons why a man wouldn't serve. The problem was either physical or mental. Mr. Fischer was able to work in a factory, so if there was a problem, it wasn't with his body."

"What the hell are you doing here?"

I jump and spin around to look behind me, almost spilling my tea. Glaring at me from the doorway is the woman from the store.

"Rhonda, that isn't how we greet a guest," Mrs. Janssen says. "This is my daughter, Rhonda, and this is . . . tell me again?"

"Clare, hi." I reach my hand out, but Rhonda ignores it.

"We've met, Ma."

"Would you like some tea, dear?"

"Had coffee at the store," she says, then holds up a plastic bag. "I brought lunch."

"I'll wrap it up," I say, smiling at Rhonda. She doesn't smile back. Instead she crosses over to the counter and starts taking out plates, banging the cupboard doors as she does.

"Clare is asking about local history," Mrs. Janssen says.

"Oh yeah?" Rhonda says, not turning around. "Well, my mother is just a fountain of knowledge on that subject."

I stand up and start putting my coat on. "Thank you so much, Mrs. Janssen. I really appreciate you giving me your time."

Rhonda spins around to face me. "What exactly is it that you want to know?" Her mother starts to protest, but she cuts her off. "No, first you're in the store asking me all sorts of things, and now you're at my house bothering my mother."

"I'm sorry—I wasn't trying to—"

"She wasn't bothering me."

"I know she was your friend," Rhonda continues, ignoring her mother. "But it has nothing to do with us. Yeah, we own that goddamned house."

"Rhonda!"

"Come on, Ma. The place is a lawsuit waiting to happen." She crosses to the microwave and shoves a Lean Cuisine into it, then slams the door shut and punches in the time. "I've told you kids go in there."

"There is a fence," Mrs. Janssen says. "Mr. Farley boarded it up after that terrible business. It is on private property."

"Yeah, and the police told us there was garbage all over the place. Lots of people have been in there over the years. You think it's a big secret, but people find out about it. I hear things, Ma. There's always enough people who know about it that the information gets passed on."

"The whole town traipsing through there like it was a carnival sideshow when it was a crime scene," Mrs. Janssen says, more to herself than anyone else. This is an old argument.

"I'm not just talking about back then," Rhonda says. "I'm saying they still do it." At the store Rhonda was so still—caged, I realize now—held in behind her counter with the sagging lawn chair and her trolls. Here, she's like an animal storming around the kitchen. She turns to me and jabs her finger in my direction. "Did you go in it when you were a kid?"

"Yes."

Mrs. Janssen turns to me and furrows her brow. "You said you thought the house was fascinating."

Rhonda snorts. "Is that what she told you? She may have thought it was 'fascinating' but not in the way you're thinking." She tosses knives and forks onto the table with a clatter and turns to me. "Am I right?"

I have backed myself up against the far counter, trying to stay out of the way. "I'm just trying to learn a little about the history," I say. "For my friend."

"What good's a history lesson going to do her now? You were asking me about the basement."

"No." Mrs. Janssen's voice is so quiet I almost miss it. "Not there."

"What is it?" I ask her. "Do you know something?" But she won't look at me.

"What's it matter?" Rhonda asks. "The point is, she was there, and she had no right to be, and now my mom and I are dragged into some druggie's overdose—"

"Abby's not a drug addict. She went there for a reason."

"I don't know what you think is in that place. Your friend was obviously a head case; I could tell the moment she walked in the store, all jittery and hyped up." She turns to her mother.

"All it'll take is some idiot kid falling through the floor and their parents'll sue you, Ma."

"There's no legal case if they've been trespassing."

"You keep telling yourself that. Jesus. You'd better hope that chick wakes up, because if she doesn't and her family decides to press charges . . ." Rhonda stomps back to the microwave and pulls out the steaming food, then shoves the next meal in. "What's it going to take to convince you? There is no value in that house. There is absolutely nothing there worth all of this trouble."

"Enough." Mrs. Janssen hits the table with her palm, making the cups and saucers shake. "I made a promise that I would keep that house standing, and I intend to keep that promise. It's a beautiful house—"

"How would you know? You've never even gone inside."

"Yes, I have."

"When?"

"It doesn't matter when. I have been inside." There's something in her voice. Fear? Anger? I can't tell which, but there's something she's not saying. Something she saw.

A memory is waking up in my head. The moment between light and dark, like Taylor said. Movement on the edge of a shadow.

Rhonda turns to me. "I was just a kid when those murders happened, but I went with my parents to clean it out after. Mom was there too, and she refused to go inside. Wouldn't even leave the car." She puts her mother's food in front of her and goes to the sink to get water. "And you've never been since. That was over fifty years ago, Ma. I've been out there."

"I told you, you stay away from that place."

"I'm a grown-ass woman, and as long as our name's on that piece of shit, someone's got to check on it. Last time I saw it, the roof'd caved in. But you're still 'taking care of it.' If you were really taking care of it, you would have sold it decades ago so that people could actually live there."

Mrs. Janssen goes to stand, but she falters, and both Rhonda and I rush toward her. Rhonda gets there first.

"Come on, let's get you in bed. I'll turn on the TV and you can rest."

"I'm fine," her mother snaps.

"No, you're not." Without another word to me, and with surprising gentleness, Rhonda leads her mother out of the kitchen.

I wait a moment, and then, shakily, I walk through the dark hallway, fumbling toward the front door. When I pull it open and light comes in, I keep my eyes away from the picture of George Sumner, the man who built the Octagon House. I don't want him to see me.

I stand on the front step for a moment, blinking in the bright light and taking huge gulps of fresh air. Memories are roaring to life: I'm standing at the top of the basement stairs, and I see eyes, a painted face. A doll. There is an old doll lying at the bottom of the stairs. I can just barely see it looking up at me, tempting me to come down and get it. And I want to; I want to desperately.

But there's another memory, pushed down under others because it was too impossible, nudging its way into my consciousness. Whose doll was it?

Go back to the beginning to find the end.

Taylor was right. There was something else down there, waiting.

10

BEN

Another memory of that long-ago August night surges out of his dreams, and he's reaching for his sketchbook and pencil beside his bed.

He's home late from work and everyone in the house is asleep. The night air is cool relief after the heat of the day, and the moon is bright. He goes up the stairs, avoiding the creaks that could wake his sleeping children. Sleep is a precious thing in this house. First he checks on Molly. She's curled up, her bum in the air, her fingers jammed in her mouth. Her sheets have been kicked onto the floor, so he picks one of them up and gently spreads it out over her and kisses her lightly on top of the head.

Joan's room is next. He doesn't dare go in. Open on the floor beside her is the book he gave her to record her findings, and lined up along the windowsill he can see the silhouette of the fallen bird's nest, a long feather she insists belongs to an owl, and a collection of rocks, each one closely studied and sketched. Joan has had so much trouble sleeping, but she doesn't move now. Her body faces the wall. He stands in the doorway for a long moment anyway, watching the even movement of her breathing. He thinks about what she told him this morning—something she found in the basement. Did she tell him what? He hadn't registered it because he was rushing to work, but now he remembers: she had found a doll. Didn't the woman who sold them the house say that no one had ever lived here? He shakes his head to make the thought go away. Probably nothing. Something left behind from when the house was built. And Joanie's a good kid. He made it clear she couldn't go down there without him. Besides, she's more interested in what's out in the woods.

"She'll have forgotten all about it by the weekend," he mutters to himself softly. Then he can install a new lock on the basement door, like Natalie's been asking him to. High enough that the girls can't reach it.

Exhaustion settles over him with sudden finality, and Ben turns and goes into the master bedroom. There is his wife. She's got the wallpaper up—something old-fashioned with delicate vines and stripes that she found on sale—but she hasn't hung the curtains yet. Moonlight streams onto the bed, making her skin glow stone white. How desperately he wants to touch her, to press himself into her the way he used to, but she is such a light sleeper now that he doesn't dare. He hasn't been able to touch her in months.

———

His pencil stops moving and he looks at the sketch. His mind has been going into the memory of that night while his hand has been working independently.

There is Natalie, but the lines that he started drawing as the bed frame have turned into stairs. Her body isn't resting in sleep; it is twisted at a strange angle on the basement floor. What was supposed to be hair fanning out from her head has turned into a spreading liquid. And all around her, crosshatched over the rest of the page, is darkness. The reality of that night asserts itself into the sketchbook, insisting he see it again.

11

CLARE

July 25, 1998
5:30 P.M.

When they got to the main road that led into town, Monica and Lori biked ahead of Clare and waved when they turned off toward Monica's house. They'd been hatching plans for the evening and made no effort to include her, not that she'd wanted to join them anyway. The exertion of biking loosened the chill over her, and by the time she got into Sumner's Mills, she was sweating again.

Getting to her house meant she would have to bike past Abby's. As she approached, she saw that the grandparents had just arrived; everyone was standing on the side steps going into the house. Abby's father was shaking the grandfather's hand, and a small woman with a wide bottom and thick calves was hugging Abby and gesturing at the large perennial garden. It brought the group's attention out toward the street. Clare knew Abby must see her, but she didn't wave. Mitchell was opening the trunk of the grandparents' car, pulling out fat blue suitcases.

Mitchell was everything Abby was not. He was sixteen but had a kind of grace and confidence that made him seem years older than the middle sibling, Paul, though there was barely a year between them. He was smart and popular and could play any sport he wanted to. Just like Mitchell,

Abby had skipped a grade, but the age difference between her and her friends was always obvious. With Mitchell, even older kids thought he was cool. Most of the time he ignored his little sister, but every once in a while, and for no apparent reason, he would suddenly notice her and become playful; he'd grab Abby and swing her over his shoulder, then pin her on the ground. She would squeal and protest, but Clare knew how happy she was to be the object of his attention, even if only for a moment. She was so small he could tuck her under one arm and carry her around and threaten to put her head in the shower and turn it on, or stuff her in a closet.

The first time it happened, Clare had almost followed them upstairs from the basement, but something had told her to let this belong to Abby alone. Abby would escape and run downstairs, then perch on the bottom step, ready to run away again when he came down, but he never came back. Sometimes she'd call out to him, trying to egg him on, then they would hear music come from his room two floors above. Abby wouldn't say anything; she would just come to the couch and sit down silently, returning to the movie or rerun or whatever they had been watching. Once Clare had suggested they go and find him, but Abby turned to her and said, "Don't be stupid. Of course not."

The last time had been in the spring. Mitchell had grabbed Abby and thrown her over his shoulder, and while she was hitting him and shrieking, "Put me down," he turned and looked at Clare as if seeing her for the first time. Then the edge of his mouth curled up into a smile. "Hey, Clare. What's up?"

She was so surprised he'd said anything to her—that he even knew her name—her mouth dropped into a stupid O and she didn't say anything, though he probably didn't notice because he didn't wait for a response.

Now it happened again. This time he smiled and waved, distracting her. At that exact moment, her bike wheel hit a tree branch in the road, and she lost control and flew through the air over the handlebars, landing on her back.

She lay on the pavement, unable to breathe, then the air rushed into her lungs. Mitchell leaned over her, smiling. "You planning on staying down there?"

The rest of the family had missed her fall and were in the house. Had he run over to her? The two suitcases were by the car, the trunk still open.

"What?" she gasped.

"Are you okay? You hit your head or something?"

"I think so. I mean, I'm okay."

"Okay. Well, maybe you should get up, since it's a road and all. Here." He reached out to her but then, seeing the state of her hands, pulled his away.

"There was a stick." She was dizzy, but more from the rapid chain of events than from the actual fall.

"No kidding," he said, nodding at the offending branch. "I'd say it was a little more than a stick." He nodded toward her hands. "That's going to hurt."

"Oh. Okay."

"Road rash is a total bitch. You need to wash it right away."

"Okay."

"Your knees too."

"Okay." Stop saying okay, she thought to herself. You sound like an idiot.

He was looking at her, his eyebrows raised. She started to get up, but as soon as she put her hand on the asphalt, pain shot through her arm. She gasped. He reached out and hooked his hands under her elbows, then gently pulled her to her feet. She closed her eyes while the world spun.

"You sure you're okay?" he asked.

"Yeah." She opened her eyes and tried to make her voice sound normal. "I'm fine."

"How far is your house?"

"It's another mile or so. I'll be fine."

"Come inside. I can drive you home. We'll throw your bike in the trunk. Looks like you made out worse than the bike did."

He picked up the bike and put it over his shoulder, then started walking toward the house. Clare stood still.

"You coming? You really shouldn't stand in the road. Cars fly around that curve."

"Yes." And she followed him in, walking slowly in case the ground decided not to meet her feet.

The house smelled like roast beef, which made her stomach start to tighten and churn. Voices emanated from the living room, but Mitchell led her away from them to the downstairs bathroom. "Try not to bleed all over the place, okay?"

"Sure. Don't want them to think you tried to murder me."

"Exactly." He smiled and leaned close to her. A conspirator. "We've got the grandfolks here. Don't want them seeing all that blood and having a heart attack."

She smelled his shampoo and another smell. It was the smell of metals in hard water, cool and clean.

"I'll get you a towel you can bleed on," he said, and bounded down the hall.

Clare went into the little bathroom. It was the guest bathroom, without the accumulations of stray hair bands, old toothpaste tubes, and razors, like she saw in the family bathroom upstairs. In a bowl on the vanity were heart-shaped soaps that no one actually used. She'd been in this bathroom before, but now it felt different, like she was in a new house because she was here as Mitchell's guest, not Abby's friend.

Mitchell. She closed her eyes and made herself breathe slowly. Mitchell would come back, and it would be just the two of them.

She thought of Monica wanting to go into his room earlier today, trying to catch a glimpse of him after his shower. She understood why. And that was why she didn't want Monica going anywhere near him.

Clare had always been drawn to Abby's oldest brother, but a few months earlier, it had grown into a full-blown crush. She was sleeping over and had just stepped out of Abby's room on the way to the bathroom when the door opened and Mitchell walked out, wrapping a towel around him as he moved. He was muscular in a way she hadn't seen before; not bulky, like men on TV, but defined and smooth. His waist was narrow, and she could see a thin trail of dark hair starting just below his navel and disappearing under the towel. She froze at the far end of the hallway, then stepped back into Abby's room.

"What?" Abby had asked, not looking up from her book.

"Nothing. Forgot my toothpaste."

Abby didn't respond, and when Clare heard the click of Mitchell's door closing behind him, she went into the hall and padded silently past his room and into the steamy bathroom. It smelled of soap, and his clothes were in a pile where he'd peeled them off after his run. She bent down to touch them and picked up the T-shirt, then dropped it. He would notice if it looked like it had been moved, and how would she explain touching his dirty laundry? But she let her hand rest on it, feeling the dampness of his sweat on her skin, and she felt a pulse start between her legs.

She knew about sex, of course—Monica talked about it all the time—but it was always a distant thing that happened to other people, no more real than traveling to a foreign country or thinking of herself as an adult. This was different. She moved her hand to her crotch and pushed into the pulse, and that both relieved it and made the pulsing stronger. When she got to Abby's room, she was sweating. She had lain awake for a long time that night, trying to imagine what it would be like to touch his warm, taut skin.

Just thinking about it now and knowing he was about to come back into the bathroom to help her make her feel dizzy. She turned on the tap and put her hands under the water, then immediately pulled them out. The sting was like electricity. Don't cry, don't cry. He thinks Abby is a kid. Don't let him think you are, she thought. She put her left hand in the water, slowly. The bolt of pain shot up her arm again, but she kept it in the water, and the pain turned into a throbbing.

Mitchell poked his head around the door. "Whoa, you look like you're going to faint."

"I'm okay."

"You don't look it. I had a bike accident last summer and broke a rib, but it was this shit that hurt the most. You've got to clean it well, though, or you'll get an infection, and that's nasty, trust me."

He was there and his hand was on her back, holding her steady, but then the sink began to move and the sounds got far away. Her stomach heaved, and her legs gave way.

"Okay, there."

He caught her and guided her onto the floor. She'd always thought fainting was the most romantic thing anyone could do, but now all she could think was: Please, don't vomit on him. He'll hate you. "I'm going to be sick."

"Here." He turned her around to the toilet and lifted the seat. "You stay there. I'll get my mom and—"

"No!"

"What's wrong?"

She was shocked by how loudly she said it. "Can't you do it?"

"Me?"

You're being weird, she thought. But everything was still swimming, and words came out of her mouth unbidden. "I don't want to interrupt. Your grandparents."

"Don't worry about them."

"I'm okay," she said. He wouldn't want to be near her if he thought she was going to puke. "I just needed to sit." The cool floor felt like relief against her skin, and she resisted the urge to lie down on it.

He took a washcloth and wet it with cool water, then knelt down to dab at her bloody knees. She didn't even feel the pain. It was like she was floating above the room as she watched herself reach out and touch his hair.

He looked up suddenly. "What? Too hard?"

"No—it's fine. I'm sorry."

She'd actually touched him. He was real. This was actually happening.

"I thought you guys were hanging at our house," he said. "Then you disappeared."

He'd noticed that they had been there and then left? Clare was always acutely aware of him, but it never occurred to her that people—and Mitchell, at that—might also be aware of her. But he had meant "you" like the group of them. Probably he thought Monica was hot. Everyone else did.

"Yeah, we were going to stay here, but then we went to check out a haunted house."

"What?" He gave her an amused smile. "A bunch of girls?"

"Yeah, a bunch of girls. We went in too."

He whistled. "Impressive."

"Why, you wouldn't?"

"Sure, I would. Was it scary?"

"It was . . ." How could she describe that house in a way that sounded cool? "Yeah. It was pretty creepy. A guy murdered his family there."

He sucked in his breath. "No shit."

"It was a long time ago. I can tell you how to find it. There's this old road through the woods that leads to it but it's almost impossible to see. You have to know where to look." Don't mess this up. Don't sound too eager.

"Yeah?"

"Sure."

"Maybe you can take me sometime."

Clare was so busy trying to figure out how to react, she didn't answer.

"That is, unless you're too scared." He grinned at her.

"I'm not scared," she said. "Besides, I've already been in it. You haven't."

She waited for him to make some kind of retort, but he just looked at her. Even the other times had felt like he was only partly registering her, the way he might notice a piece of new furniture but not have any feelings toward it. This felt different. She started to feel a pink heat travel up her neck and wondered if he could see it.

"How's your hand?"

"Hurts."

"Let me see." He reached out to take her hand but kept his eyes on hers. He was so close to her, she could catch that scent again. He smelled like a water fountain on a hot day when you lean over it and drink and drink.

"Oh my God! What happened?" Abby was at the door.

Mitchell dropped her hand and pulled away. Abby looked confused, then turned around and yelled, "Mom? Mom, come here—Clare's had an accident."

The voices in the living room stopped. Mrs. Lindsay thundered down the hall, and then she was there at the doorway with Abby. The bathroom suddenly felt claustrophobic. The nausea started to rise again.

"Clare? What happened? Look at you."

"I bet Mitchell beat her up."

"Shut up, Abby." Mitchell's voice had an edge to it that Clare was used to hearing from the middle brother, Paul, but not from him.

"What happened, honey?" Mrs. Lindsay pushed her way into the bathroom past her son.

"She fell off her bike. I was trying to help her," he said, but already Clare could tell he was disengaging himself from her. He threw the washcloth in the sink and washed his hands. "Can you drive her home?"

"No," she wanted to say. "You were going to drive me home." But she didn't say this, and Mitchell left the room without looking back at her.

"She's bleeding a lot," Abby said, peering around her mother.

"Oh, sweetheart."

"I'm fine. It's just road rash. Mitchell was helping me."

"You look like you left a lot of skin on the road. Did you hit a pot-hole or something?"

"A branch."

"How come you didn't see it?" Abby asked. "It was pretty obvious."

"Abigail," her mother said sharply. "You're not being helpful." Then she turned to Clare. "I'm always telling Ted we've got to call the county about those old trees. They drop branches every time there's a storm. I'll drive you home. Unless you want to stay for dinner. Do you want to stay? Abby's grandma and grandpa are here, and I've made a roast."

"You're going to be covered in scabs," Abby said, leaning over Clare to examine her. "You're going to have to hold your handlebars with your elbows—"

"Enough," Mrs. Lindsay snapped. "Make yourself useful and go get the hydrogen peroxide." Abby jolted straight and left the bathroom without saying anything else.

With much fussing from Abby's grandparents, it was decided that Mr. Lindsay would drive Clare home, with Abby going along for the ride. Mitchell was nowhere to be seen. Mr. Lindsay helped Clare get into the car, and he put her bike in the trunk, but now she felt resentful of the concerned attention and just wanted to get away from this loud family and back to her quiet house.

"What did you girls do today?" Mr. Lindsay asked as he pulled onto the road. Usually Clare was in the backseat with Abby, but she was being given special treatment and Abby was sitting by herself. She tried to catch Abby's eye through the mirror, but Abby was focused out the window.

"Nothing much. We just rode around," Clare said when Abby didn't answer.

"Well, I hope your little tumble doesn't slow you down."

"Where did Mitchell go?"

"Who cares," Abby said. She was sunk low in the seat and picking at a loose bit of vinyl on the door.

Mr. Lindsay glanced at her through the mirror, then turned to Clare and said, "It's his last summer at home. We're trying to give him a little more freedom."

"His last summer?"

"He's going to school in New York in the fall. Didn't Abigail tell you?"

"I told you," Abby said.

But she hadn't, because Clare would have remembered.

"He's going to do his senior year in a college-prep program in engineering. It's a great school. I tried going there when I was a senior but had to transfer out. Mitch takes after his mother, not his dumb old dad." He winked at Clare.

"I guess I forgot," Abby mumbled.

"Your father is lucky, Clare. He's got a few more years with you before you move away. It's tough to watch your kids grow up. Makes you realize how much time has passed."

Mr. Lindsay did this. It was like he'd forget that she was only a year older than Abby, and he'd talk to her like she was an adult. She liked it when Abby wasn't around, but it was strange to be held separate when she was there to hear it.

It took only a few minutes to get to Clare's house. Whether from a sense of obligation or because the resentment was loosening its grip, Abby got out of the car and walked with Clare to the door while Mr. Lindsay put the bike in the garage.

"Does it hurt?" Abby asked.

"It stings, but it's okay," Clare said. "I guess I won't be riding my bike for a while, though."

She thought about everything that had happened at the Octagon House. Did Abby think it had been on purpose? She hadn't said anything to Monica and Lori about Clare daring her, or about seeing something. Normally she blabbed without thinking, so her silence was strange.

"What?" Abby asked.

"I went up to the room at the top of that house," Clare said. "I saw you. You were just standing there."

"I got confused. I couldn't remember where the path was at first. And I wanted to make sure you were going to come out."

"Why wouldn't I come out?"

"Because—" Abby stopped, then looked at the ground.

"It honestly was an accident," Clare said. How desperately she wanted to convince herself that this was true. "The door just jammed."

Abby shrugged. "I figured you were pretty mad at me because of the picture."

Now it was Clare's turn to look at the ground. "Okay, but, like, I just don't want you thinking that I'd do something like that on purpose."

"I saw the doll."

Clare's eyes opened wide.

"That's what you thought you saw, right?"

"How could you have seen it when it was pitch black?"

"I saw it the second before the door closed. I was trying to get to it and then it all went dark."

"You must have been so scared," Clare said.

Abby didn't answer.

"What?"

"I thought . . . There was something else—"

"Abigail, your mother needs us to get back," her father called from the car. Abby turned and started walking to the car. Clare limped after her. Her body was quickly becoming stiff from the fall.

"Hey, what are you doing tonight?"

Abby shrugged.

"Monica and Lori are going to your brother's game," Clare said. "They were talking about it after you left."

Monica and Lori had been hanging out with Paul and his friends more and more since the summer had started, preparing themselves for the social jump to high school by being friends with sophomores. Monica had already stated that freshman boys would be beneath her.

"Are you going?" Abby asked.

"Ugh, no." Clare didn't want to say that she hadn't been invited. Abby rolled her eyes and smirked. Maybe the weirdness of the day was gone. "Want to watch a movie or something that's actually fun?"

"Sure," Abby said. "Just get your dad to drive you over whenever you're done with dinner."

It was the closest they were going to get to normal for now, but it was enough.

12

Go back to the beginning to find the end. First the emails: five mysterious messages sent last spring, always arriving in the middle of the night. "Do you remember?" "Do you remember?" Always questions, no answers. Then, last week, Mrs. Lindsay's email: "She said your name." And now the note pushed through the mail slot in my father's door. Her last message to anyone before she walked through the woods to that house.

These woods.

I'm parked where she must have parked her car. It took me a few wrong turns, but I've found my way back. Running beside the woods is the old fence Lori's grandfather put up. The wire is rusty and the wooden posts are mottled and gray, but the fence holds. Normally the entrance to the old road is hidden—knowable only by a small marking on the post where the wire can be unhooked. Now it's marked with yellow police tape that flutters in the wind and tells anyone who would drive down this empty road: "There's something in here." The wire has been reattached, but I see where the ground has been churned up by the tires of police cars and the ambulance. They must have had to carry Abby out; there's no way a car could get down that path now.

She wrote me that note. She knew something might go wrong. She needed to leave a sign of where she'd gone so someone could come find her.

So I could come find her.

I remove her note from my coat pocket and unfold it. *Go back to the beginning to find the end.* I found the beginning. I talked to the sister of the man who built the house, but nothing she told me clears up why Abby came back here—or what she wants me to do.

I turn off the engine and pull my jacket tighter around me, wishing I'd grabbed one of my dad's old winter caps. I doubt he took them with him; he won't be needing them in North Carolina. I bet if I opened the coat closet, I'd find one stuffed into his winter coat. It would smell like him. I close my eyes, trying to imagine what my father would say about all of this. He and I didn't have the kind of relationship where we laid it all out in long heart-to-hearts. His comfort was indirect. Quiet. Steady. Like him. Toast and tea and telling me about some book he'd been reading on arctic exploration or medicinal plants coming out of the Amazon or some distant constellation that had just been identified, and somehow, at the end of the conversation, I would always end up feeling a little more able to handle any problem I was wrestling with.

I take out my phone to call him, but it sits in my hand. I wish there was someone I could talk to about this. Not that anyone else could give me answers—I don't even know if there are answers—but just to put all the pieces in front of someone else.

I want to talk to Josh.

No. That's just habit. That's just—

I clench my teeth hard. I put my phone away.

Abby's note sits in my lap. *The dreams came back this spring.*

Spring. The dreams came back for me too. And then everything fell apart.

———

I found out I was pregnant last February. I didn't even tell Josh at first. I was afraid if I said it out loud, if I allowed myself to believe it, it would disappear. A false positive. Everything changed with those two little lines. I waited another day and took another test, then another. In all, I took seven pregnancy tests, and they all said the same thing, so I told Josh. His look of amazement turning into such pure joy made it feel a little more real. Still, I wouldn't let him tell his parents, and I didn't tell my dad or anyone else. I made a doctor's appointment and the sky didn't fall, and I started ticking off the weeks, following her development from lentil to chickpea to blueberry on one of the many pregnancy blogs I was devouring daily. I felt sure it was a she, surer than I had felt about anything before.

Finally, one Saturday morning last April, I let myself wander into a baby boutique and buy a blanket. It was yellow with sheep on it, and it was the softest thing I'd ever felt. I was standing in the shop with my head buried in it and the saleslady came over and put her hand on my arm and I started to cry and when she asked if something was wrong I said, "I'm going to have a baby." The words wobbled in front of me, as magical and delicate as bubbles. She squeezed my arm and said, "I can tell you're going to be a great mom. I know. I have a feeling for these things." I knew she probably said this to every pregnant woman who came into her store, but I wanted to believe her. I needed to. I bought the blanket, but when I got it home, I left it wrapped up in the bag and pushed it to the back of my closet.

That night I got my first email from Abby. There was no subject and the message was only a line. It said, "Hi Clare, I found you!" She didn't sign it or say how she'd found me, though she had written to my school email account, which was public, so she must have done a search.

There were a hundred questions I wanted to ask her, but I didn't know where to start. Exhaustion hit me hard in the first trimester, and I fell asleep typing and erasing and retyping and erasing my reply.

I dreamed about the Octagon House for the first time in years. In my dream, Abby and I were back in the basement, but I could only just make her out in the flickering light of a dim flashlight. I was an adult, but she was still thirteen, frozen in time. Her back was to me, but I knew the T-shirt she was wearing had a rainbow on the front that ended in a puffy cloud with "Camp Winnetowa" stamped on it. Her favorite T-shirt. Her hair was tied in its usual ponytail, and her skinny legs stuck out of her shorts and glowed in the greenish light. She was holding something in one hand, but I couldn't make out what it was, something small that hung limply in her hand. She started walking across the basement, away from me, so I followed her.

The floor was packed earth, and everything in the place stank of old water and rot. She was walking toward the corner, and when she came to the wall, she ran her free hand along the stones, looking for something, then her hand disappeared into darkness and her body followed. It was a narrow opening that looked like a shadow until I saw her walk through it. I followed her. The room we entered was smaller than the one we had just been in, and this one had no stairs in it. She walked diagonally across the room to the opposite corner and did the same thing, stepping into a shadow, another opening. She stayed just in front of me, just out of reach, and we passed through another room and another, each room shrinking.

I tried to keep count of how many rooms we were passing through so I could find my way out. Dream logic told me she would lead me in but she wouldn't lead me out. Ahead, she disappeared through another dark opening. I squeezed through it, but as soon as I passed into the next room, the flashlight died and I was in absolute darkness.

I spun around blindly and reached out to feel my way to the opening. I scraped my hands along the wet stone walls. They were solid. I tried to scream and realized there wasn't enough air to get a full breath. I opened and closed my mouth, trying to swallow air, but there was nothing. I was suffocating—

I woke up screaming, sending the cat flying off the bed. It was three in the morning. Josh was away, so I turned on every light in the apartment; then I saw my laptop, hidden under the covers in the bed beside me. When I opened it up, "Hi Clare, I found you!" was still on the screen. I kept myself awake for the rest of the night, terrified that if I fell asleep, I would find myself back in that tomb.

I was tired and irritable all the next day, but I'd sworn off caffeine and was too cautious to even take an aspirin for the headache. A window slammed in my classroom and I let out a little scream, which made the students laugh, and instead of laughing it off with them, something I was normally able to do, I felt a flash of anger and snapped at them to get back to work. Josh came home from his trip, but I was too exhausted to have more than the shortest conversation with him. I didn't want to tell him about my nightmare because then I'd have to tell him about Abby and the Octagon House, and I had never told anyone about that place.

It took a few days for the remnants of the dream to subside, during which time I did finally send a short message to Abby, asking her general questions about what she was doing and where she lived, and avoided saying anything about myself. Three days later, she sent another email. This one was also one line long: "Clare, I've been remembering our last summer together and that crazy house."

That night the dream came again, but this time Josh was there when I woke up screaming. He held me and stroked my hair. I tried to focus on his hand and not on what I was seeing in my head, but he soon fell asleep, and I was left wide awake and terrified with his limp arm draped over me.

The third email came a week later. No subject again and a one-line message: "Clare, do you remember what I told you after that night?" I couldn't get the dream out of my head. The logical response would have been to block her, but I couldn't. Whatever was going on with Abby, it was at least partially my fault. I knew that. So I read the message and wrote a short reply, asking benign questions to try to get her off this topic. I owed her that much.

But my brain was in a fog; I was terrified to let myself sleep. The headaches were a constant now. I started making mistakes in class, losing my place in the lessons. I forgot to give a major test and was late for school twice.

Two weeks passed and I was just starting to think that maybe the game Abby was playing had finally ended when the fourth email arrived. "Can't stop thinking about that house and what I saw there." Another dream of that basement, another night waking up screaming. Josh tried to be understanding, but I could see the cautious way he was treating me. He was starting to dread nighttime as much as I did. And still I couldn't tell him.

Then, a week later, the fifth: "Clare, I know you saw it too. Do you remember?"

This time I responded quickly: "I don't remember and I don't care. Grow up. Don't contact me again." I pressed send and slammed my laptop shut.

The dream changed.

Everything in the dream was the same until the end, when I passed into the final room. This time Abby was there, and the flashlight didn't go out. She was still, and I walked up behind her and put my hand on her shoulder. She was so cold. And then she turned around and she wasn't Abby. She was my mother, but her face was sunken in, the skin pulled tight and thin over the bones, and her eyes were blank mirrors that reflected the dim light. I jerked my hand away from her and she screamed, and in that sound was so much pain. Blood poured out of her mouth, so real I could smell it: thick and metallic. Something clenched in my stomach and I doubled over, then I was in our bed and I was the one who was screaming. I clamped my hands over my mouth so I wouldn't wake Josh, and that was when I realized my hands were covered in blood. Not hers.

Mine.

I stumbled into the bathroom and collapsed on the floor. Blood everywhere. My blood. My baby's blood. Leaking out of me and onto the white-and-black bathroom floor of our apartment. It was hot and brilliant red, and I knew it would stain the old, cracked epoxy between the tiles and I would always see it. Josh appeared, kneeling in front of me. "Don't step on her." I pushed him away. He had blood on his bare feet. I was scraping up the clots with my hands, trying to gather the blood as if I could put it back inside me, and he grabbed my arms and told me to stop. He was crying. I could see he was crying. I could see he was scared, but I was seeing it all from far away, and the person who was on that bathroom floor, who I knew was me, thought: *I hate you.*

He wrapped me in blankets and half carried me to the car. No need to do a D&C, the doctor said after the exam. My uterus was empty. My baby was gone.

It was the first week of May. When we left the hospital later that morning, the sun was too bright and too warm. We drove back to our apartment and I stared at all the people basking in the first taste of summer's warmth, the sidewalks covered with hastily set-up patios outside every restaurant and café. I sat in the car and watched them while Josh went into our apartment and removed every trace of blood, every sign that we were going to be parents. There weren't many—I hadn't allowed myself many. The office hadn't been converted into a nursery yet, there was no crib or stroller to deal with, just the reminder of the next doctor's appointment on the fridge door, and the bag holding the softest yellow blanket I'd ever felt, hidden in my closet. He didn't take the blanket because I hadn't told him about it. That blanket is the one little bit of my daughter that I have let myself hold on to through all of this.

There was only a month left in school and I was given a leave of absence. An elite prep school in Evanston is not the place for a teacher terrorized by dreams. The sleeplessness of the past month had led to poorly planned lessons, missed meetings, and mismanagement of my classroom, which was filled with teen girls who could smell emotional chaos like wolves. The principal was sympathetic about the miscarriage, but a month later I got a letter saying that they had decided not to renew my contract. At that point, I barely registered it.

The irony was that after the miscarriage, I wanted the dream to come back. In the dream, all of the ugliness and horror was outside me. When I was awake, it was inside, and that was much, much worse. But the dreams stopped. So did Abby's emails, until the one I got a few days ago from her mother.

In the hospital that May morning, I was so cold that I felt like I would never be able to get warm again. The doctor who examined me had warm hands. It was the one thing I was able to register. She was cleaning up when Josh suddenly cried out, "But why?" Josh who was polite to everyone, who followed the rules, who never questioned authority. He had barely said anything the whole time we'd been there. "Why did it happen, can you at least tell us that?" I could hear the waver in his voice. He was on the edge of something ugly and I didn't want to see it. I braced myself for the doctor to tell him about the percentage of pregnancies that end in miscarriage; to quote statistics about incompatibility, about fetal abnormality—all of it a betrayal by my body—but instead she looked right at us and said firmly but kindly, "Sometimes these things just happen."

But I knew why.

Abby had returned me to the Octagon House in my dreams. She had opened up what I had kept tightly sealed for years. Those dreams were like none I've ever had. I smelled it. I know you're not supposed to be able to smell in dreams, but I could *smell* the basement.

I didn't lose my baby on that bathroom floor. I lost her in the Octagon House.

———

I'm brought back to reality by my phone buzzing. A text from Lori. **How's Mrs. J? She sell you a house?**

Didn't ask.

Thinking over my conversation with Marion Janssen, I wonder how much of all of that Lori knows or cares about. She's more interested in knocking the house down than figuring out why Abby went there. Then I think of something that will spark her interest.

Told me about the family who died there. The Fischers.

It takes her a bit to respond, and I assume she probably doesn't care or is busy, but then my phone buzzes again and she's sent me a link to a crime blog. I respond with a question mark. She writes:

Just thot interesting. Gotta go. Kids have hockey tonight. Come by tmrw?

I click on the link. It takes a while; the signal is spotty at best out here on these country roads. Eventually it loads enough for me to read it. It's a post from over a year ago. Whoever wrote it covered half of Upstate New York, but I scroll down until I see a subtitle: "Sumner's Mills: Family Killer Goes Home." It's only a few sentences long, but it says that Benjamin Fischer, the man who was accused of killing his family in 1965, was being exonerated of his first-degree-murder charges due to "attorney errors" and "insufficient evidence." And because of his deteriorating health and lack of family, he would be released to a nursing home that was coincidentally close to the scene of the crime.

I drive home, in part because I don't want to spend any more time near the Octagon House, and also because I'm cold and hungry and I need a better cell signal to do my research. Thinking about what happened last spring and what part Abby's obsession with this house played into it makes me angry at her all over again. I can't go and see her yet. I'm going to take the chance that Mitchell hasn't mentioned seeing me to his parents. Given how our last interaction went, it's a safe bet.

I can't just sit around my dad's house; I need to do something. Everything goes back to that fucked-up house. Go back to the beginning, Abby said.

I remember what that house felt like, and it felt that way because of what happened there years before we ever stepped foot inside. I'm going to find Benjamin Fischer.

13

A better signal quickly reveals that there are no nursing homes in Sumner's Mills, as I suspected. I widen my search to anything within fifty miles and get three. The first place I call doesn't have any Fischers in residence, but when I call Three Pines Seniors' Residence and ask to be transferred to Mr. Fischer's room, there's a slight change in the nurse's voice, like she's caught off guard, and then she says, "One minute, please. I'll put you through."

I pace around the kitchen as the phone rings on the other end. My heart pounds so hard, I have to force myself to close my eyes and take a deep breath. I have no idea what I'll say, but I don't have a chance to find out, because the nurse comes back on the line. "I'm sorry, his phone is off. He must be sleeping. Would you like to leave a message for him?"

"I can just try again later."

"Oh." She sounds disappointed. "Are you related?"

"I'm his niece. Great-niece." I say it before I can second-guess myself.

"We didn't think Mr. Fischer had any family. He will be so happy to know you've called."

"Actually, can I come and visit him?"

"Of course. Visiting hours are eight to six, every day."

"Okay, thanks." I'm about to hang up when there are some muffled sounds like the phone is being moved around. Another woman comes on.

"Who is this?" she hisses into the phone.

"I'm Mr. Fischer's niece."

"Bullshit. He doesn't have any nieces. Is this Abby?"

So, Abby found Mr. Fischer too. I only have to think for a second. "Yes."

"I told you before: leave him alone."

"Why?"

"I don't know what you want, but I never should have let you in there alone. He's been messed up ever since."

"I need to talk to him."

"Is this some kind of game for you? He's not well. You can't just come in here and get him worked up and disappear. Did you even think about what that might do to him?"

She's winding herself up to slam the phone down, so I say, loudly so she'll hear me, "I'm not Abby. Abby's in the hospital. She's in a coma."

She's breathing hard, but she doesn't hang up. "What happened?"

"She tried to kill herself."

There's an intake of air. An intercom calls out behind her, distant electronic voices. "Ah, fuck," she says quietly.

"My name's Clare. I'm Abby's friend. I need to talk to Mr. Fischer."

"No, you don't. Just leave him alone." Before I can ask anything else, she hangs up. I close my eyes. The immediate spike of adrenaline vanishes as soon as I'm off the phone, replaced with a heavy feeling, like water filling a hole.

———

Three Pines is almost an hour's drive away. If websites are anything to go on, it's the least fancy of the three facilities in the area, but I guess that's not surprising given that the state is paying. And after fifty-odd years in prison, Mr. Fischer's standards are probably pretty low. It's one of those squat cinder-block buildings that's more about function than aesthetics. The residents whose rooms face the road look out over a sprawling parking lot, but the ones in the back must have a semi-decent view of a stand of pines. I can see the treetops waving in the wind over the roof.

Someone has taped Halloween decorations over the front desk, and a wilting scarecrow leans at an awkward angle against the wall, holding a sign that says "Welcome." I don't know if I'm going to meet resistance when I tell them who I'm there to see, but the nurse just points to a sign-in book and continues what she's doing, barely looking up. An older nurse pecks away at a computer, her back to me. The visitors' book is a large binder almost running out of pages. I start to flip through it to see if I can spot Abby's name, but the first nurse pulls it away.

"Can I help you?" she asks.

"A friend of mine was here a little while ago. I was trying to see when."

"That's not the kind of information we give out," she says, and the older nurse glances over her shoulder to see what's going on.

"She was visiting Benjamin Fischer." I don't know how many former convicts this nursing home gets, but I'm guessing that his name might stand out.

"I'm sorry, but we get a lot of visitors, and we can't—"

"She was here last week or maybe the week before," the older nurse says. "Mr. Fischer never gets visitors, that's why she stuck out." She looks at the other nurse. "You remember. I think she came once before that too. Last week, though . . ." She sucks her teeth.

"What do you mean?" I ask her.

"Oh yeah," the first nurse says. "Her. Must have had too much coffee or something."

"That wasn't coffee, honey," the older one says, shaking her head and returning to the computer.

"Do you know why she was visiting Mr. Fischer?" I ask.

"Ruth Ann just about had a fit," the younger nurse says to the other, ignoring me.

"Ruth Ann?" I say.

"She's one of our assistants. Taken a real shine to Mr. Fischer."

The older nurse just smiles and shakes her head again, like they have an inside joke, then looks past me. "How can we help you, Mrs. Elliot?" An elderly woman has shuffled up behind me.

"My daughter, Annie, was supposed to take me out to dinner, and she's late, and I'm worried that something has happened."

"Your daughter is coming next week," the first nurse says in a way that makes it clear they've had this conversation before. "See, it's on the calendar. We made you this calendar so you'd know when she's coming."

The older nurse gets up and comes over to me. "His room's down the end of this hall on the left: 104."

"No, it is today," Mrs. Elliot says, and her voice rises in panic. "Something terrible has happened, I know it."

I want to find out more about Ruth Ann, or what they thought was wrong with Abby, but Mrs. Elliot isn't going to be easily calmed, so I turn and walk down the hallway in the direction the nurse pointed. Most of the doors are closed, but a few are open—small rooms stuffed with framed pictures, afghan-covered chairs, potted plants, and a bunch of balloons in one. Others are filled with medical gear—oxygen tanks, tubes and wires and bedside tables loaded with pill bottles—and always, always a TV. I'm almost at the end of the hall when I come to 104.

The door is slightly ajar, and at first glance, it looks empty. Bare walls, no furniture besides the standard hospital bed and bedside table. I knock softly, then push the door open a little farther, and there he is, deeply asleep. The bones of his face are clearly visible, and thin wisps of white hover over his wrinkled scalp. With his hands clasped over his stomach and the sheets pulled tight, I would think he was dead if not for the rhythmic sounds of the oxygen machine and the heart monitor. His room faces the pines behind the building, and his curtains are pushed wide open. I can see why he'd want to see the outdoors after spending fifty years in jail, even if he's too old and sick to be in it. While his room seemed depressingly bare at first, now I can see that without any distractions, the freedom and beauty of what's outside is all the more visible.

I stand over him. The man's breathing is shallow but steady. I can just hear it under the machines, the precarious sound of air being sucked in through a tiny opening. This man was accused of killing his family in cold blood. This is the man I thought would be able to give me answers about what happened that night and why Abby needed so desperately to go back. She must have thought the same if she came here to visit him. Maybe she saw that in him, but I can't. Every time I try to understand more about what Abby did, I just get more confused—everything makes *less* sense.

I turn to go and almost crash into a woman charging into the room with a pile of folded towels in her arms. She jumps back, hugging the towels tighter to her chest. "Who are you?" she asks. Before I even have a chance to answer, she spits out, "You're the one who called."

Her face is young, but her eyes and body have the puffy slackness of someone who has never had what she deserves: the food, the education, the people. I see it so often in towns like this one. Who would this woman be if, say, she grew up in a family like those of the girls I taught in Evanston? Or how would they be if they were here? Instead of stressing out about internships and their college applications, they'd be stressing out about keeping the heat on and buying diapers. This woman is standing in the doorway, legs spread wide, shoulders hunched and ready, like she's expecting me to try to bolt.

"Sorry to startle you," I say. "I wanted to talk to Mr. Fischer."

"He's asleep," she says, jerking her head toward him for emphasis. "They should have told you that. He can't be disturbed."

"I wasn't—"

"I told you not to come here."

"You told Abby not to come here. I'm not here to cause any trouble." I hold up my hands. "Honest."

She looks like she's thinking that over, which is fine, she can think all she wants, but she's also blocking the door and seems like she isn't going to move.

"Are you Ruth Ann?"

Her eyes narrow, but she doesn't answer.

"The nurses at the front desk said there's a Ruth Ann who works here and knows Mr. Fischer really well. I thought maybe, if I can't talk to him, I could talk to her. Is that you?"

"I'm working," she says, but she still doesn't move. She checks the hallway behind her, then turns to me.

"No, of course. I can see that," I say. "I could just leave a note. Would you give it to him?"

"Depends. He doesn't need any more problems."

"I'll just say who I am and leave my number." I look at him lying in the bed. Is he really going to be able to have a phone conversation? "Or I could just come another time. Is there a time when he's usually awake?"

"Leave a note," she says.

It seems she doesn't trust me to leave it with anyone but her, so, with her watching, I rummage through my bag and find a pen and a crumpled receipt. I write my name and cell number on it and then: "I would like to talk to you about your house in Sumner's Mills."

She takes it and reads it, obviously not concerned about privacy.

"Thank you," I say as she folds it up and stuffs it in the pocket of her scrubs. "It's important. You are going to give it to him, right?"

"I said I would, didn't I?" She steps aside so I can leave.

"Right. Okay, well, thanks." I take one last look at Mr. Fischer, who hasn't moved throughout this entire conversation, and leave. I bet she will watch me until I turn the corner back to the entrance.

I return to my car and am trying to figure out my next move when I see Ruth Ann come out of the building, tugging her coat around her in the wind. She takes out a pack of cigarettes and disappears around the side. I get out of my car and go after her.

"Hey," I say. I'm at a distance so I don't scare her. She looks startled to see me, but she doesn't move away. She's huddled against the wall to protect herself from the wind.

"I feel like we got off on the wrong foot," I say. "I'm sorry about saying I was Abby on the phone. I don't know why I said that. I'm just— I'm kind of flailing here. I drove all the way here from Chicago two days ago, and I'm just trying to figure out what happened. When I found out Abby came here, it seemed important that I figure out why."

She doesn't say anything, but she's listening.

"I think I'm partly to blame for what happened to her, or what led to the attempt she made. I'm involved somehow, and I'm trying to figure out why."

She takes a drag of her cigarette, then lets the smoke out in a steady stream. She seems different out here, older, more grounded. "You can't blame yourself if someone's an addict." She considers her cigarette and takes another drag. "That's what you want to do, but that means you're not understanding what addiction is."

"She's not a—" I stop myself. Is Abby an addict? The emails, the note, the overdose. Maybe Rhonda and the police are right. Even Lori seemed to be implying that's what was going on.

Ruth Ann's looking at me, waiting for me to finish. "My brother was an addict. I recognize the signs." She blows out more smoke into the wind, and it whips it away from us.

"Oh."

"The way she was when she was here last week? He'd get like that sometimes. All hyped up like that. It looks like it's being driven by something good, like they're excited about something. It's a trick. It's fear."

Driven by fear. Abby's obsession with the house has just seemed . . . obsessive. Illogical. I think about Taylor and how terrified she is of what she thinks she saw, and yet she can't stay away.

"I don't mean to say anything bad about your friend," she continues. "And I am sorry she's so hurt, but Mr. Fischer—he's got no one. I don't think he's had anyone for a long, long time. I don't know how she found him or what she said to him, but, well, I know what my brother was like. When he was bad, he'd do just about anything for money. Things he never would have done, just to get it. I thought maybe she was going to try to get money out of him. I figured that must have been what happened. She promised to do something for him, and maybe he gave her some money—that's why he didn't want me to know—but then instead of doing it, she took off."

"I don't know why she came here," I say. "I didn't even know she had until you told me."

She looks confused.

"On the phone. You said, 'Leave him alone.' I figured—"

"Are you, like, a cop or something?"

I laugh. It surprises me, but it's actually a genuine laugh. She looks confused at first, but then a small smile comes over her face. I say, "Oh my God, no. I'd be the shittiest cop ever."

"Then . . . ?"

I try, as simply as possible, to explain to her about the Octagon House, how we went there when we were kids and what happened, and how Abby went back last week and pulled me in after her. "I'm just trying to figure out why I'm even here," I finally say.

Ruth Ann drops her cigarette and stamps it out with her toe, then leans over to pick it up and put it in her pocket. Standing up, she grimaces, and her hand shoots to her lower back.

"Are you okay?"

"Yeah. The floors here are concrete, and I can't afford the fancy shoes the nurses wear, just these cheap-ass tennis shoes." She indicates her sneakers, which look like dollar-store rip-off Keds. "I must walk ten miles in every shift. Ever since my kids, my body's just gone to shit."

"How old are they?"

"Eight and six," she says. I would guess she's under twenty-five.

Another blast of winds whips around the building, and my hair flies up all around me. I try to huddle closer to the wall without making her feel crowded.

"Do you got a couple of minutes?" she asks me. "There's something I could show you. I don't know if it'll help, but you said you wanted to talk to Mr. Fischer about a house. You know he was in prison, right?"

I nod. "It was a house he lived in a long time ago. It was where—" I stop myself. Outside of what she's just said, I don't know how much she knows about him.

"His family?" she asks, guessing the reason for my hesitation. "I know about that. When they sent him here, some of the nurses were real freaked out. There's still some who won't go into his room. A few even tried to get him sent somewhere else, but that didn't get far. Doesn't matter that he's innocent. They said maybe he just said that to get out—like it's that easy. It's fucked-up." She looks off, shaking her head slowly. "I swear, some of them don't even like the residents. Like why work here?" She turns back to me. "Mr. Fischer's dying—cancer. He barely moves, except to look out his window and to draw. I just do what I can to keep him comfortable. I figure, after that many years in prison for something he didn't do, it's the least someone can do for him, you know?"

I nod again. I can no longer hide the fact that I'm freezing, and my teeth start chattering.

"Anyway," she says, "there's something I could show you. Like I said, I don't know if it helps you, but I think it's got something to do with why your friend was here."

"Really? That would be— Thank you."

"Sure. I gotta go back in to get it. Where'd you park?"

———

It's drizzling outside. Five minutes later, Ruth Ann taps on the window of my car, clutching a plastic bag with what looks like a book inside it. She slides into the passenger seat and pulls a large black sketchbook out of the bag. "I gotta be real careful not to get any drips on the pages from my coat. You hold it."

I turn on my phone flashlight and open the book to the first page. It's a sketch of a bird. The lines are light and soft, like it was drawn quickly by someone who knew what they were doing. It looks real, each line adding depth and texture to the bird's body. I turn the page and there's another bird. They're labeled with scientific names in spidery writing under the pictures.

"He drew me pictures just like these," she says. "I never noticed birds before, but now I see them all the time. It makes it nicer, you know, even if you're just going for a walk, like in a place where you walk all the time, or just sitting and looking out the window. I used to think that was boring, but there's so much to see. That's what he's taught me."

"They're beautiful," I say, hoping I don't sound disappointed. I turn the page and there's another bird, then another. This is what she thought Abby was interested in? "So detailed."

"My son, Ryder, he's autistic. Mr. Fischer gave me a bird picture to take home, and I gave it to Ryder 'cause he loves animals. He's not so great with people, but ask him anything about any kind of animal, and he can tell you. He loved the picture and put it up in his room, and when I told Mr. Fischer, he gave me more. Ryder's got a whole wall in his room covered with 'em now. He knows all their names. When he's getting worked up, he goes and looks at those birds and says all their names over and over until he feels better. I taught him that. Works better than all those things the counselor said to do."

She's watching the raindrops turn everything outside into blurry blobs of gray. Her face has hardened, but not in a bad way. She doesn't have the look she first had of being on the defensive, like she's expecting someone's going to accuse her of being too dumb or too slow. She looks down at the book and points to the page I'm on, a small squat bird on a pine branch.

"That's one of my favorites: the white-breasted nuthatch. There's a few of 'em that live back there in the trees. Mr. Fischer always wants to keep his curtains open—even at night. He gets real upset if someone closes them. He wants to see the birds."

I turn the page again. "That's a woodpecker, right?"

"A male, yeah, I think. It's hard to tell 'cause it's just pencils. Males have red here"—she points to a place on the bird's head—"but the females don't. He taught me that. He's taught me all sorts of stuff."

"My dad tried to teach me about birds," I say. "I could never remember them, though."

"When your friend came, he stopped drawing them. Ryder's been bugging me for new pictures, but Mr. Fischer won't draw them now. It's hard to explain to a kid."

"Why'd he stop?"

"Like I know. He just . . . changed. He barely even talks to me now."

"When did Abby first come?"

"August. I don't remember exactly when, but I know it was August. And then again, beginning of last week."

Abby must have come here right before she went to the Octagon House. "It was just the two times?"

"Yeah. That was enough."

"And you have no idea why she came here?"

"No one tells me anything." The anger is back in her voice. I turn the page, and there, instead of a bird, is a woman's face. "That's what he draws now," she says.

Even in just a rough sketch, the beauty of the woman comes through. She's sitting at a table with her long hair falling over her shoulders. Her head is turned and she's looking at something in the distance. I flip the page. More sketches of the same woman, some looking posed, some not. Then, on the next page, two children appear: a taller one, all knees and elbows, and the younger one still soft with baby fat, her curls falling over her face. At first I assume the larger child with the short hair is a boy, but in a close-up of her face, I see she's a girl. She's crouched down, examining the leaf of a plant with a magnifying glass. There's another of the younger girl curled into her mother's lap. These sketches, like the ones of the birds, look like they were done quickly. In some of them, I see the house as it was before it was ruins. He hasn't drawn it in detail— it's clear the focus of the pictures is the people—but it's there, framing them in the background. There are curtains in the downstairs windows, and in one picture, the smaller child sits in its shade, conducting a tea party with stuffed animals. Parts of his subjects are missing, an incomplete mouth or a body only half done, but there's always enough that my mind can fill in the rest.

I turn the page again. This one is from outside the house, looking in on the family. The figures inside are just shadows: two children at the table and their mother nearby. At the top of the page, in the same shaky hand, he has written: "August 22, 1965. Morning." I don't know the date of the murders, but I know it was in the late summer of that year. Abby came to visit him, and he started drawing his family—more specifically, he started drawing his family at the Octagon House, right around the time of their deaths.

"He just sits there and stares out the window or sleeps. He always has to have that book near him, 'cause he draws as soon as he wakes up. Once I moved it into a drawer 'cause I didn't know, and he got so angry . . ."

I'm only half listening to her. I stare at the faces of the children and the woman, waiting for something to click. Whatever is wrong with the

Octagon House is connected to these three and their deaths there. The doll I thought I'd seen—it must have belonged to one of his daughters. But there was something else down there too. That shadow just beyond the border of memory. Or was that because I was a child? I'm confusing my memories with Taylor's and Abby's.

"Has he said anything about these?" I ask.

She shakes her head. "He doesn't know I've seen them. The book was open once and I started to ask, but he closed it and wouldn't say anything." The hurt is clear. Ruth Ann has never had anyone take the time to show her birds, to share something with her just for the joy of it. Then Abby showed up and she was pushed out.

I turn the page, and this time we both gasp. This picture is different. The lines are jerky, the angles hard, like he was pressing the pencil into the paper. Initially it looks like a woman lying asleep. But the angle of her arm seems off. The jagged lines behind her—which seem incomplete at first—form a staircase. Her body is small, drawn in the bottom corner of the page, while the rest of the space has been filled in with heavy lines smudged together by the hand pulled across them.

"This is new," Ruth Ann says quietly.

I turn the page. There, drawn in thick heavy lines, is the basement door. I recognize it immediately. It is open, and framed in its gaping doorway is darkness. I almost smell the decay of that place and how it felt like it was alive. Like an animal, smelling me so it could remember. I assumed his family was killed in the kitchen, or maybe, if it was late at night, in their beds. But what if they died in the basement?

The last few pages have been ripped out, their tattered edges still attached to the binding. I'm about to start flipping through again when I feel the edge of something under the inside of the back cover.

I crack open the book all the way.

"Be careful—" Ruth Ann says, reaching to take it, but that's when I find the slit, right along the inside edge of the binding. I pull it open and slide out four items: an envelope addressed to Benjamin Fischer at Auburn Prison, an official-looking envelope addressed to Mr. and Mrs. Desrochers in Manhattan, and two folded pieces of paper that look much newer. I open the official-looking envelope with the typed address first. The yellow paper is delicate; it looks like it could come apart at the folds just from being opened.

CERTIFICATE OF DEATH

Name: Joan Natalie Fischer   **Age:** 10

Date of Birth: June 5, 1957   **Date of Death:** February 17, 1968

Father: Benjamin Fischer

Mother: Natalie Fischer, née Desrochers (Deceased)

Place of Death: Lewis County Institution for the Insane

Length of Stay: 2 years, 3 months, 15 days

Cause of Death: Pneumonia

"Holy— Was that his daughter?"

"Yeah," I say, but there's a catch in my throat. This girl didn't die in the basement. Whatever happened to her, she'd survived but been institutionalized. Immediately I think of Rhonda calling Abby "a head case," and the nurses I'd just talked to. And even me. My last words to Abby: "Grow up. Don't contact me again."

"How'd a kid end up in an insane asylum?" Ruth Ann mumbles, more to herself than to me.

I open the second envelope. It's also old, written in cursive with a fountain pen. Inside is a single sheet of thick paper that was probably once creamy white but is now a dull brown. The letterhead at the top is embossed in silver and says Evangeline Desrochers with a Manhattan address.

March 2, 1968

Ben,

I'm writing with bad news. I don't know if this is the sort of thing they tell you in there, but I wanted you to know and to hear it from me. Joanie has died. It's terrible, I know, but in many ways, it is a blessing. She never fully recovered from her injuries. The doctors said it was a miracle she was alive at all, but your daughter always was a fighter, wasn't she. I don't think she ever understood what happened to her mother and sister, or to you. I visited her as much as I could but she never recognized me.

I don't know how else to say this: Joanie was haunted. The doctors had to sedate her each night because the nightmares would make her do terrible things, not to others but to herself. A new director took over at the facility and he had some fancy new ideas about how to treat the patients. They stopped restraining her at night, so she got out. They found her on the road in her pajamas and brought her back but she died of exposure. I know what the death certificate says but I wanted you to know the truth: she was trying to return to that house, I'm sure of it. I think she must have been trying to find her family. Some part of her mind must have remembered. I've become friendly with one of the nursing staff and she was with Joanie at the end. She made her as comfortable as she could: I want you to know that.

Joan is buried next to Natalie and little Molly. She is finally with her family again. I hope you can find some comfort in that.

Mother and Father obviously do not know that I have sent you this certificate but I believe it is your right to have it. And if you do ever decide to try to appeal, you may need it.

Yours, Evangeline

I want to read and reread both pieces of paper, but Ruth Ann starts shifting around, whether from the contents of the letter or the need to get the book back without being discovered, so I pass them to her and move on to the next two.

The two newer pieces of paper are printouts from a microfilm of a newspaper called the *Post-Sentinel*. Words are circled and underlined in red marker, and it takes me a moment to realize that the date I'm looking at is thirty years earlier than I'm expecting.

APRIL 13, 1936

Sumner's Mills – Residents of Sumner's Mills have been searching for three days now in hopes of solving the mysterious disappearance of Miss Alice Carey, age 21, and her six-year-old daughter, Grace. Mother and child were last seen leaving Reynolds General Store on the afternoon of April 6. Miss Carey was reported missing by her fiancé, George Sumner, on April 10. Anyone with information is asked to contact the Franklin County Sheriff's Office immediately.

APRIL 20, 1936

LETTER TO THE EDITOR

Dear Sir:

As many of the fine citizens of Sumner's Mills know, this marks the ten-day anniversary of the disappearance of Miss Alice Carey and her daughter, Grace, and yet what has happened to the search for them? The police tell us it has been called off but give no satisfactory answers as to why. I urge your readers to demand the search be resumed and not be stopped until these two are found. The citizens of Sumner's Mills must be vigilant to the dangers that lurk within our community and prey on the innocent, and we all must reject the gossip that this young mother, with her life before her, has simply vanished by her own choice. While Miss Carey was new to our community, I can assure your readers that she was a young woman of upstanding character, despite unfortunate circumstances. "Judge not, that ye be not judged." (Matthew 7:1)

Sincerely,
A concerned citizen
Sumner's Mills

"Has Mr. Fischer been doing research?" I ask.

"I told you, he can barely move. Look." Ruth Ann points to the bottom of the page. "See? Printed at ten oh-eight a.m. on July fourteenth." Next to the time stamp, it says, "Buffalo and Erie County Public Library, Printer 2." "Why was your friend bringing him old newspaper articles?"

"I don't know," I say. "It has to be connected. I'm going to keep these." I fold the newspaper articles and put them in my bag.

Ruth Ann is delicately tracing the swirling letters of Evangeline's name with her finger. "I get glimpses sometimes," she says. "The people in here. They all had lives, you know? Families, babies, marriage . . . It's easy to forget when they're like this."

I take the death certificate and letter, slide them into the hidden pocket, and give the book to her. She puts it in the garbage bag and opens the passenger door.

"Thank you," I say. "I'm really sorry for any trouble Abby caused."

"Yeah," she says. It sounds like she's going to say something else, but she doesn't.

"I hope he goes back to drawing birds for your son."

"Me too," she says, then she closes the door and jogs into the building, hugging the book to her chest to protect it from the rain.

14

ALICE

April 6, 1936

Alice held the delicate cotton between her fingers and rubbed gently.

"Soft, ainnit?" the young boy behind the counter said. "Daddy just got that in. Some guy looked like a bum traded it for a box of tobacco. S'probably stolen, but it's so pretty, Daddy says he don't mind. Folks been admiring it all day."

She smiled but didn't say anything. From a distance, it just looked white with a hint of blue, but when you looked more closely, you could see the blue was coming from tiny paisley swirls covering it. They reminded her of the shells on the beach at home. From the moment she'd seen it, she'd wanted to buy it. Alice was always drawn to pretty things. "All eyes and no brains," her mother used to yell at her. Well, she was dead and gone now. Died two years after Alice left home and never met her granddaughter. Served her right. No invitations to the new house for her. She'd have been impressed by that. A big new house, shaped like an octagon. "The newest design," George had said. Mama was only ever impressed by one thing: money. George was spending money to build this house, which meant he loved her.

"It would make a pretty dress for your little one," the boy said, then he leaned over the counter and spoke to Grace. "Would you like your mommy to make you a pretty dress?"

Grace stared at him but didn't say anything. She blinked once, twice, and kept staring. Then her eyes moved from the boy to the display of ribbons on the counter. Her hand absentmindedly picked up the end of her braid and stuck it in her mouth, where she sucked on it, a disgusting habit, the ladies at church said: "Who knows when that hair's been washed."

Alice thought she could make curtains, the prettiest curtains. For the kitchen. George would see that she was making an effort. He couldn't say she wasn't.

A woman and her daughter came in, and Alice automatically dropped the cotton and faded back toward the darker part of the store. The woman looked down at Grace, who hadn't noticed them, wrinkled her nose in disgust, and then gave her directions to the shop boy. As if your daughter's nose never ran, Alice thought. Dirt just found Grace, that's how she thought of it. She could be minutes out of a bath and she'd have dirt on her somewhere. Dirt doesn't hurt children. Alice was dirty plenty enough when she was a kid, and it didn't harm her.

A whole six months she'd been living in this village, and how many of the upstanding citizens of Sumner's Mills even knew her name? Sumner's Mills wasn't where she'd thought she'd end up, it was only a stop on her slow migration west to a big city like Buffalo, or maybe even Chicago, a place where a young woman trying to feed and clothe her child and doing it without a man wouldn't get the looks and whispers that happened here.

But then she'd met George Sumner.

George told her the house he was building would be hers—she never had anything that was hers—and he asked her to marry him. But she knew that even becoming Mrs. Sumner, having twenty children, and living the rest of her life here wouldn't be enough. She and Grace would always be outsiders.

"Daddy got in some fine cotton, Mrs. Graham," the boy said while he was wrapping the paper around the woman's purchases.

No, that was hers.

"Said he got the last bolt," he continued. "And that there's all that's left."

Mrs. Graham instructed her daughter to look at the cotton and decide if that would work for her dress. The daughter sulked and said she wanted a premade dress.

"You're lucky to have anything new," her mother hissed at her. "There's better ways for that money to be spent."

The sullen girl looked at the cotton and shrugged. "Maybe."

Alice didn't hesitate. She stepped forward and put her hand on the cotton. The girl looked at her and said, "Cut me three yards."

"Sarah Jane, she doesn't *work* here," her mother said. She sniffed like she'd just smelled something expired and looked at Alice's worn dress. It had been pretty once, with pale pink and yellow roses. Now it was a dull gray that she couldn't get white again, no matter how hard she tried. But her hem was neat, and the small rips and tears had been repaired with such delicate stitches that they were invisible unless you knew where to look. Her boots were old, and there was a hole in the sole where the water came through, as it always did on the dirt roads around here. She didn't have any polish, but she was always careful to wipe them down each night to remove the worst of the mud.

"Sorry, it's not available," Alice said. "I need five yards, and there isn't enough."

"Have you paid for it?" the girl asked. Now that she couldn't have it, she had decided she wanted it.

"I was just about to," Alice said. She turned to the shop boy, who was clearly thrilled at how much more exciting his afternoon had become. "Please measure and cut five yards—no, six."

Her heart was beating fast. Six yards would be $1.62; $1.50 was what she had in her pocket for the week's groceries. Her mind was working fast: she still had enough cornmeal that she could make it stretch, and they could go without milk or vegetables for the week. She might be able to borrow a can of beans from her landlady. "Sorry," she continued, "it should be five."

The boy held his long scissors over the material. "You sure about that, miss?"

"Yes. Five. Thank you," she said, and smiled at him. Alice's smile had a way of lifting her entire face. When she wasn't smiling, she was pretty, but when she did smile, she was undeniable.

The boy blushed and nodded. "Well, if you're sure, then. I wouldn't want to cut it wrong."

She kept smiling at the boy. It was making him nervous, but that could work in her favor. Perhaps, if these other two left, he would tell her he'd accidentally cut six yards but she need only pay for five.

Mrs. Graham was staring at her, ignoring her daughter as she huffed about the other bolts of dull muslin. Alice's hand automatically went up to her cheek. In the past two days, the deep purplish blue had faded into a greenish yellow. It was dim in the store, and her hat created a shadow over her face, but she had a feeling the other woman saw the bruise.

———

"Stay here tonight," George had said when they had finished their picnic three days earlier. "Picnic" was his term for it. Eating bread and cold beans on the ground was hers. He had assured her there would be furniture after the wedding in May.

"You know how people already talk," Alice said.

George laid his big hand on hers. "No one can see us. No one even knows you're here. That's why I chose this place: no prying eyes." He smiled at her, but when George smiled, it was only his mouth that moved. At first she'd been moved by his seriousness. She was used to the flattery of men, trying to woo her into their beds with words or cheap trinkets, if they could afford them. George did none of that, and he had money. Family money that wasn't gained and lost easily, like that of so many these days. He didn't flash it around, but Alice knew that she and Grace would never be hungry with George.

"You and Grace can sleep together, and I'll sleep in another room," he continued. "There's nothing improper about that."

Alice blushed. "The house is cold," she said. "Grace is coming down with a chill, and we aren't properly dressed."

"There's plenty of blankets," George said. "A house is supposed to be filled with life, that's what makes her warm. I do all this for you, and you barely step foot in her."

"We're out here several times a week."

"You know what I mean," he said. "She needs *life*."

"I can't, George," she said, pulling her hand away and starting to wrap the bread so it looked like that was what she'd intended to do.

The darkness that came over his face was almost immediate. That was how she would have described it, if she'd ever had need to put words to it, if she ever had someone to tell. His face literally got darker as the blood rose under the skin, like he was controlling something, but only just. His pupils grew and almost canceled out the brown of his eyes.

"Sweetheart," she said, making sure to keep her voice light and airy, "you know I would love to stay." The closer they got to the wedding and to him finishing the house, the harder it was getting to bring him back from these moods.

"You don't appreciate what I'm making for you. You don't *appreciate*"— he practically spat the word—"one bit."

"I do." She put her hand on his arm. "You know I do."

He pushed her hand away so hard that she fell forward, catching herself with it. "You got no idea the work I put into this house. All for you. Everything for you. You say you want a room on the top—I build it for you."

"I know—"

"You want a porch, you want the sink by the window, I do it all for you—"

"And it's wonderful, it really is—"

"I'm overlooking your past, your bastard kid. You should be grateful."

"I am grateful." She tried to ignore every instinct in her body that told her to tense up and run. He would see that. The only way to diffuse George's anger was with sweetness, but this time it wasn't working. He had been fine when they arrived, but something since had set him off.

"Then prove it to me," he growled.

It was true. She always gave him a reason—too much sawdust, or the afternoon being so warm—but she never wanted to spend time inside the new house. She would let him take her around it to show her the trim he'd installed, or the view from one of the bedrooms, but she always went outside as soon as she could. She thought he hadn't noticed.

"May's coming soon, Alice."

"My love, I dream about how wonderful it will be to set up a home for you and Grace—"

"And *our* kids."

"Yes, of course, and lots more children."

How was she going to do it? The reality of their upcoming marriage and moving into the house had gone from being a distant niggling problem to being only a month away. Every night she would lie in bed, sick with fear and disgusted with herself for being in this situation. There was no other choice. There was absolutely no other choice. She couldn't go back home now, illegitimate child in tow. No, she was being foolish. There was nothing wrong with the house. She would add her own touches and make it a home, and this feeling she had would disappear.

"It's getting late. We should go," she said, standing up. "Grace," she called out. Grace was probably exploring in the woods, getting herself dirty, the way she liked to do; she often spent hours in her imagination, concocting wild adventures for her and her doll, Tabitha.

"Grace!" Alice called again. She looked down at George, who remained sitting on the blanket. He was absolutely still, watching the woods.

"What is it?" she asked him.

"Huh? Oh, nothing. Thought I heard her." Then he turned and looked up at her. "Maybe you're just going to need a reason to stay."

Alice stared at him. As worried as she was, she had always believed she had the situation in control. She just had to keep him happy enough. She felt like a stone had dropped into her stomach.

"Grace! We need to go, now!" The forced lightness was gone, but she didn't care if he could hear the worry in her voice. It was a three-mile walk back to Sumner's Mills. George would drive them out, but he'd never drive them back. It would be dark by the time they got to the house where they boarded. "Where is she?" Alice muttered.

First she circled the house, looking in the woods. Grace never went more than a few feet inside the trees. Alice circled the perimeter of the clearing but didn't see her daughter, which meant she must have gone into the house. Grace hated the house more than Alice did, but she also kept her distance from George, and it was getting cold out, so she must have gone inside. She had started crying at night whenever they talked about how they would move in after the wedding. It was a new kind of crying. She would hug Tabitha to her and make a low kind of half hum, half moan while rocking back and forth. It wasn't like any sound Alice had heard a child make before.

It frightened her.

The more frantic Alice got, the stiller George became. He was obviously mad at her. Fine. She would find Grace herself. It was easier than having to deal with his moods.

The kitchen was dark, and she stood in the doorway a moment, letting her eyes adjust. It smelled like freshly cut wood, and she could see the cupboards coming together. George had said he'd spent the day working on them. He really was building a home for her. She shook her head. Whoever would have thought that she, Alice Carey, "comin' from nothing and goin' to nothing," as Mama used to say, would have a house being *built* for her. She had to find ways to show George that she did appreciate the work he was doing. Maybe he was right to be hurt.

"Grace?" she called out. Her voice echoed in the empty room. If this was a new game, it was one that would have to stop immediately. "Grace, we will be walking in the dark if we don't leave right this instant, and I will NOT hold your hand, no matter how scared you are—do you hear me?"

Still no answer.

The downstairs was divided into two large rooms. Alice had never been in a house with such huge rooms. Opposite the kitchen was what George called the "drawing room." She had tried to imagine elegant couches and high-backed chairs, and maybe, if he allowed it, a large radio, but no matter how she tried, she couldn't picture it. She went upstairs. In the master bedroom, he had moved in a high iron-framed bed with legs that looked like the paws of a large cat, claws exposed. Across from the bed was the door that would lead to the room at the top. She peered up into it. It wasn't completed yet, just the skeleton of the walls were up, and she could see the first star showing itself in the evening light.

The three other bedrooms—each large enough to hold two children, George had told her—were empty. The knot in her stomach tightened. Grace must have gone into the woods and wandered farther than she'd thought. They were so dense, if she got turned around, she could be in there for hours. She was only six years old! What kind of a mother lets her daughter wander in the woods by herself? *A mother like you, Alice,* the voice in her head said. Her mother's voice. *A no-good whore-bag of a mother.*

Alice ran downstairs and out the door. George was still sitting on the picnic blanket, but now he was watching the house, as if waiting for something.

"She's not in there," she said. She couldn't breathe right. "She must be in the woods. Do you have the lantern?"

"I'm not wasting the oil," he said.

"Then help me!" she said. She was trying not to let her voice rise. He'd told her before how her "screeching" grated on him.

She turned and marched back into the house. She would find the lantern herself. She didn't have time to waste on playing his games. Her daughter was alone in the woods. It was getting dark, and after that the temperature would plunge quickly. Nothing was as important to George as his damned house, not even a child.

She was moving around the kitchen when she saw the basement door. He had added it only last week. It was a strange door for a house because it was metal. It was a little larger than a regular door and very heavy. He'd told her he got it from the factory he owned—Sumner's Metals and Lubricants. She had wondered if maybe they could paint it so it didn't stand out so much, but George seemed offended at the suggestion, and she hadn't mentioned it since. Now she stood in front of it, staring. She touched it. It was cold, not just the cool that you'd expect from metal, but cold, as if it had ice inside. Had it been open earlier today when they were looking at the cupboards? She couldn't remember. She turned the handle and tried to pull, but the door wouldn't budge.

"Grace," she called, banging on the door. "Sweetheart, are you down there?"

She thought she could hear something, but it sounded so far away. She pulled the door again, using all of her body weight.

"There's a sort of vacuum effect," George said. He was leaning in the kitchen doorway, and his huge frame blocked what little was left of the light. "Makes it real hard to get open."

"Help me!" she cried, but he just looked at her. She had never seen him like this. His anger she was familiar with, but this was different. This was like a part of him had turned off.

"George! Please, I think she's down there." She banged on the door so Grace could hear. "I'm coming, sweetheart. Mommy's coming to get you!" She tried again, pulling so hard that her hands slipped off and she fell backward.

George laughed.

She stood up. There was a white heat inside her now. She would rip this door off its hinges if she had to. She pulled again. The door resisted at first, then swung open. Alice fell back again but was immediately up and starting down the stairs. The basement was pitch black, but she could hear Grace moaning below.

"Grace? Grace? Come to the stairs, sweetheart. I'm going to get you out of there."

The moan intensified.

Alice moved down the stairs slowly, one arm swinging into the darkness ahead of her, the other touching the stairs behind her to keep her balance. There was no railing, and the stairs were steep and uneven. Why would he build them this way? It was like he wanted to make them dangerous. "I'm coming, sweetheart, I'm coming," she kept saying, over and over, until her feet touched the dirt floor. Grace moaned again, but Alice couldn't see her. "Where are you?"

"Mama," Grace said. Her voice wasn't much more than a whisper. "Help me."

Alice could barely see anything. The light coming from the kitchen wasn't strong enough to reach more than halfway down the stairs. She was disoriented, and her skin registered the movement of air, like there was a window cracked open. But that was impossible.

"Mama," Grace said again. Her voice was in the darkness, all around, impossible to locate. How could she be so close and not here at all?

"Sweetheart, come to the stairs. I can't see where you are. You have to come over to me."

Another moan, this time sounding like it came from the right. Alice got down on her hands and knees, sweeping one arm out in front of her, groping blindly into the darkness, and then suddenly Grace's tiny hand found hers. Alice pulled Grace to her and stood up as the little girl wrapped her thin arms and legs around her. Slowly, bent over so she wouldn't fall backward, she climbed up the stairs while Grace buried her face in her mother's neck and whimpered.

"Ah, there she is," George said. Alice looked at him, a huge lump of a man. That was what he was. He had enjoyed watching her panic. He had known all along. "You should be careful where you're wandering," he said to Grace. "That door's got a mind of its own."

"You animal! She could have been hurt down there!"

George towered over her, pulled his hand back, and punched her in the face. She staggered to the side. Her head hit the wall, and her vision blurred. Grace screamed and dropped to the floor.

"I'll show you hurt, you ungrateful bitch." He raised his arm to hit her again, but before she knew what was happening, Grace was tearing at his clothes, trying to hang off his arm. He turned to her and roared, "This is all your fault, you little shit."

In the second when she saw his fist about to come down on Grace, she screamed, "Grace, run." Grace shot across the room toward the exit. Distracted by the girl's escape, he wasn't able to catch Alice, who stumbled after her daughter. She caught up with Grace, grabbed her hand, and they ran as fast as they could into the woods toward the road.

There was still light in the sky, but the sun was down. It didn't matter. She made them keep running. When Grace stumbled over a branch, Alice scooped her up and continued to stagger forward along the rutted access road. At any moment, she expected to hear the roar of George's car behind them, and she tried to stay on the side of the road so she could dive into the trees, but the woods remained silent.

When they reached the main road, she put Grace down and then stood, frantically pulling air into her chest. Her arms, her legs, her back, every part of her was screaming for oxygen, and her face was stinging from the impact of the punch, but they were out. She wouldn't cry. She would not let Grace see her cry. She bent down and said, "Can you walk now, sweetheart?" Grace nodded, and they started walking toward the village.

When they were well past the patch of woods and it was clear George wasn't coming after them, she asked her daughter what had happened.

It was Tabitha, her doll, Grace said. She'd put her down, just for a minute, so she could tie her shoes, and then she'd been looking at a bird outside the window, and when she looked down, her doll was gone. "George took her," she said.

"Did you see him take Tabitha?"

"No, but I know he did."

"Grace, it's a sin to accuse someone falsely."

"He took her."

She had looked all around and couldn't find her anywhere, then she'd passed the basement and seen the doll on the stairs, three down from the top.

"Maybe you dropped her there." But even as she said it, Alice knew that wasn't what had happened. Her daughter never would have voluntarily gone near the basement.

"No, he *put* her there."

"But that doesn't make any sense, sweetheart."

George had been in and out of the house when they were setting up the picnic, but surely he wouldn't do something like that, no matter how angry he was with her. Alice tried to think of what she had done to set him off.

"He doesn't like me, Mommy."

She couldn't answer because she knew it was true. She had known it all along but had hoped that George would come to like her daughter and treat her the way he treated his younger sister, Marion. With her, he was protective—strict, even—but always kind.

Marion was thirteen and had been the one who introduced Alice to George. Unlike the other girls in the town, she thought Alice's independence was exotic and exciting. She and her brother had lost their parents years ago, and she quickly made Alice her older sister and confidante. In the times when Alice thought about calling off the wedding, it was the thought of how devastated Marion would be that made her stop.

"Did you call out for me?"

"I called as loud as I could." Grace started to cry again. "I called and called."

Alice pulled her daughter into her arms and held her tight.

A mile outside of town, a pickup truck passed them, then pulled to the side of the road and they got in the back. The moment Grace sat down, she was asleep. Alice carried her up to their room in the boardinghouse, took her shoes and socks off, and slid her into bed with her clothes still on. Grace was clutching Tabitha the whole time, but Alice detached the doll and took her over to the basin to rinse off the worst of the dirt. If she laid the doll close to the vent, it would be dry by morning.

Her mind was churning as she held the doll under the water, when she looked down into the basin. Blood was washing off of it. She was sure the color of the water was more red than brown. She went over to Grace and pulled off the blankets. Gently she examined each limb and her head, but she couldn't find any cuts; then she opened Grace's curled fingers. Three of her nails were shredded, and the end of each finger was almost black with dirt. She had been clawing at the door. That was when Alice finally let herself cry.

The next day, as the bruise bloomed across her face, they stayed inside. Alice washed every speck of dirt off Grace and played with her all afternoon until some feeling of normalcy returned. She would have to go back into the world at some point, but not until she knew what she was going to do.

On Sunday, they stayed away from church, but at noon there was a knock on the door. She didn't want to answer it, but then a young girl's voice whispered, "Alice? It's Marion. George told me the two of you had a fight. He's such a wreck about it."

Alice opened the door a crack to make sure Marion was alone. As soon as she saw Alice's face, she began to cry. "Oh no, poor you," she said, coming in and gently touching Alice's bruised cheek with her small hand. "What happened?"

Instinctively, Alice backed away, her hand going up to her face. "I fell. It's nothing. I'm fine." Her big brother was all the family Marion had. She'd be devastated to know what he'd done.

"George keeps saying that he's lost you. He hasn't eaten anything in two days. He doesn't know I'm here, but I had to see you."

"I'm all right," Alice said. "It was a bad fight. We both said things we shouldn't have."

"I know he has a temper, but it's because he's been on his own since our parents died. He hasn't had any guidance, and that's so much worse for a man. Alice, please forgive him. He needs you desperately, and he loves you so much."

Alice tried to tell her about the feeling the house gave her, but she didn't tell her about Grace getting shut in the basement. There must have been an explanation for that. The more she tried to explain the feeling, the more ridiculous it sounded. "People make mistakes," Marion said, and Alice knew she was talking about her now. "I know you've had it rough, but it will all change once you get married."

She was right. Marriage, a house, money: those were real. A bad feeling wasn't. How could she throw it all away because of one bad afternoon? George was probably just exhausted because he was working so hard to get the house completed on time. Her house.

In the end, Alice agreed to see George. Marion cried again and hugged her and promised to bring some ointment for her cheek. When she left, Alice closed the door quietly and leaned her head against it, and then she heard Grace behind her.

She turned around and smiled at her daughter, but then her smile faded. Grace was just staring at her, her eyes wide and frightened and accusing.

"What is it, sweetheart?"

"He doesn't like me," she said. "He said it's 'cause of me you don't like the house."

Alice crouched down so she was eye to eye with her daughter. "I know he got mad, but men do that sometimes. George is a good man. Remember? He gave you your doll."

Grace shook her head. "Marion made her."

Alice sighed. "It will be all right, I promise." Her daughter was only six, she thought. She didn't understand the situation, and she'd had a bad scare, but this was the way it had to be, and she would make it work.

———

And now Alice was standing in the shop buying material for pretty curtains. She would sew them tonight and put them up at the house the next time they went out and surprise him. And she would pick some wildflowers when they bloomed and put them on the windowsill. She would add the little touches that would make the house a home. Their home.

Mrs. Graham and her daughter had left the store by the time the shop boy was done cutting and wrapping the cotton. Alice was counting out the money when he held out the blue ribbon to Grace. "Would you like it for your dolly?" he asked her.

"Grace, no," Alice said.

"No charge," he said. "Go on, take it." He winked. Grace reached up and pulled the ribbon off the rack and then tied it around Tabitha's waist. And then she smiled her lopsided smile that Alice hardly ever saw.

George's mud-spattered Buick was sitting outside their boardinghouse. He was behind the wheel, hair combed and slicked, a fresh-pressed shirt on. He smiled tentatively when he saw them and waved, and they walked over.

"It's a beautiful afternoon, isn't it," he said.

"It is," she said. "I thought you'd be working on the house."

"I finished your special room," he said. "Put the glass in this morning. Windows all around, like you wanted. I was wondering if you'd like to come see it."

"That would be fine," Alice said. She opened the passenger door, but Grace didn't move to get into the car. She looked up at Alice, her eyes huge. Alice touched her small, trusting face. "Come on, sweetheart," she said quietly. George was watching them. After a moment, Grace got in. Alice sat down in the front, hugging the package of material to her.

George started the car and then turned to her, put his hand on her knee, and squeezed. "I'm never going to lose you again. You're coming home now. You're coming home."

15

CLARE

July 25, 1998
9 P.M.

After dinner and a second dose of antibiotic ointment, Clare went back to the Lindsays' house. Abby's parents and grandparents were on the porch with the remnants of dessert spread out around them. Mitchell was nowhere to be seen and Paul was at his game, so Abby and Clare had their choice of places to hang out unbothered. By nine o'clock, they were sprawled on the basement floor, playing Monopoly. They had made hot chocolate because the basement was permanently cold and damp, and they each put in five marshmallows, so the tops of the mugs were sticky with the melted sugar. The road rash on Clare's hands and knees had softened to a dull throb that she could almost forget if she didn't make any sudden movements.

"Does Paul like Monica?" Clare asked, carefully licking the marshmallow off her fingers.

"I guess so," Abby said.

"Do you think something's going to happen between them?"

"I don't know. Maybe." Abby was silent a moment. "It would be kind of awkward."

"She'd start hanging out with him and his friends."

"Lori would too."

They were both quiet. Here in the basement, it was easy to forget the baseball diamond and whatever might be happening there. It was easy to forget the house and that basement. And it was easy to forget this was the last summer of being a kid, because in a little over a month they would start high school, then everything would be different. In some ways, Clare wanted it to happen now, just to get it over with, but in other ways she wanted to press pause and stay in this familiar world forever.

She was about to roll onto her back and close her eyes when Abby suddenly sat up, took a deep breath, and said, "I'm sorry about the picture."

Clare didn't know what to say. *It's all right?* Except it wasn't—it never could be. But she was also relieved that Abby had been the one to say it.

"When I took it, I never meant . . . It just happened, but I didn't mean for it to. I mean, I thought you might have shown them yourself . . ."

"But why did you take it?" That was what she hadn't been able to figure out—which bothered her more, that Abby had taken the picture or that she had shown Monica and Lori?

"I just wanted to look at it for a little bit."

"But why?"

"I just like that picture."

"She's not your mom. You never even met her."

"I know."

"So, it's weird. You're being weird about her." Talking about it was making Clare angry again.

Abby picked at the carpet pile. "It's just sometimes I wish . . . Like you had your mom and your dad and it was just you. You've told me about how you used to go camping and go on hikes and your mom knew all this stuff about plants and stars and like my parents are just— It's always about my brothers. Mitchell's perfect at everything and everybody idolizes him, and Paul's just an asshole for no reason, so he and my dad are always yelling at each other. Sometimes I just think, like if I went away or something, they'd forget about me. My mom would probably be happy. Like she has this idea of what a daughter is supposed to be and I'm just not right."

"That's not true."

"Yeah, it is. If I knew how I was supposed to be, I could change or whatever. Your mom loved you so much, even before you were born—you can see it in that picture. And so sometimes I pretend that I'm you, or, like, not *you* but that she was my mom too."

Clare picked up the little silver dog that was her Monopoly piece and rolled it between her fingers.

"Please don't be mad at me," Abby said.

"It's okay," Clare said, and she meant it. The hollow feeling was back in her stomach, but it made the anger go away. The hollow place had formed about a year after her mother had died. It was what the pain had turned into: absence, a part of her eaten away the way the cancer had eaten away at her mother. That hole deep in her gut threatened to pull the rest of her into it. It wasn't as strong as it used to be, more like a persistent ache now, but sometimes, when she was tired, she felt like it might be easier to just let go and slide into it.

"Monica said you look like her."

"No, she didn't."

"She did. When you went to the bathroom, she said it. Your mom was so pretty."

Clare felt tears welling in her eyes. Maybe Abby could tell, because she jumped up and said, "You want to watch a movie or something? This game gets boring after a while."

"Are you mad at me for what happened at the house?"

Abby shook her head.

"Okay. Good."

"Are you mad at me?" Abby asked.

Clare shook her head.

"So we're even," Abby said, and she grinned.

While Abby hunted through VHS tapes, Clare sat on the couch. She looked like her mom. It had been something she'd wanted so badly, she'd hardly dared even think it, and Monica had confirmed it. It made her mother feel both further away and closer at the same time. Inside her stomach, the hollowness gnawed.

As the opening credits for the James Bond movie rolled, Abby curled up next to her on the couch, her legs tucked under her and her head on Clare's shoulder. There was nothing unusual about them watching a movie—they had done it hundreds of times—but Clare realized she couldn't remember the last time they had let their bodies be close like this. Around Monica and Lori, they were naturally more guarded, but that protective separation had started creeping into their alone time too. Clare sighed. It was nice to feel the warmth and weight of another person.

Abby took Clare's hand, careful of the bandages on her palm, and traced a triangle on the inside of her wrist. Their signal.

At some point, years ago, one of them had found a book about hoboes during the Depression. Clare couldn't remember how old they were, or what school project they were supposed to be working on, only that it was raining outside and the two of them had curled up on one of the orange beanbags in the corner of the library and read this book. Maybe it was the idea of people who could go anywhere, who were never stuck in one stifling tiny town like they were, but instead could follow their restlessness, moving through the world on its edges, like ghosts.

"Look," Abby had said. She was pointing to what looked like a triangle, but instead of meeting at the points, the lines crossed over one another. "It means a disordered state of mind." She traced it on the page, and then she took Clare's hand and traced it in her palm. Slash, slash, slash.

Then Clare took Abby's hand and traced a triangle with the lines meeting in points. "All is well."

From those two signs, a form of secret communication grew between them: their little act of rebellion. Sometimes Clare would open her locker to find a note with the broken triangle tucked into it and she would know she needed to find Abby and help her put the edges back together. Or they would be in the backseat of the Lindsays' car and Clare would take Abby's hand and trace a triangle on her palm. It was a way of telling her they were safe, they were together. "I am here." "I see you." "All is well." Those two simple symbols could say many things. On days when the hollowness took over, she wouldn't need to say anything, but she would feel Abby trace that triangle on her leg as they sat at lunch in the cafeteria, Monica and Lori across the table having no idea. Small acts of rebellion making them feel strong.

Abby had drawn a triangle, points meeting. When she was done, Clare took her hand and turned it over. She hesitated a moment, then she drew her triangle. *I am here too.* Inside her, the hollow feeling grew a little smaller.

—————

They were halfway through the movie when Abby pressed pause and announced she was hungry and went upstairs to make a snack. Clare lay on the saggy couch. If Abby didn't come back soon, she'd be asleep. She heard the basement door open and sat up just in time to see Mitchell coming downstairs, bringing the smell of Abby's microwave popcorn with him. He was home from his job at Dairy Queen and must have just showered because his hair was damp.

"Hey there," he said. "What's up?"

"Not much. We're watching a movie."

"I see that."

She felt dumb. Of course he could see that. Sean Connery was frozen on the TV, jumping from a speedboat.

"How are your injuries?" he asked, coming over to the couch and sitting near her. Clare smelled his shampoo and something that might have been aftershave. His T-shirt was the kind of soft cotton that fell over his body, showing the shape of muscles underneath.

She held out her hands, palms up, and he touched the bandages. "Make sure you keep them clean," he said softly.

"Okay," she said. Her voice caught in her throat and it came out as more of a squeak.

"But you look like a badass."

"Are you going out?" she asked, then immediately worried that he'd think she was nosy.

He shrugged. "There's a party I might check out. I don't know. Probably going to be lame, you know?"

Before she could think of a reply, he jumped off the couch and went into the back part of the basement. "Hey, can I grab you for a moment?" he called to her. "I gotta get my old hockey bag, and it's buried."

Standing up, walking toward him, felt so easy. The drowsiness was gone. She was an equal and could help him as easily as he could help her. She wasn't his little sister's friend.

"Thanks. It'll save me pulling all this shit out. It's under a pile back here, so if I hold stuff up, maybe you can get in and pull it out. Can you use your hands, or do they hurt too much?"

"They're fine," Clare said, though the thought of anything touching her raw palms made her wince.

"My brother's a pig. I'm only using it as long as there's nothing growing in it." He was looking around, pushing boxes aside. "Jesus, this is a dump."

She could only partly see him by the light of the frozen movie and the hanging lightbulb at the other end of the room.

"Aha. Victory!" he cried out.

She came over beside him. He was next to a pile of mattresses leaning against the wall, with stacks of blankets and sleeping bags on top. He held them away from the wall. "I can sort of see it. If you can grab it, that would be aces."

She squeezed in past him, feeling blindly for the hockey bag, and using just the ends of her fingers grabbed what felt like a handle. "I've got it."

But just then the movie unpaused itself and Sean Connery finished his leap into the moving speedboat with an orchestral crashing of drums. It surprised them both, and Mitchell dropped the mattress he was holding. The pile of blankets and the mattresses came down on Clare.

"Oh, shit—I'm so sorry," he called. "Are you okay in there?"

"Yeah, I just don't know if I can get out. My leg's pinned."

He was laughing. "Where are you? I can't see you."

"In here."

Then she felt his hand. It reached in through the pile and grabbed her arm.

"Is that you?" he said.

"Can you pull me out?"

His hand kept moving, though. She could hear him laughing, but he stopped when his hand quickly brushed her breast. She felt a jolt of heat rush up from between her legs. His hand had gone right across her nipple; had he known? Maybe he had just thought it was her arm.

He moved enough of the stuff off her, and she was able to crawl out, then he reached in and yanked the bag out, pulling more of the stuff down from the pile.

"Hey, thanks," he said. "Sorry about that. I didn't mean to—"

Mean to what? To drop all the stuff on her or to touch her? She could feel how hot her face was.

"It's okay," she said. "At least you found it."

"Yeah. Thanks."

He took the bag and unzipped it. A moldy stench immediately rose out of it. "Gross," he said, and closed it, then tossed it on the pile. "Paul's such a fucking slob— Oh, sorry."

"I don't care."

Please, please don't go back to thinking of me as a little kid, she thought. If he saw her as an equal, he wouldn't apologize for swearing.

The movie blared into the back of the basement. They both stood in the dark. It was hot and stuffy. He was breathing heavily; she was too. She still felt where his hand had brushed her. How long did they face each other in the dark? He was almost a foot taller than she was. If she were someone else, someone more sophisticated, she might be able to reach out and put her hand on his chest. She wanted to feel his heart to see if it was pounding as much as hers. And she desperately wanted to say something that proved she wasn't a kid—anything that wouldn't sound stupid.

He reached out and tousled her hair and said, "I don't know if it's you or me, but one of us sure is accident-prone." Then he walked back toward the TV. She followed and went to the couch as Abby came downstairs, carrying a bowl of popcorn.

"Awesome. How'd you know I was hungry?" Mitchell said and grabbed a large handful of the popcorn, causing more of it to fall on the couch.

"Hey, you hog, that's ours," Abby said. "Mom made it for us."

"Haven't you learned yet that you have to share with your older brother? It's part of the deal."

"The deal? I don't know about any deal."

"Sure, you do," he said. "The deal is you give me whatever I want." He grabbed another handful and bounded up the stairs.

"Give that back!" Abby yelled after him, but she was smiling. She sat down and put the bowl between them. "We need to rewind it. I just missed that part."

She was so happy, she didn't notice that Clare's face was sweaty and she was smiling too.

———

The movie was just finishing when they heard Paul come home. Then they heard Monica's and Lori's voices. Clare and Abby looked at each other.

"Is Abby here?" Monica asked.

"How would I know?" Paul growled, or at least that was a fair assumption of what he'd said.

"She and Clare are in the basement with a movie," Mrs. Lindsay called out. "You girls go on down."

Mrs. Lindsay loved it when her children's friends came over. And even though Mr. Lindsay liked to complain that it already felt like they were feeding a small nation with the appetites of their two teenage sons, he'd always add, "Well, I guess it doesn't make much difference to add a few more."

"I made some popcorn, girls," Mrs. Lindsay said. "I can make some more. Did you want to stay over?"

"Jeez, Ma—chill out, we're not staying," Paul said. Monica giggled. It hurt even from down in the basement to hear that.

Mrs. Lindsay said, "Well, I just meant it's late." Her voice sounded different.

Then Mr. Lindsay's voice: "Don't speak to your mother in that tone."

Paul said something else, quiet.

"I don't care, Paul. It's not acceptable, and you know that."

"Sorry, Ma."

"Paul!"

"I'm sorry, okay? Why's everything have to be such a big deal?"

Then Monica and Lori came downstairs. They'd obviously been hovering at the basement door, trying to listen to as much of the argument as possible.

"Hey," Abby said.

"Hey," Monica said. They slouched onto the other chairs.

"What's up?" Lori asked.

"Nothing. We were watching a movie," Abby said.

"We heard."

"What happened to you?" Lori asked, pointing at Clare's bandaged knees and hands.

"Bike accident."

The door at the top of the basement stairs slammed, and Paul came down looking pissed off. "Sorry. My fucking parents can't ever give it a rest."

"Mine are like that," Monica said.

"So, are we going or what?"

"I haven't had a chance to ask them." She turned to Clare and Abby. "There's a party and we're going. We were wondering if you wanted to come too."

Clare felt her stomach jump. Was it the same party Mitchell was going to?

Paul turned to Abby. "I just want you to know, if you're coming, it's because these two want you to come. I'm not babysitting."

"Of course we want you to come," Monica said. And as if anticipating the next question, "I've told my mom I'm sleeping over at Lori's."

Abby looked at Clare.

"Call your dad and tell him the same thing," Monica said to Clare. She sounded impatient.

"Come on," Lori said. "It'll be fun."

"Sure," Clare said. "How do we get there?"

"Mike's got his dad's car," Paul said. "Unless you're too injured."

"I'm fine," Clare said. "We'll come." Abby's eyes widened, but she wisely didn't say anything.

"If you're coming, we're leaving now. Mike's waiting outside."

They went upstairs, and Clare called her father from the kitchen phone. The lie came out easily, and her father didn't question her, just told her to have fun. Abby still hadn't said anything. Paul went into the living room and told his parents something, but Mrs. Lindsay followed him into the kitchen. "How long has Michael had his license?"

"Jeez! I don't know. Long enough."

"How old is he?" Mrs. Lindsay asked.

"He's sixteen. He might even be seventeen. He failed a couple of grades," Paul said, and Monica giggled. "Mom, it's like three miles away. It's fine. He's legal, don't worry."

Mrs. Lindsay turned to the girls. "You girls can have a sleepover here. We've got lots of space."

"That's okay, Mrs. Lindsay," Monica said. "Lori's mom already rented the movie."

"We have movies," Mrs. Lindsay said, turning to her husband, who'd come to the doorway. "And my parents are here."

"But Mom, they're asleep," Abby said.

"Caroline, it's fine," Mr. Lindsay said. "Abigail, be home by breakfast."

"Paul and Mike are dropping us off so Mrs. Farley doesn't have to come over," Monica continued.

"Okay, well, have fun," Mrs. Lindsay said. "And Paul?"

"I know, be home by midnight."

They waved to her while they piled into the car. Mike was scowling behind the wheel. "Took ya long enough," he grumbled.

"Your mom's cute," Monica said.

"Thanks," Abby said, and Monica's smile tightened. She'd been talking to Paul.

The four girls squished into the backseat, and Paul sat up front with Mike. The car smelled like cigarettes and wet dog. There were old papers and coffee cups on the floor. Mike sped through the quiet village and onto the interstate.

Abby was hunched on Clare's lap and squeezed her leg when they turned onto the entrance ramp. "Ow, watch it," Clare said quietly.

"Sorry."

The excitement of possibly seeing Mitchell again had turned into a sick feeling. Wherever they were going, it was far. The exits were ten miles apart. How was she going to get home? What if Mike started drinking? What if he got in an accident? How could she do that to her dad? What if the police pulled them over? What if Mike drove away and left her behind?

"Where are we going?" Abby asked.

"There's a bush party. It's not far," Lori said. Was she scared too? Did she actually want to go? It was so hard to tell with her what was real and what was an act; the act was so convincing, so complete, that it became real. Why couldn't she be like that? Clare thought. She wanted to be easygoing and able to adapt to any situation. Monica adapts the situation to herself; people and events form around her, as if they need to please her. But Lori is a chameleon. She blends into any crowd. If she just pretends everything is fine, then maybe everything will be. Clare breathed out.

"Am I too heavy?" Abby asked.

"Yeah, you should lay off the popcorn, there, porker," Paul said from the front seat.

Mike took the first exit and they pulled into another small town. Ryan, the third member of Paul's gang, was waiting outside a gas station. He had a large bag with him. They pulled up to him, and he threw the bag in the trunk.

"Careful, man," Paul said.

"Hey, ladieez," Ryan said as he squished his way into the backseat and stretched his arm out behind them. "I don't know why you're sitting up there, Lindsay. It's way more fun back here." Lori elbowed him and he pulled her hair.

Instead of getting on the highway, Mike went through the town and stayed on smaller roads. After a few more miles, he turned onto a dirt road.

"You recognize where we are?" Paul said. He grinned back at them.

"Duh. We're near my house," Lori said. "Why'd you go this way?"

"The guy at that gas station doesn't card," Ryan said.

"See? You didn't lie to your parents," Paul said. "You can all go to Lori's house after."

Mike pulled over on the side of the road, where there were a few other cars. There was no sign of a party. He heaved the bag out of the trunk, which made the bottles inside clink together, then walked off the road into the woods. The others followed. Paul put his arm around Monica's shoulders and used his other hand to fend off Ryan, who was jabbing at him.

It was a relief to be in familiar territory. They'd biked along this road. If she had to, Clare knew she could find her way home. But as much as it was a relief, there was a new nervousness as she followed the guys into the woods. Through the trees, she saw a fire and heard voices. As they got closer, she began to see faces, but she didn't see Mitchell's. People were standing and sitting around the fire. Voices came out of the darkness. There were more people here than she'd thought.

"You want a beer?" Paul was holding a bottle out to Monica.

"Fuck off, Lindsay," Ryan said. "We don't got enough of those for you to be sharing."

"Chill, Richardson. She can have one of mine."

Ryan turned to the other girls. "If you girls want beer, you gotta pay. Those weren't easy to get."

"I don't have any money," Clare said.

"There's other ways to work off your debt." Ryan was looking directly at her.

Paul burst out laughing. "Holy shit, look at her face. As if."

She felt her face going red, but hopefully they couldn't see her in the dark. "I don't want any."

"Yeah, me neither," Abby said.

"Well you weren't getting one anyway," her brother replied.

Monica poked Paul. "I thought you said you weren't babysitting." He wrapped his arm around her neck and fake-wrestled her away from them.

"Can we lose the children now?" Clare heard him ask, and Monica laughed. Ryan and Mike followed them. Lori gave them a look, then shrugged and followed the others into the crowd of shadowed figures.

There was a breeze sending sparks up from the fire to explode in the dark. Abby and Clare moved toward it. The grass was wet, and whenever the wind changed direction, the smoke would move over them, but once they were sitting by the campfire, it felt good. They were here; this was what they'd been wondering about. These were the people who would matter next year. Abby kept shifting and looking around. Clare knew she was wondering if there was something else they were supposed to be doing. Were they giving off some signal that they didn't belong?

Across the fire, there was a couple making out. They'd stop, swig their beer, then keep kissing each other. People drifted in around the fire and then back out into the darkness. Everyone had a drink. Everyone seemed to fit.

A girl sat down next to them. She had really short hair and big eyes. "Hey," the girl said. "Okay if I sit here?"

"Sure," Clare said.

"I don't want to be over there next to the make-out twins."

Abby laughed.

"What happened to you?" the girl asked Clare.

Clare wished she'd changed into pants. The bandages on her knees made her look like a kid. "Bike accident. I'm a klutz," she said, trying to sound light.

The girl laughed. "Yeah, me too. Are you guys new to the school?"

"We're—" Abby started, but Clare elbowed her before she could say "freshmen."

"Yeah," Clare said. "We're sophomores. We're transferring." Even though it was dark, she could tell that Abby had opened her mouth to correct her, then closed it again.

"Cool. Maybe we'll have classes together. I transferred last year," the girl said. "I started there last January so, you know, it's kind of annoying to have to start then, but it's okay."

It was this easy? To say you were something, someone, different and to be taken for that?

"You two want to smoke?" the girl asked. "I've got a joint. You ever smoke before?"

"No," Abby said.

"This is pretty gentle. Here." The girl lit the joint and inhaled deeply, then passed it to Abby. Abby looked at Clare, unsure. The girl smiled, and the smoke looked like moving clouds coming out of her mouth. "It's okay. You might cough a bit, but it won't fuck you up."

Abby took the joint and held it to her mouth. The tip glowed red when she inhaled. She immediately started coughing, and the smoke came out of her mouth. The girl laughed, then passed it to Clare.

"I'm okay," Clare said.

"Come on," Abby said, still coughing. "Try it."

The girl looked at Clare, smiled, and took the joint again. "No, that's cool. More for us, right?"

She and Abby passed it back and forth between them, Abby coughing each time. "You'll get used to it," the girl said. Abby smiled at Clare, then puffed the smoke out. She didn't look as elegant as the girl, but at least she didn't cough.

"That's it. I'm Lesley, by the way."

"I'm Abby, this is Clare."

"Hey there, Abby and Clare."

Clare didn't understand. It was so obvious that Abby didn't know what she was doing, why was she the one fitting in? "I'm going for a walk," Clare said, and got up. She needed to know if Mitchell was here, and besides, it was clear Abby was more interested in getting high with some girl she didn't know than being with her.

"A walk?" Abby said, still coughing a bit. "Why?"

"Because I want to."

"Don't be like that."

"Like what?" Clare asked. Now Lesley was going to think there was something wrong with her. She stood up, brushing the wet grass off her legs.

"Let her go if she wants to go," Lesley said, then looked up at Clare. "If you're going to piss, I'd recommend that direction. Fewer people." She pointed off to the right.

A guy came over and stood by them. "Hey," he said, taking the joint, "I told you to wait for me."

"Chris, this is Abby. I'm teaching her how to smoke."

"S'up Abby?" Chris said. Abby giggled. Clare was standing right by them, but he didn't seem to notice her. He passed the joint back to Abby, and she inhaled, then immediately exhaled.

"You gotta hold it in longer than that," Chris said. "Or it won't do anything. Here, lean close to me." He took a long inhale, then leaned in to Abby's face, almost like he was going to kiss her. "Open your mouth," Lesley said. Chris blew smoke into Abby's open mouth.

Clare walked away. Abby didn't even turn her head. She was so engrossed with her new friends.

———

Clare didn't think she'd get lost. She spent a few minutes walking in the woods, then grew tired and turned around. She tried to go straight toward the sound of the fire, but she kept hitting fallen trees and having to go around them, which confused her sense of direction. Then she saw someone ahead. She stepped a little closer. It was Paul. There was a girl kneeling in front of him with her head almost touching his crotch. His hand was on the back of her head, cradling it. Clare stumbled backward and snapped a branch, and the girl's head whipped around. It was Monica.

Paul stepped away from Monica, fumbling with his pants. "Fuck off, Clare. We're busy."

"Clare? What the fuck are you doing?" Monica hissed.

Clare took another step away from them, but her mind was moving slowly.

"Stop staring. What are you, some kind of pervert?"

"No—" Clare said, but it didn't really come out.

She turned and ran, then tripped on the undergrowth. She fell and a stick dug into her palm, just missing the bandaged road rash. She wanted to cry out but didn't want Paul and Monica to hear her. The look on Paul's face. He hated her. He hated her and he would never forgive her for this. It didn't matter that it was an accident. And Monica would hate her too because Paul did and Monica and Lori would never want to hang out with her again and—

She was gasping and hiccupping and running blindly, tripping over branches and getting smacked in the face with tree limbs, and then she stopped and stood, pulling in air in huge gulps.

There had been enough light coming through the trees that she'd been able to see the spit dripping down Monica's chin. Her lipstick had been smeared around her mouth and her hair was sticking out in all directions. She looked like a demented clown. And Paul's face? That moment of complete befuddlement coupled with his pants being around his knees. Clare started to laugh. She pushed her hand over her mouth so they wouldn't hear her. Wait until she told Abby.

Then she remembered what Abby was doing now with her new friends, and just as quickly the giddiness disappeared. She was utterly and completely alone. She wiped her eyes and sat down, pressing her thumb into her palm to make the sting go away, and for the first time, she started to feel calm.

Screw them. Screw all of them. From now on, she was only going to do what she wanted to do. Even if it meant having fewer friends, or no friends. Who cared if Lori and Monica never talked to her again. They hardly talked to her now; they just talked to each other and let her listen. And Abby? For all her clinging to Clare earlier, she had discarded her as thoughtlessly as Monica would have.

Clare missed talking about real things like she used to. Now all she and her friends talked about were people they went to school with or high school kids. When her mother was still alive, they would go on camping trips. Her mother had taught her how to make a fire and the names of the plants and how to recognize edible mushrooms and berries. They'd bring their sleeping bags outside and look up at the stars, and her dad would help them find the constellations, and if he didn't know the story of a constellation, he and her mom would make one up. Her family being whole like that seemed so far away, almost like it had been only a dream. She looked up at the stars. "Big Dipper, Little Dipper, Cygnus, Cassiopeia . . ." she whispered. She knew them, so that memory had to be real.

In the distance, she heard the pop and crack of the fire. A hundred feet overhead, the highest leaves moved against each other in the breeze, and above them, the stars exploded silently. The woods at night didn't scare her, so she would stay here until everyone went home, and when the sun rose, she would walk home and start being the person she wanted to be, the curious, imaginative person she'd been when she was little. Only this version would be older and stronger. And this version of Clare wouldn't need anyone.

16

The phone vibrates off the bedside table and lands on the floor with a thump as I reach out to find it. I'm disoriented, blinking in the dark, looking for the lights that used to come in through the high bank of windows of our bedroom in Chicago. For a moment, I think I hear Josh breathing beside me, but it's just the rhythmic whirring of my phone continuing to vibrate into the carpet. Still stupid with sleep, I grab for it and swipe the screen open. "Hello?"

"Clare?"

It takes my brain a moment to catch up. I hear the sounds of the hospital, but visiting hours are over; Abby's mother would be calling me only if it's an emergency. I'm too late. I was a coward and didn't go to see Abby and now it's too late—

"Clare, are you there? It's Caroline Lindsay."

"Yes, sorry, yes, I'm here. What's happened?"

"You need to come to the hospital. It's Abby. She's waking up."

Forty minutes later, I'm pulling into the almost empty parking lot of the hospital. No hesitation this time, I'm running. Over the past twenty-four hours, her mother told me as I struggled to pull my clothes on and get out of the house, the doctors began decreasing some of the medications, and Abby started to show signs of consciousness. She's coming, she's coming back.

Mrs. Lindsay waits for me in the lobby with a pass that will get me upstairs. As soon as she sees me, she rushes toward me, arms open.

"Oh, Clare, you came. I knew you'd come." She holds me out at arm's length. "How are you? When did you arrive? It's going to mean so much to Abby that you're here." Before I can respond, she hurries me toward the waiting elevator. "Come on, let's go up to her room."

"Is she awake?" I finally manage to ask.

Mrs. Lindsay is stabbing the elevator button repeatedly. "No, not yet, but soon," she says. The doors whoosh closed, and we start to move up. "She started showing signs around dinnertime. We had just left. It was one of the nurses who noticed. She was giving Abby a bath. We're going to stay with her all night, all the way through this. They said not to get too hopeful yet. There are tests scheduled for the morning, but this is such a good sign."

"How long will it take before she's fully awake?"

"They don't know. They are going slowly so they can monitor her. Clare, she's coming back to us." She's grabbing on to my coat and looking at me like I'm the grown-up and she's the child, practically vibrating with excitement. "I can't believe you came, you actually came."

"But you asked me to—"

"When Mitch told us you were in town, I knew, I just *knew*, something was going to shift for Abby."

"I was going to come later today," I say. I feel like I've got guilt written all over my face, but she's too excited to notice.

The elevator doors slide open on the fifth floor and Mrs. Lindsay bursts out, striding toward Abby's room with me scrambling to keep up. In some ways, I'm grateful. There's no time to be nervous. Mrs. Lindsay's excitement is infectious, and I have to stop myself from believing that Abby's going to be sitting up in bed smiling at me. To think it could all be that easy. The floor is quiet. The lights in the hallway are dimmed and the nurses' station glows. They look up when we move past, and nod to Mrs. Lindsay. Abby's been in here for a week. I'm sure they know the whole family well by now. The doors to rooms are all closed except for one at the end on the right. I can hear a man's low voice coming from inside. Mrs. Lindsay pushes it all the way open and there she is.

Abby is suspended in a web of tubes and machinery. Tubes in her nose, an IV in her arm, another tube coming from the back of her head, and more snake out under the bedclothes, all connected to machines that rhythmically beep and whir—a landscape of white noise. A thick bandage is wrapped around her head. On the bedside table is a large vase with flowers, and leaning precariously against it is a bright blue teddy bear. The only illumination is coming from the fluorescent light on the wall above the bed, and it glows a soft purple and makes the white of her sheets shine. I'm still in the doorway taking it all in as Mr. Lindsay jumps up from the chair beside the bed and comes over to hug me.

"Clare!" Like Mrs. Lindsay, he looks smaller than I remember. The skin over his face is pulled tight and the bags under his eyes are deep and permanent, but his grip on my arms is firm. "It's so good to see you again. It means so much to us that you've come, all the way from Chicago, is that right? Is your father still here? How is he—?"

"Ted," Mrs. Lindsay says, "let her talk to Abby."

"Can she hear us?" I ask.

"They don't know for sure, but she's showing more signs of responsiveness. The doctors are very excited. Very," he says. He's still gripping my arms. "I'm reading to her just so she has something to hold on to. Go on and talk to her. She'd love to hear your voice."

"Um, sure," I say.

He lets go of me and goes over to his daughter. "Sweetheart," he says quietly to her. His hand brushes her forehead. "There's someone very special to see you. Clare's here, baby doll. It's Clare."

Abby's parents look at me, waiting for me to do something, so I go over to the other side of the bed and reach out to touch her, then pull my hand away, hoping the Lindsays haven't noticed my hesitation.

"Hi, Abby. It's me, Clare."

Nothing happens, of course. I look at them. Mrs. Lindsay is smiling like she knows something amazing is about to occur. Mr. Lindsay nods. "Keep talking to her," he says. "We have to keep talking."

I open my mouth, but nothing comes out. What can I possibly tell her? I feel self-conscious, like I'm supposed to be some kind of miracle worker who, through words alone, can cut through all the damage and wake her up. Who am I kidding? Abby and I haven't even been in touch for over twenty years. I know nothing about her life besides this. I shouldn't be here. I step back from the bed.

"Here." Mr. Lindsay is holding out a Winnie-the-Pooh book. "Just so she can hear your voice."

"But . . ." I'm no one, I want to say.

"I've been reading to her for two hours. She's probably sick of me," her father says, still holding the book out. "It was her favorite when she was little."

Abby's parents are so hopeful and expectant, while her thin, damaged body lies between us. "Okay," I say, and take the book obediently.

I perch on the vinyl chair Mr. Lindsay has just vacated and open the book to where the page is bent down.

" 'One fine winter's day when Piglet was brushing away the snow from in front of his house . . .' " I stop and look up. They're still watching me, watching Abby, as if at any second she's going to pop out of bed. Didn't they listen to the doctors? They said it could take time.

"That's great, Clare," Mr. Lindsay says. "Really great." His wife nods emphatically.

I put my head back down and keep going. " 'He happened to look up and there was Winnie-the-Pooh. Pooh was walking round and round in a circle, thinking of something else . . .' "

———

An hour later, I am still reading. Mrs. Lindsay has finally succumbed to exhaustion and fallen asleep in the armchair in the corner, and Mr. Lindsay is pacing. Every thirty minutes a nurse comes in to check on the machines and record any changes, and once a doctor has been in to do another examination. I tried to hear what he said to her parents in their conversation in the hallway but couldn't make out anything. It's almost two in the morning. I don't know how much longer I can keep reading or how I'll be able to drive home. At this point, all I want to do is crawl into the backseat of my car and sleep.

"Just another little bit," Mr. Lindsay says, "then Caroline can take over."

At the sound of her name, Mrs. Lindsay wakes up. "Clare, can you stay for a bit?"

"No, we—" Mr. Lindsay starts to protest, but it's clear he's as exhausted as she is.

"I'm sorry to ask this," Mrs. Lindsay says, "but if we could just have a few hours to get some rest."

"Carol, we can't leave."

"The doctors said it could take days. We have to take care of ourselves or we won't be any good to her when she wakes up." She turns back to me. "We're at the Howard Johnson just down the road. It's three minutes. If I could go and sleep in a bed for a few hours and have a shower—"

"Well, I'm not leaving."

"Ted."

"I'm not." The anger between them is palpable.

"Fine, but go to the waiting room, where you can stretch out. I'll bring you fresh clothes."

"It's fine, Mr. Lindsay," I say. I desperately want them to leave. I have no idea what I'm going to say to Abby, but I need to be able to be with her alone. I can't think clearly with the Lindsays watching me. Their anxiety is exhausting. I wonder if Abby can sense it too.

He looks at me, unsure, then sighs. "It seems like a lot to ask."

"It's fine, really. I want to be here."

And it's true. It took me so long to get in here to see Abby, but now that I'm with her, I don't want to leave, as tired as I am. I desperately need answers from her.

"If you need me, I'm down the hall. It's just past the elevators on the right. I'll tell the nurses that I'm going to be there. If anything changes, *anything*."

It's a relief when they finally go. I'm so tired I feel drunk. I dim the light and drag the armchair out of the corner next to the bed.

Taped to the rails around Abby's bed are pictures her parents have brought from home. There are pictures of Abby with people I don't recognize—glimpses of her as a sixteen-year-old; at twenty. Some with boys who start to look more like men. Most of them are family pictures. Paul with his wife and three kids—hard to imagine—and one of Mitchell with a beautiful woman on a beach that looks far more exotic and sunny than anything you'd find around here. They have their arms around each other and are laughing and wet, having run into the sea with their clothes on. I make myself look at it for a moment and my stomach twists, then I move around the bed to look at the ones on the other side.

The pictures are arranged in chronological order: her childhood, her teenage years. In one of them, we're at our eighth-grade graduation. I'm wearing makeup and pumps that I could barely walk in. Abby's in a cotton dress her mother made for her. I was much taller than she was by then; my growth spurt was right at the start of puberty. I realize, seeing the two of us side by side, that the last summer we spent together, she still looked like a girl, while I was a teenager. She wore a bra, but I knew it was padded. But it wasn't just physical. Going into that final summer, something was starting to move us apart. If I had known what would happen, would I have been able to stop it? Was it just that we were developing at different stages? Or was it a series of things, each small on its own, adding up to what happened that day, and then that night in July, just a month after this picture was taken?

Sometimes, when I sensed the growing space between us, I told myself that I didn't need her. At the time, I felt strong. It's the same feeling I had when I pulled away from Josh. There have been other times when I've felt myself pulling away from a relationship, drifting quietly and irrevocably apart. I used to think it was brave to be alone. But now I know it's just lonely.

I sit in the stiff armchair. The steady rhythm of the machines, the faint in and out of her breathing, almost lulls me to sleep, but I sit up when the intercom turns on—a nurse calmly paging a doctor. When I get up and poke my head into the hallway, there's no sign of anyone. It feels like the world is asleep.

Abby's right hand has the IV tube taped onto the wrist and is strapped to the bed rail. Her left hand lies free. A white bandage covers the tip of each finger. At first I thought the bandages were a precaution against her trying to pull out any of the tubes and lines, but now I see that the pinkie finger on her left isn't bandaged and there's something on the end of it. I turn on my phone flashlight and gently straighten her fingers. The nail of the pinkie is torn down to the quick, and the skin has the shiny redness of new skin. If this finger wasn't considered bad enough to be bandaged, the others must be much worse. The evidence of violence in those hands is in direct opposition to her eerie stillness now. Her fingers tell me what she can't. The basement door was closed. She was in complete darkness. If I close my eyes, I'll see the rusted door, its surface pockmarked with old chipped paint, broken off in slivers. Abby tried to scratch and claw her way out.

Gently, I take her hand and open her curled fingers so I can see her palm. With my finger, I trace a triangle, lines meeting at the points. Our old symbol.

Does she remember?

In this hospital room that feels suspended in time, in space, in memory, will this get through?

I press harder on her cool palm and her bandaged fingers automatically curl over mine. I spread them open and trace the triangle again.

"Abby, can you hear me? I am here."

17

CLARE

July 25, 1998
11:30 P.M.

Clare's shorts and shoes were soaked with the dew and she began to shiver violently. One of the cuts on her knees had reopened when she'd fallen, and the road rash was throbbing. She got up stiffly and walked toward the sound of the fire and voices. She had no idea how long she'd been gone. It felt like hours. As she got closer, she heard male voices, fighting. She stepped into the clearing. The fire had gone down and everything was much darker. The two guys arguing were silhouetted against the dying embers. Other people were starting to come out of the woods and gather around them. Abby stood by herself, struggling to find her balance.

"Abby," Clare called out, and her friend lurched around to look at her, confused.

"Look," Abby said. She gestured drunkenly to the fight and Clare realized it was Mitchell and Paul. "Where'd you go?"

Clare didn't answer because at that moment, Mitchell swung his fist and hit Paul in the face. Paul staggered backward, holding his eye, and then ran toward Mitchell and pushed him. Mitchell was taller and more athletic, but Paul had been lifting weights for months, and his bulk took Mitchell down. Paul straddled him and pulled back his fist, when some of the others restrained him. Mitchell jumped up, shoving people reaching out to help.

"Why are they fighting?" Clare asked.

"'Cause of me," Abby said. She tried to grab Clare's hand but ended up missing. "We shouldn't have come. Why'd you go before?"

"You were having a pretty good time on your own," Clare said.

Abby turned fully to look at her. "You're mad at me?" But a group of people had clustered close to them, trying to see the fight, and Clare let them get between her and Abby.

"You're such a fucking loser—" Mitchell yelled at Paul, breathless.

Paul lunged again, pushing away the people who were holding him. He ran at Mitchell, but Mitchell was ready and Paul was drunk. Mitchell threw him down on the ground, falling on top of him.

"We can't all be perfect like you, you fucking fag," Paul cried out.

Mitchell punched him again, then stood up. Paul took longer to get up. A few people went to him—it looked like one of them was Monica—but he pushed them away and stomped off into the woods.

Mitchell came over to Abby and grabbed her arm roughly. "Come on. We're going." The crowd was already starting to disperse.

"Where's Clare?" Abby's voice sounded light and far away. He said something Clare couldn't hear, so she stepped closer to them, and he saw her.

"There you are. Are you fucked-up too?"

"No," she said. "I didn't take anything."

"Why'd you leave her alone? She didn't know where you were." He was angry, but at least he wasn't talking to her like a kid.

"I just went into the woods to pee. She was with another girl."

"Lesley—" Abby interjected.

"And then I got lost."

"Do you guys even know these people?" Mitchell asked. He was trying to maneuver Abby through the dark and had to half carry her.

"We know Lesley," Abby said, but her speech was slow and slurred.

"Lesley? You want to meet my brother?" But Lesley had disappeared into the darkness.

"Come on," Mitchell said. "The car's over there."

As they walked away, Clare saw people settle back around the fire. They were passing around another joint, and someone turned the boom box on again.

The car was parked a little way down the road. Abby wanted Clare to sit in the backseat with her, but Mitchell said, "No, sit up front with me. I already feel like a fucking taxi." When Clare slid into the front, he said quietly, "Sorry. I'm not mad at you. My brother's a shit."

"You saaaved me," Abby said from the back. She lurched forward and threw her hands over Mitchell's shoulders.

"Get off me," he said, pushing her hands away. He was glaring at the road. He had blood on his nose and his lip. "Do you have any idea how much shit you're going to be in?"

"Don't tell them," Abby said. It came out as a whine.

"It's pretty fucking obvious," Mitchell muttered, but Abby didn't respond. She already seemed to be falling asleep.

"I'm sorry I left her," Clare said. "I really did get lost."

"It's okay." He turned to look at her. "You're not her babysitter." He pulled the visor down and opened the mirror to examine the damage to his face. "That fucker," he muttered. He looked around for something to wipe his face with and ended up using the bottom edge of his T-shirt.

"Does it hurt?" she asked after a moment.

"Nah. Even when he's sober, Paul can't punch for shit. I got him good, though."

"Do you two fight a lot?"

He shrugged. "We did when we were young. Most of the time we'd just be messing around, and then he'd get all worked up and actually try to give me a black eye." He looked at her again. "Do you have siblings?"

"No, just me," she said.

"Thought so. You're lucky."

Clare didn't answer. He rolled down the window and they could hear the low murmur of voices coming from the party. Abby was leaning her head against the window, her eyes closed. Clare glanced back at her, wanting her to sleep.

"I'd decided not to come, then I heard my parents arguing. My mom's all worked up about Paul being a dick. Just didn't want to listen to it, you know?"

Clare nodded, although she didn't know.

"They just have to chill. Does your mom get all uptight?"

"My mom died when I was eight. Cancer."

She never knew how much to say when someone asked. Some people automatically asked, "How?" and others didn't. A long time ago, she had decided it was easier to just offer the reason and get it out of the way.

"Shit. I'm sorry. That sucks."

"Yeah."

"I thought I'd heard that, sorry I forgot."

"Heard it?"

"Like in passing." Abby, she knew. Abby entranced by the enigma of a family of two. She was as fascinated by Clare's family as Clare was drawn to hers, though for different reasons. "Does it bother you to talk about it?" he asked.

"No. I mean . . . I don't, much. But that's 'cause everybody knows. It's just one of those things now." Stop. Don't make it small. It wasn't small. She thought about how she felt looking at her mother's photo earlier that day. About thinking that her mother had left her a sign.

"That's why you seem older," Mitchell said.

"Well, Abby skipped a grade, so she's younger than everyone."

"No, you seem older than all those girls. Especially what's-her-name, with the makeup."

"Monica?"

"Yeah. She's . . . something," he said. "Sorry, I know she's your friend."

Clare shrugged. Was Monica her friend? She thought about what she'd seen in the woods, and what Monica had said to her, and about how sure she'd been that she could go forward without them. She looked at Abby, who was sound asleep. Maybe not without Abby.

A car drove toward them. It slowed when its lights hit the parked cars by the road. Clare watched the taillights until they disappeared.

"We should get out of here. Whoever that was might call the cops." He started the car. "Can we take her to your house?" he asked. She felt a lurch in her chest; she didn't want this to be over. "It's better my parents don't see her like this, especially with my grandparents there," he said. "Will your dad be up?"

"He'll wake up if we come in this late."

"Fuck," he said under his breath.

"Have you ever seen the sun rise?" she asked.

"Sure. Haven't you?"

"Yeah, of course."

"I used to deliver papers," he said. "I had to get up at five in the morning. I hated it, but I saw a lot of sunrises. Why?"

"I decided I wanted to see the sunrise this morning. I haven't since I was a kid." She felt him turn to her, waiting. "I haven't seen a sunrise since my mom died."

"Oh. Sorry."

She immediately felt bad for saying it. It was a dirty trick to use her mom like that, even though in this case it was true. "I just meant . . . I haven't seen it in a while."

"Neither have I."

They were both quiet on the drive into town, but it was an easy silence. Clare kept her focus on the darkness outside. In the reflected glow of the dashboard lights, she saw him look over at her a few times, but she kept her gaze forward. She felt strangely calm, like this was perfectly normal, she and Mitchell driving together down these dark roads. She wasn't just his kid sister's friend being driven home from a party they shouldn't have been at; she felt like an equal. At the same time, another part of her mind knew that tomorrow this would seem impossible.

Remember this. Remember, remember, remember.

Mitchell parked a block away from his house and turned off the car. It was past midnight and the houses were dark. The sounds of summer night bugs floated in the air. Somewhere, a dog barked. He hadn't taken her home. Was that because they hadn't figured out what to do with Abby or because he didn't want this to end either? A car passed and they instinctively slid down in the seats. She laughed.

"Shhh," he said, and reached over to gently put his hand over her mouth. "You'll wake her up." She tasted the earth on his palm from when he'd fallen in the fight. "Sorry." He pulled his hand back. "I guess we're hiding."

"I guess we are," she said. She could still taste the earth and something salty—sweat or blood—under that. They stayed down in the seats. The streetlight over them shone on their faces at this angle. "You have a bit of dried blood," she said, pointing to her own nose.

"Yeah?" He dabbed at it with the corner of his shirt. "I bet Paul's face is worse." He sighed. "No matter what, I'm going to have to explain something to my parents. I just want to keep Abby out of it."

"That's nice of you."

"I don't know if I'm trying to be nice," he said. "Maybe. I don't know." He glanced back at Abby to make sure she was still asleep, then turned back to Clare. "There's something going on with her. Have you noticed it?"

"I don't know," Clare said. Had she? She had always just taken Abby as being Abby: impetuous, irritating at times, intensely loyal.

"I just get this sense that she's, I don't know, reckless? Something. Sometimes—most times—she's just my goofy kid sister. Paul picks on her, but she brings it on herself half the time. But then other times, little things she says, they just don't suit her. I wanted to ask you about it."

"What has she said?"

"Like last week, she said she was going to come and visit me in the city on her own. And I said Mom and Dad probably wouldn't let her do that, and she was like, 'I'll hitchhike. I've almost done it before.'"

"She was probably just saying that."

"Yeah, probably. But I'm worried she's going to do something stupid, like tonight. She's impulsive. Doesn't think things through." He shifted uncomfortably. "I've gotta sit up, I'm getting a cramp in my neck." He turned to her. "Hey." Then he stopped himself, but he was smiling. "Nah. It's stupid."

"What?"

"Nothing."

"What? Now you have to tell me. That's the rule."

"What rule?"

"What were you going to say?" She was sitting up now.

"That house you told me about. The one you went to today?"

"The Octagon House?"

"Yeah. Do you wanna show it to me?"

The thought of going to that house in the middle of the night was terrifying. But she would do anything to stay in this car with Mitchell.

"Never mind." He laughed. "Dumb idea."

"No, I can show you. But it's a ways off the road. We'd have to walk in."

"I thought you said there was an old road."

"It's pretty overgrown."

He shrugged. "I don't know. Let's decide when we get there."

He started the car and drove out of the village back toward the party. They were both quiet again, but instead of the easy silence, Clare felt almost giddy. This time, when he looked over at her, she looked back at him and they both grinned.

"I can't believe you said yes," he said.

"Were you secretly hoping I'd say no?"

"Are you calling me a chicken?"

"Hey, I've already been inside," she said. "If anyone should be scared . . ."

"I know, I know," he said, and turned to the road, smiling.

They drove a half mile past the party—no sign of police being called—and then around the bend in the road. "It's right around here," she said when they reached the patch of forest where the house was hidden. The car slowed to a crawl. "If you can point the lights at the fence, I can find the post where the wire's cut."

Mitchell pulled over and Clare got out and walked to the fence. The air felt cool after the close warmth of the car, and she shivered. In the headlights, she walked along beside the fence, testing the wire at each post to find the one that was just hooked over the nail. Her heart raced. What if she couldn't find it? What if she had misjudged completely and it was still far away? In the darkness, everything looked different. She was just about to give up when she came to one more post, and this time, the wire popped off the nail. She gave a thumbs-up, then turned away. She probably looked like an idiot doing that. She pulled the wire back wide enough so the car could fit through. Mitchell carefully maneuvered it off the shoulder and bumped onto the grass, then nosed it through the opening into the forest. She reattached the fence wire to the post and got back inside.

"Do you think you can drive through?" she asked.

"I'm not sure," he said. "But I don't want to leave the car on the road with Abby asleep in it, and I don't want to wake her up." He opened his door. "I'll go see."

She watched as he walked ahead to the edge of the high beams. His shadow leaped up like a giant reflected on the trees. He bent down and lifted a huge branch, then threw it off to the side.

"It's pretty overgrown," he said when he got back in. "But I think we'll be okay if we go slow. Try to watch for branches and rocks, okay?"

He put the car in gear and they rolled forward. He squinted into the forest at the overgrown path while the trees on either side leaned in toward them. The bright beam from the headlights bounced as the front wheels sank into a dip, and something scraped along the bottom. Mitchell swore quietly but kept going. Branches scraped the sides, as if the woods were getting tighter the closer they got to the house. Miraculously, Abby slept through it all. Then the path turned to the right and they rolled into the clearing and there it was.

Only a few hours past their first visit and Clare's mind was already trying to move the house into something only imagined, but seeing it rise up out of the darkness made it very, very real.

"Ho-ly shit," Mitchell said quietly. "You weren't kidding."

Clare just nodded. Something jumped deep in her belly, that ancient animal brain where fear lives. The house seemed larger somehow. Looming. Utter darkness. And just as strong was the sudden urge, the need, to go inside. *Something down here for you.* The same feeling she'd had before. It wasn't overriding her fear; it was woven into it. The need to run and the need to move toward it. Her hand was on the door handle.

"Whoa—" Mitchell said, louder than he should have, then he switched to a whisper. "What are you doing?"

"Don't you want to go in?"

He gave a little laugh. "Slow down there, tiger. What are we going to do with Abby?"

"Do you think she's going to wake up?" Please, she thought, please don't wake up. That would ruin everything.

"Probably not, but . . . let's have a drink first. Then we'll decide. Have a little liquid courage."

"You're just trying to stall."

He didn't reply, just grinned. He hopped out, opened the trunk, and got back into the car with two bottles of beer. He twisted off the caps, and beer started to fizz out the tops.

"Shit," he said, but he was laughing. He used his shirt to mop up the spilled beer. "Should have thought of that." Seeing her hesitation, he asked, "Do you even want a beer? I should have asked first."

"Sure."

"Have you ever had beer?"

"Yeah, of course."

"You ever been drunk?"

She hesitated for a second, then said, "No. Have you?"

He laughed again. It was getting easier to make him laugh. "Just drink slowly. Maybe just drink half."

"What if I accidentally drink the whole thing?" she asked.

"Okay, here." He tipped her bottle of beer into his mouth so the lip of the bottle didn't touch his lips. He poured half of it into his mouth, then handed it to her. He swallowed. "Consider me your self-restraint."

"How did you do that?"

"Practice."

"I didn't know you drank," she said.

"Everybody drinks. I just don't get caught, unlike my brother. Cheers." They clinked bottles quietly. The beer was warm and bitter, but she got used to the taste after a few sips. For the rest of my life, she thought, I will remember this moment.

"How did you guys find this place?" he whispered. Had he felt it too, the sense that the house was listening to them?

"Lori. This is her family's land."

"And it's just been sitting here?"

"Yeah. Her dad wants to get rid of it, but he can't."

"Why the hell not? I would," Mitchell said.

"It's cursed. I mean, that's what some people say."

"Shit." Saying it was cursed at this time of night didn't seem so strange, and Mitchell had lost all of his earlier skepticism. He finished his beer, so Clare took two quick sips and finished hers too.

"So, what do you think?" she asked. "Do you want to go in?" In the few minutes they had been sitting there drinking their beer, the feeling in her gut had calmed, but now it came fully to life. Its energy rippled through her. She wasn't dumb enough to think that a half bottle of lukewarm beer had made her drunk. It was being here with *him*, it was whatever was inside that house pulling her toward it, it was the feeling that if they went in there together, then no matter what happened, she and Mitchell would always have that.

"Okay," he said. "I can't believe we're doing this, but okay."

"What about Abby?"

He turned to the backseat. She was sleeping with her mouth open. He reached out and touched her shoulder. "Abby?" She didn't even move.

"If we just go in for a couple minutes, she'll be okay," he said. "She's been asleep for less than an hour. Pot will make you crash for way longer than that."

"Maybe we should leave her a note," Clare said. She knew if she woke up and the first thing she saw was that house, she'd freak out. "Do you have a pen?" She opened the glove compartment. "Aha." She pulled out some old bills and a pen and wrote: *Stay in car. Back in a minute.* She considered writing *Clare & Mitchell* but then decided on *Clare*. She also found a flashlight, which she turned on, and left the note on the seat next to Abby.

They got out, closing the doors very softly, and walked across the clearing to the house. As they got closer, the open doorway became visible. "In there," she whispered. "I think it was the kitchen. There's a bigger door on the other side, but it's boarded up."

"So, the front door is at the back?" he asked.

"I guess so." She hadn't thought about it, but unless there was another access point through the woods that Lori hadn't mentioned, he was right.

They were at the door. Mitchell looked quickly toward the car, then said, "Okay, let's do this." He reached over and put his hand on the small of her back.

The kitchen was pitch black, but dim moonlight shone through the spaces in the boarded-up windows. They stood in the doorway, breathing in the mildewed smell of the house, letting their eyes adjust to the added darkness. Clare's eyes glanced toward where she knew the basement door was, but from this angle, she couldn't tell if it was open.

"Shit," he said under his breath. "We should have brought that flashlight. I could go and get it."

"No!"

He laughed. "Or not."

He had been standing right behind her, and feeling him there felt safe, but he stepped around her and walked farther into the kitchen. Cold air descended on her, sending shivers down her spine. She turned suddenly, looking back outside. Had something moved out there? Could someone be watching them? The party wasn't far, and there might be others there who knew where this place was.

"What is it?" Mitchell asked. His voice had a trace of panic.

"Nothing, sorry."

"I'm going farther in," he said. "We've come this far. Might as well explore."

"Maybe we should go check on Abby."

"She'll be fine," he said. "We've been in here for, like, thirty seconds."

"How will we know if she wakes up?"

"If she gets out of the car, we'll hear the door. We'll go right back to her." He crunched across the kitchen over the leaves and broken glass, heading toward one of the two doorways that led to the other room. He stopped. Even without seeing it, Clare knew he was touching that metal door.

"Don't—"

"What is it?"

"Nothing. Sorry. It's just the basement." She didn't want to go near it.

He pulled on the latch, but the door didn't move. "How do you know? It's jammed shut."

Relief coursed through her. "Come on," she said, a little louder now. "I want to show you that room at the top." The basement was closed. It would stay closed. They could be here, they could have this, and whatever was down there—

Stop. There was nothing down there. She shivered.

Mitchell whistled the *Twilight Zone* theme as he walked toward her, but her eyes had adjusted enough that she saw he was smiling. They walked to the base of the stairs and stood observing the second-floor landing. Mitchell was in front of her, running his fingers over the old wallpaper that lined the stairway.

Suddenly, out of the corner of her eye, Clare saw or sensed movement outside the window. The faint bit of moonlight coming through the crack had been momentarily broken. She gasped. Mitchell whipped around. "Jesus!" he said. Then he leaned toward her. "Sorry, I'm jumpy."

"Me too," Clare said. She desperately wanted to go back to the doorway and check the car, but she couldn't risk being separated from him. When they were close, this felt doable. He must have felt the same way because he reached his hand out and took hers, holding it gently so he wouldn't disturb her bandages. He squeezed her fingers and they started moving up the stairs. They had just arrived at the top when she heard a *click*.

"Did you just hear something?" she whispered.

He stopped and listened, then laughed nervously. "Stop trying to freak me out."

On the second floor, the moonlight streamed through the windows unimpeded, and the empty bedrooms glowed. Clare didn't know if he would want to explore each room, but she wanted to get as far away from the basement as possible.

"This must have been the master," he said when they stepped inside the biggest room. It was airy, with three windows. With the moonlight pouring in, it was almost serene.

"The top's through here," she said, opening the door that led to the narrow staircase. Mitchell came over and peered up at it, then stood back and held out his hand. "After you."

There was no banister because the stairway was so narrow, so she braced her hands on the walls and climbed up. As Mitchell climbed out after her, he whistled. "This is amazing."

Just like it had that afternoon, the room at the top felt completely different: maybe because it was so far above the basement, or because it lacked the dirt and debris of the first floor, or because there were windows all around. It smelled different too. It was dusty, but the smell of damp rot that had permeated the rest of the house hadn't made it up here. Clare went to the window and looked down toward the car. There was no sign of Abby, but she'd been lying down on the backseat so there wouldn't be a way to see her anyway. Clare couldn't tell if she was seeing the glow of the flashlight she'd left on the seat, or if it was just moonlight reflecting off the windows.

"Stop worrying," Mitchell said. "She's sound asleep." Clare nodded, willing herself to believe him. He knew the effects of pot better than she did, after all.

He sat down, then lay back on the floor. "It's almost a perfect panorama; we just need a skylight."

She sat down against the wall.

"Not over there, you won't be able to see it all. You've got to come to the center. Just don't fall down the hole."

She slid closer to him. "Now," he said, "lie back." She did. "Isn't that amazing?"

"Yeah."

They lay there for another moment. She listened to the sound of Mitchell's even breathing, and hers automatically started to match his. Her body was fizzing with electricity, every part of her attuned to him. He was so close; if she just moved her hand, she could touch him.

"Clare, Clare, Clare," he whispered. "You're so quiet."

"Sorry."

"No, it's nice. I like quiet."

"Me too."

Clare thought about Abby, but how could she break this? This would never, ever happen again. She would never be alone with him again.

She felt his hand brush her leg, and all the hairs on her body stood up. For a second she thought it must have been an accident, but then he touched her leg again, and this time his hand stayed there. He turned his head to look at her, but she kept looking straight up.

"Clare?"

"Yeah?"

He rolled over on his side so he was now above her. She smelled the beer on his breath and his shirt. She probably smelled the same. His hand moved up her leg, over her shorts, and under her shirt, but he kept his eyes on hers. He moved his fingers across her stomach, and she felt tiny charges of electricity surge over her skin wherever he touched.

"Can I kiss you?"

"I— Uh . . ."

His hand stopped moving and he pulled away slightly.

"Yes." It came out like a croak, her throat was so tight.

He leaned down over her and kissed her. His lips were softer than she'd expected. A light kiss, barely touching.

Her mouth was closed, but then she opened it and his mouth matched hers. She felt him run his tongue along her teeth. The tips of their tongues touched, and she pulled hers back but then tried again. His hand on her stomach had been still, but as he kept kissing her, he started moving it again. There was more weight to the kiss now, and as he shifted, more of his weight came onto her. It felt good.

His hand moved up her side until he got to her bra, then he traced the outline of her breast. He rubbed his thumb across her nipple. She gasped.

"Is that okay?" He pulled away again.

"Yes."

"Just tell me."

"Okay. It's . . . okay."

"Only okay?" He smiled down at her.

"It's nice. It's good." Was she supposed to say something dirty? If she were older, if she were more experienced, she'd know something better to say than "okay" and "nice."

He stayed above her and watched her face as his thumb circled her nipple again. She wanted to look at him. She wanted to tell him how the nerves he was touching were exploding in her stomach and between her legs.

"Close your eyes."

He kissed her eyelids. Then her nose, then her mouth again. And the whole time his hand was on her breast. Then she remembered her hands, just lying there beside her. She found the edge of his shirt and touched his bare stomach and his chest. His skin was warm. She could feel his heart. Then her hand moved down to the waist of his pants. She was feeling that line of hairs when her fingers traced under his waistband.

"I'm not . . ." She couldn't tell him that she had never done this before.

"It's okay," he whispered. "Just lie back. Enjoy it."

He sat up beside her and pulled her shirt up and over her head. The air on her skin was cool, and she could feel the grit from the floor pressing into her. He leaned in and kissed her neck, down to her collarbone, and to the edge of her bra. He was holding himself up with one hand, but his other hand was still on her stomach; then it slid down over her shorts and onto her thigh. The warmth of his breath hovered over her bra, and without realizing she was going to make a sound, she moaned.

His head shot up. "What was that?"

"That was me."

"No. I heard another sound."

She started to sit up, but he pulled away from her and held a finger to his lips. As quietly as she could, she sat up, wrapping her arms around herself. Mitchell crawled to the edge of the stairway and listened.

"What was—?" she started to ask, but he held his hand out to silence her.

"Shhh. That. I just heard it again."

She hadn't heard anything. She scrambled to pull her T-shirt on, but it was knotted and her hands weren't cooperating. Then she heard it too and she froze. Something was moving downstairs over the broken glass and debris. It moved slowly, stopped, then moved again. All the heat on her skin evaporated in a second and she started shivering.

"I'm going down there," he said.

"Wait. Check the car first."

She stumbled over to the window and squinted out to the car. The moon had gone behind a cloud again and it was impossible to see anything but the outline of its shape.

"The doors are closed. We didn't hear a car door."

"Fuck," he said quietly. He started down the steep stairs.

"Wait, I'm coming," she whispered, and hurried after him. When she got to the bottom of the stairs, he was already moving across the bedroom in long silent strides. He stopped in the doorway and listened.

"I can't hear it now." Cautiously, he walked out into the hallway. The clouds broke up again, and light came into the hall from the window at the end. They went to the landing over the kitchen. He took a step down, but it creaked, so he pulled his foot back up.

"Hello?" His voice cracked and came out a half whisper. They waited. There was no reply and no other sound.

Clare's stomach was a pit, as if her insides were going to drop out of her. He took a step down, then another and another, and she followed. Nothing responded. But there was something there. Something was listening to them.

"Stay here," he whispered when they'd reached the bottom.

She stood pressed against the dirty wall of the stairwell. She didn't want to breathe and tried to picture where he was in the kitchen. They had to get out of here.

He came back to her. "It's probably an animal, like a raccoon or something. Let's go to the car." He walked across the kitchen to the outside door without waiting for her. That was when she heard it again.

Like a sigh or a groan, the sound of air escaping a body, moving over vocal cords. Then a different sound, the dragging of the heavy basement door opening wider, beckoning her. She froze. "Abby?"

A sigh of cold air exhaled from the basement, and even halfway across the room, she felt it move across her skin.

Clare turned and bolted out of the house.

Mitchell was across the clearing and had almost reached the car. She was breathing hard now, running as fast as she could, not caring how much noise she made. She caught up to him as he took the key out of his pocket, and that was when they saw it. The back door. Wide open.

"Oh, fuck. Oh, fuck. Oh, fuck me. No." He spun around, wild-eyed. Looking at her, the house, the car. Abby was gone. The note was there, but the flashlight was missing. "Fucking fuck." He slammed his fist into the roof of the car.

"She's got the light," she said.

"Would she go into that house by herself?"

"No. No way. She didn't even want to go in with us in the daytime."

"Okay. So, she's out here somewhere. Maybe she's gone out toward the road."

"Except . . ."

"What?"

"If she thought you were in there, then she'd probably go in."

"Which is it?"

"I think we should check the house first."

"Okay." He started walking toward the house. She knew she should tell him about the basement, but she couldn't. She couldn't say it out loud because that would make it real and none of this could possibly be real. When they got to the kitchen door, he turned and said, "You stay here and keep an eye out in case Abby's around. I'll go upstairs."

"I'll come with you."

"It's faster if we split up."

"No! Please don't make me stay down here on my own."

"Just stay here by the door," he snapped. "Sorry." He put his hand on her arm. "We need to cover as much ground as we can."

Tell him, but she said nothing. Even if the basement door had opened on its own, she couldn't imagine Abby going down there.

He went to the bottom of the stairs and called up to the second floor. "Abby?" His voice sounded strange in the house. It didn't echo the way it should have but was absorbed into the walls. "Abby? Call out and tell me where you are."

Clare's eyes darted from the woods to the clearing, then into the kitchen, to where she knew the open basement door waited. To look in one direction, she couldn't see the other. She pushed herself against the rough doorframe, feeling the jagged wood poking through her thin shirt.

Mitchell came back downstairs. "She's not up there. She has to be outside. Fucking hell, how big are these woods?" He walked across the kitchen. "Stay here. I'm going to circle the house."

Keeping her body against the wall, she turned inward to face the basement door, but she couldn't see it from here. She needed to know for sure if it was open. Just one quick peek. She began to walk across the kitchen.

"Help me." The voice was so small, almost inaudible, but there was no mistaking where or whom it was coming from.

Abby was in the basement.

"Mitchell." Clare tried to yell his name, but her tongue was thick and stuck in her mouth. She ran back to the outside door. "Mitchell!" Louder this time, but there was no response from him. He could be on the far side of the house, or in the woods—

"Help me."

Clare couldn't wait for him. She had to go into the basement herself.

She took a gulp of the outside air and ran, stumbling across the kitchen, beelining for the basement doorway. The smell was stronger, and the air coming up was thick with mold. She stepped onto the first stair. Instinctively her hands swung to the sides, looking for a banister or wall, but there was only open air. It was so absolutely dark that she couldn't see the steps below her. She forced herself down another step; it felt like stepping off a cliff into oblivion. She half sat, half fell onto her butt. At least this way, more of her body was in contact with the stairs, but if something came up those stairs at her, she wouldn't be able to move quickly enough.

Stop it. She slid down another step and another.

"Where are you?" Clare said into the darkness. "Turn on the flashlight."

"I can't. It'll see." Abby's voice was so small in the darkness.

It?

Then she heard Mitchell come into the house again. "Mitchell!" She tried to yell but couldn't get enough air. "Mitchell, down here!"

"Clare?" He was nearby. "Clare! Where are you?"

She crawled back up a few stairs, using her hands to guide her. "Down here. She's down here."

And then his silhouette was in the doorway above. "Fucking hell," he said, coughing at the stench. "Where's the light? Abby, are you down there?"

"She won't turn the light on."

Abby made a sound that was like a whimper.

"Abs," Mitchell called out. "We can only get you out if you turn on the light."

Abby whimpered, then there was a click below and the weak beam of the flashlight came on and hit the right of the stairs. It was only bright enough to light the small space around it, but it was enough. Clare's eyes traced the silhouette of Abby near the wall, her skinny legs pulled into her chest.

"Go, go." Mitchell was right behind her now. "That thing's going to die any second."

Pushed from behind, Clare moved quickly down the last of the stairs. As soon as her feet hit the ground, she felt the damp of the earth floor through the thin soles of her tennis shoes.

"Clare, you grab the light. I need both hands for her."

She crawled toward Abby and reached out for the flashlight lying on the floor, and that was when she saw the doll. It was sitting in front of Abby. She crouched down and picked it up. It felt like a tight bundle of cloth. She held it farther into the beam of light and gasped. The face—it was the face she had seen earlier that day. Eyes painted wide open, a mouth like an O. The cloth was smudged with dirt and the features were faint, but she could still make them out. Its hair was made out of yarn and pulled into a braid, and it was dressed in a long skirt and apron with some kind of ribbon around its middle. But this couldn't have been a sign from her mother. Her mother would never leave her anything as hideous as this. It was a trick—a trick to get her down here.

"What are you doing?" Mitchell said from somewhere behind her. "I said, get the light."

He was moving toward the stairs with Abby in his arms. Clare dropped the doll and grabbed the flashlight, swinging it around, trying to find him.

"Shine it on the stairs, for fuck's sake."

How could he move so fast down here? She was pulling air in, trying to breathe. Her limbs felt like they were made of wet clay.

Help me.

She froze.

Don't leave me.

Who are you?

She didn't say it; she thought it, just like she knew the words she was hearing were not being spoken out loud. Whatever was down here was speaking directly into her head. She swung the light around to find the doll again, but it was gone. Was that where the sound was coming from? Impossible.

Mitchell was partway up the stairs. There was enough light coming from the kitchen to guide him. He was going to reach the top and the door would close and she would be stuck with whatever was down here and she deserved it. She was the one who'd put Abby in here.

"Hurry." Mitchell was at the top of the stairs. Abby was collapsed in his arms.

Clare dropped the flashlight and, using both hands, clawed her way to the top of the stairs and out into the kitchen. And then they were running, through the kitchen, out of the house, and across the clearing to the car.

Mitchell set Abby down in the backseat, but as soon as she was in the car, she began tearing at her clothes. "Get them off me. Get them off."

"What are you doing?" Mitchell yelled at her. But Abby was frantic. She was trying to pull the T-shirt off her body, but it was like she didn't know how.

"Help me," she screamed. "Get it off me. I don't want it touching me."

Clare pushed past Mitchell and got into the back. "Here," she said to Abby, and grabbed the bottom of her T-shirt and yanked it over her head. She dropped it on the floor of the car.

"No, no, no," Abby said, pointing to it. "Get it out of here." Clare picked up the shirt and threw it out of the car. "Don't touch it. Don't get it on your hands."

"It's okay, there's nothing—"

"Blood. There's blood."

"What the fuck—"

"It doesn't matter," Clare said. "Just get us out of here."

Abby's body shook violently with the cold. Mitchell ran to the trunk, got out a blanket, and threw it in to them. Clare pulled Abby down to lie on her lap and wrapped the blanket around her as tightly as she could, but Abby didn't respond to any of it, she just stared straight ahead as they drove away.

They bumped over the branches and rocks on the old road, but Mitchell kept going, his hands gripping the wheel as he leaned forward, trying to see what lay ahead. When they got to the fence, he jumped out, unhooked it, and pulled the wire open as wide as he could. Once free, he got back in and slammed his foot on the gas. The car tires spun in the dry earth for a moment, then lurched forward, leaving the gaping hole in the fence behind them.

Mitchell drove quickly. His eyes would flick up to the rearview mirror, but Clare kept her focus on Abby. She was squeezing her hand, but Abby wasn't responding. With her other hand, she smoothed Abby's forehead and whispered, "Shh, shh, it's okay. You're going to be okay."

Abby's breathing was shallow and quick, and she was staring at something far away that Clare could not see. At one point, Clare looked up and caught Mitchell's eyes in the mirror, but they both broke away as soon as each saw the other. Just before they got on the interstate, he pulled over, opened the door, vomited, wiped his mouth, and kept driving without saying anything.

It was almost two in the morning when they reached the Sisters of Mercy Hospital. Mitchell pulled the car up to the emergency entrance, lifted Abby out, and rushed her inside without looking back. Clare stayed in the car. She watched the doors swish shut behind him. She would wait here until someone told her what to do next.

18

I press my forehead against the cool window and look out at the parking
lot far below. I try to imagine the three of us, frantic and freaked out,
pulling into this same lot. The hospital has been taken over by a large con-
glomerate and renovated since then. Now, if I were to go into the lobby,
there would be pale blue faux-leather chairs; large tropical plants tucked
into the corners; and tasteful watercolor prints framed on the walls. But
for all the design, would the feeling of the place be any different?

That long-ago night, the main thing I remember about the waiting
room was that it was empty. That I was in it says that at some point
Mitchell came back out and parked the car, and I went inside with him.
What we talked about, if we said anything, is lost to time. There was a
silent TV up in one corner, hanging too high to change the channel. The
vinyl chairs were cold under my bare legs, so I sat perched on the edge.
Mitchell didn't stay in the waiting room with me. I saw him at the phone
booth down the hall, then he went outside and paced in the parking lot.
There was a vending machine, and I desperately wanted something to
take the horrible taste of beer and adrenaline out of my mouth, but I
didn't have any money and didn't want to ask him.

Mr. and Mrs. Lindsay arrived a little later. Mrs. Lindsay was crying,
and I kept hearing her say to the doctor who came out, "But I don't
understand, what happened?" I'd chosen a seat that was tucked around
a corner, where I figured it would be hardest to see me. Mitchell stayed

outside. I couldn't hear what the doctor said, but then they followed her down the hall and went into a room where Abby must have been. A few moments later, Mr. Lindsay came out and went outside to Mitchell. I heard him yelling: "First Paul comes home beat up and drunk, and now this."

"I'm sorry. I didn't know she—" Mitchell's arms were wrapped around him, and he was staring at the ground.

"What the hell was going on tonight?"

Mitchell said something else, too quiet to hear.

"She's thirteen! What was she even doing there?"

This time the response was louder. "Paul's the one who took her. I was bringing her home."

"If you were bringing her home, she'd have been there hours ago. Not catatonic in the emergency room."

Mitchell put his head down again and said something I couldn't hear.

"That's not good enough, Mitch."

Mrs. Lindsay came out of the room where Abby was. She went outside and the yelling stopped, then she came in and saw me. "Clare? Oh my goodness, honey, you're here too?" She hugged me. I hadn't realized how cold I'd felt until she held me. "Look at you," she said. "You're all covered in dirt." She took off her jacket and put it over me.

"Is Abby okay?"

"She's sleeping now. The doctor said she's had quite a scare. Can you tell me what happened?"

I tried to tell her about the party and how I came out of the woods and Mitchell and Paul were fighting and how we wanted Abby to sleep it off, but as soon as she'd hugged me, it was like something very tight that I'd been holding on to suddenly let go. I started crying. I knew I wasn't making sense; my nose was running and I was gasping for breath. I didn't know what Mitchell had told them. Had he talked about the Octagon House? How we'd gone inside and left Abby? How we'd left her a note?

"Clare." Mrs. Lindsay grabbed both of my arms and held them firmly. "Did something happen to Abby at this party?"

"No!" I said. "I mean, she smoked some pot, but—"

"You have to tell me. Do you understand?"

I nodded mutely.

She narrowed her eyes. "Mitchell said something about an abandoned house?"

"I know we should have brought her right back. We didn't want her to get in trouble—"

"But what were you doing there?"

"Just looking around."

"Why would Mitchell take you girls to a place like that? With Abby in that state?"

"No, she was asleep in the car. We just went in for a few minutes. Just Mitchell and me."

"But why?"

I had no answer for her. No answer that would make sense now.

"Then how did Abby get into the basement?" Mrs. Lindsay asked.

"I don't know. We were upstairs. We didn't hear her come in—"

"But she's afraid of the dark." Mrs. Lindsay was trying not to cry. I had only ever seen adults cry once, at my mother's funeral, and the response in my gut was immediate. No matter what, I couldn't let Mrs. Lindsay cry. I had to stop this.

"Ever since she was a little girl," she continued. "She's always had to have a night-light unless you were with her. But you weren't—"

"I'm sorry—"

"It doesn't make sense. None of it makes any sense."

"Mitchell heard a sound," I said. I couldn't make sense of it for her; all I could do was keep telling her what little I knew so she'd stop asking me why. "We thought it was a raccoon or something. We looked all around and couldn't find anything, and then we went to the car and she was gone. And we came back to the house, and that's when we checked the basement."

"What's in the basement?"

"Nothing. I don't know."

"You didn't go down there?"

"I did, but it's dark. There's nothing there. It's empty."

"But she must have thought you were down there."

"No, I wouldn't—" The events of the afternoon rose to the front of my mind. Me, saying I saw something. Me, telling her to go first. Me, closing the door.

"But why, Clare?"

I didn't know what to say. She got up and went outside. After a few minutes she returned, followed by Mr. Lindsay and Mitchell. She said, "Ted will drive you home. Your father must be worried sick."

"I told him I was sleeping over at Lori's."

As soon as I said it, her face changed. I don't think she'd realized until then that this whole night had started in her house. Abby had told her the same lie. She'd had us all there at the start of it, we had all been in on it, and look what had happened. Lying to my father was one thing. You expect to lie to your own parents, but lying to another parent seemed far worse.

"Is Abby going to be okay?" I asked.

Mrs. Lindsay didn't answer. Instead she turned around and walked away. Her husband put his hand on my shoulder.

"She's going to stay here overnight. We'll bring her home tomorrow if the doctors decide that she's ready. Before we go, though, my son has something to say to you."

Under the fluorescent lights of the hospital, Mitchell looked much younger than I'd ever seen him. There was still a little dried blood by his nose, and his eyes were puffy and red. His clothes were covered with dirt, as were mine. He came closer and looked down at me hunched in the waiting room chair. I felt so small and dirty. My face was probably splotched pink because I'd been crying, and my nose was running.

"Hey, Clare."

"Hey."

"I'm sorry."

Sorry for what? For having kissed me? For talking to me? For being nice to me?

"I shouldn't have taken you to that house," Mitchell said.

"But—"

"So, sorry for that." He was looking straight at me. Had he told his parents that it was his idea to go inside? Whatever he'd said, I didn't think he wanted me to say any more with his dad standing there, so I just nodded. He stuffed his hands in his pockets, turned, and walked away.

That was the last I saw of him for a long, long time.

My dad was waiting for me in the driveway. Mr. Lindsay left the car and they exchanged a few words before turning to me. I got out and walked toward the house, barely acknowledging the shoulder squeeze as Mr. Lindsay passed. What I needed was my dad. I needed him to demand that I tell him, to yell at me and make me explain myself. Or else I wanted him to hug me and to feel how strong he was, how much bigger than me he still was. Most of all, I wanted him to forgive me, but that would happen only if I could tell him.

None of that happened. That was the way it always was for us. There would be no confrontation, no raised voices, no words. And because of that, there would be no ending, just a gnawing—a humming, this constant worry that someday I'd come home and my father would be gone just like my mother was. Or I would be. I'd look in the mirror and there would be no one there. I'd fall into the hollow inside myself and never come out.

Maybe I was the one who started it. When I decided not to cause any ripple in the surface of my damaged family—when I went quietly into my room and closed the door and bit down on my pillow—maybe I was starting something that would continue throughout my life. Maybe I was to blame. I don't know.

What I do know is that at the beginning of that night, I was still a child, and by the end I was something else. Not an adult—it wasn't like in some movie—but I would never be able to go back to the ease of playing a board game in the basement with my best friend. Or to keeping everything else safely in fantasies and dreams.

As much as I wanted to fall asleep, I couldn't, so I did end up seeing the sunrise, just not the way I'd planned. I was filthy. The campfire's smoke was in my hair, I was covered with dirt from the woods and the house, and the cuts on my knees and hands needed cleaning again, but I couldn't get out of bed and take a shower. Partly because I didn't want to move, but also because those smells and that dirt were the only tangible evidence that the night had even happened.

———

A nurse enters Abby's room and we both jump. She's young, probably just out of nursing school. Maybe that's why she gets the night shift. A hot-pink scarf is wrapped around her head; even in the dim light of the room, its color pops against the muted tones around her. "Sorry," she says. "I didn't realize there was still someone in here with her."

"Her parents asked me to stay. They thought someone should be with her at all times, you know, just in case."

She doesn't say anything, just nods slightly and moves around Abby, checking numbers on the machines, running her fingers over the lines that are running in and out of Abby's body. It is comforting, watching her movements: light but deft.

She picks up one of Abby's hands and looks at me questioningly.

"I think . . ." I start to say. "She was trapped. She was trying to get out."

The nurse's other hand goes up to her mouth, and her eyes grow wide. "Trapped?"

"Yes. In an old basement."

She looks at Abby and strokes her forehead. "Poor thing. I had no idea." She turns to me. "They just moved me up to this floor today. I didn't know." She gently prods the bandages again. "Tomorrow morning, we'll get these off and make sure her fingers are healing under there." She makes a soft clicking sound with her tongue and lays Abby's hand carefully on the bed.

On her way out, she turns back to me. "Do you need anything? A blanket or a pillow?"

I shake my head and she leaves. I don't want to get comfortable. I need to stay awake. To remember.

———

In the days after that terrible night, Monica and Lori left messages and even stopped by the house, but my father told them I was sleeping, and after a couple of attempts they gave up. I knew I was making myself an outcast for my freshman year of high school, but that no longer seemed so bad. It would be a relief compared to negotiating the politics of our supposed friendship. Even after my road rash healed, I left my bike in the garage and stayed home. I read and watched reruns on television and waited for the summer to be over.

I saw Abby two more times. Her mother called me about a week after she got home from the hospital and asked if I would like to see her. She was on an antianxiety medication that they would soon realize was too strong, so she was dozy and out of it. We watched a movie and she fell asleep fifteen minutes in. I wanted to leave but didn't dare, so I waited for the movie to finish and moved only when Mrs. Lindsay finally came down and quietly told me that I should go home.

Before I left, I went up to Abby's bedroom. If anyone had asked what I was doing, I could have said I was looking for something I'd left behind, but no one would ask because it was as normal for me to be in that room as it was for Abby. Or it had been. The summer before, we had entertained ourselves one rainy afternoon by writing our names on the inside wall of her closet with leftover paint from a home improvement project. I didn't have paint this time, but I grabbed a marker from her desk and opened her closet, which was in its usual state of chaos, with clothes falling off hangers and lying in piles on the floor. I pushed the clothes aside and drew a large triangle—points meeting—on the wall, right at eye level: *I am here.*

I was so sure she would see it and that it would be able to cut through whatever was in her head. I had no idea what had been started that night. None of us did.

As the days passed, I began to question if what I remembered had happened. Did I actually fool around with Mitchell? Did I really think my mother had left me a sign in that house, or that the basement door had opened and closed on its own? The more I thought about it, the more impossible it all seemed, except . . . why had Abby gone down to the basement?

As much as I tried to believe she had gone down there of her own free will, I knew something had begun when I had followed that horrible impulse and closed the door on her.

A week before school started, Abby called me. At first I thought she'd finally seen what I'd put in her closet, but it soon became obvious that her mother had put her up to it. We went for a walk, both on the lookout for anyone from our school who might have heard what happened. Without meaning to, we ended up at our old meeting place at the corner of her road and mine, halfway between our two houses. We had never told Lori and Monica about it, unintentionally intentionally. A place for just the two of us. We lay down in the grass and stared up at the sky, and I wanted desperately to say that I was sorry. But sorry for what? Sorry for leaving her in the car to go into the Octagon House with Mitchell. Sorry for the thoughts that had come into my head that night and so many times before, when I told myself I didn't need her to make myself feel stronger. Sorry for liking Mitchell so much and wanting him to like me more than anybody else, including her. Sorry for telling her to go into the basement and closing the door on her. As much as I tried to convince myself it was an accident, I knew I had done it, I had proved myself capable of cruelty. Of all the horrible things that had happened that summer, that was the worst. Sorry for a hundred things I couldn't say because I was scared and confused and fourteen.

There were high-stacked cumulus clouds above us. I watched as a speck of an airplane flew into one, then appeared a moment later. In the end, what I said was, "You were so scared when we got you out of that basement the first time, why did you go back?"

"No, *you* were scared. You were the one who was crying." She didn't sound angry. She was talking in this slow singsong voice that I had never heard before. It must have been the drugs they had her on.

"I know, but . . ."

"I was scared at first," she said. "It was so dark I couldn't breathe. But then she talked to me."

"She?"

"She wanted me to be her friend."

"Why do you keep saying 'she'?"

"It was like she knew me. She has a secret. She was going to show me, but then you guys opened the door."

"Who are you talking about? Why didn't you tell me any of this?"

"Because," she said.

"Because why? I'm your best friend. I tell you everything."

As soon as I said it, I braced myself for her response, but she just kept looking at the sky; and then in the same spaced-out way, she said, "I wasn't sure that first time, if it was real. But then after the party, I woke up in the car and we were at that house again. I thought I was dreaming at first."

"Mitchell didn't know what to do with you, and we got to talking about it, and he wanted to see it—"

"You and my brother went into the house and you left me alone in the car."

"We just went to look around. It was only for a couple minutes."

"I wanted to sleep, but then I heard her calling me, so I went too."

"We got back to the car and you were gone and we freaked out. We looked everywhere for you." I was sitting up now, ripping up fistfuls of grass.

"She needs help."

"There's no 'she.'" I was getting frustrated. She didn't sound like any version of Abby I had ever heard; she didn't sound like little Abby, like follower Abby. She was medicated, yes, but it wasn't just that. She sounded so terrifyingly sure, like everything she was saying was a fact. It didn't matter whether I believed it or not.

"She was going to show me her secret, but then there was someone else. Or something. She was so scared. That's when I called out to you—"

"There was nobody down there besides you."

"Oh, Clare, you were standing right next to her."

That feeling of not being able to move. Of the coldness seeping into my body through the floor.

"She's still in there," Abby said. "She's trapped. We have to help her. We have to go back—"

"Stop it!" I grabbed her shoulders and shook her hard. She looked at me, but I wasn't sure she saw me. "Are you talking about the doll? That's what I saw before, okay? It was just a stupid doll."

"That was her doll."

"Who? You're not making any sense." Abby just looked at me like I was the child, like I was the crazy one. "You can't answer because there is no *her*. It was just a fucked-up creepy place."

"She spoke to you too."

"No one spoke to me except you."

"She wants you to help her."

"No, no, no."

"Why won't you believe me, Clare?"

Because. Ghosts are trapped. If they exist, then it means my mother could be a ghost, which would mean my mother is trapped and there's nothing I can do about it. Ghosts cannot exist. This belief was forged through childhood grief—built in the nights and weeks and months after my mother died. Building it was how I was finally able to sleep without nightmares. It was how I was able to return to school, and play, and laugh, and grow up. A belief built that way is rock solid. It has to be, because everything depends on it.

"Because there's nothing down there," I said. "Pot makes you hallucinate. You were scared and you were high and you saw that doll and thought it was talking to you but it wasn't real. None of that was real."

"You think it's all in my head?" She was angry. I had cut through the fog, and now she looked like she wanted to hit me. "You sound like the doctors." She practically spat when she said it.

I looked her in the eye and held my face as emotionless as I could. "There is nothing down there. Ghosts don't exist. It's all in your head."

Then she stood up and walked away without looking back.

I jumped up to follow her, but she didn't stop, and we walked in silence. When we got to the end of her driveway, she said, "My mom said I should tell you we're moving back to Buffalo. I'm going to a special school. We're leaving tomorrow."

"Buffalo?" That was all I could think to say.

"Yeah. It's a school for crazy people. My parents think I'm crazy too."

"I didn't say that—"

She turned around and walked toward her house.

"I'll call you," I said, or maybe I said I'd write to her. Or maybe I didn't say anything.

A part of me refused to believe that the Lindsays would actually move away. As ridiculous as it was, I felt like they'd left me behind and soon they'd realize and come back and get me. A few days later, I walked to their house and watched the movers pull everything out onto the lawn and pack the giant truck. It didn't look like the table I'd eaten at, the couch I'd sat on. Separated from that family, it was just stuff. I watched until they locked the door and drove away.

I thought about that sign I'd drawn in Abby's closet. She had never acknowledged it, but I knew she must have seen it.

I am here. Now it had another meaning:

I am waiting.

Our friendship had been effortless. It was everything and then it was gone and the silence it left behind was like white noise: empty, but blocking all the other sounds out.

19

Deep memories. Like being able to see to the bottom of a lake if the water becomes still enough. I look at Abby lying motionless in the hospital bed. As a child, she was never still. Always fidgeting, jiggling her leg, or playing with a pencil or hair band or whatever was at hand. Even in her sleep she would kick and turn, sending blankets and stuffed animals flying. It was part of what made her seem so young.

Her hand is limp in mine. I straighten my spine and stretch my neck. Abby's stillness helps me remember. There are the familiar memories—the argument we had the last time we saw each other, watching the movers empty their house—but other memories are new. Abby talked about a "she" in the basement. And she said there was someone else too. Someone, or something, that scared her. Scared her so deeply, she's back in this hospital. All these years later, here we are again.

I squeeze her hand, hard. "Abby." My mouth is dry and my tongue is clumsy. I swallow and try again. "Abby, I remember what you said now. What did you see in that basement?"

She doesn't respond. *Of course she doesn't respond, you idiot.* But she's listening. Maybe I'm delusional to believe it, but I know she's listening. Her breathing has changed; it's getting faster. Her heart rate too. Machines can't lie.

I lean in and put my mouth right next to her ear. "Abby, it's Clare. I remember what you told me. I need to know, what did you see in that basement? Is that why you went down there again?"

And then I feel it: the slightest movement of her fingers, a twitch.

"Abby? Abby, can you hear me?"

Her fingers twitch again, a tiny but undeniable spark of energy, of life. I look at her closed eyes, her mouth, anything to tell me something is about to happen, but there's nothing.

"What am I supposed to do? I came back. I got your emails. I got your note, but you're not telling me enough. How am I supposed to help you if you don't tell me how?" My voice has risen without my meaning it to. "You have to tell me how to help you. You have to tell me."

The change is instantaneous. One moment she is limp; the next, her entire body is rigid with electricity. Her fingers jerk harder this time, and then her hand slips out of mine and begins to twitch. Her hands spasm into claws and she tears at the blanket in spastic movements. Her back arches and her face contorts into a grimace as the muscles and tendons in her neck tighten.

"Abby? Abby!"

The machines in the room are squawking out high-pitched beeps.

"Open your eyes. Open your *eyes*." I don't even realize I'm yelling until I hear myself. I fumble around looking for the call button, but even before I've found it, the bell's ringing at the nurses' station at the far end of the hall.

Then Abby's eyes open.

Her pupils are huge and black, and her mouth opens into a scream, but no sound comes out. It opens and closes, opens and closes, like she's being puppeted by someone else, and then—

She's looking at me. Her eyes are still huge, but she is looking right at me.

A harsh gasping sound escapes from her dry throat. She's moving her mouth—*she's* moving it now, and it's not a spasm, it's her.

"What is it?" I grab her shoulders and squeeze hard while her body shakes and spasms under me. "What is it?"

Strong hands grab me from behind and pull me away from her. A team of nurses closes around her. They call out instructions as the machines grow louder and louder. Abby's body flails, held in the grip of something so much more powerful than she is.

They've pulled her blankets off, and between their bodies I see her, an apology of grayish-white skin, hip bones sticking up. Her father is in the room now, crying out, trying to push his way to his daughter. "What's happening to her? Someone has to tell me what's happening to her."

The nurse with the pink scarf takes me by the elbow and leads me out. "You have to go now," she says.

"But—"

The door closes in my face. Over the intercom, someone rattles off a code, and more people appear from nowhere and move quickly toward Abby's room. I stand and watch the closed door, trying to understand what just happened. She saw me. I know she saw me. There was recognition. She knows I'm here, so now what?

I can't go home until I know what's going on, so I end up in the lobby on the first floor. Despite the new color scheme and the art, the little alcove hidden from the main entrance is still there; without even thinking, I go there to wait. When I look at the chair in the corner, I see myself at fourteen, dirty, freezing cold, and in shock. Waiting to find out what's next.

———

Fifteen minutes later, I hear Mrs. Lindsay's voice. She's talking to someone and moving quickly. I get up stiffly and peek around the corner. Trailing her is Mitchell. She turns and says something to him, then gets in the elevator and the doors close. Mitchell stands there for a moment, rubs his eyes, and walks into the waiting room. He takes a seat in the main area. I stay hidden where I am. He sits with his elbows on his knees, head in his hands. He's wearing a tattered sweatshirt and track pants under his long gray coat. His face is rough with stubble. Twenty minutes ago, he was probably sound asleep when his father called and his mother dragged him out of bed to drive her here. She's going to be back down soon, then either she'll stay down here or he'll go up to Abby's room. Either way, I'll have missed my chance. I take a breath and step out from the alcove. "Mitchell?"

His head jerks up. He stares at me for a moment and smiles, but it fades. "Clare."

"I'm sorry to startle you."

"No, it's— I'm glad you're here." He sounds genuine.

"I figured I should stay until I knew what was going on," I say. "I was with her when it happened."

"I know," he says. "My dad told us. Are you staying over there?" He smiles tentatively. "I've spent a lot of time in this place lately, and all the chairs seem the same to me, but if you've found a more comfortable one . . ."

I feel my face turn pink. I'm acting weird again. "I didn't know if you wanted to be alone. And after last time . . ."

"Actually, I don't want to be alone right now. I mean, it's three in the morning, so I'm sure you want to go to bed, but if you're going to be staying, I'd love the company."

We go outside. It's cold enough that I can see my breath, but the cool air is waking me up. After hours in the hospital, I need the fresh air to clear my head. We find a bench close to the entrance. The lights of the hospital are behind us and our faces are in shadow. It's easier to talk here instead of under the waiting room's unforgiving fluorescents.

"I'm really sorry about yesterday," I say once we're settled. "Or the day before—I've lost track of time."

"It's fine," he says. His voice is low and warm. The bench is small enough that there's only a few inches between us. I want to touch him, to feel the solidity of his presence, but I can't and I won't. He continues, "I meant what I said about it being good that you came back. It means a lot to my parents."

"Yeah, but—"

"Clare." He turns to look at me. There are smile lines around his eyes. His hair has receded a little, and I know from seeing him before that it's graying around the temples, but the exhaustion hanging over him is on a body that is strong and lean. The years have changed him from a charismatic boy to a man who makes you want to draw closer. "Whatever happened tonight," he says, "it had nothing to do with you."

"I don't know—" My voice breaks before I even realize that I'm going to cry. "Shit." I clench my teeth to make myself stop. He waits. He doesn't put his hand on my back or hold my hand or anything, but he's there. "Sorry," I say again. "I'm okay."

"Can you tell me what happened?"

I try to describe what I saw, but it was all so fast. It's hard to know. "I was talking to her," I say. "And she could hear me."

"The doctors say that she probably can."

"But what if what I said—"

"My parents have been talking her ears off ever since the doctors said they were going to start to bring her out of the coma. They also said there could be setbacks."

We let that sit in the air before us, neither of us willing to say what it could mean.

After another moment, I ask, "How are you?"

He shrugs. "The past couple of weeks have been hell. I'm glad I'm here. I'm going to have to go overseas again soon."

"Oh." The disappointment hits like a stone in my gut. I close my eyes and reflexively hunch into myself. I think of that picture taped to Abby's bed: Mitchell and some beautiful woman, an exotic beach, the way they're looking at each other in the picture.

"Are you cold?" he asks. "We can go back inside."

"No," I say. "I'm fine."

He takes his phone out and checks it. "My mom's going to text when she knows what's going on," he says, slipping it in his coat pocket. "I've been having this recurring nightmare," he goes on. "I'm in the basement of that house and Abby is curled up on the floor—like she was when we found her—but then she gets up and walks away from me, and she just keeps walking. She's always just at the edge of my flashlight light. She gets to the wall and she just moves through it, like it's no big deal, and I follow her. I try to count how many rooms we pass through so I can find our way out, and then suddenly she's gone and I am trapped."

I realize he's stopped talking and is looking at me. "Are you okay?" he asks.

"I've had the same dream," I say.

"About Abby in the basement?" he says. "I guess that's not surprising. It's not something you forget."

"No, not just that. The rooms. Following her, and getting trapped. I started having it last spring, when Abby sent me these emails out of nowhere." I describe my dream as best as I can, but I don't tell him about the miscarriage, or about Josh, or how the dream changed in the end. "When did they start for you?"

"Last week. When she disappeared. I had it each night until we found her. And again tonight. Right before Mom woke me up to tell me what happened."

"Do you think. . . ? It's probably just coincidence."

I'm expecting him to agree with me because that's the easier answer. Just like it's easier to believe she went into the basement with the intention of swallowing that bottle of pills, like Lori is telling herself. But he doesn't say that.

He's quiet for a moment, then he says, "I'm the one who found her." I turn to him, but he's staring out at the parking lot. "I've been coming home more, the past six months. Well, I guess you knew that." I feel my face turn pink again, but it's dark and he's looking straight ahead. "So, I was home when Abby disappeared. And I had that dream. Scared the shit out of me. My dad was frantic, but I kept trying to convince myself that she'd call with the usual bullshit excuse. But then another day passed, and she didn't call, and I had the dream again. On the third day, I drove out here. I didn't tell Mom and Dad because I figured it was such a long shot. I phoned the police on the way. Someone had called in the car sitting on the side of the road, and they'd been out to look a few hours before but hadn't seen anything. Just gave it a warning tag. They were state troopers—not from around here. I told them about the house. I wasn't sure if it would still be standing, but they agreed to come back out. She'd been in there three days, and that whole time I was ignoring what I knew."

"But you didn't actually know," I say. "They're just dreams."

But they're so much more than just dreams. Look what happened to me. I think about what happened upstairs: Abby's open eyes looking at me—just for a second but *seeing me*—desperately trying to tell me something.

Mitchell looks at me like he's about to say something, then he gets up and walks toward the parking lot. I have to fight every urge in me not to jump up and go to him, to throw my arms around him. After a minute, he turns back around but stays where he is. "You should go home, Clare. You should get away from here."

I don't know if he's sending me home because he feels sorry for me or because he doesn't want me around. Either option hurts.

His phone buzzes, and he pulls it out and looks at it. "I can go up," he says. He's about to say something but then thinks better of it. Instead, he walks toward me. "Get some rest. We'll call you tomorrow and let you know how she is." He puts his hand on my shoulder, and instinctively I reach up and put mine on his. Just touching him feels like relief. This is what my body has been starving for. Then his phone buzzes again and he pulls his hand away, brings his coat around him, and goes into the hospital.

I sit on the bench for a long time. The stars overhead are endless. Somewhere in the hospital behind me, Abby is floating between darkness and light. Behind the hospital, the ancient mountains of the Adirondacks rise up, indifferent to all of us who live in their shadows.

———

When Abby told me that her family was leaving Sumner's Mills, I assumed it was to get her away from any reminders of what had happened, but there was another reason. Late one night, about a week after she was released from the hospital, Abby slipped out of the house and started biking to the Octagon House. Mitchell got home around midnight and found the side door open. At first he thought it was from Paul coming home late and not closing it properly, but an instinct told him to check on his sister. Her room was empty. He woke his parents, who called the police and began to search for her. That was when Mitchell went into the garage and saw her bike was missing.

He got back into the car and drove through town and out onto Route 31. She was almost at the break in the fence when he found her. "It was like she was in a trance," he said. "Her feet were bare, and she was just wearing light pajamas and it was cool that night, but she didn't seem to notice the cold. She was moving really slowly, thank God. Otherwise, I might not have caught up to her in time." When they got home, the police were at the house. "After that, my father put a lock on the outside of her bedroom door and started checking on it throughout the night. A few days later, my parents told me they were moving back to Buffalo."

I learned all of this at a hotel bar in Indianapolis three months ago when my past almost literally walked into me in the place I least expected it. Mitchell was there for a conference; I was there for a wedding. Josh had flown home to Chicago that morning because of work, but I'd wanted the change of scenery and, having nothing to return to, had opted for a later flight. What neither of us said was that we also needed some space from each other.

The moment Mitchell and I saw each other and he asked if I wanted to get a drink, my crush, which had been dormant for so many years, roared to life. Neither of us knew that three months later, we'd be back in Sumner's Mills with Abby comatose in the hospital.

I told him about teaching in Chicago; he was working for an engineering company overseas; each of us was selective about which details we shared. We moved further into the past, talking about college, places we'd lived, and eventually why his family had left Sumner's Mills so abruptly all those years ago. I wanted to know what was going on with Abby now but didn't want to tell him about the emails she'd sent in the spring.

"Do you see her much?" I asked. "Where's she living?"

"She's at home—Buffalo. Sometimes with our parents, sometimes on her own. Kind of depends on where she's at mentally. She has trouble holding down a job, so she's usually broke. To be honest, I don't think she has any interest in seeing me."

"I doubt that," I said.

"No, she's changed a lot," he said. "Like, a lot. My folks were always so worried about Paul, but he's fine. Abby's the one they obsess over now."

"Obsess?"

"Well, my dad. He's a worrier. My mom too, just in different ways. I mean, in this case, they're right to worry."

"Why? What's going on?"

"Well, earlier this week, right? She takes off and is gone for hours and doesn't answer her phone. She got home at like two o'clock in the morning and then couldn't understand why my parents were so pissed."

"Yeah, but she's an adult. Does she have to report in?"

"My sister does not behave like an adult. There's a lot going on . . ." He trailed off and took a sip of his beer. "I guess I deserve it, though, right? I mean, she and I never talked about what happened at that house, but I know that's part of it."

"It wasn't your fault," I said.

"Yeah, it was."

"I shouldn't have left her. I was her best friend."

"But I was the responsible older brother. Supposedly." We were several rounds in and he'd taken off his suit jacket and tie. His body still had the easy grace that I remembered from when he was a teenager. He pulled off a strip of the beer label and smiled at me. His smile was still the same. "I was distracted."

I had pined after him for most of high school, even though he was gone. I assumed it was because he was my first full-blown crush. My first kiss. That left some kind of an imprint on a person. As I sat across from him, it felt surreal to have those old feelings awakened. I thought maybe it was the beer and the stress of the past few months. A teenage crush felt so simple compared to the painful mess my relationship with Josh had become.

"I was distracted too, I guess," I finally said. "And I couldn't believe I was going to go back into that fucking house, *again*. All to impress you."

"What? I was trying to impress you," he said. "I kept hoping you'd change your mind, but you were formidable."

I laughed. "I don't think 'formidable' is the word I'd use to describe myself at fourteen."

"Fourteen!" Two businessmen at the bar glanced over at us. "Fuck," he said quietly. "That's so young."

"Sixteen's not a lot older."

"I know. Paul's oldest is going to be fourteen soon. I still remember when he was born. And now I officially sound like an old man." He chugged the rest of his beer and smiled. "I'm a little drunk," he said.

"Me too." I was starting to think I was more than a little drunk.

"Are you tired?" he asked. "You have some early-morning meeting or something?"

"Nope." I had decided not to mention my unemployed status. "My flight's not until the afternoon."

He looked at me for a moment and cocked his head, then said, "So, what's in Chicago?"

"Nothing."

He raised his eyebrows. He wasn't wearing a wedding ring, something I had noticed almost immediately. I wondered if he'd noted the same about me.

"What about you?" I asked. "What's in . . . ?"

"Riyadh," he said. "It was London for a while, but it's Riyadh now. And nothing. Well, I mean, work, tall buildings, a lot of money. But . . . you know."

We were quiet for a moment, trying to figure out what the next move would be. Though I knew I couldn't drink any more, I didn't want this to be over. I excused myself to go to the bathroom, but as soon as I stood, the room spun. In the bathroom, I splashed cold water on my face. My cheeks were flushed and I could feel my pulse, like all of the blood in my body, being pushed through at a higher speed. Every part of me was alive in a way it hadn't been in months.

When I came out, Mitchell was coming out of the men's room. We looked at each other, and then he moved toward me and I don't know if I kissed him or he kissed me. We fell into the wall of the little hallway. He still smelled the same.

"I took care of the tab," he said. "Let's go up to your room." I nodded and took his hand to lead him to the elevator.

When we got to the door of my room, he grabbed my arm. "I saw an ice machine."

"You'll need a bucket," I called after him, but he was already moving down the hall.

I went into the room and raided the minibar, pouring whiskey into the flimsy plastic cups. I didn't want it and I didn't think he did either, but I had to do something. He knocked on the door holding a handful of rapidly dripping ice.

"I tried to tell you—"

"You did, yes." He came inside and leaned up against me, dropping the ice on the carpet. His hands were freezing and wet. He slid them under my shirt and rubbed them across my back and I felt the shock go through me.

I led him over to the window and opened the blinds. We were up on the eighteenth floor with the lights of the city sprawling out below us. Our hands moved over each other, pulling, undoing, sliding our clothes onto the floor. Naked, reflected in the glass of the window, I saw my body and watched his hands move over me, felt him pressing himself into me.

"Clare," he whispered. "Clare, Clare, Clare." And then he was inside me.

It was the first time I'd had sex since the miscarriage two months earlier. Josh and I had tried a few times, but I always ended up pulling away. It wasn't that it hurt. I knew the statistics on miscarriages; I knew women often went on to have healthy pregnancies. None of that mattered. My body had betrayed me. Maybe it had known, on a cellular level, that I didn't deserve to be a mother, so something in me had rejected that tiny bit of life. Josh wanted to try again. When I'd pull away, he would say he understood, we could wait, but what I couldn't tell him was that it was never going to be okay again. With Josh, my body felt like it was moving by rote, going through the motions in the hope that if I acted like everything was all right, maybe it would be.

With Mitchell, I didn't have to think. My body just responded. Neither of us said anything, but we clung to each other like two drowning people, touching every part of each other, eyes open and looking at the other. I knew I was cheating. There was never a second when I didn't know I was cheating, and it wasn't that I didn't care—I did—but for the first time in years, my body was alive. It wasn't just a teenage crush. I had loved Mitchell. Maybe it was misplaced, but it was real, and it had never gone away, and now I was feeling it again.

After, we dozed off in bed. A few hours later, I woke up and Mitchell was sitting on the edge of the bed, his head in his hands. I watched him for a moment, trying to tell from the shape of his back what was going on. I reached out from the warm cocoon of the duvet to pull him to me, but he moved away when I touched him.

"I have to go," he said.

"It's three. Stay."

"I think it's just easier."

I turned on my side, away from him, and looked out the window. What he meant was, it would be easier not to deal with this, with expectations, with the past. He dressed in silence, then came over and put his hand on my shoulder.

"Clare, can we talk about this?"

I closed my eyes.

"Things are complicated for me right now," he said.

His hand was warm. All I could focus on was that warmth and weight on my skin.

"I'm sorry," he said.

I couldn't open my eyes. If I saw him, I knew I would start crying and I might never stop, so I kept them closed, and after a moment he took his hand away and left.

=====

I went home and told Josh. I didn't know how he would react. After everything we had been through, after how patient and steadfast he'd been through all the terror of the spring, I knew I should feel wretched, but all I could feel was numb, like I was watching it all play out from far away. Maybe he was the same because he didn't cry or even get angry. He just sat quietly on the couch while I told him everything.

"We were drinking, but I knew what I was doing," I said. "I wish I could say that I didn't, but I did. I'm not going to lie about that."

He said, "Okay," and got up and left. He didn't stomp around or slam the door. He just left.

After, I sat on the couch for a long time. Long enough for it to get dark around me. I heard residents at our low-rise coming in from work, their noise echoing in the hall. Everything was different, I knew that. It was just one night, one drunk fuck, if I wanted to put it crudely, but it wasn't, and I would be lying if I pretended it was. Maybe it was that to Mitchell. He hadn't asked for my email or cell number and he hadn't offered his. It doesn't matter, I thought. *It doesn't matter it doesn't matter it doesn't matter.* Something had changed. Am I a naive fool to call it love? I don't know. I only know that something woke up in me that night with Mitchell; a part of me that had been asleep for over twenty years was finally awake. Hurting and longing but awake.

Josh came back much later that night. He told me not to get up because it wouldn't take long to say what he needed to say.

"It's not the cheating. Stuff happens, I know that. It almost happened to me once. I never told you that. Maybe I should have. It's the way you looked, Clare, when you told me who it was. I've never seen you look so . . . happy. It was different from anything I've ever seen, even when things were good between us. Am I right?"

I nodded.

"Do you love him?"

"I— I don't know. I haven't even thought about him in years. I didn't know I still felt this way."

"Are you going to see him again?"

I shook my head because I knew I wouldn't be able to say that out loud without breaking down.

"It doesn't change anything, does it?"

I shook my head again.

He went to the sink, got a glass of water, and stood there, his back to me, drinking it all, then he turned around. He was crying, but his voice was under control. "I need you to leave. Go to Jenna's or something. Just for the next few days."

"Okay," I said.

"I'll move out," he said.

"No, I should be the one—"

"No. Dan and Myra are coming over. They've still got a bunch of boxes from when they moved, and they've got a truck. I want to do it now."

"It's ten o'clock."

"Yeah. I called them on my way back."

"What did you tell them?"

"It doesn't matter, Clare. Just go, please."

I got up, grabbed the suitcase that was sitting by the door from where I'd dropped it, and left.

I saw Josh two days later, when I was at the apartment packing up my stuff. We'd both decided to leave and had been exchanging business-only texts about our comings and goings to avoid each other, but I'd lost track of time and was in the midst of sorting pots when I heard his key in the door. His coolness and calm from the first night were gone; he looked terrible. He had puffy bags under his eyes and his fingernails were bitten raw. I made us tea and we sat at the table, trying to talk about logistics—who would call the utilities companies, who would get the cat—when he started crying, and suddenly he was kneeling in front of me with his head in my lap. I stroked his head and looked down at him sobbing uncontrollably. Josh was such a good person. He was everything I wanted in a partner. A few months earlier, I'd thought we were going to be parents together, and I was so happy, wasn't I? And now I had severed everything.

I could end this now. That's all I could think. All I had to do was tell him I had been wrong, tell him I wanted to try again, and he'd do it and all that pain I was causing would stop, but I would not say those words. I could not. I knew I would probably never see Mitchell again, but it didn't matter. What had happened between us had been one shining moment, but I had to take from it what was being offered, which was a window into a truth: that's what love can feel like. Maybe someday I would find it with someone else, but I wouldn't be able to manufacture it with Josh, so I held him as he cried but I didn't say anything, and after a few moments, he got up and went to the bathroom to clean himself up and I made sure to be gone before he came out.

———

"Clare?" Mrs. Lindsay is shaking me awake. I had folded myself into a chair in the waiting room. It was too cold to sleep in my car and I didn't trust myself to drive home. Outside, the first traces of light are in the sky. "We thought you'd gone home. I just came to gather Abby's things."

"Is she okay?" I check my phone. Just past six o'clock. Around me, the hospital is starting to wake up.

"She's stabilized."

I struggle to sit up, but my entire body hurts. "It all started so fast. I didn't know what to do."

Mrs. Lindsay sinks into a chair across from me. She looks twenty years older than she did when she met me in the lobby, and I realize that her hair is completely gray.

"It was a seizure," she says. "We were told it might happen, but this one was severe."

Abby's thin body spasming on the bed, bandaged hands clawing at the air, her eyes like black holes.

"When they first got her in here, she started having them in the ER. The paramedics administered Narcan, but she wasn't coming out of the overdose, and then the seizures started. That's why they put her in the coma."

"I was trying to talk to her. I was just telling her I was here. If it was something I did—"

She shakes her head. "The doctor said there were probably a number of factors." She sighs. "They don't know. They don't want to say that, but that's the truth of it. All of this technology and there's still so much they just don't know."

"But is she going to be okay?"

"We don't know yet. Increased seizure activity isn't a good sign. They're concerned about brain stem involvement. They had to put in a breathing tube. The next forty-eight hours are crucial. They took her by air ambulance to Buffalo and they'll do more testing there. There's a neurological intensive care unit there that is able to handle it better than this little hospital can. It's where she should have been all along. We were afraid to move her before, but now there's no choice. Ted's gone with her. I'm leaving as soon as we're done here."

She starts to get up but then collapses back into the chair.

"Mrs. Lindsay?" I jump up and go to her, but she waves me off.

"Why Abby?" She speaks so quietly, I can barely hear her. "I don't understand. Why is this happening to her?"

"I don't know."

"What did I miss? I must have missed something, something that was probably right in front of me. If I'd just been paying closer attention, I could have stopped it . . ."

"I . . . I don't . . ."

"I don't mean what's happening now, I mean a long time ago. This must have started somewhere. I know mental illness is complicated, but even with all of that, there must have been a beginning. When she was a girl. And I didn't see it, but if I had, if I could have intercepted it, got her into therapy or onto medication sooner or something. Anything."

"Maybe there wasn't anything you could have done."

She looks at me sharply. "Then what kind of a mother am I? The one job, the *single most important job* a parent has, is to keep their child safe, and I failed. And now we might have to . . . to decide . . . if she doesn't wake up, if she can't ever swallow or, or *breathe* . . . Ted says life above all. Life at any cost. But that's not a life. Being kept alive by machines? The whole time the doctor was talking to us, all I could think was, what is a life? And what is just being alive?"

Behind us, someone wheels a trolley down the hall. Farther away, the intercom sounds, footsteps, voices, another emergency, another family.

"Mitchell's gathering her things upstairs. I told him I'd get the car." She stands up, absentmindedly fumbling in her purse for the keys.

"I'd like to come to Buffalo," I say. "If I can see her again. Is that okay?"

She nods, pats my arm, and then shuffles off toward the doors and the growing light of morning.

20

NATALIE

August 22, 1965

The shelf over the kitchen door was too high for the children to reach, which made it a perfect place to put the keepsakes from Natalie's childhood: a miniature rosebud tea set that her grandmother had brought from England; the crystal dog her sister, Evangeline, gave her on her eighteenth birthday—stolen, she suspected, from some friend's vanity, but she loved it and her sister, and that made it worth the insignificant crime—and a small vase that held the dried flowers she'd picked from her mother's garden on the dawn of her wedding day.

Every morning when she came into the big kitchen in their new house, she looked up at these items. The window over the sink was east-facing, and the sun would be streaming in. In the mornings, she could almost forget all the doubts of the night before; she could almost forget the inconveniences and "quirks," as her husband called them, of their new house. But at night, with lamps burning in every room to ward off the darkness, all of those doubts and the anger would return.

How in 1965 could they have bought a house without a phone? Or updated wiring? The man who had built it had done it himself with Depression-era technology, and half of the light switches didn't work, but rewiring the place was out of the question at this point. They had been assured that the telephone lines would be coming, but three months in and she was yet to see a sign of any crews out on the road. Yes, their apartment in the city had been too cramped for a family of four, and yes, the children now had fresh air and open space to play in, but the days were going to get shorter and colder, and she was the one stuck in this darkness night after night. And in that darkness, her thoughts were becoming wild. Unrecognizable.

And so, every night before she carried the lamp upstairs, she looked at the items on that shelf. They were a tangible reminder of a previous life, a good childhood with loving parents. Now she was a mother with her own two, and that was good too. Maybe someday her girls would have their own memory shelves. Joanie's would be filled with desiccated birds' nests, feathers, and arrowheads. Molly's would have her collection of colors: the piece of pale green glass she'd found and put in her window, a dried red leaf, a clump of quartz that sparkled with flecks of gold and purple and blue. Maybe she'd be an artist like her father.

She would put these knickknacks somewhere safe until a time when she could have them out again. In their place, she had put the rifle that Ben had bought from a man he worked with. Imagine her, owning a rifle. But it didn't seem as strange as it once might have. Joan was always talking about mountain lions and black bears and wolves. Ben had told her that the largest animal around was probably a coyote, but Natalie couldn't get the thought out of her mind.

And it wasn't just wild animals she was afraid of, was it? Last week when she was cleaning the windows, she had seen a footprint in the dusty soil outside one of the living room windows. At first she assumed it was Ben's, but it was larger than his would have been. She wanted to tell him about it, but she didn't. Why? Because he'd tell her it was in her head, just like he did in those dark months after Molly was born. So she didn't say anything. If someone was prowling around, well, she had the rifle now. And she wasn't afraid to use it.

It was one of those summer evenings when it felt like the light would never leave the sky, though the sun had already dipped below the tree line. The children were in bed but awake, tossing restlessly with the thin sheets sticking to their bare legs. Ben had finally found a job at the local factory and was picking up extra hours. He wouldn't be home until almost midnight.

She had just placed the rifle on the shelf when she realized that a car had slid through the opening in the trees and stopped. She froze. No one ever came here. What was this feeling—excitement? Fear? She wasn't afraid of strangers. But how long had it been since she'd spoken to a stranger? The summer days passed easily, with the routines of the children and housework and trying to coax their small garden to produce something besides chokeweed. She hadn't noticed, but the solitude of the place was growing around her like ivy, pulling her into it. And now here was a stranger entering her secluded world, and her first thought was to grab the rifle. She shook her head to clear it. "You're being paranoid," she told herself. She smoothed her hair, wiped her sweaty hands on her pants, and stepped outside.

An older woman, wearing a hat and gloves despite the heat, was standing next to her car, holding a plate with a tea towel draped over it. Natalie waved, and the woman smiled but didn't come any closer. They looked at each other across the clearing, and then Natalie walked toward her. She realized the woman was probably only in her forties, but her style of dress gave her a formal, older look.

"I hope it's not too late, I know you have children," the woman said, holding out a gloved hand. "I'm Marion Janssen."

"Marion Janssen . . ." Natalie couldn't place the name.

"I sold you this house. My brother, George Sumner, built it."

"Oh," Natalie said, "yes, of course." The transactions had all happened at a bank, but the names did sound familiar.

"I'm sorry I haven't come earlier—I've been meaning to. I wanted to give you these." She thrust the covered plate toward Natalie. "A small welcome present."

"It's very kind of you. Can I offer you a cup of tea?"

"No, I'm fine, thank you."

"Water, at least?"

"No, no, I won't come in. I just wanted to make sure you were getting settled. Is everything with the house all right?"

"It's getting there." Natalie bit back the impulse to lie and say everything with the house was just lovely. This woman had sold them a financial mess. Yes, it had been cheap—all they could afford, if the truth be told—but there were other costs besides money. "It will be helpful when we can get a phone line in."

"Hmm, yes," Marion said. "Strange it's taking so long." She didn't sound like it was strange, though. "Is that your boy?"

Natalie turned. Joan was standing in the doorway in her pajamas, her short copper hair standing straight up on one side. "Girl," she corrected automatically. "Joan's our eldest. Her sister, Molly, is three." She sighed, then called to her, "You might as well come over, since you're out of bed already."

They watched as Joan took long gangly strides toward them. Her legs were skinny, with knees covered in scabs, and her skin was tanned a deep brown from spending every waking minute outside. She was as long and thin as her little sister was round and soft.

"Hello, Joan," Mrs. Janssen said. "My brother built the house you live in. Do you like it?"

"There's a swallow's nest in the eaves outside my window," Joan said. "I saw them hatch, and now they're getting ready to leave the nest."

"Joan is a real nature buff," Natalie said. "Living out here is perfect for her."

"My brother liked nature too," Mrs. Janssen said. "He was always more comfortable here in the woods than in town. That's why he chose this spot. You know, he used to come out here to hunt squirrels when he was a boy. My family owned all this land." She waved a gloved hand vaguely around them.

"He'd hunt squirrels?" Joan asked, confused as to why anyone would do this.

"Sure. Squirrels, rabbits. He caught a baby fox once."

"But why?" Joan's voice was rising, and Natalie grimaced. Her daughter was an adamant protector of all living creatures, which was part of Ben's point about not having a rifle in the house.

"For fun," Mrs. Janssen said. "It's what boys did. Why, George could hunt or track just about anything."

"Things were different back then," Natalie said, hoping to calm Joan down.

To her relief, Joan let it go. "There's a brown owl that lives in the woods. Did he see the owl?" she asked Mrs. Janssen.

"He never lived here," she said. "He built the house, then he went to war."

"Does he want to see the owl now?" Joan asked. "I've seen it come out of the woods there." She turned and pointed to the woods on the other side.

"He was lost in France a long time ago," Mrs. Janssen said. "But maybe he saw owls when he was building the house. He spent nights out here."

"Joan," Natalie said. "You need to get back into bed."

"I can't sleep."

"Lie in bed and close your eyes." Joan was starting to put up a fight every night about going to bed. "You won't fall asleep standing out here."

"You need to count the sheep," Mrs. Janssen said. "That always works for me."

"But Mommy, the sound will come back."

"There's no sound, it's just your imagination."

"But if I fall asleep—"

"That's enough," Natalie said sharply. "Go in the house and get into bed. And don't wake your sister."

"But—"

"Now."

Joan scowled and walked back into the house. The two women watched her go.

"She's a real tomboy," Mrs. Janssen said.

Natalie stiffened but refrained from saying anything. This woman was obviously from another generation who expected girls to run around in dresses and penny loafers. Yes, she missed Joan's long hair, but part of her admired her daughter for having the guts to hack it all off in the spirit of rebellion.

"I wondered how you all would adapt, coming from the city."

"The children love being in the country. Next she'd be wanting to show you her bug collection," Natalie said, turning to Mrs. Janssen. Joan's complaints about a mysterious sound had started a few weeks after they'd moved in. At first it had been inconsistent, but now she was complaining about it almost every night. Natalie had considered taking her to the doctor to have her ears checked, but it seemed a waste of money when it was clearly something her daughter was imagining.

"George would be glad there's someone living here who loves these woods as much as he did," Mrs. Janssen said. "What did she mean by the sound?"

"She's got an active imagination, that's all."

"So it's not real?"

"No, of course not," Natalie said. "It's probably just the wind."

The older woman nodded and looked out at the house and the still trees beyond it.

"Are you sure I can't offer you anything?"

"No, I have to go. I don't like driving in the dark," Mrs. Janssen added. "I'm glad you're comfortable here. I feel better knowing you are." She stopped speaking but didn't make any move to get back into her car.

"Is everything all right?" Natalie asked.

"I just wondered—I hoped, I mean—I hope you're happy here. This house was very dear to my brother."

"The kids have lots of space, and that room at the top will make a great studio for my husband. He used to be a painter."

"Mmm," the older woman said, but she didn't seem like she was listening. She pulled an envelope out of her purse and was looking at it as if unsure what to do with it.

"Mrs. Janssen?" Natalie asked.

"There was a woman," she started, then trailed off. When she spoke again, her voice had changed. It was quiet and urgent, with none of the forced cheeriness it had a moment before. "This was a long time ago now, and it was probably nothing, but I, well, I feel like you should know. My brother had a fiancée, Alice. She had a little girl too, a bit younger than your Joan. The child had been born out of wedlock—I'm not judging—but Alice wasn't one to be turning down an opportunity for security, is what I'm saying. George was so proud of this place, building it all himself. He was basically building it for her. But she didn't seem to like it."

"That must have been disappointing for him," Natalie said, not sure where this was going. She felt odd being out of the house with the children inside and wanted to get back in.

"Alice and I were friends. We knew each other from church, and I had introduced them. George would bring her out here to show her what he was doing. That little room at the top"—she pointed up to the studio—"he built that because Alice wanted it. But one time she came out here . . . I don't know what happened, but she was just so . . . agitated afterward. She kept saying, 'There's something wrong with that house, there's something wrong.' It didn't make any sense, and I told her that. Perhaps I was too sharp with her. I told her to give the house another chance, to give my brother another chance. She agreed she would, but then . . ."

She trailed off. She was looking past Natalie at the house behind her. Suddenly she gasped as if she had seen something. Her face went pale, and she stuffed the envelope back in her purse.

"Let me get you some water," Natalie said, reaching out to touch her elbow, but she shrank away. "Maybe the heat is getting to you."

"What? No." Mrs. Janssen stared at Natalie like she had no idea who she was. She looked around, confused. Perhaps she was older than she looked and going senile. Except a moment ago, she had seemed perfectly fine. "I have to go," she said, and started rummaging for her keys.

"But—" Natalie started. Now she wanted to know. "Did something happen to that woman?"

"No. I don't know. I never saw her again. She just . . . disappeared."

"What do you mean?"

"Well, I mean she probably ran off. My brother was never the same after that, and he couldn't bear to live here. I shouldn't have mentioned it. Ever since you moved in, I've wondered if I should say something, but . . . Well." She gave a nervous laugh that stopped as suddenly as it had started. By now she had found her keys and was back in her car, fumbling to get them in the ignition.

"Thank you for . . ." Natalie didn't know how to continue. What exactly was this woman trying to tell her? "We're fine."

"Of *course* you are. George would be so happy to know a family is living here. He always said, 'She needs a family.' "

"She?"

"I just wanted you to, um, hear it from me. I don't know if anyone else has said anything to you."

"No," Natalie said. The people in the village barely spoke to her, never mind sharing decades-old gossip. "I should get inside."

"Oh dear. I shouldn't have said anything." Mrs. Janssen touched her forehead and closed her eyes. "I just didn't know . . ." She got the key in the ignition and the car roared to life. She started to back up with a jerk, almost hitting a tree, then did an awkward turn and sped off down the access road between the trees.

Natalie walked into the house with the covered plate. In a flash of anger, she threw the whole thing—plate, cookies, and towel—into the garbage bin. What was the purpose of that visit? Was Mrs. Janssen trying to scare her? So, George Sumner's fiancée ran off after he built this house for her—what did that have to do with their family?

Maybe the poor woman saw how isolated she would be and got out while she could. Natalie considered telling Ben about the strange visit when he got home later that night, but then remembered they were still arguing about the rifle. She glanced up at it, sitting on the shelf over the door. Upstairs, a floorboard creaked. Joan had probably been watching from the window. Hopefully she hadn't heard, though the windows were all open. Natalie was too tired to go and scold her, and she didn't want to hear Joan complain about the sound again.

"There is no sound." Saying it out loud made her feel better.

Natalie looked around the long kitchen. There was still a little light in the sky, but the room was dark. She lit the lamp on the table and the other on the counter by the sink, and the kitchen became warm in the pools of lamplight. The cupboards at one end were well built, and she'd given them a fresh coat of white paint when they'd moved in. The counters gleamed with the mineral oil she rubbed into them every night. Molly's stuffed animals were spread out mid-game at the far end by the woodstove, and Joan had left her growing leaf collection on the table, but the room was large enough that it never felt cluttered. Mrs. Janssen had been right: a house did need a family.

The basement door latch clicked, and the door scraped open.

Natalie froze, and the skin on her arms turned to gooseflesh.

The house had quirks, there was no doubt about that. One of them was that the basement door kept opening on its own. Ben thought it was something to do with the foundation shifting. The latch didn't line up properly, so there would be a click and it would slowly open. At other times, the door was almost impossible to open, like it was being sucked closed. She'd never been nervous of dark places, not like some girls she knew, but she avoided going near that door as much as possible and never went down into the basement. She had gone down only once, when they had first moved in. The smell was one thing, but also, she was three steps from the bottom when something—a feeling or premonition—had filled her with panic. She'd turned and run back up.

The children weren't to go down there either. She had asked Ben several times to put a different lock on the door—what if Molly fell down those stairs?—and he always promised to, but he kept forgetting and the door kept opening and every time it did, the kitchen filled with that horrible rotten smell.

Last night she had caught Joan coming out of the basement. She'd scolded her harshly, but nothing she said seemed to have any effect on her eldest daughter now. Earlier this evening, she'd heard Joan whispering to her little sister about finding something. Whatever it was, it made three-year-old Molly very excited, but when Natalie tried to find out more, both girls clammed up. Thank goodness school was starting soon and Joan would be out of the house during the day.

Natalie got up, went to the basement door, and pushed it. For a moment it resisted, but then it gave way and the latch clicked into place. She jiggled the handle, but the latch stayed shut. The house creaked and settled with the heating and cooling of the days. That was all Joan was hearing—layers of sound, crickets and cicadas chirping, night birds squalling, leaves rustling, and far beyond that, the low rumble of a truck or car moving past, its passengers oblivious to the dark house hidden among the trees.

Natalie was exhausted. Since they'd moved here, when the tiredness hit, it was all she could do to get herself upstairs and into bed. She poured herself a glass of water and lowered the lamps, leaving them on for Ben. She moved up the stairs, being sure to avoid the creaks and wake the children. She was almost at the top when she heard the distinctive click again. She stopped, but she was too tired. Ben would close it when he came home. It was her last thought before she fell into a restless sleep.

———

Downstairs, the basement door slid open again, and the darkness called. Joan, almost asleep, opened her eyes. The sound was back.

21

Abby's father must have been watching for me, because when I step out of the car on the small cul-de-sac in Buffalo late the next day, he's already striding toward me, oblivious to the rain pouring down in sheets. When I agreed to go to Buffalo, I thought I would drive out and back in one day. But between the weather and my state of mind, it's taken me longer than I thought it would to get here, and I've missed visiting hours. Mr. Lindsay insisted I stay with him: "Don't waste your money on a hotel. I've got an empty house." At my confusion, he added that he and Mrs. Lindsay recently separated, and Mitch is staying with her.

I don't know if I want to see Mitchell or not. Part of me does, desperately, but each time has only made it worse, and the more I think about what he said last night, the clearer it becomes that he doesn't want me around.

Four hours on a highway is a long time to think. The closer I got to Buffalo, the more I started to question why I offered to do this. Was it just guilt? Abby's in worse shape now—possibly because of me. How is my seeing her again going to make anything better? But there's something else, something about being around this family again. The Lindsays always invited me in and seemed to be happy that I was around. I slept over at Abby's far more often than she ever did at my house; I ate at least one meal a week there, usually more. After what happened to her that summer, I felt shut out. And I deserved it, even if no one else knew what had happened. I knew. I missed Abby and was pining for Mitchell, but it was more than just them—it was the easy way they could make a place for me at the dinner table, the way they were so entirely themselves in front of me because I wasn't a guest, I was part of the family.

When Mrs. Lindsay reached out to me after so many years and asked me to come home, it was the first time in a long, long time that I thought I could actually help. I could be a part of something.

"Give me your keys," Mr. Lindsay says now and holds out his hand. "You can't park there. I'll put your car in the driveway, and we'll head out in mine."

"I thought visiting hours were over."

"You've come all this way. I'm going to give you the grand tour."

We drive in silence for a few moments. Every minute or so he turns and looks at me, smiles, and then goes back to the road. I expected him to be exhausted and distracted with worry after last night, but instead he seems calm, even happy. "She's in a good place," he says, like he can read what I'm thinking. "And she's home. She's *home*. I didn't realize how awful it was, having her so far away, until we got her back here. She's in the best place she can be. I think she's going to pull through."

"Mr. Lindsay—"

"Ted. No more of that now."

"Ted, I'm so sorry about what happened. If I had anything to do with it—"

"That was nothing to do with you, do you understand?" He takes a hand off the wheel and grips my arm tightly, looking right at me. "Do you?"

"Yes, I know, yes," I say, more to get him to look at the road than because I agree.

"You being here is a good thing, not just for Abby but for me too. Seeing you, seeing the woman you've become, it gives me hope, do you understand? And it reminds me of how things used to be when Abby was just a carefree girl."

Was Abby ever a carefree girl? Maybe to the adults around her, but I know otherwise.

To keep the conversation off me, I ask, "How are Paul and Mitchell?" Just saying Mitchell's name, I can feel my neck growing pink, but it's dark in the car, and Mr. Lindsay is focused on the road.

"You know Paul's got a wife and three kids now. They're down in Phoenix. Gorgeous down there. You ever been?"

"Just the airport."

"And Mitch is all over the place. Goes wherever his company sends him, but he loves his work. He's in charge of a big project in Saudi Arabia."

"That's awfully far away." I am working hard to keep my voice even, conversational. Thinking of that picture on Abby's bed, I desperately want to ask if he's married, but I don't trust my response if the answer is yes.

"He's been there for over a year now." He glances over at me, but I keep my gaze forward. "Abby adores him. Just worships the ground he walks on." I nod. That hasn't changed, despite what Mitchell thought. "A few years ago, I got him to come home on vacation. I thought if he spent some time with her, he might be able to reach her, since her mother and I couldn't."

"I bet she loved that."

"Oh, she was so excited about him coming out—talked about it for days, about what she'd show him, what they'd do—but then he gets here, Caroline makes a great dinner, and Abby doesn't show up. Doesn't even answer her phone. We finally get through to her around eleven at night, and she's furious."

"Why?"

He rubs his hand over his eyes. "Abby is, um, sensitive. I mean, we all are, but she was—is—hurt easily. And she had it in her head that Mitch should have picked her up first before coming to us. She was living out by the airport at that time. They'd never talked about it, but that didn't matter. She thought him coming to us first meant we'd be talking about her. I don't know. I think she was just embarrassed. She'd gained a lot of weight and was losing her hair. The pills they had her on . . ." He shakes his head.

"But she looked so thin."

"Every time they switched her medication, it was a whole new roller coaster of side effects. With some, she couldn't sleep; with others, she couldn't stay awake. They messed up her metabolism, so she'd gain and lose weight. These last ones they had her on, she had no appetite, and you remember, she never was much of an eater even before that. I was making her drink one of those Ensure drinks each day, but I don't think it was doing much good. It's not healthy, I'm telling you. How is a person supposed to recover when their brain is a chemical war ground?

"Thank goodness Mitch was here for this. He's been like a rock for Caroline. Like I said, my daughter has gone through hell, and her mother and I have been through it with her."

We zigzag our way through the city as he points out a place Abby worked one summer, the apartment of a friend from high school, the restaurant where they'd celebrated her thirtieth birthday. He talks to me as if I am so familiar with all this that I can't ask things, like when did he start to notice the changes? When did she start taking medication? He refers to her friends and events in her life as if I know who and what he's talking about. I nod and stay silent. He assumes we kept in touch. I can't tell him I barely knew the Abby he's talking about.

We pull into the parking lot of Buffalo General Hospital. "This isn't where she is now. The first time she tried to kill herself, I brought her here. She swallowed a bunch of pills and then called me. She called me right away and said, 'Dad, I've done something bad.' I was across the city, but I drove like a maniac—ran about three red lights—and I brought her in here and they pumped her stomach."

"Why didn't she go in an ambulance?"

"Refused. She wanted me to take her. Abby was always like that. When she was a little girl, if she had a nightmare, I was the one she'd call out for. That really hurt Caroline, but that's just the way she was. Caroline had been so excited when we had a girl, but Abby was always mine. Mitchell was Caroline's baby."

"What about Paul?"

"If Paul ever had a nightmare, I didn't know about it; he certainly never called for one of us. But Abby always turned to me, even when she got older. They kept her overnight and then admitted her to the psychiatric hospital. She stayed there for about a month. I tell you, that month was a relief. I always knew where she was."

We leave the hospital but haven't gone far when he stops again at a dingy bar called the Lucky Horseshoe, though some of the letters are burned out, so it's the "Lucky Ho shoe." He turns off the engine next to a gutted phone booth, wires hanging down where the phone has been ripped out, like arteries going nowhere.

"Some junkie must have done that. That's where she called me from the second time. It was about six months after the first time. She'd been drinking and had a fight with some asshole boyfriend. The way those guys treated her. I tried to go after one of them, but Caroline convinced me there'd be no point. I should have done it. She wasn't supposed to drink with her meds. Eleven o'clock at night, and they kick a young woman onto the street because she's getting a little rowdy. She was messed up, and she'd fallen in the parking lot and cut herself pretty bad on some broken glass, and she thought she'd cut her wrists. I don't know, maybe those cuts were on purpose, that's how the hospital treated it. She lost her cell, so she called me from this phone booth, and I came and got her and took her back to the General. They took her into triage, and then this young doctor comes out and he asks if we can talk. He wants to know if I've ever heard of borderline personality disorder.

"'She's on meds for bipolar disorder and anxiety and so on and so on,' I say, and he says maybe some changes could be made. In the meantime, he says, I should go home.

"'I'm staying with my daughter,' I say. 'She needs to know I'm here.'

"But he says that may be part of the problem. If it is BPD, and he seems to think it is, she's going to keep making these attempts. It's her way of saying she needs help, and if I give her attention now, I'll just be reenforcing it. So, when she does this again, and she probably will, I have to drop her off and then leave. *Leave* her." His voice sounds strangled, like there are hands wrapped around his windpipe. "I'm her father. But I left her. Doctor's orders."

"I had no idea." My voice is small and dry.

"No one does." His hands grip the steering wheel even though we're not moving. "Leave her," he says again. "It's unnatural." He starts the car. "That phone booth saved her life. After that, I made her promise to always keep her cell charged and on her, and that was the one promise she kept. Until this last time."

"She didn't have her cell with her?"

"She left it in the car."

"Maybe it was an accident. I'm always losing my cell."

"It wasn't an accident."

I turn to him to say something, but I see the hard set of his jaw and turn back to look out the window. We drive for another ten minutes. I've lost any sense of direction. Then we come over a hill and I can see Lake Erie, stormy and thrashing ahead of us.

"Did she take anything with her into that house?" I finally ask, breaking the silence.

He's quiet for a moment, then he says, "A can of Coke. I guess she needed something to help her swallow the pills. Whole new bottle."

"She always had those on her, right?"

"Yeah," he says. "She always had those."

Her family, like the police, accept that this was another suicide attempt. It's easy to see why they would.

We drive beside the Buffalo River, then he pulls over. There are signs for the Coast Guard station ahead.

"Abby loved it out here. She said this was her favorite place to think. I used to bring her here all the time. We'd come here after her appointments. About two years ago, I found a doctor who was willing to treat BPD. She was the first doctor Abby trusted. Dr. Beth. She was South African and had this amazing accent—Abby would try to talk like her after appointments. We had a ritual; I'd bring her to her appointment with Dr. Beth, and then after, we'd go get a milkshake and come here. Dr. Beth was a good listener, she said. I think that was the first time she felt like she was actually being heard."

"Dr. Beth sounds amazing."

246 · JENNIFER FAWCETT

"She was. She was just here on a yearlong program. She went back to South Africa last December."

"How did Abby take it?"

"At first I thought she was doing pretty well. She started spending a lot of time at the library, doing research, she said. I thought that was a good sign, taking the management of her disease seriously. She switched to another doctor, Reinhold, but he didn't listen the same way. She made another suicide attempt in February, and Reinhold admitted her, then she stabilized and he let her out after a few weeks. But she wasn't stable. She was pretending."

"Pretending?"

"She was good at it."

Her emails to me came two months after this attempt, I think, trying to place my own timeline within hers.

"That's one of the symptoms or features of this disease," he continues. "Manipulation. It wasn't Abby doing the manipulating—it's like she was possessed. It was living inside her, and it drove her to do these things. She didn't want to do them. That's why she always called me after she'd made the attempt."

"She told you that?"

"She said the only way to make it go away was to give in to it. Then, as soon as she did, it would go away, and that's how she was able to call me. The day she disappeared, she switched her appointment date without telling me. She had a car, but we kept the keys, and Caroline left them out. Such a goddamned stupid mistake. Reinhold saw her, renewed her prescriptions, and sent her on her way. I've read his notes from the visit. One line read: 'Patient appears to be stable.' And then some comments about dosages. That's all he gave her. He's supposed to be trained to see through the bullshit. Abby had so much bullshit; she was buried in it. She couldn't tell where the bullshit ended and the truth began.

"I got home from work, saw her car was gone, saw her note saying she was going to her appointment alone. I told myself it would be okay—I tried to convince myself. It was a beautiful day, I thought maybe she'd come here, but then it got dark and she still didn't come home, didn't answer her phone, didn't respond to texts. I started panicking. I went to all the places I've taken you. I ended up here. I went into the water—didn't even feel the cold. I just kept diving, trying to move my hands along the bottom. It's all algae, you can't see a thing. She'd once told me that she had this fantasy about getting a boat and sailing off to the horizon. Just disappearing out there and starting somewhere new. Somewhere fresh."

He opens the door. Rain and wind blast into the car. "Come on. I want to show you the lighthouse."

He starts walking down a dirt path with his head ducked against the wind, and I scramble to get out of the car and follow him. The dark lake and sky make the horizon almost disappear except for the whitecaps breaking far out in the water, the waves crashing against the breakwater. By the time I catch up to him, we're both drenched and freezing, but he doesn't seem to notice. He turns to me and grabs my arm. He has to yell over the wind. "The first time she tried to kill herself," he says, "I begged her to never do it again. I got down on my hands and knees and I begged. And she promised. She always gave herself an out. The methods she chose were slow—overdose, poison, cutting herself—reversible, if you caught them in time. And she would call me and I'd take her to the hospital. 'See, Dad,' she would say, 'I kept my promise.' But the last time, she drove four hours away. She left her phone in the car. She broke her promise. Why did she change the cycle this time?"

"I don't know."

"Why did she go back to that house?"

"I don't know. I'm trying to understand, but—"

"Why didn't she give herself an out? There has to be a reason. You don't have to protect me, Clare—I just need to know."

"I don't know. Please, you have to believe me."

"But you were her best friend."

"When we were kids."

"What the hell is in that house that she had to go back?"

"There's nothing."

"That's what the police said. That's what Mitchell said. But you— If anyone knows, it has to be you."

I have nothing. I came back here fooling myself that it was to help, but I have nothing to offer, nothing that makes any sense at all. I came back here thinking I was being brought back in. What if my being here only makes it worse?

We stand there, wind and rain lashing against us, Abby's father clutching my arm like he's drowning, and then he drops his hand, turns, and walks back down the path, not waiting to see if I'll follow.

I stay out by the lighthouse as long as I can stand it. When I get back to the car, my fingers and toes have gone numb. Mr. Lindsay doesn't say anything, but he doesn't seem angry anymore, just tired. We sit in silence for a few minutes with the heat blasting, and then in a dull voice, he says, "Okay, let's get you some dry clothes."

At his house, he gives me a pair of pajamas—Abby's, I'm guessing—and I throw my clothes in the dryer. I left so quickly, I didn't bring extras to change into. He turns on the TV and warms up dinner, but I can barely keep my eyes open and excuse myself before I can finish.

He leads me down the hallway to Abby's room. When we get there, he goes in to turn on the light, but I stop at the doorway. On the outside of the door is a heavy bolt.

"Everything all right?" he asks.

"Sure, yes. I'm just tired."

"I hope you'll be comfortable in here. Just yell if you need anything. Bathroom's next door."

He looks at me for another moment, like he wants to say something, then he nods and leaves. I know I should look around—maybe there are clues about why Abby went back to the Octagon House—but the room looks clean, not just tidy but cleaned out, and I'm too exhausted to keep my eyes open. I hear the news coming on downstairs in the living room and the sound of him rattling around in the kitchen as I drift off to sleep.

=====

I wake up with a jolt. It takes me a minute to remember where I am. The alarm clock that glows beside the bed says it's past one. Outside, the rain has let up, but the wind blows, the kind of gusts that knock down tree branches and send garbage cans flying. Maybe that's what woke me.

No. It was something else. Then the doorknob clicks, and the door opens slowly and silently. I'm frozen, not breathing. A silhouette—Mr. Lindsay—in the doorway. He doesn't move. He doesn't say anything; he just stands there. Beside me, the alarm clock clicks over to the next minute: 1:23.

"Mr. Lindsay?" My voice is a cracked whisper.

"Sleep well, baby doll," he mumbles.

Then he pulls the door shut and closes it softly.

I wait. My heart pounds. The cliché is true: it really is loud when you need to be quiet. I can't tell if he's still out there; there's no light on in the hallway to cast a shadow. I breathe out slowly but don't move. Another minute clicks over, then another. Outside, a gust moves through the old tree in front of the house, and its branches creak in protest. I listen farther out. The house is silent. When the wind dies down, I can hear cars on the road behind the cul-de-sac. I try to listen for the sounds of the city. Somewhere in a hospital downtown, new machines surround Abby, beeping and humming their white noise. And somewhere beyond that, the waves of Lake Erie pound the shore.

I have to get out of here. The need is so strong, so immediate, that I don't even question it. I could go for a drive, find my way back to the lake. I understand why Abby liked it there, all that open space, the horizon that seems so close. I open my door slowly, but the other bedroom doors are closed. I imagine Mr. Lindsay lying in bed, listening. I hold my breath and creep down the stairs.

My coat and shoes are still damp, but I put them on over my pajamas. My keys aren't in my purse or my coat pocket, and then I remember giving them to Mr. Lindsay so he could move my car. They're not on the table by the front door or in his coat pocket. I use my phone flashlight and check the floor all around the door, the dining room table, the bookshelves—all of the places he could have absentmindedly put them. But he had said, "We kept the keys." So, not absentminded. Purposeful. The tightening feeling of claustrophobia starts to grow in my throat. I go into the kitchen and open every cupboard and drawer. I shake the boots lined up by the back door and slip my hands into the pockets of each coat hanging there. My movements are getting louder, sloppy. I don't care. I want him to wake up so I can demand that he answer why he's trapping me here. Is this what he would do to Abby? Watch her sleep, lock her in her room, take her for a milkshake after her doctor's appointment like she's a child? That is insanity-making. With all the crap she had to deal with, those mind games would have only made her worse.

I'm making my way back toward the stairs through the living room. A large bay window looks out on the empty street, but then a neighbor's security light goes on, and I see the silhouette of Mr. Lindsay sitting in a large chair, facing the street. He's been there this whole time. He listened to me quietly curse and stomp around, and he didn't do anything. I walk up to his chair to demand that he give me my car keys.

He's asleep.

The Winnie-the-Pooh book is in his lap.

My paranoia extinguishes. He's not playing mind games. He's a father hovering on the edge of grief so deep, he has to know that if he goes in, there is no escape. I think about the daughter I will never know. I never even got to see her face, but I know that I would have done anything to protect her.

Anything.

I take a blanket that's folded over the couch and gently spread it out across Mr. Lindsay's lap.

I am not trapped.

I am not being held hostage.

I think of Mrs. Lindsay's face when she talked about the horrifying decision they might have to make about Abby. I think of Mitchell, gritting his teeth, refusing to look me in the eye. And Mr. Lindsay on his knees, begging his daughter "never again." And his vigil here, born out of years of worry, of desperately trying to hold on to someone intent on slipping away—someone caught in the grip of something so much bigger than all of them. I came back to be a part of something. Instead, I am a witness to the shattering of a family I once wanted to be mine because I thought it was unbreakable.

22

The next morning, I wake to Mr. Lindsay politely tapping on my door.

"Clare? Sorry to bother you," he says from the other side. "But visiting hours start soon, and I'd like to get there."

My dry clothes are folded neatly outside the bedroom door, and when I get down to the kitchen, coffee in a travel mug and a toasted bagel are waiting for me with my car keys sitting next to them. If he heard me moving around downstairs last night, he isn't saying so. I'd planned to drive myself so I can leave straight from the hospital, but he insists we drive together. He says parking is a nightmare, though after what I saw last night, I think it's because he doesn't want to be alone.

In the car, he puts the radio on quietly and we drive in silence. We're stuck in a slow-moving turn lane when he says, "I'm going to knock out a wall in the living room."

"Oh?"

"I decided last night. There's a sunroom in the back, you didn't see it, but it's south-facing and is just gorgeous when the sun is out. It's winterized. I'm going to make that Abby's bedroom. It looks onto our back garden. There's a whole drama that unfolds around our bird feeder between a pair of blue jays who think they own the entire backyard, some tenacious sparrows, and one very crafty squirrel. Abby used to sit back there for hours, watching them, and then she'd play out the whole drama to me over breakfast, you know, giving them all voices and characters. She was so good at it. I never thought of her as being the dramatic type, you know, she was always so shy, but she really got into those characters. So I'm going to put her back there so she can watch them. And if she can't see—they said there's a possibility of blindness—then I'll narrate it to her, and she can see it in her mind.

"It isn't up to us to decide the quality of a life. That's selfish. That's so *selfish,* and Caroline . . ." He clenches his jaw, then massages it. "We have very different views on this. She thinks I'm being delusional for being hopeful. About our child. Our little girl. Jesus Christ, what else is there but hope? There's nothing, Clare, I'm telling you. Nothing. The second they let me, I'm bringing her home. I don't care what it costs. If I have to hire a private nurse to help care for her, I will. It's just money."

He's quiet for a moment and then whispers, "My daughter is a fighter. That's why she never was able to do it. A part of her didn't want that. A part of her wanted to stay alive. That part is still in there, and goddammit, I am going to do everything, *everything,* to help her."

We pull into a towering parking garage across from the glass and steel monolith that is Abby's new temporary home. No wonder Mr. Lindsay feels more hopeful about her prognosis now that she's here. He slides the car into a spot, we get out, and he pops the trunk.

"Caroline and I have been gathering things to bring to her hospital room. To make her room feel more familiar, for when she wakes up."

"I saw the pictures."

He nods. "There's more here. This room's a bit bigger, so I figure we'll bring this up."

He takes a large box out of the trunk, but as soon as we're in the building, all of his exaggerated buoyancy is gone. He's hunched over, and I don't think it's from the weight of the box.

Abby looks the same as she did before, except now there are more machines, more tubes. The most noticeable one is coming out of her mouth, and next to the bed is a ventilator, breathing for her. The clock started ticking two nights ago. The next twenty-four hours will determine whether that deep animal part of her brain that keeps her heart beating and her lungs moving will recover, or whether she will need to be on life support forever. The moment we get into the room, Mr. Lindsay does a sharp inhale of breath.

I reach out and put my hand on his arm, and after a moment, he puts his hand over mine.

Her fingers are still bandaged and I'm not allowed to touch her, even on her hand. She's at risk of infection. I'm wearing a mask and have scrubbed my hands and put covers over my shoes, but even with those precautions, I cannot come any closer than a few feet from her bed.

I have nothing to offer this family. That's what I learned last night. As I stand here watching machines keep Abby's body alive, it becomes even more clear. After all of this, rushing here because she said my name, the hope that I might actually be able to beat advanced medicine and wake her up, by what, the sheer force of my presence? What an egotistical joke. I'm a fool. I didn't rush back here to save Abby; I rushed back to Sumner's Mills because it's the one place in the world where I existed once, and I need to exist again. Abby saying my name made it feel like maybe I still existed for her, within whatever dark, silent hole she is in, but maybe she said my name only because I am a memory.

She was calling on the past Clare, and past Clare is gone.

The doctor pokes his head in. "Ah, Mr. Lindsay, shall we have a quick chat?"

"I can step out," I offer.

"No, the hallway is better, I think," he says. He's Indian, and his accent gives his words a warmth that must be helpful in a unit like this. "After all, we cannot know exactly what is being received." He nods toward Abby.

Mr. Lindsay follows him out. I look down at Abby.

"Where are you?" I whisper. "Where am I?" It feels like the last time I actually knew who I was, knew where I belonged, was when I was with her, when we were just girls who had no idea what we were about to walk into.

To pass the time, I start to go through the box of things Abby's father has brought along. Inside are framed pictures of her family, more formal than the ones that were taped around her bed. I recognize some of the older ones from when we were kids, and more have been added since. There's another of Mitchell and that beautiful woman. My heart does a flip-flop, but I make myself look at it. It's the same scene, but this is before they went fully into the water; they're just in up to their shins. In this picture, it's undeniable: Mitchell is married. He's wearing a pale-tan suit with a flower in his lapel. She's wearing a white sundress that floats around her and is holding a bouquet of flowers. I close my eyes and take a long, slow breath. Let the hurt rise. There's no way to stop it. For me, our sleeping together was the final break that I needed; for him, it was a mistake.

I put the picture back in the box. The reality of Abby's current state is enough—not to make the hurt stop but to help me focus. I'll make myself useful, keep Mr. Lindsay company until his wife arrives, then I'll drive back to Sumner's Mills, pack my car, and leave. Whatever I thought I could do here is past. Abby's recovery has nothing to do with me now.

Most of the books in the box are dog-eared paperback romances, but there's one book that catches my eye because it's larger than the rest. It's called *American Cloth Dolls Through Time*. Several pages are turned down, marking rag dolls with long dresses and painted faces. I put it aside and keep looking. At the bottom of the box, under the knickknacks and a folded quilt, is a spiral notebook with loose papers sticking out of it.

I sit with the doll book in my lap and the notebook tucked inside so I can close it quickly when Mr. Lindsay comes back in. Inside the notebook are printouts from Etsy and Pinterest with more pictures of old-fashioned homemade dolls. Under those are three more newspaper articles printed from microfiche, like the ones Mr. Fischer had. They're covered in Abby's telltale red circles and underlines, like gashes demanding the text open itself up and reveal its secrets.

Post-Sentinel

AUGUST 23, 1965

BRUTAL MURDERS SHAKE TOWN

Sumner's Mills – The sleepy hamlet of Sumner's Mills woke up to horror this morning as it learned of a gruesome midnight murder. Mother and wife Natalie Fischer (née Desrochers), 31, was found dead in her home with two children, aged 3 and 8, also deceased. Husband, Benjamin Fischer, 34, is being held for questioning.

"It was cold-blooded, that's the only way to describe it. Right in their own home," said Lt. Charlie Eastham of the Franklin County Sheriff's Office. "I've done police work for fifteen years and spent three years in the South Pacific. I've seen bad, but this was just plain cruel."

Although no official statement as to the cause of death has been made yet, anonymous sources have told the *Post* that the deaths were caused by gunshot wounds.

The Fischer family was new to Sumner's Mills, having moved only months earlier from Yonkers. Mr. Fischer had been working at the local factory, Sumner's Metals. Associates describe him as "quiet" and "keeping to himself." Little else is known about the family, who have no known relatives in the upstate area. They were perhaps best known for their unique house, which is in the shape of an octagon.

The brutality of this murder has rocked this small, close-knit community. "They kept to themselves, but that's nothing too unusual up here. They didn't go to church, but the kids were always well dressed and well behaved whenever I seen [*sic*] them," said Doris Blackburn, a longtime Sumner's Mills resident.

Authorities are asking anyone with information to come forward.

Post-Sentinel

AUGUST 27, 1965

HUSBAND CHARGED IN TRAGIC
DEATH OF CHILD AND MOTHER

Sumner's Mills – Benjamin Fischer, 34, has been formally charged
with two counts of first-degree murder in the deaths of his wife,
Natalie Fischer, 31, and daughter Molly, 3, and the attempted
murder of daughter Joan, 8. The elder child remains in critical
condition after suffering severe wounds to the head.

While there was initial speculation about an outside suspect,
police quickly suspended their search, citing a lack of evidence.

Mr. Fischer is being held without bail at the Franklin County
Jail until trial. The district attorney will push for the maximum
penalty due to the severity of the crime. Mrs. Fischer's family has
issued a statement requesting privacy at this difficult time.

Albany Times-Union

JANUARY 5, 1966

HUSBAND GETS LIFE FOR MURDER OF FAMILY

Albany – After a three-day trial, Benjamin D. Fischer, 34, of
Sumner's Mills, NY, was found guilty of second-degree murder in
the death of his wife, Natalie Fischer, (née Desrochers), 31, and
daughter, 3, and attempted murder of his elder daughter, 8. Last
August, the village of Sumner's Mills was shaken by the brutal
attack on the family in their home, though it was quickly estab-
lished that there was no evidence of an outside suspect.

While it was originally reported that all three were victims of gunshot wounds, the coroner's report showed that Mrs. Fischer died of internal injuries due, it is believed, to a fall down the basement stairs. The two children were in the basement at the time of their respective death and injury. The youngest child died of a gunshot wound. The older child suffered life-threatening injuries and remains hospitalized. The district attorney has requested that in the case of her death, her father's sentence be reexamined.

Mr. Fischer broke down during the sentencing but otherwise made no statement throughout the trial, despite entering a plea of not guilty.

Presiding Judge Charles M. Littleton declared that while there was no question of the guilt of Mr. Fischer, citing a lack of evidence of premeditation, the death penalty would not be sought and the original charge of first-degree murder amended to second.

Sources who wish to remain anonymous have hinted that this may not be the first tragedy to befall the house where the Fischer family was living. Built in 1936 by local resident and self-taught architect George Sumner, the house remained unoccupied until it was purchased by the Fischers. Mr. Sumner is MIA, last known to be in France in 1941. His fiancée and her child were declared missing in 1936; however, no charges were ever made, and foul play was not suspected. Attempts to contact the Sumner family have gone unanswered.

Under the last article, in blocky letters—the pen's ink seeped into the pages—is one word: CURSED.

I open the notebook. Pages and pages of drawings of the doll, each one getting more detailed as it became sharper in her memory. On the printouts of the doll pictures, she has circled the eyes of one, the dress of another, trying to get the right match—

I understand what Abby is doing: trying to draw the doll in the basement. The eyes painted wide open, eyebrows arched like she's frozen in a moment of surprise, the red button mouth that makes a tiny O. I look back at the doll history book and at the printouts. All of the dolls she has noted are from the 1930s. I always assumed that whatever was haunting that house was from the murders that happened in 1965, but what if there was something before that? Someone. That's what is being hinted at in the newspaper article: *This may not be the first tragedy to befall the house . . .*

And what she told me she had seen in the basement. What I had denied her.

There are three torn sheets. I recognize them immediately: the missing pages from Mr. Fischer's book. They're just simple sketches, done quickly with a pencil, but they hold so much pain that they're hard to look at. The first is a silhouette: a woman standing in a doorway with a rifle. She's faceless, but I assume it is his wife, Natalie Fischer. Then another of his wife, but this one is a close-up. There's something wrapped around her, like a blanket. Her eyes are huge, terrified, and one hand looks like it is reaching off the page toward me. I turn the page over quickly. The final picture shows a child in a hospital bed, covered in bandages. Eerily familiar to the scene in front of me.

I stare at the block letters spelling CURSED, imagining Abby carving that word into the page. Did she think she was cursed by the house? Was the Fischer family cursed too?

Stop this. I don't believe in curses. And I don't believe in ghosts.

No. I don't *want* to believe in ghosts.

If she can't escape, neither can I. If I can't escape, neither will you. Abby's riddle.

The murders in 1965 happened in the basement. Everything that happened to Abby happened in the basement. No matter what I believe or don't, if there is a source for this—a beginning—it is there. All of her searching, these old newspaper articles, finding Mr. Fischer—it was all to try to figure out what was down there. And then she went back. And she made sure that I knew she went back, not to punish me but to help her if it didn't work.

"I know why you went back," I say to her quietly.

All of the exhaustion and defeat I was feeling have disappeared. I feel electric. For the first time since coming home, I'm starting to understand why I'm here. To finish what Abby couldn't.

I tuck the notebook and newspaper articles into my bag. When I leave Abby's room, Mr. Lindsay is nowhere to be seen, and I don't want to wait around for him. I've got my car keys back, so I'll take an Uber back to his place, retrieve my car from his driveway, and get back to Sumner's Mills.

———

I'm leaving the basement cafeteria armed with the largest coffee I can find when I almost walk into Mitchell, who is balancing a tray with two mugs and muffins. He's looking more awake than when I saw him last, but his stubble has grown thicker, and his familiar gray coat is open to reveal a fraying sweatshirt that looks like he's had it since college.

"H-hey," I stammer.

"Hey," he says. "Mom mentioned you were coming in to see Abby."

"I stayed with your dad. I didn't know they . . ."

"Yeah. Happened a few months ago."

"I was just up there. Your dad's with the doctor."

"I'm here with Mom," he says, nodding toward the other side of the room. Mrs. Lindsay is on her phone, fortunately with her back to us.

"I have to go. I'm driving back," I say. I suddenly want to tell him; I need to tell him. He was there too. He saw the basement that night we got her out, and he knew to go back there to look for her. He has the dreams too. He can help.

"Oh," he says. "Well, thanks for coming all the way out here. Like I said, it means a lot." He's talking to me, but he's not looking at me. His eyes dart around. "Look, uh, I wanted to tell you. I have to go back to Saudi sooner than I thought."

"I know, you're married," I say and immediately regret it. I don't even want to talk about this right now.

"What? No, I—"

"I saw the picture, your wedding on the beach."

"I was married. We divorced over a year ago."

"Then why—? When we saw each other, you said it was messy."

He sighs. "I didn't just mean about that. Yes, there's that, but there's other stuff too."

"I just wish you'd told me," I say. I know I sound like a petulant child. There's the part of me that desperately wants to get back to Sumner's Mills, and there's the other part that wants to drag Mitchell to some quiet corner and demand he explain how we had one impossible night and then he walked away.

"Yeah, well, you weren't single either." Off the look on my face, he adds, "I looked you up. There's pictures of you and your husband all over Facebook."

"No—we weren't married. And those are ancient. We—"

"It doesn't matter. Things are messy. *I'm* messy. I can't talk about this now."

Mrs. Lindsay has turned around, probably wondering what's taking him so long, and she sees me. She waves but doesn't get up. He starts to move away from me toward his mother.

"Mitchell—" I call after him. He turns around but doesn't come back to me. "I think I know why Abby went back to that house."

I'm expecting disbelief or confusion or resigned tiredness, but instead he looks angry.

"Just leave it, Clare. Nothing is going to change the situation, so there isn't a point in dwelling on whatever you think happened—"

"She said my name—"

"I'm the one who thought she said your name. It was when we were getting her out of the house. I might have misheard; she was barely conscious."

"And she left me a note. Before she went into the house, she left a note for me. She's asking me to help her. And when she woke up—"

"She didn't wake up. It was a seizure."

"But she saw me."

"If you want to help her, visit her. Read to her. Bring her flowers. But forget about that fucking house." He pivots, but I reach out and grab his arm.

"Look, if you're mad at me, I'm sorry, but I need you to listen to me. She didn't go back there to kill herself. There's something down there—"

He pulls away from me, spilling one of the coffees on the tray. "For fuck's sake." He clatters the tray onto the table beside us, then leans in close to me. "My sister is sick, okay? Really sick. You haven't been around her for the past twenty years, but I have." His voice has risen, and I'm aware of people near us turning to watch. "Her theories were crazy enough—I kind of expected them from her—but you? Jesus Christ. Grow up. This is real for us, not fucking teenage games, okay? If you can't understand that, then stay away from my family."

He walks away from me, leaving his tray behind. Mrs. Lindsay glances at me, confused, and follows him out of the cafeteria. A cluster of med students sitting a row over watch me. I burst into tears. I don't care. One of them starts to stand up, to say something to me, but I don't stick around long enough to hear what it is.

23

JOAN

August 22–23, 1965

The sound was loud in her head, insistent, that moaning hum that buzzed the inside of her skull. Finally both parents were in bed. Her mother had gone to bed shortly after that lady left, but her father had come home later than usual. She had to concentrate to hear past the sound, but she had heard, or maybe felt, when he'd stood at her door to check on her. Part of her wanted him to catch her awake—maybe he'd come in, sit down on the side of the bed, say, "You still up, Joanie?" and it would be just the two of them, the way they used to be when he didn't work double shifts all the time. But tonight she needed to get back down to the basement, so she faced the wall and forced herself to breathe slowly until she heard the soft creak of him shutting her door.

Five minutes passed with no sign of either her parents or her sister waking up, so, moving as slowly and silently as she could, she got out of bed, positioned her pillows under the sheets to reassure any sleepy parent checking on her, and crept to the top of the stairs, the hum notching up another note like a guitar string being pulled tighter. Her little sister appeared in her doorway, rubbing her eyes and holding her stuffed owl, Mr. Peeps.

"Go back to bed," Joan hissed. Molly stuck her thumb in her mouth and shook her head, her curls shaking around her. Joan knew there was no point in arguing with her; it would only risk waking their mother up. She would just have to take her into the basement. She never should have told her about finding a doll; of course Molly wouldn't let go of that. The basement door was open, waiting for her. It had to be tonight.

"Fine, then," she said, holding out her hand to take Molly's. "But you have to be really quiet."

———

Joan had been four and a half when Molly was born and had only a few memories of her mom before pregnancy. They were always out of the apartment among people, looking in shopwindows or playing in a park or driving somewhere in a taxi, Joan's gaze fixed on the passing buildings reaching into the sky. Skyscrapers, her mother called them, and promised someday to take her to the top of one, where she'd be as high as the birds. These memories were snapshots, like moving photos, never more than a half moment of time that her brain had captured and stored.

And then her sister was born and her mother changed. She cried a lot or got angry about little things that had never bothered her before, or sometimes, the worst times, she just got very quiet, like she wasn't even in her body. Joan had known there were problems. She knew her parents fought about money. She knew her dad wanted her mom to go and see a doctor, and her mom refused. But even though their apartment was small, Joan was only partly aware of the adult drama playing outside her child's world because that was when she and her dad started their long walks. Her dad would say, "Let's give Mom some space," and he'd bundle the baby into the carriage. Baby Molly would gurgle and stare up at them as she and her dad walked through the park and he pointed out birds. Her dad knew every bird there was, Joan was sure of it, and he taught her how to identify them by the markings on their wings or their chests, and by their calls. They would keep moving until the baby fell asleep, and then they'd find a park bench and eat the sandwiches he'd made, saving the crusts to entice nearby birds. They would sit very still until the birds got used to them and started to come closer, and then her father would take out his sketchbook and begin to draw. First she just watched him. She loved seeing the pictures come to life under his pencil, starting out as nothing more than a few lines before becoming real. It was like magic. Then he started to teach her how to draw. They would stay in the park until the baby woke up, hungry and crying, then they would walk back home.

Molly was a sweet child, all ringlets and dimples. She had chubby arms and a little toddler belly that she thrust out in front of her. It was impossible to stay mad at her, as infuriating as she could be at times. Joan had stretched into a long, gangly beanpole. She had her father's dark red hair, and now that they'd been living in the country and she'd spent every day outside under the sun, darker constellations of freckles appeared on her nose, her elbows, and all over her calves.

Joan turned eight at the beginning of June, and her father gave her a beautiful leather-bound book filled with alternating blank and lined pages. "You can draw on your own now," he told her. "And don't forget to record where and when you saw the bird." I don't want to draw on my own, she wanted to say, but she didn't because it would have seemed ungrateful. Soon she was drawing more than just birds; she drew bugs and plants and even a few rare animals she'd spotted. Every night she would show her father what she'd drawn. Initially he was very interested and would ask her about it, but as the summer went on and he started working at the metal plant, he got more tired and distracted and sometimes he'd forget to ask, or if she'd offer to show him, he'd say, "Later, later."

So, a few times she made up what she'd seen—wolf tracks that probably just belonged to a coyote, or the claw marks of a black bear on a tree, probably just cracked bark. She knew she was doing it to get attention and it was babyish, but she didn't care. Her parents believed her.

That was when they got the rifle. Joan hated it because it was meant to kill an animal. She knew they had it because of what she'd said, but she couldn't take it back now. Besides, there might be more than animals in the woods.

The woods that surrounded their house were thick, and her mother was easily nervous, so Joan never went too far into them, but one afternoon a few weeks ago, she'd gotten distracted and gone farther than usual. That was when she saw the man. His clothes were old and dirty and hung off him like he was a scarecrow. He stood still next to a tree, so she almost didn't see him. He was taller than her dad, with long, stringy gray hair and dark eyes—he was watching her. He held a finger to his lips. Then he pointed up into a tree. She looked where he was pointing and saw a bird's nest—much larger than usual. Maybe an owl, or even a hawk? When she looked back, he was gone.

She didn't tell her parents about the man. Made-up wolf tracks were one thing, but this was different. If her mother thought there was someone out there, Joan would never be allowed in the woods again.

———

The girls were forbidden to go into the basement. That hadn't stopped Joan from trying, but whenever she jiggled the latch, it moved up and down without catching, and the door remained sealed shut.

Last week she had been downstairs moving slowly through the house at night, the sound drilling inside her head, and the basement door had opened. There was a puff of air, like something being released, and the door slid open a few inches. Joan froze. She went closer and the sound got louder. Slowly, being as quiet as she could, she crept toward the opening. She was two feet away when, suddenly, the door sucked shut. The sound stopped. Joan stood in the dark kitchen, her heart pounding so hard she could feel the vein in her neck pulsing, because now she knew. The sound was coming from the basement.

Last night the door opened again. She was ready for it, waiting with a flashlight. The door made a sound like the latch clicking, even though the latch didn't work, and then it slid open. As soon as that happened, she jumped out of her chair, making too much noise, but she didn't care. She aimed the flashlight into the basement, but she couldn't see anything. The darkness was thick. She would have to go down.

The stairs were uneven, and there was no banister, so, using one hand to hold the stairs behind her, she inched her way down. She was over halfway when she saw it.

A doll. With a painted face, lying on the last step looking up at her. Joan didn't care much about dolls anymore, but this was an amazing find. This was better than the bird's nest, better than the baby rabbits, better than any animal or insect she'd been able to find. As soon as she saw it, the sound changed from a drone into a pulsing *nah nah nah nah nah nah*

No no no no no no no

Joan stopped. She was two stairs above the doll. If she sat, she might be able to reach down and grab it—

No no no no no no no

Why not? She found it, finders keepers. It wasn't like it belonged to anyone else.

The sound shifted again.

Go go go go go go go

The door began to close. She turned around and started to scramble up the stairs, dropping the flashlight. It was less than a second—a flash as the light arced down—but in that flash, she saw a girl standing beside the stairs. Not a ghost—the light would have shone right through, like it did in comic books—but an actual girl. Her mouth was open. "Go go go go." The sound was coming from the girl.

A girl. A friend. A secret friend.

Joan reached the top of the stairs and turned to look down, but it was only darkness below her, then she slid through the gap before the basement door closed her in. As soon as she stepped through the doorway, her mother grabbed her arm and dragged her away from the basement. She was breathing hard and digging her fingers into Joan's arm.

"What the hell are you doing?"

"Ow." She tried to wriggle her arm away, but her mother's grip was like iron. "Mama, you're hurting me."

Natalie held tight and shook Joan. "You know you're not allowed down there."

"I was trying to find the sound."

"There is no sound," her mother hissed into her face. "There is no sound, do you hear me?"

"But I heard something down there, like an animal." She hadn't planned to lie, it just came out, but it worked because her mother let her go. Joan fell onto the floor. She skittered away, rubbing her bruised arm. Was her mother going to hit her? She knew kids whose parents hit, but hers didn't. It was so outside the realm of possibility—until now.

Everything had gone wrong since they'd moved into this house. Her parents were like aliens, they barely knew she existed, she couldn't sleep, her mother didn't sleep, and now there was the very real chance that her mother would hit her and there was nothing she could do about it. There were no other kids. No Grandma and Grandpa or Aunt Evie, her mom's sister, who always brought her presents and could get her mom to laugh and make everything better and brighter.

Her mother was just looking down at her, unmoved by her tears, like she didn't even recognize her. Then she turned and pulled one of the chairs out to sit down. Joan thought maybe she would ask her to sit, to talk to her. She didn't care if she got in trouble, if her mother would just talk to her. Instead, fixated on the dark woods outside, her mother said dully, "Go to bed, Joan. I don't want you down here."

Joan had lain in bed, her arm still sore, her mind buzzing from what had just happened. A doll, a girl in the basement, her mother growing angrier and more distracted every day. "There's something about this place that's very wrong," Joan once overhead her mother saying. "I can feel it." Her father had said something she couldn't hear, and then her mom had said, "But I'm not getting better. It's worse here."

Then Molly had climbed into her bed, and she'd hugged her little sister tight to her and whispered a story about a secret girl who lived in the basement and came out to play at night and they had amazing adventures together underground. She thought her sister would be satisfied with a story, but Molly was smarter than she realized. She figured out that Joan had come from downstairs—maybe this girl was real. And Joan had told her that the girl had a doll, so now Molly was determined to go into the basement too.

===

Moving down the stairs quietly, with Molly in tow, Joan carried a half-burned nub of a candle and a book of matches, since she'd dropped the flashlight in the basement. When they got into the kitchen, the basement door was open. An invitation: *Come, play.* They stood at the top of the stairs, Molly holding tight to Joan's pajamas as she lit the candle. It took a couple of tries because her hands were shaking. The candlelight was different than the flashlight because it flickered. Instead of a pathway of light, they were in the center of a glowing orb.

"Go slow," she whispered to Molly. She grasped the candle in one hand, her sketchbook jammed into her armpit, and held Molly's small hand with her other. The little girl's legs wavered as she took a big step down to the first stair.

"Go down on your bum," Joan whispered to her.

Molly shook her head adamantly.

"It's safer."

"Dirty," she mumbled, and squeezed her stuffed owl closer to her. Her eyes were huge, the candlelight reflecting off them.

One step at a time, they made their way down. Going this slowly, being concerned for Molly, Joan was less aware of her own fear. She swung the candle from side to side, trying to spread the light as far as possible, to find the girl, but she was nowhere to be seen. When they got two thirds of the way down, Joan saw the doll. It wasn't on the stairs now; it was on the floor a few feet away from the stairs. The sound seemed quieter down here, she realized, like it was muffled by the thick black air. They reached the bottom step. Joan kept looking back, checking the door to make sure it was staying open. If it started to close, she'd have to grab Molly and run for it. They couldn't stray from the stairs.

As soon as they reached the ground, Molly let go of Joan's hand and started toward the doll, but Joan grabbed her, almost dropping the candle. She hadn't touched the doll yet. She didn't know what would happen when she did touch it, but if it was going to be something bad, she didn't want it to happen to her sister. They were both watching the doll, Joan holding the candle high with one hand and Molly with the other, and then out of her peripheral vision she saw something—movement or shadow—and swung the candle around, and there was the girl.

Right beside them, reaching out to Molly.

Instinctively, Joan pulled her sister close. Molly's head spun around, but she couldn't see the girl. "Is it her? It is the girl, Joanie?"

"Shhh."

Close enough to touch, she appeared younger than Joan, probably five or six years old. She was drowning in a dress that fell past her knees, stopping just above black lace-up boots. The collar looked like it belonged to a sailor. She was real-looking, except everything about her was the same dull gray-brown color—her skin, her dress, her hair hanging limply in two braids. Her eyes were huge and had a pale gray film over them that reflected the flickering candlelight.

She would give the girl something for the doll—a trade.

"Give her Mr. Peeps," Joan whispered to Molly, but she just hugged the owl tighter. So she set down the candle and pulled the owl out of Molly's hands. She started to protest, but Joan clamped a hand over her mouth. When Molly stopped squirming, Joan crouched down and put the owl next to the doll.

It all happened so fast.

Joan had picked up the candle and stood, hoping the girl would accept the trade, when she heard movement at the top of the stairs. There was a yell—her mother's voice. She realized this just as a sound exploded from above. Joan dropped the candle and the light extinguished as Molly crumpled in front of her. Both happened at the same time, like they were the same thing. *My sister is a candle.* It was her last coherent thought, then the animal part of her mind took over. Hide. *Hide.* She tried to pick Molly up, but she was suddenly so heavy that Joan could only drag her deeper into the basement. She felt herself screaming—jaws widening—but she couldn't hear the sound because of the ringing in her head, then something tight wrapped around her neck and pushed her into the earth floor. Molly fell out of her arms. Hands—*whose?*—pressed harder around her neck and she kicked and clawed, trying to pull them off her, trying to find her sister, the girl, her mother, but finding only darkness—darkness in her eyes and the ringing silence in her head and her lungs squeezing and squeezing.

Go in and the pain will stop.

She stopped fighting, and the darkness poured in.

24

BEN

The first time Abby visited Ben with her questions, her memories about the house, with newspaper articles he had never seen, he had been so surprised that someone was visiting him and so confused through the fog of medication that he hadn't been able to do more than lie there and listen. He cursed the pills that made him slow and stupid. She had so many questions for him: What did he know about the house's origin? What had it been like to live there? Had he heard anything unusual? Seen anything unusual? What had actually happened the night his family died? Who or what had killed them? This was the most surprising of all: She didn't think he'd done it. She thought there was something else, someone else, in the house that had done this to his family, because it had done something to her.

"Remember for me, Mr. Fischer," she had said, then she reached over and picked up his limp hand. Her hand was so small and warm. He began to cry, and she pulled away, apologizing. He tried to protest, to tell her that her hand in his felt like his daughter's, but all he could do was mumble incoherently, and she was already ringing the buzzer for a nurse. Ruth Ann, who had been pacing outside the door, her cheeks bruised pink with indignation, was back in his room within seconds.

She promised she would come again. And although he could only nod, he promised her he would clear his head and let the memories return. When the nurse brought him his pill that night, he pretended to swallow but held it under his tongue. They didn't check closely in here. When she left, he spat it into a tissue and pushed it under his mattress.

After a few days, his mind felt less cloudy, and the memories came back in dreams that etched an image in his mind. If he moved quickly enough when he woke up, he could sketch it before it faded. It felt good to have his mind sharpening again. The pain was a price he was willing to pay, though he had to make sure to hide it so they didn't put him on morphine. The cancer was advancing quickly now. Let it come, he thought, if only Abby would come back.

For weeks, the collection of discarded pills under his mattress grew. And he dreamed about his family, about that house, and finally, about that awful night when everything had gone wrong.

=====

It was just past midnight, August 23, 1965. He had come home late from work to find the lamps turned low, his family already in bed. He hadn't been asleep long when Natalie woke him up because she'd heard someone or something moving around downstairs. No, outside, maybe. It could be an animal. He asked if she had remembered to put the stone on the garbage can beside the house. She didn't know, so he got out of bed, pulled his clothes and shoes on, and went outside to check.

No sign of animals. He should have gone back to bed, but he stayed outside. Why? Because the night air felt good on his skin. Because there was a strange beauty to this house in the moonlight, and he wanted to be able to look at it, to know that it was theirs—really theirs. No more cramped apartments or noisy neighbors. He walked across the clearing to the edge of the woods and turned to look at his house.

In that time, he supposed, Natalie had left their bed, gone downstairs, and seen that the basement door was open—something he had missed. So she retrieved the rifle from wherever she had stored it after their argument that morning and aimed it down into the basement, the basement, where, for some reason—a reason he will never understand—

Joan had taken her little sister. After, the police had found a candle on the floor near their bodies. He can imagine them, a three-year-old and an eight-year-old, holding off that darkness with a single candle that made their shadows leap on the walls and appear monstrous to their mother.

Is that why she aimed the rifle into the darkness and fired? Was it the kickback that caused her to fall, or had she realized in that horrible second what she had done and run down the stairs and tripped? He will never know.

In his mind, he watches Natalie do this, but on the actual night, he was standing at the edge of the woods when he heard the shot. It sounded like it came from the house, but how could that be? He bolted across the clearing and into the kitchen. It was empty. The basement door was wide open, and the kitchen smelled like gunpowder. He lit the lantern on the table, his hands shaking so much that he dropped the match twice before it took. Then he shone that bright light into the basement and saw his wife lying at the bottom of the stairs, the rifle beside her.

He left the lantern at the top of the stairs and stumbled down calling her name, willing her to respond, but the basement was silent. He lifted her up to cradle her head and felt the warm blood pooling beneath her. None of it made sense. Had someone shot her? Had someone broken into their house? But if that had happened, how had the rifle ended up beside her? He wasn't thinking about fingerprints or evidence. All he knew was the rifle was dangerous and he had to get it away from her, so he threw it across the basement.

He carried her upstairs, placed her on the kitchen floor, and wrapped a tablecloth around her to keep her warm. She was losing a lot of blood, but she was alive and looking at him. Her mouth moved soundlessly. She reached up and grabbed the front of his shirt, but he took her hand away—she had no strength left—and he said he was going to get help. "I'll be right back," he promised. "I'm going to call an ambulance. You're going to be all right, my love." The children were upstairs asleep, he thought. He thought about getting her in the car and taking her straight to the hospital himself, but he didn't even know where it was.

He wrapped the tablecloth tighter around her. Her face was so pale now and her body shook with cold, even though the night was sticky. Then he ran to the car and drove to the Farleys' house because his house still didn't have a phone installed, one of the many things Natalie had worried about. He pounded on their door until the elder Mr. Farley, rifle cocked and aimed, opened it a crack. When he saw Ben covered in blood, he grabbed the terrified man and pulled him inside. "Phone, phone," Ben managed to say. By the time he was off the phone, Mr. Farley's boots and coat were on and he was waking his son to start a search for the person who had broken into the Fischers' house and shot Mrs. Fischer. Others had heard on the party line, and soon more cars showed up, and local men, armed and hungry for the hunt, began to fan out into the woods and the Farleys' fields.

Ben got back to the house as the police arrived. "Hurry, hurry," he called to them as they swarmed the house. An officer was asking where his children were. "Upstairs, asleep," he said.

But a minute later voices yelled from down in the basement: "There's two more down here."

After that, his memory splinters into fragments—voices and images that cannot, will not, ever fit together. He is only ever left with these fragments: trying to get to his wife, she needed to know he was still there, but her eyes were open, unblinking, and then the sickening blankness of the sheet pulled over her still face. The kitchen filling up with men in heavy boots, the low, excited voices of veterans back in combat; the red lights of the ambulance bouncing off the trees, the bodies of his daughters being carried up from the basement—"But they were in their beds; I saw them in their beds"—and then the hospital and a doctor with a quiet voice telling him about Molly, "There was nothing we could have done, Mr. Fischer." Everything had gone wrong, yet here was the sun, rising again just like yesterday, when his family was alive. And then another doctor told him that Joan was still alive, in critical condition but *alive*. He was in the room with her when the police came in and asked him to come to the station. They told him there was no evidence that anyone had broken into the house, but with

Mr. Farley's search party, there had been footprints everywhere. The rifle had been taken for fingerprints. "And whose prints are we going to find?" Then they said the doctors had noted bruising around Joan's neck. "You know what happens to guys in prison who hurt little children, Mr. Fischer?"

The more they asked him questions, the more confused he got. He had been outside—he was sure he had been outside. But none of what happened made sense without him being at the center of it.

And by the time they arrested him three days later for shooting his daughter, attempting to kill his other daughter, and pushing his wife down the stairs when she tried to wrestle the rifle out of his hands, he didn't know if what they said had happened was true or not.

For all these years.

Now here was Abby—a stranger—who knew about his family, who knew his house, and who didn't think he had done it.

When Abby finally came two weeks ago, he had a sketchbook of drawings to show her. The last three he had drawn as he'd woken from this last memory: his wife at the top of the stairs with the rifle, her face as she lay dying in the kitchen, and Joan in her hospital bed covered in bandages.

Just before Abby arrived, the nurse had made him swallow the pill in front of her; they were catching on now, though they hadn't found the ones he'd hidden under his mattress. He could feel the dark edges of the medication starting to move across his mind. He thought he could hold it off long enough to tell her what he had remembered, but Abby was behaving differently this time. As he told her the story, she couldn't stop moving, sitting then standing, going to the window and looking out, looking at the sketches again, moving, fidgeting, energy sparking off her.

"But why were your daughters down there? There had to be something—"

"Joan had found a doll down there. She was excited about it."

She stopped and stared at him. "She found a doll?"

"Yes, she said something to me that morning about finding a doll in the basement. She was always finding things, but usually it was leaves and rocks."

Abby pounced on her large bag and rifled through it. "Where the— Fucking hell, I can't find anything in here," then she dumped the entire thing on the floor. Pens and pencils, makeup, pieces of paper, tampons, loose coins, batteries, a half-eaten chocolate bar, an empty water bottle, and three full bottles of pills all spilled out. She grabbed a spiral notebook and flipped through it. "This. This." She pushed a rough drawing of a doll in front of him.

"I don't know," he said. "I didn't see it. She wanted to show it to me but—"

"Did either of your daughters have a doll like this?"

"No," he said.

"You're sure? You're absolutely sure?"

"Yes," he said, but was he sure? Had he ever paid attention to his daughters' toys?

"Jesus fucking Christ," she said. "It's got to be her, then. I saw this doll in the basement, but I assumed it belonged to your kids. It's connected. It's got to be. The doll, the *doll,* I *knew* the doll was important, but I couldn't *see* it—it was right in front of me and I couldn't effing see it. The doll was hers."

"Whose?" he asked, but she didn't hear him. She was moving faster now, or he was slowing down. She shoved everything back into her bag, then she turned to him. "Can I have those?" She pointed to the sketchbook. "Not the whole book. Just those last ones. Of that night. Can I have those? I'd like to be able to look at them longer. Maybe there's something else there that will, you know, ring bells or whatever, right?"

He nodded, but she was already reaching for the sketchbook. She ripped out the last three pages and tucked them into her notebook, jamming the whole thing in her bag.

"Will you come back?" he asked, hating how desperate it made him sound.

"Yes, sure, yeah, of course. If I get out alive." And she laughed, but it was a laugh that scared him. "I'm going back to the house."

"Now? But—"

"Hell yes, now. The time is now. I'm psyched. I have these feelings—" She shook her head, impatient with him or herself, he couldn't tell. "It's too complicated to explain. It's just a good time for me, now, to go. It's like a, like a power surge, you know? And I've been kind of adjusting my medication so I'm more . . . I'm more, uh, I'm not numb and dumb, the way they like me." That dark laugh again. "And I've got a car. I mean, we're only like an hour away from Sumner's Mills. Do you even know that? How close we are right now? I can practically feel it. So I'm going to go in. I'm going to find her, and I'm going to exorcise her the fuck out of there and out of my head, and then this will be over."

"Find who, Joanie?" he asked, fighting the heaviness pressing down on him. Too strong to hold off any longer. But he had to tell her to stay away from the basement. He had to tell her that he and her mother had strictly forbidden her to go down there . . . He had to fix that door, to close it permanently, to get some boards and hammer them across that basement door so it could never open again . . .

She looked right at him and said, "Don't you see? It's Grace. Grace is the beginning and the end."

Then she promised to come again soon and she left.

———

It's been almost two weeks now. She hasn't come back.

25

My anger and humiliation keep me focused for a good half of the four-hour drive to Sumner's Mills. After that, there's the thin bitter coffee of rest stops. Mitchell sends me two texts asking if we can talk, but I don't respond. Maybe this is what I needed to get him out of my system. I know the angry high I'm on isn't going to last. When I crash, it's going to hurt. But haven't I known this all along? There was never any hope for us. Maybe now I can finally move on.

Lori texts too, asking if I want to get together. She's out of town at a hockey tournament but will be home tonight. At the rest stop, I send her a quick message saying yes, I'm leaving Sumner's Mills tomorrow, so tonight I'll come by to say goodbye.

What's the hurry?

Long story. Better over beer.

That gets another series of emojis involving a palm tree, a clock, a lightning bolt, a jigsaw puzzle piece, and a random selection of others. Lori uses emojis like hieroglyphs, a language that makes sense only to her.

I don't know how much I'm going to tell her about what I've learned. She's already freaked out about that house. Maybe after. Right now, I have to get rid it. Whatever is in there, assuming there's anything, has a hold over Abby and Taylor.

And you too.

Destroy the house and the hold gets broken. Doing that means talking to Marion Janssen, so she's my first stop. If she won't listen, I'll figure out plan B.

Although Rhonda also wants the house gone, I don't want to have to deal with her. I need to talk to her mother without her storming around. When I get into Sumner's Mills, I drive by the gas station but can't tell from the outside if she's working, and I don't want to go in. It's early afternoon on a Saturday, so I figure the odds favor me, and I drive to the Janssens' house.

There's no car in the driveway, which is a good sign. I go around back to the door Mrs. Janssen said they use more often, and knock. No answer. I pace, trying to figure out if I can look in windows without being seen. If she's napping, she won't hear me. I knock again, louder this time.

I can't put this off until tomorrow. By then I may be second-guessing myself. I need to leave here knowing that the house is coming down, that I have accomplished at least that, and I want to leave as soon as I get up in the morning.

On a whim, I try the doorknob. I push, and the door opens. The stale smell of the house hits me as soon as I stick my head in. "Hello? Mrs. Janssen? It's Clare."

There's no sound, then I hear something being knocked over. "Mrs. Janssen?" I call out. "Are you all right?"

From down the hallway, a small voice calls out, "Hello?"

I step inside and close the door but keep my hand on the doorknob. "It's Clare. From the other day. I was wondering if I could talk to you again. I knocked, but no one answered."

"Come in," she calls out. "Third door on the right. I'm in bed."

Mrs. Janssen's room is as dim as the front of the house. The same heavy curtains are in here too, and only a thin line of afternoon light sneaks in. She's sitting up in a large bed with thick curling bedposts. Next to her is a table—the hospital kind that can swing over the bed—and on the floor is a cup of spilled water.

"I was trying to find my glasses and it spilled," she says as I come in. She's attempting to move the tray so she can get up.

I walk over to her. "I'm so sorry to disturb you," I say. I get some tissues from the box near the bed and mop up the water as best I can.

She's covered in heavy quilts despite the stifling warmth in the house, one up to her waist, the other wrapped around her. If it's possible, she seems older than she did a few days ago. The smart cardigan and blouse are gone, and she's not wearing any jewelry. There's a pile of magazines on the side table, and sitting on top is a seven-day pill organizer with one full compartment remaining.

"My pharmacy. Please forgive me for not getting up. I am not well."

"I'm so sorry. I'll only take a minute of your time."

"When you get to be my age," she says, "you spend many hours in bed. It is very boring. I hate television, and the radio is nothing but garbage. I read, but my eyes get tired easily." The bones of her face seem more pronounced in the dim light, and her eyes and the hollows of her cheeks are just dark patches.

I pull Abby's notebook out of my bag and flip to the last picture of the doll, then click on the bedside light for her to see. "Do you recognize this?"

She squints at it. "I used to have a doll that looked like that. A lot of girls did. There were fancier ones, but these were always my favorite."

"I saw this doll in your brother's house. Could it have been yours?"

She looks up at me, and I'm expecting a rebuke or denial, but she just sounds sad. "No, that wasn't mine. I was thirteen when George built that house. Too old for dolls."

"I thought it was from the Fischer girls, but they weren't the first children to be in that basement, were they?"

She nods, a tiny, almost imperceptible movement. "Tabitha. She called her doll Tabitha."

"Who did?"

"Grace. Sweet, lost little Grace." She exhales. I wait. Then she takes another breath and says, "Grace was Alice's daughter. George was going to marry Alice, and he was desperate for Grace to like him, but she never took to him. He thought she was turning her mother against him."

"Was she?"

She's silent for a moment, then she says, "I don't know. She wasn't a mean little girl, not at all. But she hadn't been shown much kindness in her short life, so it took her a while to trust. I made that doll for her sixth birthday. Such a simple thing, but she'd never had anything like it. She always had it with her." She smiles. "She used to call me her big sister. I always wanted a sister. I let George give it to her, but she knew it was really from me . . ."

"And you think this doll is the same one?"

It's just a whisper, but she says, "Yes. Oh . . . oh, that poor little girl."

I take the picture back and put it in my bag. The fizzing electric feeling I've had ever since leaving Buffalo is changing, no longer sparking in all directions. The pieces that refused to fit together are falling into place, which means that my place in all of this—my place now—will start to become clearer.

"I would like to show you . . ." she says. She tries to lean over to open the bedside table drawer but gives up. "Could you?"

I open the drawer. Inside are more pills, old bottles of lotion, more magazines, and a Bible. "In there," she says, indicating the Bible. I hand it to her, and she opens it to pull out an aged envelope. She lays it on her lap, both hands over it as if she's soothing it. Then she begins to speak.

"My brother raised me. I barely remember my parents. They died in an automobile accident. George was with them. I was supposed to be too, but just before we left, he insisted that I go and stay with the neighbor. I never knew why, but he saved my life. I was seven, and after that, it was just George and me."

"My mother died when I was eight," I say.

She nods and gives me a little smile. "You and I share many similarities, I think," she says. "We both lost our mother. You said you had no children. Is that . . . Do you want children?"

"Yes," I say. I have to swallow before I can go on. "Very much. And it almost happened. But this past spring, I lost her."

She reaches out her hand and I take it, and I'm surprised by her strength. Her skin is like tissue paper, the bones almost exposed.

"I know," she says. "I had a feeling. When I asked if you had children before, your face . . ." Then she leans her head toward me and says, "You still can."

"Yes, well." I pull my hand away. "We'll see." This is not what I came here to talk about, and the sudden swell of emotion is unnerving.

"I lost five. My mother lost children too. That's why there is such an age difference between George and me." She points to a line of framed pictures on the wall opposite the bed. I get out of the chair to examine them. No, not pictures; they are samplers, cross-stitched with names and dates: Louisa Marion, February 13, 1941; Margaret Rose, December 2, 1944; Robert George, July 29, 1946; Marion Judith, November 2, 1947; Delmar George, November 10, 1950. I step away and return to the bed. I can't imagine waking up each morning to this morbid gallery of names. I have never said out loud the name I secretly chose for my daughter. I don't know if I will ever be able to.

"My angels," Mrs. Janssen says, looking at the samplers in a way that says these unborn children are still very present for her. "It is a punishment, isn't it?"

I start to protest. I hear all the things that well-meaning friends said to me, but then I stop. "That's what it feels like."

"In my case," she says, "it was. Punishment. And yet I kept trying, and finally I was blessed with Rhonda." She picks up the envelope and offers it to me. "I decided that if you came back, I would show you this."

The envelope is addressed to Miss Marion Sumner, but there's no return address. Carefully I remove a single sheet of brittle paper and hold it in the beam of sunlight. The writing is spidery and slanted, the ink blurred in places.

Dearest Marion,

I need your help. Grace has disappeared.

Yesterday, George brought us out to the house and insisted we stay the night and after our fight and what you told me, I couldn't bear to see him upset again. When I woke up this morning, she was gone. George says she's run away but she wouldn't do that. He won't go to the police. He's brought me

back to town to pack some of my things for the house. He says
we must stay there now. I will leave this with Mrs. Mills and
hope it reaches you. If Grace comes to you, please help her, and
please say nothing to your brother.

I think of you as a sister and hope you feel the same for me.

With all my heart,
Alice

I read it again and then again. "Alice and Grace were reported missing. I saw the newspaper article. But the search was called off."

She doesn't say anything, just looks at me.

"You told me your brother's fiancée ran away."

Still nothing. Then—

Help me.

The voice from all those summers ago echoes in my head. "The Fischers weren't the first to die in that house, were they? If the doll belonged to Grace and it was in the basement . . ."

She remains silent. Even in this dim light, I see how clear her eyes are. I imagine her as the girl I saw in that picture with her brother, trying not to move. At last she takes a breath and begins to speak.

"It was just George and me for six years. He wouldn't let anyone take me away. He said he'd be my father and mother and big brother, and he was. We took care of each other. Over the years, there were other young people he would find and take in. Strays, he'd call them. Orphans, out in the world on their own. Things were very different back then. They'd come through on the train and he'd find them somehow. Sometimes they'd stay with us for a few days, but then they'd disappear. I was always so sad when they went away, but George would say, 'It's better, just the two of us.'

"Then he met Alice. She was someone *I* found." She smiles a little and then continues. "My brother fell in love with her very quickly and very hard. And you would think I'd be jealous, but I wasn't. I loved her too. I thought of her as my older sister. Alice was very beautiful, but it was more than that. She was the strongest woman I'd ever met. The other women in town were not kind to her—I knew what they said about her showing up with a fatherless child—but I didn't care. George didn't either. And then, I don't know exactly when, but he started to change. It was small at first, but I knew him well. Something I'd never seen before—he was fierce about her."

As she continues, her voice changes. It's lost the tremor and breathiness it had before. She sits up straighter in the bed, like telling this story strengthens her.

"George built the house for her. They were to be married in May, and he was working frantically, but Alice didn't—I don't know why—she didn't like the house. Shortly before she disappeared, something happened. They had a horrible argument. George was distraught. He thought he'd lost her. I had never seen him lose his composure like that. He was like . . . like an injured animal. Have you ever been around an injured animal?"

I shake my head.

"They are vicious, but it's fear. It's all fear. He was my brother and I loved him. I'll always love him, no matter what." She pauses. "So, I went to Alice and I begged her to give him a second chance and she agreed. And that was the last time I saw her.

"A few days later, I was in the church, where I helped with the Sunday school. I was cleaning up from our Easter celebration when Mrs. Mills brought me that letter. Old Mrs. Mills was Alice's landlady. She said Alice had asked her to get it to me, and she was worried enough that she walked it over instead of putting it in the post. I didn't know what to do. I was seeing my brother less and less by then; he was always at the house. I had no way of getting in contact with him—it wasn't like now—so I borrowed a friend's bicycle and rode out there.

"George's car wasn't there. I thought Alice might be inside, but when I knocked, no one answered. I should have just gone home but . . . I didn't understand that if I learned something, I wouldn't be able to unlearn it. But I was thirteen. I didn't know anything. So, I went in.

"There was hardly any furniture yet, just a few chairs. The downstairs is just two large rooms—well, I suppose you know that. I stopped at the basement door. I don't know what it looks like now, but back then it was so out of place. Everything in the house was made out of pale wood; it would have been such a beautiful home—but that door. It didn't belong there.

"I went upstairs. In the large bedroom, there was the bed, which was not made up properly, and an open suitcase sitting on a chair. The clothing in the suitcase was obviously Alice's, but it was hanging out, all disheveled, like someone had torn through it. The bed had a gray wool blanket pulled across it, but the pillows had the embroidered covers that I recognized as my mother's wedding set. I think I was embarrassed, to be seeing this, knowing they weren't married yet and what people already said about her. That was why I wasn't thinking clearly. I was going downstairs when I saw . . . I saw . . ." She falters, takes a breath, then continues. "Blood. On the wallpaper. A smear of it, like it had been swiped accidentally by someone moving down the stairs. I hadn't seen it on the way up because the staircase was narrow and my body had blocked the light, but now with the sun hitting it, there was no doubt. And that's when I realized what had felt so odd in the bedroom: the pillowcases were there but not the quilt that went with them.

"I don't know how I did this, but I went back into the bedroom. My hands were shaking, but I lifted that gray blanket up and it was just the bare mattress underneath. It was surreal, like I knew what I was going to find the second before I found it. There was a large dark bloodstain. I . . . I touched it. In the center it was darker, it was still wet. I didn't know what to do. I was just a child. The person I had always gone to for comfort, for answers, was my brother, but now I was alone. I knew that no matter what, I couldn't let him know that I'd seen this, so I pulled the blanket back over it, and I don't know if it was intuition or a guardian angel, but something told me to get out of the house *now*.

"I ran down those stairs and out the door to my bicycle. I tripped on my skirt and hurt my ankle, but I barely even noticed until later. I was getting on the bicycle when George's car pulled through the gap in the trees and there he was. He was alone. He saw me, and his face—it did something odd. It was just for an instant, but he didn't look like my brother. He got out of the car and came toward me. He had a cut on his face, like a scratch down the side of his cheek, and his hand had a bandage on it. He asked what I was doing there; he was trying to be friendly, but I could tell he wasn't happy I was there. If I'd already been on the bicycle, I could have pretended I'd just arrived, but he'd seen me getting on. I tried to laugh, to pretend nothing was wrong, but I couldn't breathe. I said I had wanted to surprise him and Alice, and as soon as I said it, I realized I'd made a mistake. 'Alice?' he said. 'But we're not married yet, why would she be out here?' He tried to make some little joke to embarrass me. It was awful, both of us pretending that nothing was wrong. Then I looked down at my skirt and realized there was blood on it. I had wiped my hand on my skirt without thinking. I made some excuse and got away as fast as I could. There was this narrow road through the woods that connected the house to the main road. It was so bumpy and filled with rocks and tree roots I couldn't ride my bicycle over it, so as soon as I got out of sight of the house, I jumped off the bike. Something made me turn around. I ducked in between the trees so I could see the house. It was so stupid, so dangerous, but I wanted to see what he was doing. He was standing in the kitchen doorway, watching the opening in the trees that I'd just gone through. He was so still."

She stops and reaches for her glass, her hand automatically cupping the empty space.

"Hold on," I say, getting up. "I'll get you more water."

I fill the glass in the bathroom off her bedroom and bring it to her. She reaches out for it thirstily, but her hands are shaking, and she has to hold it with both of them. "Thank you," she says.

"Can you go on?" I ask quietly when she's done drinking. I can see that this is costing her, but she nods and continues.

"Two days later, I came downstairs in the morning and he was sitting in the kitchen. He looked awful. He told me that Alice and Grace had run away. He asked me to go with him to the police."

"Did you show them the letter?"

"How could I?" she cries out. "My brother was standing beside me. He was my only family. I decided that I could not believe what I had seen. Something must have happened, but I couldn't know for certain, don't you see?"

"So, what did you say?"

"I told them that Alice mentioned having second thoughts about the marriage, which was true. And that she was planning to leave. She would have, if she'd had the chance.

"I was a thirteen-year-old girl. They wouldn't have listened to me. No one knew who she was, she'd just drifted into town and stayed. Most people thought my brother was a saint for planning to marry her and taking in her child. She was a lesson on the dangers of loose morals. And it was better to . . . It was easier to believe that something else had happened."

I rummage through my bag and pull out the printout of the newspaper articles that Abby had given to Mr. Fischer. "But it says here there was a search. Did they search the house?"

"There was no real search. A police officer went around and asked a few questions. Everyone assumed she'd left the same way she'd arrived."

I hold out the letter to the editor. "But what about this one. 'A concerned citizen'—is that you?" I think somewhere I hoped that, even as a scared kid, she had done the right thing. I think of myself as a scared kid: Did I do the right thing? Mrs. Janssen doesn't take the article, and I let it drop into my lap.

"No, that wasn't me." She sounds resigned.

"I guess there was at least one other person in the town who cared about Alice and Grace."

"No," she says. "It wasn't because they cared about them. There were rumors . . . I'm sure I didn't hear most of them, but some made their way to me."

"About what?"

"About my brother. He spent a lot of time in the woods—that patch where he built the house. The rest of the land had been sold before I was born, but that little piece of forest he refused to part with."

"But why were there rumors? There's nothing wrong with liking the woods."

"In small towns like this, people talk. Nothing is private. Farmers out in their fields *think* they see or hear something, they go home and tell their wives. Their wives tell their friends. The children hear. Whispering in the schoolyard behind my back. But we were the Sumners. We owned the factory. No one could *do* anything, so they whispered."

"About your brother."

"And about those strays." In a singsong voice she recites, " 'If Georgie asks you to walk in the woods . . .' " Her hands are fists, blueish veins sticking out.

"Do you think any of it was true?"

She looks at me like suddenly she's not sure she can trust me. The kindly grandmother is gone.

"Mrs. Janssen." I'm trying to keep my tone even, gentle. To sound patient, even if I'm not. Rhonda could return at any moment, and that'll be the end of this conversation. "You kept that letter. You told me about what you saw."

"What is it that you want from me?" she asks.

Her question catches me off guard. I take a breath and look straight at her. "The house is dangerous. Not because it's falling down. It's more than that. You need to get rid of it. You need to bulldoze it to the ground and get rid of every scrap. And fill the basement in with concrete. I came to beg you to do that."

She holds my gaze before turning her head. "I know."

We're both quiet for a moment and the dense air of the house holds the silence close to us. Then I say, "You were taking care of it for your brother. But he's gone. He wouldn't know."

Her head snaps to me and her eyes widen, then she says, very, very quietly so that I can barely hear her, "Yes, he would."

She says this so certainly. Coldness slides down my back. "That's not possible," I whisper, more to myself than to her.

"George went away after all of that. I don't know where. I had no communication from him. I was sent to an aunt's house. I wanted to stay and wait for him, but they wouldn't let me. Three years later the war broke out in Europe, and he sent me a letter telling me he was going to volunteer. He sent the deed to the house, signed over to me. He asked me to keep it for him, and so I did."

"Until 1965."

"My husband insisted we sell. Said it was obvious by then that George wasn't coming home. I couldn't bring myself to go in. I hired some young men to clean it out, make whatever repairs were needed. They came back and said it was empty. Absolutely empty."

"But what about the basement?"

"Sealed shut, that's what they said. They had tried to go down there and the door wouldn't open for them."

"But it wasn't shut when the Fischers were there."

"I'm telling you what they told me. They were big men. They said they'd tried, and I believed them."

Her hands are shaking, the water in her glass threatening to spill all over her. But at the same time, she sounds solid and strong. I don't know how to understand the mixed messages her body is sending: the frail old woman whose memories are terrifying her, or the iron-willed woman who has lived with this knowledge for decades and has found some way to bear it. Fear and anger, each keeping the other in check.

"When I learned that the people who'd bought it had young children, I tried to warn them."

"But why would you need to warn them? Even if what you think happened to Alice and Grace actually did. Your brother was killed in the war."

"No, he was missing in action. I'd been trying to find him, but the military had nothing."

"But for you to warn them . . . you must have had a reason."

She looks away, annoyed.

"I'm just trying to understand."

"I had no proof," she finally says. "It was a feeling. The men who went to clean out the house said it wasn't just empty, it was in good shape. It had been unoccupied for thirty years, but nothing was broken, no sign of animals . . . It was like no time had passed. And sometimes, here in town, I would feel like I was being watched. In my house too. But I couldn't tell my husband that. He would have thought I was crazy. So we sold George's house, and I thought I'd do what I could do. If I could warn them to be careful without scaring them."

"Did you tell them about Alice and Grace?"

"More or less. I had taken this letter, but then I saw . . . I thought I saw—" A shudder goes through her, but she grits her teeth and continues. "He was there. I saw him there. I saw him in the woods on the other side of the house. He was looking right at me. I looked away for a second and he was gone."

"So he came back?"

"I don't know." It's the loudest I've heard her speak. "Don't you see how I have agonized over this? With everything that has happened at that house? He was my brother. I desperately didn't want any of this to be true. But what if it was? If he thought that I knew what had happened, he would have hurt me. He would have hurt Rhonda."

"But he loved you. You said he raised you."

"You don't understand. George's love is a possessive love."

My phone buzzes with a text and I just about jump out of the chair. Maybe it's the lack of air in the room, or having spent so long in the past with her, but I feel like I'm in a trance. I fumble for my cell as it vibrates with another message, and then another.

It's Taylor. U said to text.

It's bad. Have to go there.

Help me.

I stand up, abruptly spilling Abby's notebook and loose papers onto the floor. "I have to go. Shit—I'm sorry—I have to go." I'm feeling around on the carpet for everything that's spilled out of my bag and the phone buzzes again.

Going now.

I try to text her back, but it takes three attempts because my fingers are clumsy.

Wait for me. I'm coming. DON'T GO.

"It's my friend's daughter. She's going into that house. It's going to happen again."

"Again? No—"

"Yes. And there will be another after her. And another. This keeps happening."

I'm half out the door when Mrs. Janssen calls out, "Clare—"

I spin back around.

She's sitting up again, looking straight at me. "Make this end. Destroy it."

26

Punishment. The word keeps running through my mind as I race to my car and out to Lori's. I try calling Taylor, but each time it just goes straight to voicemail. I call Lori—no luck. I text her.

On my way to yours. Taylor wants to go to O-House. Going to stop her.

Usually Lori is so quick to respond, but in the five minutes it takes me to get from Mrs. Janssen's out to Lori's place, there's no response. Her message said she was out of town at a hockey tournament. I envision her wrangling a team of small children in hockey gear, the echoing noise of an ice rink with hundreds of parents and kids in it—it could be hours before she thinks to take out her phone.

I scramble out of the car and run to Lori's door. It's locked. I bang on it and call out, "Taylor, it's me—let me in." Inside, the dogs go nuts, slamming themselves against the door. She's not in there; I know she's not in there. There's a mess of bikes on the lawn; I have no idea if one of them is hers. Then I look across the road. Taylor doesn't need to go the long way, on the road. She has a shortcut. She can go straight through the fields to the woods.

For a second I think about trying to follow her, but the woods are dense and I don't know my way through them. I could miss the house entirely. I jump back in the car and send gravel flying as I screech out of the driveway. I don't know how fast Taylor is moving, but at this point, she has to be close. I almost miss the place in the fence that leads to the old road, but fortunately the police tape is still there, fluttering in the breeze. I could try to drive in, but if the police and ambulance didn't think they could get through, there's no way my shitty hatchback will make it. I park the car, make sure I have my phone in my pocket, and run into the woods.

I know I should be yelling Taylor's name, but every time I open my mouth, the words get stuck in my throat. I feel like I'm being watched. It's the old superstition, the old fear. It's everything Mrs. Janssen has just told me, except that has to be impossible. She couldn't have seen her brother all those years later. She felt guilty and confused. I'm breathing so hard, I can't get enough air to yell loudly anyway. It takes me too long to get there and it doesn't take long enough because I'm not ready. I will never be ready. Everything in me has been running away from that house ever since I was fourteen and here I am, running toward it—

And then I see it.

I stop on the edge of the clearing, my chest heaving. The outside walls of the house are completely gray now. The little room on top has collapsed into the bedroom below, as if a giant hand came down from the sky and crushed it. The kitchen door is a black hole directly in front of me. There's more yellow police tape stretched across it. When I was here before, that was the only way in. I hope it still is. There's no sign of Taylor.

I take out my phone. No signal. A sharp jolt of panic shoots into my gut. Alone, alone, alone. Abby left her phone in the car. Maybe she knew. She couldn't have called for help if she'd tried.

A bird shoots up from the opposite side of the clearing and startles me. I have seen this before. A moment later, a girl steps out of the woods. "Taylor!" I call out. This time my voice works. I step into the open so she can see me, and just as I do, two more birds screech up out of the trees. Then an entire flock of blackbirds lifts into the sky and swarms over the house, and for a second we're both frozen, watching this explosion of movement where there was only stillness. Just as quickly, the birds scatter and are gone.

"Clare?" she calls out. She looks so small.

"Stay there," I yell, and I run to her, keeping to the outer perimeter of the clearing.

She's wearing rubber boots caked with clumps of mud from the fields she has tramped through. Her hair is blowing wild around her and there are leaves stuck in it. Her face is splotchy from crying, and as I get closer, she starts to cry all over again.

"I couldn't take it anymore. It's been so bad. Every night—I can't sleep—it's all I can think about."

"I know. It's okay. I'm so glad you texted me."

"Mom's with Chloe and Jake. She thinks I'm at my friends', but I came home. I had two of these, but they're so heavy I had to leave one behind. Do you think it'll be enough?"

Confused, I ask, "Enough what?"

She lifts a battered gas canister from a patch of long grass behind her.

I stand there stupidly. I've been thinking large machinery—backhoes and cranes and dump trucks to haul it all away. But Lori's been threatening to come and burn the place down for months now. I look at the house. Is it too damp with mold and rot to do anything but smoke, or would it go up like a massive bonfire?

"I have no idea," I say, taking the canister from Taylor. "Look, you have to go."

She shakes her head violently. "Then it'll never end."

"I'm going to get the house torn down. I talked to the woman who owns it. She's agreed."

She's still just staring at me and shaking her head. Even though they're not related, she looks too much like Lori—her stubbornness.

"I texted your mom. She's going to be so worried—" I say.

"You told her?"

"Of course I told her."

"I have to do this now. I can't wait. It has to be *now*."

I grab her shoulders with both hands, feel how thin she is under the oversize coat. But in some ways, we're mirror images. We feel this house inside us. We hear it. We saw the doll revealed in the shadows—an offering of sorts to us. The Fischer girls in the basement—I wonder if they saw the doll too.

Taylor has come to destroy this house on her own. She lugged a full gas canister through mud and thick undergrowth. Abby was strong enough to come back here too, arming herself with information. But in doing so, she came out barely alive, threatening to take her family with her. Anger grows in the pit of my stomach. Good. I need it. That will make me strong enough to go in there and do whatever I need to do to end this. Taylor can't be here. It will ruin Lori.

No one should lose their child.

I'm still squeezing Taylor's shoulders; I release my grip. "It's too dangerous. You can't go in there. Look what happened to Abby."

"Please."

"Go back to your house. As soon as you get reception, call your mom and tell her what's happening. Once she gets my text, she's going to be crazy with worry."

"She'll just yell at me."

"She loves you, and she's scared."

"My mom isn't scared of anything. She's just mad all the time."

"She's scared of this house."

Her eyes well up again. "But what about you?"

"I'll be fine."

"Can't we just do it together? Isn't that safer?"

"No."

Because I have to go back inside the house. I can't tell her this, but I know it's true. I've known ever since I came home. It's what Abby was telling me in her note. It has to be me, not for the house—it doesn't actually matter who lights the match—but for me. Because I've been haunted by this too. And the only way to break that is to go back to the source and do it there. I know it's not realistic or smart or even vaguely sane to blame everything bad that has happened to me on this house, but it has left a residue, and it's time I leave that behind once and for all.

I don't say any of this to Taylor. I pick up the gas canister, and with my other hand, I nudge her toward the woods. "Go."

I stand at the edge of the woods until I can't see her moving through the trees, and then I turn around and face the house. I realize she might not do as I've instructed, but I don't want to be here any longer than I have to be, and the faster I get this done, the faster I can get out of here and call Lori myself.

"Okay, you fucker," I say to the house. If I focus on the anger, I can do this. "Let's do this."

But by the time I'm at the kitchen doorway, I feel like I'm fourteen all over again. I stand, blinking, letting my eyes adjust to the dim light filtering in through the cracks in the boarded-up windows. Dust hovers in the air in those thin beams of light, waiting for me to walk through it, to send each particle colliding into another, creating a ripple across the room, letting the house know that someone has entered. The only way to know if the basement door is open is to go in to it. The canister hits the side of my leg as I walk, and gas sloshes inside. I focus on what's real: the rough plastic handle, the smell of the gas, the crunch of my feet over broken glass and dead leaves.

I walk diagonally across the kitchen toward the basement. I smell it before I see it. Damp earth and stagnant water and something else, something festering under that. The basement door is partway open, and written on it in chalk is a broken triangle.

It's not big, and if the police saw it, they probably just thought it was a kid adding to the vandalism of the place, but I know Abby slashed those lines there.

Our sign: a disordered mind. But hers? Or is she trying to warn me about what waits below?

Standing in the doorway, I turn on my phone flashlight and shine it into the darkness. It just barely reaches the bottom. To see what's beyond, I'm going to have to go farther down. I step onto the top stair, then the next, and the next: the slightest hint that the door is closing, and I'll be able to get out in a matter of seconds. But it's not far enough. The darkness feels dense; it absorbs the light as if I'm shining it into water. If there is something waiting for me down there, it has enough dark to hide in.

The wood stairs are slick with dampness, and with no banister, there's nothing to hold. I have to put the phone in my pocket so I can edge my way down, holding the gas canister in one hand. Halfway down, my heel slips and I fall back heavily, almost dropping the canister. I leave it and take out my phone, my cold, fumbling fingers threatening to drop it into the nothingness below me.

From here, I see the basement wall. The stones of the foundation glisten between black fingers of mold. Instinctively I check the door, but it hasn't moved. Keep going. Down, down, down into darkness.

What am I supposed to do down here? Is just coming down here enough, Abby? Have I made my amends?

I want to keep my back to the stairs. I scan the light from side to side, trying to shine it in all places at once, but that's impossible. I need to see the doll. I need to know if it was real. *And if you find it?* the voice in my head asks.

Then I'll have proof that Grace was real. And will that mean that my memory of the voice speaking to me is real too?

Panic bubbles up in my throat.

The stairs are like an umbilical cord to the outside world. As long as I'm touching them, escape seems possible. Or maybe it's their solidness: they are real, while everything else around me is empty darkness. There's no evidence of anyone else ever being down here, and yet I know police and paramedics were down here two weeks ago. No gum wrappers or crumpled receipts or anything that might have fallen out of a pocket when latex gloves or a flashlight were being pulled out. Upstairs, the floor is so littered with the detritus of all the years of trespassers—animal and human—but down here the floor is bare. The basement opens only for some. And, in my limited experience, it doesn't stay open for long.

I move my light in wider arcs with each pass, trying to cover as much space as I can. Then, at the farthest point, my light catches something. Abby left another broken triangle chalked onto the wall.

My breath catches in my throat. Whatever she wants me to see, it's there. I let go of the stairs and shuffle my way toward the far wall, counting my steps, listening for a sign of something moving in the dark, but all I hear is my own breathing. Part of the wall seems to be crumbling. I run my hands over it, feeling its bumps, then a stone dislodges. I lift out the loose stone and air moves over my skin. An opening. Something's behind the wall. I pull more stones away, throwing them behind me. They make a low thump on the earth floor. I try to shine my light into that blackness, but I have to make the hole larger. Moving faster now, I push the stones into the opening until it's large enough that I can reach my arm into it with the flashlight and poke my head through.

A tunnel.

It's about three feet wide and five feet high. Desiccated roots stick out through the walls. I can see it bend about fifteen feet ahead: a tunnel that goes beyond the border of the house, under the clearing, and into the woods. Somewhere, in those woods, is the entrance.

I swing the light down to the ground closer to me. There, to my left, is a low flat stone that's larger than the rest. Sitting on it is a book that looks like the cover might have been leather, the pages swollen with moisture. Next to that is a stuffed animal—maybe an owl?—a pair of woman's lace-up heeled boots, a flask, a cap, a tin cup, a pair of tattered shoes with no laces, a cloth sack, and a few smaller items I can't make out from here. The largest is a folded sheet. Impossible to tell what color it once was, but even under the dirt and mold, I can see some type of embroidery—

My mother's wedding set.

Mrs. Janssen's words. If this is the quilt that was missing from the bed, these have to be George Sumner's things. His collection. And each item here, each so different from the others, must have belonged to . . .

Strays . . . he'd find them somehow . . . then they'd disappear.

He built this house in his graveyard, and then he kept adding to it.

My stomach turns, but I force myself to move the light over the whole collection until it catches on something on the ground that makes me freeze again. It's cloth, folded neatly into a square, and newer than anything else down here. I can see part of a rainbow and puffy cloud. If I unfold it, will I see "Camp Winnetowa" written over it? Abby's shirt that I threw on the ground before we sped away in the car.

Ghosts don't pick up T-shirts and wall them into a tomb.

He was here. He was watching us that night.

The wave of nausea is immediate. I fall back out of the tunnel and sit on the basement floor. I tremble and wrap my arms around my legs to make myself as small as possible. It's so cold. I pull my jacket tight around me, but it's not enough.

This is what Abby was trying to tell me. Proof. Proof that she wasn't alone down here. Now I can leave, except I can't. The cold is working its way under my skin; I feel like I'll never be warm again. And the deeper it moves inside me, the heavier I feel.

Help me.

My head jerks up. There, on the ground about four feet in front of me, is the doll. Standing behind it is something else.

Help me.

Grace. Alice's child. She's been down here the whole time. Small and thin with long stringy braids and a dress that goes to her shins. She's all one color, like an old picture—skin, hair, and clothes a grayish brown, except her eyes, which are huge and white. Blind from all the years in the darkness. My phone must be dying because no light moves past her or reflects off her skin. She's a black hole, pulling it into her.

Take her.

You are not real. You cannot be real.

Help me. Take her.

Take the doll to Marion, not the old woman she is now but the thirteen-year-old who once showed this little girl kindness. Take her to the teenage Marion who would get this doll and understand that she needed to help, who this time would be brave enough to stand up to her brother and demand that the police search the house and help them find George's graveyard.

She's holding the doll out to me, and I lift a heavy arm to reach for it when she turns and looks up the stairs. The light at the top is bright, far brighter than it should be. And the moment the light hits her, I see the ring of black bruises around her neck.

Go, now, she says in my head. *GO.*

I stagger to my feet and lurch across the darkness to the stairs. My foot slips on the bottom step, and my phone drops out of my hand, but it doesn't matter. Nothing matters but getting out of here. I climb up on all fours, fingernails digging into the slimy wood. I slip again, banging my knee, but the pain jolts me into focus, and I scramble toward that unnatural light at the top. And then I'm high enough to see the kitchen, and it's not boarded up and filled with garbage. The sun floods through the windows and it's airy and bright and new, the floor uncluttered and clean. At the top, a man steps into the doorway, cutting off the light. His face is impossible to see. He towers over me. He reaches his arm out to push the door shut, and I hear a woman behind him.

"No, please," she screams. "Let her be—"

In the second that he turns his head, I get to the top and reach out for him. If I slip through him, I will be out of the basement and back into the kitchen as it is now. He will be gone because he is not real. He is a memory. He is a nightmare that I am both in and not in.

And Abby will stay in this basement. She will not come out of the coma. Maybe it will take months, maybe it will take years, but eventually her family will accept what the doctors are telling them, and they will turn off the machines keeping her alive. And everyone will say there was nothing that could be done. But I will know, I will know what I could have done.

So I let my hands make contact. I know he cannot be real—he is not real—but I feel the rough fabric, the weight of a body, as I grab on to his shirt with both hands and pull backward. In that second I see him, the face from Mrs. Janssen's pictures, a face shifting from rage to panic as he loses his balance, and we fall together down, down, down into the darkness. The door slams shut as my body hits the floor, breath escapes me, and then I keep falling.

Clare

Wake up

This voice is different: older. Abby? No, it's my mother. She knows I am here. But I am still sinking into darkness. It's what I imagine it would be like to dive deep, deep into the canyons on the ocean floor, beyond the boundaries of what is known. I have been falling into this darkness for a long time. Minutes? Hours? How much longer before I come to the end of it? And then?

And then I will rest. Finally.

Is this what I came here to do? I thought this would be frightening. How much time we waste being so frightened of death and now here it is and it is gentle after all. Is this what my mother was trying to tell me? Lavender. I need to remember the smell of lavender. I can't remember the smell—I have to remember the smell, but all I can smell is gasoline—

Clare

The voice is different now. Farther away. It's not inside my head.

"Clare!"

And suddenly I'm not falling. I open my eyes but there's nothing. I try to gasp in air and the smell of gasoline burns my throat. I'm on the basement floor. I feel wetness all around me, soaking into my clothes. I must be bleeding, but I can't tell from where. I try to swallow and I can't. I taste blood. I'm so thirsty, oh, God, I'm so thirsty. How long have I been down here? I blink my eyes open shut open shut but there is no light. Burning and panic. I'm going to die down here, and I don't want to die. I thought I wanted to die when I lost my baby. That thought has been in me, poisoning everything I've done since May, but now that the reality of it is here, the panic, the clawing desperation to *live*, is screaming in my head—

"Clare!"

Banging on the door high above me and now I'm fully awake. I open my mouth to call out, but no sound comes out.

"Clare, we're coming." There's a voice—no, two voices. Everything is muffled, far away somewhere. And then the door opens and two flashlight beams cut into the darkness. Two silhouettes.

"Clare, are you in there?"

They cough and gag. "Jesus, what the fuck—" A man's voice. Mitchell's voice.

"Clare! Clare!" It's Lori. Lori and Mitchell are here. I'm not alone anymore.

"Is that gas?"

"Oh my God, is she—?"

"No, stay up there. Keep that fucking door open—"

Someone rushes down the stairs and grabs me, pulls me up.

"Oh, fuck, fuck, fuck."

Grunting and coughing as my body is dragged up the stairs. I'm watching it, not feeling it. Come back now, come back into your body, it's going to hurt, but you have to come back, I tell myself. Then a second pair of hands helps pull me out, and we all fall in a heap on the kitchen floor.

"Is she breathing?"

"Get her out of here. Get her out of this fucking house."

Mitchell and Lori pull me up again, one on either side of me, my feet half dragging, trying to hold my weight as they carry me into the outside, into the evening, into the world. Air rushes into me and I feel my body. I am back inside it, and I spasm and begin to retch, but nothing comes out. I lie on my side, my body convulsing, trying to expel everything inside me onto the dirt.

"We have to get away from this place."

"Look at her; she can't move yet."

I'm gulping the clean air. I can't breathe fast enough. The sky shines purple under the low clouds. The sky, the trees, Mitchell's and Lori's faces, my own hands streaked with black—everything hurts my eyes after that blindness, and I want to take it all in: air, color, sound, the world. My stomach heaves and heaves. Everything hurts, but I'm out. I'm out. I'm out of the basement.

Mitchell grabs me by the shoulders. "What the fuck were you doing?"

"Jesus Christ, leave her alone." Lori pushes him off me and I fall back again. She pulls her coat off and puts it over me, then keeps her arms around me, holding me tight. We're on the ground and she's rocking me. "It's okay. You're okay. You're safe," she says. "It's over, it's all over."

I don't know how long she keeps repeating that to me. Mitchell has moved away from us. He's sitting on the ground, his head in his hands.

"I'm sorry," I try to say, but it hurts to speak, and I taste blood again. "I'm sorry," I croak.

"Shhh," she says. "Don't talk yet." She hands me a water bottle and I fumble with it, then I drink greedily, half of it running down my face. "Slow, now," she says. "You don't know how your stomach is going to take that." I force myself to slow down, take a gulp of water, pull the bottle away from my lips, breath, breath, take another gulp. Lori watches me, not saying anything. Finally the bottle is empty.

"That's better," she says. "You going to make it?"

I nod, my breathing more settled. The movement hurts my head.

"You look like you've been in one hell of a fight," she says.

I point to my side where the pain is the sharpest and mouth, "Fell."

"You fell?"

I nod.

"Jesus, you're lucky you didn't crack your head open. You probably broke a rib, but I don't think you're bleeding."

I want to examine myself for the source of the wetness, but it hurts too much to move.

"The floor was covered with gas," she says. "Can't you smell it?"

And as soon as she says it, that's all I can smell. Another wave of nausea rises in my stomach, but I manage to keep myself from throwing up again. When it's passed, I half whisper, half croak, "Taylor?"

"She's okay. Pretty shaken up. She's at the house with her dad. He'd just gotten in, and I threw the kids at him and came here. When she called me, I could barely make out anything she was saying because she was crying so hard, but I'd already gotten your text. I was on the way home. Mitchell called me earlier—said he was heading here. Said he saw you this morning and you were acting weird and you wouldn't respond to him either."

"He came back . . . ?"

"Why were you down there?"

"Abby," I croak.

"She's not down there. She's in a hospital in Buffalo, which you know because you were just there."

I shake my head.

"I do not understand you two and your obsession with that house."

"We saw . . . There's something . . ."

She puts her hands on my shoulders. "Stop. Whatever it is that you're doing, or you thought you were doing, stop. You could have died. If we hadn't gotten you out, you would have suffocated down there. Do you understand that?"

I nod.

"Do you?"

"Yes." And I do. The reality of that makes my stomach heave again, and this time I can't stop it.

Lori watches me but says nothing. I'm on my hands and knees, face and hands streaked with black mold and dirt, retching into the earth, utterly and completely pathetic. When I'm done, she says, "You've inhaled a lot of gas. You were in a terrifying place. That fucks with your head. But I am telling you, there is nothing down there. Okay?"

I nod and Lori says something, maybe to Mitchell, then I watch her walk across the clearing toward the house. I lie down. The clouds above are moving away; it's going to be a clear night. In my peripheral vision, I see movement and turn my head to watch Mitchell moving toward me. I make myself sit up and try to say something.

"Don't even bother," he says. His voice is choked, ragged. His eyes are raw. "How many times do I have to drag people out of this place? How could you come back here? Abby was one thing, but you? What the fuck is your excuse?"

I open my mouth to speak, but again, nothing comes out.

"Did you even think for one second about anyone else? Did you think about Lori and her family? They've just gone through this with Abby, and now you? And what about your dad? You're all he's got, but did you even think about him? And what about me?"

"You?" I croak.

"Yeah, me. Maybe in your head, that's some kind of martyr bullshit that no one cares about you, that what you do doesn't affect other people, but it does. My sister is the same, and I'm so sick of it. You're both so fucking selfish."

"Mitchell—"

"I can't do—" I hear the catch in his throat. "I can't do this, Clare." He's crying now and not even bothering to wipe the tears away. "I thought I lost you." And he turns and walks into the woods.

The vise grip is back on my head. I'm watching the place in the trees where he's disappeared when Lori runs up from behind me.

"We gotta go. Are you okay to move?"

Before I can answer, she puts her arm around my waist and heaves me up. Pain explodes in my side and I double over. She gives me all of two seconds to recover, then drags me across the rest of the clearing and into the woods.

"Hold on to me," she says. "We've got to move quickly. It's going to hurt."

I want to ask her what we're running away from, but I can't catch my breath because every inhale makes it feel like I'm being stabbed. "Just watch where you're putting your feet and keep moving," she says. I'm stumbling over branches, but she keeps her arm tight around me until we tumble out of the woods at the opening of the fence. Mitchell is there, but he won't look at me.

Lori helps me into her car and holds out her hand. "Keys. Mitchell will drive your car to my place. We're going to the hospital."

I feel drunk, and my head hurts so much it's hard to keep my eyes open, but I manage to dig my keys out of my pocket and give them to her. "Just leave it," I slur.

"We have to get your car out of here. Look," she says, and she turns and points back to the woods, and that's when I see the thick black smoke billowing up into the sky. She has a huge grin on her face. "I'll call the fire department, but I don't want them to know it was us."

As we drive away, I watch the black smoke rising higher and higher and disappearing into the evening sky.

27

In the hospital, they put me on oxygen, tell me I have a cracked rib, and after a few hours, send me home with a prescription for some extra-strong painkillers. At Lori's insistence, I am spending the night at her house. She says she's worried that I might have some residual effects from the gasoline, but really, I think it's because she knows I don't want to be alone. I'm grateful.

She sets me up on the couch in her basement and brings me soup and toast and tea, as well as multiple ice packs for my rib and my knee, which is turning a foul shade of purplish green. The family's upstairs, the kids running back and forth, excited that their father is home. I lie very still and listen to the sounds of life—chair scrapes, voices rising and falling, plates and glasses clinking, the theme music of an old sitcom, then the growing quiet, voices farther away, water running, and finally a hush settles. Someone watches a football game, but the volume is low.

Through it all I move in and out of sleep, in and out of time. It's my mom and dad upstairs, and I want to go up and spend one last night with them, the way it used to be, but I know I can't, so I stay down here and listen. I want to remember everything. It's Abby's family, the loud, loving family I so desperately wanted to be a part of. At some point when I was asleep, someone brought me a bowl of ice cream and a homemade card that said "Feel beter soon, luv Chloe" with a drawing of a dog. The ice cream has melted when I find it, but I drink it anyway and let the cool, thick liquid coat my raw throat. Lori comes down a few times to make sure I'm still breathing, she says. I can't bring myself to say it, but it feels good to be taken care of. She tells me the fire department let the house burn and just made sure the fire didn't spread.

"They'll know it was set on purpose. The gas—" I start to say, but she cuts me off.

"I told them it was probably kids. I know those guys. They're not going to look too deeply into it unless I ask them to."

"Marion Janssen agreed to it being destroyed. I'm not sure that's how she meant."

Lori snorts. "She could have done it fifty years ago and none of this would have happened."

We're both quiet for a moment, thinking about what that would have meant.

"I think she'll be relieved. It's gone. It's really gone," I say.

"I know. It is completely gone."

"How is Taylor doing?" I'm not sure if she told her mother how I ended up at the house. Lori deserves an explanation.

"She wanted to come down to see you, but I told her to wait until tomorrow. She fell asleep after supper while she was doing homework. Passed out with her face in her math book."

"I'm sorry," I say. "If it feels like I went behind your back."

I see Lori stiffen a little, but then she takes a breath and says, "Can you tell me what happened?"

"She told me about going into the house. I recognized something in her. I saw the same thing in Abby." Lori's head turns sharply toward me. "Not mental illness but the obsession, as you call it. That house had a strange pull on some people."

"I will never understand that," she says. "I'm not saying it isn't real—I know it is for you and Abby. And I guess for Taylor. But I've lived next to that place for *my entire life,* and I'm fine." She smiles. "Well, you know, reasonably fine."

"I gave Taylor my number and told her to text me if she ever felt herself being pulled there. I know I should have told you, but she seemed to trust me, and I thought that was worth it. Plus, I knew I'd call you the moment I heard from her—and I did."

"Huh," Lori says. She gets up and starts gathering the dishes I've left scattered on the coffee table, then she turns to me. "It just kind of hurts, you know? You want to think that *you're* the person your daughter reaches out for, not some person she's just met. And with all the step-mother stuff—"

"I know."

"Thank you, though. I'm not sure if I've said that. If she hadn't texted you . . ." She swallows hard. "I can't even . . ." She puts the dishes down and sits beside me. "Clare?" Her voice is quiet. Even. "Were you trying to . . . ?"

"I don't know," I say. "Right before you guys got the door open, I knew I was probably going to die, and I realized I didn't want to. Maybe I never really did, it just seemed . . . I don't know. Like a way out."

I'm expecting her to rage at me the way Mitchell did, or to stomp upstairs, but she doesn't do either. She just sits with me. After a minute she says, "And now?"

"I'm okay," I say.

"Okay. Good. But if you weren't?"

"I'm okay."

Maybe I have underestimated Lori. Maybe I'm still seeing her as the cool, sassy fourteen-year-old, and maybe I underestimated her then too. What if, instead of pulling away from her after everything that happened, I had tried to tell her? It's not even a question of *would we have been best friends all these years;* it's more about *what would I have been like.* If I'd allowed myself to be vulnerable and scared instead of running away.

She's leaning back on the couch with her arm over her eyes. I don't know what time it is, but the house is quiet above us.

"Can I tell you something?" I finally ask.

"Sure."

"I had a miscarriage earlier this year."

"Oh, shit." She squeezes my hand, wide awake now. "I'm so sorry."

"I need to . . . to start saying it out loud. Letting it be real. I thought maybe it was connected to all of this."

"To the house?" She doesn't sound skeptical, just confused.

"Abby got in touch with me, and I started having these horrible nightmares about it and then . . . I don't know. It sounds crazy when I say it, but then I lost the baby."

"It's not crazy."

"Really?"

"Fear is real. Even if what you're afraid of isn't, the fear is." Then she says, "I've lost two as well."

"I didn't know. I'm sorry." I can't see her face, but I imagine the little smile of acknowledgment in the silence between us. "The woman who owned the house, Marion Janssen, she lost five pregnancies. She said she thought she was being punished."

Lori sighs. "Tell her to look up the statistics. The rates are way higher here than anywhere else in the state. Cancer too. That's what my doctor told me. It's because of the metal factory that *her* family owned; it poisoned this place. Doesn't make it any easier, though."

"Does it get easier?"

She thinks about that. "No. And yes. I don't think about them as much now, so in that way it's easier. When I do, it still hurts. But I kind of don't want it to stop hurting, you know? Like, that hurt is all I have of them, so if I let it go, then what do I have?"

If you let hurt go, what is left? Will the memory stay behind if you allow the pain to float away? Ever since Mom died, all I've had is this emptiness. This bottomless sadness and rage—I can say that now—rage at being ripped off, of having to give up someone who I should never have had to lose. And guilt. Always guilt. Guilt for being angry. Guilt for not being good enough to fill her up with so much happiness that there was no space for the sickness to get in. I have been afraid to let all of those feelings about my mother go, because what if there is nothing left then?

I'm exhausted and still a little nauseated and I know I could sleep for three days but my mind feels clear. I realize now, sitting here in another family's house, maybe there is something else underneath the grief—

early memories moving like animated snapshots in my mind: my mom and dad sitting in the front seat of the car and her turning around, smiling at me, and pointing to something out the window; Mom rubbing dried buds of lavender between her hands, then putting her face into them and breathing deep.

What other memories are inside me, like little shoots of life in a garden long abandoned, only waiting for the sunlight to wake them up?

My phone buzzes, but it's across the room plugged into the wall, and I'm too cozy on the couch to bother getting up.

"It works?" Lori says. When we were in the hospital, she handed me my cracked phone, which Mitchell must have rescued from the basement.

"I guess so."

"You going to check that?"

"I'm sure it's nothing important."

She unplugs my phone from the charger and brings it over to me. "Answer your texts. You don't want people worrying about you." Then she goes back upstairs.

It's from Mitchell. Just checking in, he says. I ask if we can talk sometime. His answer is immediate.

I'm already here.

———

"I've been driving," Mitchell says when I get in his car. "I know I should have waited for you here, but I wasn't in a state to— I wasn't going to make any sense if I tried to explain."

"Thank you," I say. "I know that's not enough but . . . I don't know how long I was down there. I don't know how much longer I would have been able to breathe if you two hadn't pulled me out when you did."

"After I saw you this morning, I had this feeling you were going to go back there. And there was that dream I'd had."

"The one about being down there with Abby?"

"Yeah. The last time I had it, it started out as Abby, but then she turned around and it was you."

"Me?"

"I wanted to tell you before, that night at the hospital, but . . . I thought it would freak you out. That's why I wanted you to get away from this place. And then what you said this morning, and you didn't respond to my texts. I've ignored those feelings before, so this time I just decided fuck it. If I'm wrong, I can go to your house and apologize in person."

"Apologize for what?"

"What I said this morning," he says. "I shouldn't have said that. None of us want you to stay away."

"I figured out that whatever she went in there to face, I had to go and face too. I know it doesn't make sense, but I need you to know that even though it was selfish and reckless, it was the best I could do."

He's quiet for a bit, then he says, "Okay."

"Okay?"

"I don't get it, but I understand about your intentions being good."

I know what I saw but I don't believe what I saw, and I don't know what to do with that. Even if I did believe it, how can I ever explain it? Trying to make sense of it makes my head begin to pound again.

"Being down there again felt like the twilight zone," he says, "like I'm going to be forced to live through my mistakes over and over in some kind of endless loop."

"You're not the one who's made mistakes," I say.

He looks at me. "Am I— Were we a mistake? This summer?"

"No," I say. I'm so surprised by the look on his face, it takes me a moment to recover. "I thought that's what *you* thought. You said things were messy."

"Messy, yes," he says. "Not wrong. And the other day when I first saw you, you got so upset. You said you were sorry for everything, so I just thought . . ."

"So we were both wrong," I say. "Huh."

"Huh," he says too. Out of the corner of my eye, I see his mouth twitch into a little smile, but then he leans forward and grabs his phone off the dash.

"I got a message from my mom. Abby started showing some positive signs a few hours ago. She's not in the clear yet, but her odds are improving."

"That's hopeful," I say.

"The doctors are 'cautiously optimistic.'" He smiles and puts the phone down. "It really is good to see you again. Less than ideal circumstances, but I guess you can't be choosy."

I laugh, then stop because it hurts. There's still so much I don't know. "Can you tell me now? About . . ."

"About Sasha?"

I nod.

"We divorced a year ago when I took the job in Saudi, but we'd been separated for a while before that. She stayed in London. I'd told her I didn't want to have kids. That was the main reason why our marriage fell apart—at least I thought it was. It's not that I don't want kids, but seeing what was happening with my sister—it's hard to explain the roller coaster. I mainly saw it through my parents. It's been years of watching this eat away at their relationship—at the whole family, really. I don't know if any marriage could survive that. I told Sasha I didn't want kids, because what if I pass this along? They say it's not genetic, but I don't know. If it happened in my sister, couldn't it be in me too? I thought Sasha was okay with it, but then over time she wasn't, and she said she wanted out. She emailed me at the end of last May to tell me that she'd met this great guy and they're pregnant and she is so happy and blah blah blah. Everything inside me just stopped. It's like my whole life was this fantastically designed machine where every cog and wheel fit into the next, then I get this email from my ex and the whole contraption seizes.

"So I went home. But Abby wasn't doing well—something to do with a bad reaction to a change in medication, and Mom and Dad were completely consumed by that, and I'm not supposed to have any problems anyway. I'm supposed to be the easy one. When I'm really feeling sorry for myself, I think they can't even see the real me; the mess. I blamed Abby. I blamed her disease. That's something I've come to realize. I stopped seeing my sister and her disease as separate, and that's . . . fucked up."

He swallows hard but keeps going.

"And I guess, under that, I blamed myself. I've always thought I had something to do with it coming out in her. Borderline can be a result of trauma. Like it got triggered; the switch got turned on. That night when we went to the house, it's obviously connected to her going there again, and that first time was my fault. Which means my family falling apart, my marriage falling apart, my sister's life being wasted, it all comes down to being my fault."

"It wasn't your fault," I say. "None of it was your fault."

"I was the one who wanted to go there. I knew she was messed up because of the pot. She was just a kid."

"We all were."

"Yeah, but there was something about my sister that was still so childlike. And after that night . . . she changed. All because I was trying to impress you with how brave I was. What a joke. You at least left a note and a flashlight. And you kept wanting to check on her. I would have just walked away and left her there."

Nausea rises in my throat. I have to tell him. All these years, he has blamed himself for what happened to Abby when it's been my fault all along.

He goes on, "I had just had that fight with Paul—do you remember? I was pissed at my sister. I wanted to fool around with you. I was tired of being the good guy. But I didn't think she'd leave the car. Like never in a million years. I've never been able to figure out why she went down into the basement, though. The house, I guess I can understand, because she knew we were in there, but why the basement?"

"It's because of me."

"No, it wasn't."

I have to tell him, I know I do, but telling him might be the end of any connection I have to the Lindsay family. I take a breath.

"Okay. I told you we'd gone there earlier in the day, the four of us. I thought I'd seen something in the basement, and I told Abby we should go down there, but then I . . ." My voice catches. I swallow hard. *Say it.* "I tricked her. I was mad at her for something she had done earlier with this picture of—it doesn't matter—so I told her to go ahead of me, then

I closed the door on her. I was going to open it right away, it was just to scare her for a second, but then it wouldn't open. So she was in there for a couple of minutes. And while she was in there . . . she saw something, or thought she saw something, or . . ."

I can't look at him. I squeeze my hands into fists, digging my nails into my palms. The vise grip is starting in my head again.

"Clare."

"If you want me to get out right now, I will totally understand." My hand is on the door handle. "You don't ever have to talk to me again."

"No." He sounds surprised. "What? No. You were a kid, like you said. Kids do that kind of shit to each other. Are you kidding? The stuff Paul and I used to do to each other? And to Abby. Well, Paul, mainly, I was an angel, as you know." He smiles. "You couldn't have known that the door would stick. It was a mistake."

"But it started all of this," I say, and now I'm crying, big, ugly, nose-dripping, hiccuping tears. "Everything—everything started because I did that."

"Hey . . . Hey now," he says quietly, and he reaches over to me and pulls me in to him. I wince as my ribs get jostled. "Oh, sorry." He leans in and puts his forehead against mine. He smells so good. He smells like *Mitchell,* the smell I have known since I was fourteen, the smell that I have never found in another man. The smell I do not deserve.

"After she got out of the hospital, we met up, and Abby told me why she'd gone back in—that something was down there. I told her there was nothing down there and that she'd imagined it because of the pot. But I saw some things today that . . . Yeah. I don't know."

He leans back and looks at me. "You told Abby what anyone would have said."

"But if I'd listened to her, maybe I could have . . ."

"Talked her out of it? Made her better?"

"I could have told someone. I could have stopped this before it grew into what it became."

"And if you had, what do you think their response would have been?"

"I don't know, she could have gotten help."

"She had help. She's had *years* of it. She's been seeing a therapist ever since that summer. She had powerful drugs, she had a loving family, and *she* was the one who drove herself back there and went into that basement."

The questions that have been haunting me rise up in my mind: the full tank of gas, the door, the emails. But I don't say these things because what Mitchell is saying is also true.

"Do you know how many attempts she made before this one?" he asks.

"But your dad said this one was different."

"Yeah, it was, but she was ramping up. The one before it, she pushed it further that time too. If this wasn't the one, there would be another and another until she went too far, but that's the disease. That's fucking brain chemistry—it's not because of some prank you pulled when you were fourteen."

"Then why did she say my name?"

"Because you're her friend."

"I used to be."

"I think in her head, you still are." Mitchell takes my hands in both of his. "She used to talk about you."

"She did?"

"Yeah, duh." He smiles, but I can't smile back. I'm still braced for the rejection, trying to hear it under his words. "If you're telling me this because you want me to forgive you, then fine, I forgive you. But I don't think there's anything that needs forgiving. I think you were a kid; a kind but frightened kid. I don't think I'm the one you need to get the forgiveness from."

"From her?"

"No, dummy, from you. What, have you never read a self-help book?"

"No." I smile a little.

"Oh, man, don't tell my mother. She has a whole library."

"What about you blaming yourself, then? If I shouldn't, you shouldn't."

He shrugs. "Eh, yeah, maybe. Guess I should read those books too."

He releases my hands and adjusts his seat so it reclines back, then closes his eyes. After a moment, I copy him. He looks over at me and smiles.

"I just got déjà vu," he says.

It takes me a moment to catch up, but then I laugh, which hurts, but not badly. A bug lands on the bottom corner of the windshield, and I watch it make its slow diagonal progression to the top before it flies away.

"I meant what I said before," Mitchell says. "I'm pretty messy right now."

"Me too. I think more than I realized."

"Acceptance. See? That's progress." He turns his gaze to his window. Everything is dark and silent and still. We are completely alone in the world. I close my eyes and drift far away, lost in the labyrinth of memories.

"How's your head?" he asks.

"Hmmm?"

"You inhaled a lot of gasoline. Are you okay?"

"It hurts. It's not as bad as it was. Lori says hopefully I only killed the brain cells I don't use."

"You're staying here tonight?"

"Mm. She thought I should."

There's another moment of quiet, then he adjusts his seat back up and turns the car on. "I should let you get some sleep."

"Are you going all the way back to Buffalo tonight?"

"I was going to." He sounds exhausted.

"Stay here."

"Here?"

"Stay at my house. With me."

I have never been able to ask a man for anything. Never been able to make the first move. Maybe it's because this isn't a move, or maybe because it feels like everything has been stripped away and I am just me. The past is gone; it's a burned house in the middle of the woods. It's over, and we are here now, and this is all there is.

I leave a note for Lori. We drive to my house. We go to my room, to the narrow bed of my girlhood, and lie there holding each other until we both fall asleep.

28

BEN

It has been almost two weeks and Abby hasn't returned. Ruth Ann hovers around him, anxious and silent. He wants to be kind to her, but the pain has become a constant, and he does not have the energy to push his way through it to her. Easier to give in.

He is sleeping now. He knows he's dreaming because the pain is like noise heard through earplugs, muffled and distant. He is standing in the middle of the kitchen of his old house. It's nighttime and the kitchen is empty—stripped bare. The floor is covered with garbage. The windows are smashed, with boards nailed over them. This is what the house looks like now. He knows this in the sure way that one knows things unquestioningly in dreams. And then the kitchen is on fire. No, not just the kitchen, the entire house. The heat singes the hairs on his arms and the smoke burns his throat but he isn't in danger. The wallpaper is blistering, then peeling off in long strips flying all around him. As they pass him, he can just make out that where the patterns should be are words—the typeface of old newspapers, the careful penmanship of a child, the slanted lines of someone writing in fountain pen—nothing in front of him long enough for him to see what is written, only that they are words. Then each strip of paper curls in the heat and the edges turn black and it bursts into flame and floats up into the sky. He looks up. He sees the stars. The interior walls, the second floor, the roof, they are all gone. All that is left is the perimeter of the house, burning down around him, down into the ground.

Someone stands on the other side of the flames, watching. He can't see her face, but he knows it is a she and that she is a child. In the heat and the smoke, her silhouette wavers. She's waiting for him. Beyond her, there are others and somewhere among them, his family. Once he steps out of this burning house and into the cool darkness on the other side, he will not wake up.

His eyes blink open and he is back in his room in Three Pines. His bed faces the window and, as requested, the curtains are open. The sky is streaked with the first tentative bits of morning light. He squeezes his eyes shut and tries to reenter his dream, but it's gone. Anger surges within him, lending him the strength to roll onto his side and jam his hand down between the mattress and the bed frame to find the stash of sticky pills he had spat out diligently until the pain became too much and the nurses caught on to him.

His fingers are weak and stupid. They brush the tiny pills, but he can't get the muscles to cooperate and pick them up. He grinds his teeth to keep himself from screaming. That dream is so close, hovering just beyond consciousness. If he can fall asleep, he can go there again, and this time he will make sure he doesn't wake up. He rests his head on his arm, and that's when he smells smoke in the thin cotton of his pajamas. His fingers finally grip two small pills. He pulls them up and puts them in his mouth, then shoves his hand down again and gets three more. He does not know how many he saved, but when he has eight in his mouth, he decides this will be enough. They are dissolving on his tongue and the taste is bitter. It doesn't matter. He is going back. For the first time in all these years, he is going back to that house, or what's left of it. And this time he will cross through the wall of fire and take the hand of the girl waiting for him in the darkness and let her lead him into the old forest.

29

The sun wakes me up the next morning. It's streaming into the bedroom because I forgot to close the curtains. The night before comes flooding into my mind in the seconds before I am fully awake: the basement, falling down those stairs, the fire, Mitchell. Mitchell is here. But then I open my eyes and the bed is empty. I hear the shower shut off. He's leaving. He's woken up, realized the horrible mistake he made being here last night, even though nothing happened. Maybe he's realized he doesn't actually forgive me now that he's had some time to think about it. He's getting dressed and planning to drive away, probably leaving me some note about having to rush back to Buffalo, and that will be it. This realization hits me, like someone has kicked me hard in the gut, and my body curls into a ball. The bathroom door opens and I shut my eyes. If he wants to sneak out, I'll make it easy for him.

He comes in, and I hear him pulling clothes on, walking softly in bare feet on the carpet. The bed sinks as he sits, and I open my eyes just a crack. His bare back is to me, he's bent over pulling on socks. There are still drops of water on his skin and it takes everything in me not to reach out and touch him. The smell of soap. His scent. He glances over his shoulder and catches me watching him.

"Hey," he says, facing me.

"Hey."

"How are you feeling?"

"I don't know. I haven't tried to get up yet."

"Well, don't."

"Don't?"

I brace myself for what he's going to say.

"Yeah, I was going to bring you breakfast."

"Wait, what?"

He smiles. "You sound so shocked."

And that's when I smell the coffee.

"I hope you don't mind, I kind of rummaged in your kitchen."

"There's not much there."

"I noticed. I was *going* to bring you breakfast, but then I settled for just coffee. What do you take?"

He moves to get up, but I reach out and grab his wrist.

"What?"

I don't know. It's a purely physical response. And I don't know if I pull him toward me or if he leans in, but in a moment, he's hovering over me, his hands on either side, his face only inches from mine.

"Mitchell . . ."

He swallows but doesn't move away. "Hey, Clare."

"Hey."

"I made myself get out of bed so this wouldn't happen," he says.

"Oh."

"Hey, no, don't do that. Don't retreat. I want this to happen, but you're . . . what you've been through. I didn't want to take advantage or . . . I want it to be right."

"Me too."

He smiles. "This is a strange way to have a conversation."

I nod, then his mouth is on mine and my hands are on that damp skin. Our bodies feel like they move of their own will, while my mind flies up and hovers above us, watching, trying to understand that this is really happening.

"Where are you?" he whispers.

"I'm here," I say, and I return to my body. And when he enters me, we aren't drunk and frantic in the dark, and we aren't two scared kids trying to act braver than we are. We are just us, here, now. Our bodies move slowly together, eyes open and locked on each other. I feel like he can see into me: all the darkness that I have worked so hard for so long to keep hidden because it is ugly and will make anyone who sees it run. He sees the little girl whose house smells like her mother's sickness and who worries that her friends will think she's contaminated too; he sees the blood on the bathroom floor; he sees me refusing to stop the hurt while Josh weeps into my lap; he sees me shaking in the dark basement, feeling like my mind is letting go; and still he keeps looking. I see him and I see myself, here, now. I see a man who has been unraveled but who is still somehow moving forward, and a woman who has known too much death but is still capable of love—a woman who went back into the darkness and emerged alive.

After, we lie in a pool of sunlight. My drowsiness returns. Finally he shifts and says, "Your hair is making me a little high."

"Is that a compliment?"

"Uh, no. I mean, you have great hair, but I think the gasoline smell is lingering a bit."

I laugh. "I did wash it, I swear. I had a shower the second I got to Lori's."

"Yeah, well, don't go lighting any matches. I'd say you're still flammable." He sits up and reaches for his phone, then groans.

"Everything okay?"

"Yeah." He's scanning messages. "Yes." He puts the phone down and rolls over to face me. "Honestly, ten text messages from my mother over the course of this many hours is less than usual, so I'd say things are fine."

"How's Abby?"

"They're doing some tests later today, but Mom seems positive. I should go back." He sits up and starts pulling pants and socks out of the tangled sheets, then he says, "Come with me."

"To Buffalo?"

"Yeah. I mean, if you have other things—"

"No, I mean, yes, I'd like that."

"I don't know how things are going to be. It would be good to have you there." And then, as if reading my mind, he says, "For me. *I* would like you there."

We agree that he'll go ahead while I take another few days to recuperate. I don't trust myself to drive yet, and my knee is too swollen now to get in a car. After he leaves, I fall into a deep sleep, and if I dream about the Octagon House, I have no awareness of it when I wake up.

Lori gives me twenty-four hours, then sends me a series of texts so laden with graphic emojis that I'm worried I'm going to reinjure my healing rib because I'm laughing so hard. She also offers to send Taylor over after school to help me out, "as penance," but I decline. In truth, I barely get out of bed except to eat and wash my hair.

Three days later, I'm at the hospital in Buffalo again. Going up in the elevator, I'm suddenly hit with a premonition that everything with Mitchell will be awkward and terrible. We have had a three-day break with the exception of some text messages about Abby's prognosis and mine. What if what happened before was a blip, a result of adrenaline and circumstance, but now he's had a chance to think it over and—

The door opens and he steps into the elevator and pushes the button to close the door.

"You're leaving?" I ask.

"No. Just waiting for you."

"Oh."

One look at him and my worries evaporate. I take a breath. "Hi."

"Hi." He wraps his arms around me and buries his face in my hair. "Mmm, you smell so much less like a gas station."

I don't want to let go of him. We stand, arms wrapped around each other, and my body comes alive again as I breathe him in.

"I happened to notice that there's a spare bed in the room across from my sister's," he whispers into my ear. "The old lady in there is sound asleep, probably comatose . . ."

And then we're kissing again and every part of my body pulses. I push him up against the wall of the elevator just as the door dings and reopens. We duck out, ignoring the looks from the elderly couple who get on, forcing ourselves to stifle our laughter so we don't get kicked out by the nurses.

I am aware of the air moving in and out of my lungs, the weight of my body as I walk down the hospital hallway, the warmth of his hand in mine. How long have I been numb? I never want to retreat into that numbness again.

Abby is still connected to tubes and wires, but the breathing tube is out of her mouth, and there are fewer machines than there were a few days ago. It's not just the change in machinery around her, though. She looks fuller, more like someone who is deeply asleep but who will eventually wake up.

"She looks—" I start to say.

"I know," Mitchell says. "The doctors are amazed. They said they've never seen such a quick recovery from where she was." He squeezes my hand.

"But is she safe? Is she out of the danger zone?"

He turns to face me. "It's a long process, but she's in a good place. You've done all you can. Let the medicine and her body do the rest, okay?"

I nod.

"I'll be in the hall," he says. I haven't told him that I want to talk to her alone; he just knows. "Take as long as you want." And he steps out of the room, closing the door softly behind him.

I go to Abby and thread my fingers through hers. Her fingers are still bandaged, but even they don't seem as damaged as they did just a few days before.

I open my mouth to tell her about going into the basement, about what I found, about how I almost got trapped there—to tell her all of it—but I can't say it yet. She doesn't need to hear it yet. Maybe someday, but not now.

I squeeze her hand, giving it a little pressure, and then when I'm letting go, I feel the resistance from her. It's slight, but somewhere, some part of her is reaching out and holding me next to her, and it's where I want to be. I bend down and whisper in her ear. "Come back now. I'll wait for you. Come back."

30

SPRING

I'm back.

Around the curve in the road where the field stops and the woods begin, parked next to that spot where the fence is only hooked over the nails. The woods are thick enough that there are still patches of snow, but out here the first signs of spring grass are pushing through the dried remains of last fall. As I sit here in my car, the heat radiates through the windshield, and my skin soaks it in.

In the six months since the Octagon House burned down, I have avoided coming anywhere near here, so when Lori texted yesterday and asked me to meet her at the entrance to the old road, I had to think hard about whether I wanted to return. She must have sensed my hesitation because she sent another text thirty seconds later.

Worth it. Trust me.

A few days after the fire, Lori made an offer to buy the clearing from Mrs. Janssen, but in the end, she just signed it over. "I got the paperwork from Rhonda when I went in to get milk. Like it was nothing, after all these years," Lori said. A few weeks after that, I learned later, Mrs. Janssen died in her sleep. I've been thinking a lot about the choices we make when we are very young, choices made out of fear or just the innocence of not knowing. Choices that can haunt us. I hope, by letting the house go, Mrs. Janssen was able to let that sense of her punishment go with it.

As soon as the papers were signed, Lori and her brothers brought in their tractors and trucks and hauled away the remains of the house. She kept me posted on their progress and asked if I wanted to join her to ceremoniously fill in the hole that used to be the basement. She even texted me a picture of the dump truck she'd rented and told me I could be the one to release the load of dirt into it.

But I knew I couldn't go anywhere near the place. Not yet.

I thought about letting the police know that there were probably bodies buried in the woods—George's "strays"—but then I thought about what would have to happen next. I would have to explain how I knew, and I didn't think that anyone would believe me. And if they did a search, everything would be torn apart. The people who are buried in there have been buried for a long, long time. Maybe it was better to let them rest. So I said nothing.

And then I found the doll.

The night I was pulled out of the basement, I'd stripped my filthy gas-soaked clothes off at the hospital and was given a spare pair of scrubs, then I wore Lori's clothes until I got home. I assumed my clothes were thrown out, but a week or so later, Lori called me to tell me she had them. She'd washed them as best as she could, but she'd left the jacket because she thought it would have to be dry-cleaned. It was balled up in a plastic bag, and as soon as I took it out, the smell of damp earth and gasoline made a wave of nausea wash over me. The old me would have thrown it in the trash can before smelling that again, because to smell it meant that what had happened was real, and the old me would have much rather written off all of it to some horrendous, fear-inspired fever dream. But I wasn't that person anymore, or at least I was trying not to be. I made myself stand there in my father's kitchen and spread the jacket out on the table and let the smells hit me, and that was when I noticed the lump in the side pocket.

I have no memory of putting the doll in my pocket. I remember seeing it in the basement, but I don't remember taking it. I have tried very hard to remember everything that happened down there, but there are holes I can never fill in. I believe there are things I saw that my mind, in some attempt at self-preservation, did not record. I might never know these things. And I'm trying to accept that there are things I saw that logically cannot be real, and yet . . .

No matter how I think about it, it always comes back to that: "And yet . . ."

But the doll was real. So I decided that I would bury it properly. I would give it the burial that the little girl who owned it never had.

At first I thought I would buy a plot in the local cemetery, give it a gravestone, and put Grace's name on it—something permanent that people could see. But when I went to look around the cemetery, those rows of gravestones seemed so impersonal. I was sitting on my deck, wrapped in a quilt and drinking hot cocoa, trying to decide what to do, when I realized that I was looking at the perfect place: my mother's lavender garden. It was my favorite place to play when I was a little girl. If I dug around in the earth now, I could probably find broken bits of my old plastic tea set from all the afternoon tea parties I'd had with my dolls while my mother worked beside me. Grace would like that.

I filled the sink with warm water and soap, sprinkled dried lavender buds on top of it, and submerged the doll. And as I squeezed it out, the water instantly turned brown. I let it go down the drain, refilled the sink and put in more soap, and did it again, and again, and again. In all, it took six soakings until the water stayed clear. The cotton would never be white again, but it was a lot cleaner, and a little more of the face was visible. It was still covered in speckled black mold stains, and I thought about trying to bleach them out but decided not to. The mold was important; it showed what the doll had survived.

My mother had an open coffin. I do not know my father's reasons for choosing this, but even when I was a child, its wrongness screamed at me. When my mother died, her once long brown hair was in thin patches on her head. Her skin was thin and gray, her cheeks sunken. The woman who lay in the casket was wearing a horrible brown wig. The makeup was painted so thickly on her face, I swear to this day that I could see the brushstrokes. Blush in cheeks long without blood, lips painted a delicate shade of pink my mother never would have chosen, filler injected into her face to make her seem plump and healthy. But she wasn't healthy. The only reason she was in that box at the age of twenty-seven was because she lost the battle with a horrible disease. Why now, after her death, was that being hidden? When I saw her, I screamed. The adults around me assumed it was grief, but it was actually fear. Now, as an adult, I can make a logical argument that my grief-stricken father wasn't in his right mind to make decisions; that the funeral director probably did this, and my father was too shocked to argue, too shattered to resist. But it's taught me how wrong it is to try to cover up frightening things.

I cleaned and repaired that little doll, but I made sure not to make it something other than what it was: old and ragged and loved. Bits of the stuffing were coming out, having swollen from the years of moisture. Using a pair of tweezers, I gently pulled the excess out, then sewed up the seams. I undid the braid of yarn hair, combed it with my fingers, and rebraided it. When I was combing the doll's hair, I was combing Grace's. I was combing the hair of the little Fischer girls. I was combing the hair of my daughter; hair I would never have a chance to touch.

I found a box and folded the oldest, softest pillowcase I could find and used it as lining. I placed the doll in the box, sprinkled more lavender buds over it, and put the lid on. And then there was nothing more to do but bury it, and suddenly, desperately, I didn't want to be alone.

The list of people I could call had become very short. Mitchell was in Saudi Arabia for a few weeks, but even if he'd been around, this wasn't the sort of thing to bring him into. Abby was still in the hospital and, though I didn't know it then, only a few weeks away from fully regaining consciousness. That left Lori. I was about to call her when I thought of Taylor. Lori would humor me, maybe, but Taylor would understand. I still hadn't seen her. I wanted to make sure she was okay, but whenever Lori mentioned her, anything she was doing sounded so mundane, so normal, that I didn't want to disturb the peace she had found. This felt different.

I texted Lori and asked if Taylor would be able to help me with something. Two hours later, Taylor was standing on my doorstep, looking confused about why she'd been sent over to my house on a Saturday afternoon.

"You can say no," I said as I brought her in. "I didn't tell your mom—I will because I don't want this to be weird—but I wanted to ask you first. Okay?"

"Sure," she said. It wasn't dismissive. She was curious but guarded.

"I want to show you something. I think you'll recognize it." I opened the box and she peered into it. Expressions flashed across her face: confusion, fear, recognition, and then a little smile.

"That's her."

I nodded. "I want to bury her. I think it's important. I was wondering if you'd do it with me."

She gently took the box from my arms.

Taylor and I walked into the wild lavender garden and I let her choose the spot. She took a long time, going to one area, standing in it and closing her eyes, then moving on to another. Finally she declared one place to be *it*. I dug a hole that was a few feet deep and put the box inside.

"Let's put some lavender on top," she said, and she started grabbing fistfuls of the dried flowers off the stalks and scattering them into the hole. We covered the lid with purple flowers, then we both stood there as a cold wind blew dried leaves into small whirlwinds across the yard.

"Do you want to say anything?" I asked.

She shook her head. "I don't know."

"Me neither," I said.

"Can I say a prayer?" she asked. "Just a quiet one. Like, to myself?"

I closed my eyes. Words whirled around in my head. Nothing was right, nothing was sufficient. There were no prayers in my mind that could give me comfort, no words that could make me believe I was actually speaking to a higher power, and yet . . . There was something there with us. I heard the wind and felt it touch the back of my neck. It wasn't words that came. It wasn't images or memories either, just a feeling.

Rest.

You can rest now.

Afterward, we warmed ourselves up with cocoa and a bag of cookies, and sat on the deck looking out over the yard.

"Are you going to mark the grave?" she asked me, swiping at the chocolate mustache she'd given herself.

"No. We know it's here. That's enough." That and I was trying to sell the house. If prospective buyers thought there was an actual grave in the backyard, they might be hesitant. New owners would probably rip out the old lavender plants and seed the whole thing. Hopefully I'd buried the box deep enough that it would rest there undisturbed. I closed my eyes and leaned back in the sagging lawn chair and realized that I felt looser, lighter, than I had in a long, long time.

———

In the new year, I moved out of my father's house and rented a cheap apartment in another town, close enough that I've been able to get to Sumner's Mills easily but far enough away that I don't feel like I live there. Mitchell got transferred to the New York office, and so throughout the winter we've been able to see each other every weekend, which, in theory, is helping us take it slow. In reality, I have no desire to take it slow, and I don't think he does either, so the long drive between us is probably a good thing. Between seeing him and getting my father's house ready to go on the market, I have been traveling to the rehab center to visit Abby.

Abby regained consciousness in late November, but that, as I've learned while watching her go through it, was only one step in many on the road to recovery. She isn't able to walk yet, but she's determined that she will, and despite the fact that she's called her physical therapist every name in the book, he says she's his strongest fighter, and that is the best indication that someday she will walk again. It helps, she says, that he's six feet tall and gorgeous.

A few months ago, Mitchell and I decided to out ourselves to her. It was my idea, and I felt great about it until the moment we walked into her room and sat down in front of her.

"Uh-oh," she said.

"Abs, we wanted to tell you something," Mitchell said after I hadn't said anything. "Well, Clare wanted to. I was fine to keep going as we were."

Abby looked back and forth between us. The left side of her body was a little slower to respond than the right, so when she started to smile, it looked like the grin was literally spreading across her face. "First," she said, "I may have fried parts of my brain, but my eyes work just fine, and you two are pretty obvious. Second"—and this she said directly to her brother—"if you're a dick to her, I will physical-therapy myself out of this chair just so I can kick your ass."

So she knows.

Abby and I don't talk about the Octagon House. I've never asked her why she went into the basement again or what happened once she got in there. I want to know, but I am okay to wait until she brings it up. Our conversations stay in safe areas. She tells me funny stories about the people in the facility, and I tell her bits and pieces about my life when she asks, but mainly I let her talk. That's how it has been until yesterday.

I arrived in the middle of the afternoon, my usual time, bringing a bag of groceries for her. She's complained about the food at the facility enough that I finally got the hint and started bringing food each time I visit. She never tells me what she wants; I just guess. Yesterday it was a new jar of peanut butter—I'd noticed the old one in the trash—crackers, granola bars, cookies, dried fruit, and a few bags of Easter candy. Abby's got a sweet tooth, and she's slowly losing the hollowed-out look she had in the hospital. I walked into her room and was about to propose we get outside before it started to rain again when she said, "Do you remember that summer after we went into the basement? We saw each other again, right?"

I put down the groceries and perched on the edge of the bed. Just the word "basement" and all of this new normalcy—the regular visits, the easy conversations that were nothing more than gossip, the way it had seemed like we were going to be able to slip back into each other's lives after everything that had happened—suddenly it all cracked. Maybe it had never been real. Maybe Abby had only been entertaining me. Why would she have any interest in actually becoming my friend again? And if she turned on me, would Mitchell follow? Would he have a choice?

"Yes, I remember." I tried to keep my voice even, but the words were tight in my throat.

"You know, I don't even remember moving to Buffalo," she said. "It's like my memory went all wonky for a couple of months after I was in that house."

"We saw each other," I said. "Only a couple of times, though. You were pretty messed up from the drugs they were giving you."

"But I told you what I'd seen that night." The way she said it told me that despite her memory being fuzzy, that conversation was very clear. "And I asked you if you'd seen it too."

"I don't really remember," I said, which was true. I'd reinvented that last time Abby and I had been together so many times, it was hard to pick out what had really happened from what I'd wanted to happen.

"I was so mad at you." She said it matter-of-factly, not as an apology, not as an accusation. I couldn't tell if it was past tense or if some of that anger was still in her all these years later. "You'd been down there, and that girl or whatever she was, she had been down there too. I could see you both. She was practically standing next to you, then you said you hadn't seen anything, and you told me I was wrong. You told me it was just the pot and me being scared."

"I thought you didn't remember."

"I remember that," she said, and waited for me to contradict her, but I was done denying my part in what had happened.

"Had you seen her?" she asked. "Were you just saying that there was nothing there to, I don't know, make me stop talking about it or something?"

"I—I don't know," I finally said. "Honestly, Abby. I'm like you. I remember going down there to get you out. I remember being terrified, but I can't remember what I actually saw, or if I saw anything."

She studied my face. All these years later, and we were back to the question: Do you believe me? She turned and looked out the window and my eyes followed her gaze. Outside, bare tree branches were moving slightly in the breeze. It looked like it was getting cloudier. She absent-mindedly played with a loose string on the blanket covering her.

"Yesterday my therapist was talking about this idea that's part of dialectical behavior therapy. It's this therapy I'm doing in here. Have you heard about it?"

I shook my head.

"It's especially good for people like me," she said. "It's kind of their jam here. So, in DBT, they believe that it's possible for a person to hold two truths at one time. Does that make sense?" She turned and looked at me. "Up until now, whenever I thought about what happened, it was either that you were a liar or I was crazy. Either what I saw was real and my best friend lied to me about it, except there was no good reason I could think of *why* you'd lie to me. It's not like lying would protect me or prevent what happened, so why would you do it? Or, my best friend was telling me the truth and I was crazy."

"And what did you decide?"

"I think you know," she said. "I'm not crazy. Despite my current circumstances. I know what I saw down there. Even if it seemed impossible, it happened. And you just . . . you tried to erase that experience. You told me that something that was so real—that changed *everything*—that it was just in my head, but I know she talked to you too. So I tried to convince myself that you lied to me to protect me, but I could never . . . I don't know. I could never get that to sit right."

"Oh." That was all I was able to get out, because the lump that was in my throat was suddenly making it hard to talk.

"But now I think, at least, I'm coming to believe, maybe we were both telling the truth." Her eyes were very clear. I didn't say anything because I was trying to catch up. "I believe you, Clare, that's what I'm saying. I can believe you now. But I also believe me."

"I can't remember what I saw when we were kids," I said. "Honest, I'm not just saying that. But last fall, I went into that basement again—"

Her eyes got wide, and I could see her physically recoil. I hadn't told her anything. I hadn't told her about the house being destroyed or about Marion Janssen or Mr. Fischer or any of it. Now I was watching her face, because I knew that at the smallest sign of this being too much for her, I had to find a way to get out of the conversation. "And I saw things down there. I can't make any sense of them, but I saw them and . . ." I swallowed hard. Just say it, I told myself. This time you be the crazy one. "I saw the tunnel. I thought you had wanted me to see that as proof. You left our sign so I'd find it."

She didn't say anything, just kept looking at me, listening.

"I thought you were trying to prove to me that there had been someone else down there. And then. What happened next, I haven't been able to figure out. I saw her. She wanted me to take the doll. And then I saw him. And I touched him. I killed him, I think. I pulled him down the stairs with me. Except that doesn't make any sense. He had to have died a long time ago. I can't make it make sense, so it couldn't have happened, but I *felt* him. And later, I found the doll. It was in my pocket. It's this mix of real and not real, except all of the real things are dependent on the not-real things."

She didn't say anything; she reached across the blanket and took my hand. Her fingers are healed now, but the skin on the tips is a bright pink, and some of the nails are never going to grow right. Abby being trapped in that place was real too: her hands will forever attest to that.

"See?" I said. "Maybe I'm the one who's crazy."

She smiled. "You know what else is crazy? I've been totally craving those Easter cream eggs, and you *knew*. You must be a freaking psychic." She nodded toward the grocery bag and squeezed my hand. "Come on, I want to eat enough of those things to make my teeth hurt."

———

A car honks and I open my eyes. Lori has pulled up behind me and Taylor sits beside her. It's been a few months since we've seen each other, between me being away a lot and Lori and her husband trying to get their business off the ground. When Taylor gets out of the car, I notice she's grown a few more inches. She's got braces and has a bright pink streak in her hair. She grins at me as I get out of the car, and I can't help but grin back.

Lori cocks her head and looks at me for a second. "You look good."

"You sound surprised."

"No, seriously, is there something different about you? Did you do something to your hair?"

"Nope." I can't contain the smile that spreads across my face. All in good time. She looks like she's about to say something, but then Taylor bounces up to us. "I like the pink," I tell her.

"Thanks. Tell my mom she needs to do it too."

Lori rolls her eyes.

"You should," I say. "It would suit you."

Before she has a chance to reply, Taylor says, "Mom, are you going to make her do it?"

"Make me do what?"

"This is Taylor's idea," Lori says. "Just to make that clear. She's the one who discovered it, and she thinks that you should have your eyes closed."

"I brought a blindfold," Taylor says. "That way you get the full effect."

"Full effect of what?"

"You'll see."

"I can't walk through the woods blindfolded," I say.

"Exactly," Lori says. "And I'm not carrying her if she sprains an ankle."

Taylor sighs dramatically. "Fine. But can we put it on you once we get close?"

I agree and we enter the woods. They don't feel ominous this time. As promised, when we get close to the clearing, we stop, and Lori ties a blindfold around my eyes.

"Thank you for playing along," she says quietly.

"Am I going to regret this?"

She doesn't answer. They each take my hand and lead me carefully through the last bit of the underbrush. The sun warms my face as we step out into the clearing. They let go of my hands, and I pull the blindfold off and gasp. In front of me are islands of crocuses. Tiny purple, yellow, and white flowers wave gently in the wind. Around them, small shoots of green are starting to poke through the earth.

"How is this possible?"

"Isn't it amazing?" Taylor says.

"Did you plant these?" I ask Lori.

"Nope," she says. "After I filled in the hole where the basement was, we brought in a couple more loads of earth. You can see that it kind of rises in the middle there, that's covering the foundation. It must have something to do with the earth we brought in."

"It's the house," Taylor says. "It's gone, so now things can grow."

Her mother shakes her head. "I don't know. It doesn't make sense to me, but whatever. I'm not going to question it."

They offer to walk me out, but I want to stay for a little.

"You're sure?" Lori asks.

I nod. I didn't think I could come back to this place, but it's different now. Whatever that feeling was, that feeling of something watching and waiting, is gone.

After Lori and Taylor have disappeared into the trees, I step farther into the clearing so I'm fully in the sun. I close my eyes and settle into the sounds around me, the wind moving the ancient tree branches, the quiet call of birds behind me. If I open my eyes, I will be surrounded by color, by life returning. I put my hands on my belly. Life inside and out. A new life. A small heart beating inside me. Mitchell is on his way up from the city now, and tomorrow we'll tell his family our news. In the summer, we will move in together and I will start to decorate the nursery. Yellow, I think. Something to match the softest baby blanket I've ever felt. I open my eyes and see the nodding heads of spring flowers.

acknowledgments

I have been living with this book for a long time and while the creation of it has mainly been a solitary exercise, often late at night, it would never have got to this form if it weren't for the net of people around me. Some have had a direct impact on the words on the page; others have supported the creation of this through the gift of time, faith, and love. To all of them, I offer my deepest thanks.

To my agent, Victoria Marini, who has stuck by this book through so many revisions and never wavered in her support, thank you times one hundred. To my editor, Loan Le at Atria Books, who said yes and then proceeded to be the best story doula a writer could ask for (and I was briefly a part of that fierce tribe of birth doulas, so trust me when I say Loan has doula-ed this book into being), thank you many, many times over. And to the rest of the team at Atria: Liz Byer, Libby McGuire, Lindsay Sagnette, Suzanne Donahue, Dana Trocker, Karlyn Hixson, Nicole Bond, David Brown, and Maudee Genao. Thank you!

Thank you to Megan Hamilton, who encouraged me to try NaNo-WriMo all those years ago when I was in immigration limbo and had no money and no job, but lots of time (so no excuses!). To Leah State, Meagan O'Shea, Rekha Shah, Marilo Nuñez, and Raoul Bhaneja, who have known me for too many years to count and have supported not only the creation of this book but the creation of me as a writer.

Thank you to Dr. Jennifer Bonner, associate professor of biology at Skidmore College, who walked me through some coma basics, and Dr. Dana Lau in the psychology department at Skidmore College, who helped me understand dialectical behavior therapy. Any mistakes in the book are mine.

To Matt Dellapina and Sean Lewis, for saying yes before anyone else did. Thank you for making Storybrink a place for writers. And to Signe Bergstrom and Eve Moennig for a thousand+ pencils, and for being two of my earliest readers.

Thank you to my parents, Barry and Sheila Fawcett. You were the main characters in my first play, and you can rest assured, you do not appear in my first book and there's nary a goat in sight. Your unconditional support of my dream to be a writer is my bedrock. And to Chris and Ed Dolan, who welcomed me into their family and never failed to ask, "How's the book?"

And finally, to Sean and Eamon. For every hour I was at my computer, for every late night when I crawled into bed long after you were both asleep, for every time I was overcome with doubt and you gave me your love and support, thank you. I love you more than words can say.

about the author

Jennifer Fawcett grew up in rural Eastern Ontario and spent many years in Canada making theater before coming to the United States. She holds an MFA from the Iowa Playwrights Workshop. Her work has been produced in theaters across the country and published in *Third Coast, Reunion: The Dallas Review, Storybrink*, and in the anthology *Long Story Short*. She teaches writing at Skidmore College and lives in Upstate New York with her husband and son.